PRAISE FOR DRIVING FORCE

Kate Angelo has mastered a fast-paced, romantic suspense that had me cuffed to the page.

— DIANN MILLS, BESTSELLING AUTHOR OF
ROMANTIC SUSPENSE

Kate Angelo is an author whose name you'll want to remember. Her complex characters resonate from the page, and along with an action-packed plot make for one powerhouse book. I know I'll be following her career for a long time.

— LISA PHILLIPS, USA TODAY BESTSELLING
AUTHOR OF THE LAST CHANCE COUNTY SERIES

DRIVING FORCE

AN ELITE GUARDIANS NOVEL

LYNETTE EASON
KATE ANGELO

sunrise
PUBLISHING

A NOTE FROM LYNETTE

Dear Reader,

I'm so excited that the next installment of the Elite Guardians is here. And wow! All I can say is strap on your seatbelt and get ready for a wild ride, because there might be a Tesla involved.

When I was reading through all of the auditions for the reboot of the Elite Guardians series, I knew it was going to take some special authors to get it just right. And to say that Kate's audition blew me away is an understatement. She did her research for sure and crafted a premise that I couldn't say no to!

I love that the hero, Captain Grey Parker, is in a wheelchair, and that the heroine—sassy, smart, and skilled, Christina Sherman—thinks she is going to be keeping him safe...but instead has her world rocked when she finds herself guarding *his dog*. For really good reasons, of course. Okay, guarding his dog AND him—but he also has her back and is a hero in more ways than one.

And Grey, who still mourns losing the use of his legs after an overseas mission gone wrong, guards his heart with every weapon in his arsenal, only to find himself surrendering to the love Christina offers—in the midst of dodging bullets, bombs, and bad guys. Naturally.

So, strap in and get ready for a rocking good story chock full of romance and suspense. Thank you for joining us on the ride!

God Bless,

Lynette

To God,
who fills me daily with unimaginable peace and joy.

To my husband,
who is my prayer warrior, advisor, supporter, and best friend.

To my children, family, and friends,
who have taught me that family is more than blood.

May the God of hope fill you with all joy and peace as you trust in him, so that you may overflow with hope by the power of the Holy Spirit.

— ROMANS 15:13

SIBERIA, RUSSIA

DECEMBER 29, 10:29 A.M.

Today was going to be a breeze—a thirty degrees below zero in the frozen tundra of Siberia breeze.

Captain Grey Parker bounced his knee in time with the blades of the tilt-rotor aircraft as they sliced through the Arctic sky. He leaned his head back against the side of the airplane and picked at the skin near his thumbnail while he rehearsed the mission in his head.

An extraction with three hostiles and one friendly was a simple in and out job for the Special Ops Air Commando unit he led. Always the first to deploy into hostile areas, they cleared the path for other operatives by disarming explosives and neutralizing enemies. Yes, this mission was a sure thing.

So why did the hair on the back of his neck stand on end?

He sensed eyes watching him from across the aircraft. Eyes that belonged to his friend, First Lieutenant Marshall Wallace.

They stared at each other for an uncomfortable minute, each refusing to look away.

Wally broke, his perfect white teeth glinting behind a broad smile. He ran a hand over his thick beard and thrust his chin toward Grey. "Boss looks more relaxed than all of us. How's that when he's got the most dangerous job?"

The Belgian Malinois swayed his tail at the sound of his nickname. He lay on the bench beside Grey, right where he always was. Side by side, fighting together for the last four years. Boss was a sniffer dog cross trained in search and rescue. Countless times he'd saved their lives, finding an IED or tracking an enemy before he could ambush their squadron. Boss showed an eagerness to learn, so Grey started training him to detect chemical weapons a few months ago.

Grey patted the dog. "Are you kidding? He's got more bravery in one paw than all of us put together."

"That ain't sayin' much," replied Briggs, the youngest of the unit. "My niece is braver than Wally, and she's only eight!"

Wally threw an elbow to Briggs's ribs. The man dodged it and gave Wally a playful shove.

Laughter filled the aircraft, and the men took turns telling stories of past adventures. Wally brought up the time Briggs almost lost his eye when a bullet ricocheted off a rock near his head. With laughter ringing around them, Wally pointed a jesting finger at the baby-faced soldier.

Briggs snorted. "Hey, that eye patch was a chick magnet."

The tension was still there, all their nerves stretched tight, but the joking helped them deal with it.

The pilot radioed Grey to prepare for landing. "Time to rock n' roll," Grey said.

The tilt-rotor aircraft made a vertical landing in the Purinsky Nature Reserve, 150 miles north of Norilsk, Russia, on the edge of the Arctic Circle. They suited up in snow camouflage to combat the thirty-below temperatures.

Their orders were to recover Dr. Anton Kalashnik, a Russian American biochemist forced to work in a chemistry lab in Akademgorodok before he escaped to America. Russian operatives had abducted the doctor and brought him back to Russia where they held him for ransom. Drone surveillance identified a small cabin in sparse woods giving off four human heat signatures, one of which was believed to belong to the kidnapped scientist.

Grey buckled Boss into his tactical harness and patted his haunches. "Good boy. You ready to work?"

Boss wagged his tail at the word *work*.

The pilot lowered the ramp of the aircraft and a frigid wind permeated the cabin. Grey squeezed his helmet over his head and powered on the full-color night vision goggles turning the moonless night into a computerized version of daylight. He settled his rifle across his chest and loaded Boss onto the snowmobile.

"Let's move," Grey said.

Four men followed out of the plane and into the night. The dense snowfall muffled their sounds as they traveled. Six miles from the camp, Grey stopped near a cluster of spruce trees, a location he'd handpicked from drone surveillance. The massive evergreens grew in a wide semi-circle, protecting three sides.

"Simmons and O'Donnell, wait for my call. Briggs and Wally, you're with me. We'll approach on foot and request extraction once the target is secure."

He clicked his tongue, alerting Boss to watch for hand signals, and pointed forward with two fingers. Boss went to work. He wagged his tail and pulled on his leash gently, sniffing the ground as he moved forward. Once Grey cleared an area, he moved into a safe position while Wally and Briggs alternated moving into position in line with Grey. He led the team using this bounding overwatch technique, zigzagging through the snow while Boss searched for explosives.

Boss paused about two hundred yards from the extraction point and circled back, tail stiff. He slowed his pace and backtracked, sniffing and snorting in a concentrated area. His rear dropped to the ground. Grey rewarded him with a hardy pat and a chin scratch. He tagged the area with infrared paint visible through their NVG. No telling when the bomb was buried. Maybe today, or maybe ten years ago. Either way, they wouldn't be disarming it.

A hundred meters before the extraction point, Boss perked his ears and his body stiffened. Without hesitation, Grey halted and signaled danger. He dropped flat on the ground and low-crawled beneath the branches of a snow-covered conifer tree. The sharp pine fragrance made his nose twitch, but he resisted the urge to scratch.

Grey peeked over his shoulder. Good. Wally and Briggs were down, rifles in firing position.

Boss lay flat, paws outstretched. Grey drew him close and scooped snow into a mound by his face to hide his frozen breath. Grey scoured the trees for human outlines.

A crunch at his three o'clock. He swung his rifle toward the sound and saw a slight bulge between two trees. It looked wrong. Before he could squeeze his trigger, a crack of gunfire shattered the silence. A rifle dropped to the snow and a man sank to his knees clutching his throat. Blood seeped through his fingers and ran down his neck.

Gunfire erupted and a patch of snow exploded over Grey's head. More bullets sprayed the trees where he'd taken cover. Clumps of wet snow dropped onto his back. He caught a glint of light on an embankment at his one o'clock. A slight deviation in the terrain. He aimed for the protruding lump and squeezed the trigger. A red mist sprayed the snowy ridge.

The forest went still.

He slowed his breathing and studied the trees. *Two down, one to go.*

The remaining kidnapper might be inside with Dr. Kalashnik, but if it were Grey, he would take the high ground and wait for his target to approach the building. He searched the horizon for anomalies. Nothing.

He signaled for Wally and Briggs to move. No telling where this guy was hiding. Grey slithered toward the cabin, careful to avoid brushing the low-hanging branches. Boss crawled alongside, expertly mimicking Grey's movements, alert and continuing to sniff for a mark. Grey reached the edge of the clearing in front of the building and paused.

He pressed his eye against the scope and studied the trees for a hint of a target.

Come on. Where are you hiding?

He glanced to his right. Wally had made his way to the first dead sniper and had a clear view of the cabin and forest beyond. Briggs flanked the building and covered Wally.

Find him, Wally. Pull the trigger.

His chest seized as a single gunshot echoed through the forest. Movement in the trees, followed by the sound of rustling branches. A body slumped over. The impact from Wally's bullet had almost knocked the kidnapper off the well-concealed tree stand. How'd Wally even see that guy?

Wally whistled and lifted his head from behind his rifle to salute Grey. It was good to see Wally in his element. He'd changed over the last few months, after the accident, but today he seemed on his game.

Grey gave him a thumbs up. He spoke low through his coms. "Sly one, up in the tree like that."

Briggs chuckled. "I hate to break it to you, but Wally's never going to shut up about this."

"Yeah, except he'll tell the guys how he took out all three snipers with a single bullet." Wally was the best storyteller, even if he embellished every tale. It was a coping mechanism for the necessity in taking a human life. None of them took pleasure in it, but the world was what it was. And unless things changed...

Wally turned serious. "The sound travels, you know."

"Good point," Grey said. They still had a job to do. "Let's move."

Boss pranced across the snow, sniffing the ground around the building. Briggs trailed behind, with Wally falling in beside Grey. They circled the cabin, alert to any threats.

They approached the front door and Grey radioed Simmons. "Bring the buggy. We're extracting the target."

"Affirmative. Moving in."

"Mines are marked. Keep an eye out."

"Roger."

Wally secured the door and Briggs covered the forest behind them. Grey signaled Boss to search. The dog sniffed his way up the uneven steps and around the small porch, lingering around the threshold. He whined and paced back and forth, nose to the crack in the door. Grey waited for him to sit but couldn't imagine they would set an explosive on the door. Far too risky for the scientist. A slight gust of wind could blow this rickety old cabin over. A bomb? It would obliterate the building and the asset the Russians had worked so hard to kidnap.

Boss stopped sniffing. He looked back at Grey, questioning.

"What is it, boy?"

He whimpered and flicked his tail, but Boss didn't sit. Grey asked him to search again, but the dog had the same reaction. A short whine and a flick of the tail. It wasn't making sense. Boss could detect nineteen thousand distinct scents down to the molecule thanks to the specialized training with the CIA in Chemical, Biological, Radiological, Nuclear, and high yield Explosives. If there was an explosive in this building, Boss would tell him.

Wally raised his eyebrows. "What are we waitin' for? There ain't no butler waiting to open that door for us."

Wally was right. They needed to get the job done and get home. "Briggs, guard the door. Simmons and O'Donnell are on the way." He lifted his chin to Wally, who nodded his readiness.

Grey flung the door open and jumped back. Wally rushed past with his rifle up, scanning for threats. "Clear!"

Grey entered the small cabin after Wally and stared down his rifle, examining the room. It was nothing more than a box with four walls and a roof. On a cot along the far wall, a wiry old man held shaky hands up, palms out. Wally hovered over him at the foot of the cot. The stench of sweat and urine penetrated Grey's ski mask. A kerosene lamp emitted a dim light on a table where the men had been playing cards. A small kerosene heater glowed with a dull amber flame in the opposite corner.

Grey positioned himself with his back to the wall opposite the cot. He tugged the face portion of his balaclava down and blinked as his eyes adjusted. "Dr. Anton Kalashnik?"

"Ye-yes?"

"I'm Captain Parker with the United States Air Force. We're here to rescue you. You can put your hands down."

The scientist wiped the sweat from his forehead with a trembling hand. "I am glad to see you," he said in a heavy Russian accent.

Distant buzzing from approaching snowmobiles permeated the room and O'Donnell's voice came through Grey's coms. "Half a mile out."

"Copy that." Grey looked at Dr. Kalashnik. "Extraction team incoming. Sit tight."

Wally nodded and let his rifle rest at ease. He placed a hand on the doctor's shoulder. "The dog doesn't like you, man."

Grey glanced at Boss. The dog's fur was standing on end. Head lowered, eyes locked on Dr. Kalashnik.

"What is it, Boss?" Grey reached down and patted Boss on the side. The dog vibrated with a low growl and he bared his teeth.

Adrenaline shot through Grey's veins and every muscle in his body tensed. He looked to Wally, but he was busy sliding his gas mask over his face. His eyes darted from Wally to the doctor. The old man had his palms on the edge of the cot and was pushing himself up.

Grey took half a step forward. "Stop! Stay where you are—"

A blinding flash exploded from beneath the cot. The force slammed Grey against the flimsy cabin wall. The wood paneling splintered under the impact. A sharp pain surged through his back. His legs crumpled and he slid to the floor as a cloud of smoke filled the cabin.

His eyes watered and his lungs burned. The gas mask. He had to get his gas mask on before he breathed too much of whatever this was. Weighted hands fumbled at his side but refused to cooperate. He gave up and held his breath, forcing his eyes open to see through the smoke.

Relief washed over him. Wally was on his feet with his gas mask in place. Grey's eyes drifted shut. Voices and the sound of Boss snarling registered as distant noise. He tried to speak, but words wouldn't form. His body grew heavy, and his eyes wouldn't stay open.

A tugging at his shoulder. Snorting and wetness on his neck. Boss...

His world faded to black.

2

TWO YEARS LATER

COLUMBIA, SOUTH CAROLINA

THURSDAY, 3:45 P.M.

What she wouldn't give to feel the comfortable weight of her Magnum M24 long-range rifle pressed snug to her shoulder. Christina Sherman lay on the cold metal grate of the catwalk suspended in the rafters of the Federal Life basketball Arena. Tucked away like a nesting eagle, she scrutinized faces and body language discerning potential threats. No rifle this time. She was forced to patrol with a high-powered spotting scope. Too bad it was mounted on a heavy-duty tactical tripod instead of her rifle.

Her skin had flushed hot when Chief Webb denied her request to bring the M24. Didn't he know she was a former Army Special Ops sniper? Well, she wasn't about to point it out. He was in charge, and she knew how to follow orders. At least she carried her .45 caliber Smith and Wesson M&P tucked into the holster at the small of her back.

Why were so many people at a basketball game in the middle of the day on a weekday? Didn't these people have jobs or a school to attend? But then again, the weather was unseasonably cold for a February in Columbia, South Carolina. They'd probably jumped at the chance to do something inside.

The music and commotion from the spectators below floated up to the ceiling and settled around her. She'd nestled herself on the catwalk between a bank of lights overlooking the basketball court below where she could see all three thousand spectators. If anyone looked in her direction, they'd be blinded by the brightness. The blistering heat radiating from the halogen bulbs reminded her of the week she'd spent holed up in a sweltering shack in Musa Qala. Even without her rifle, this assignment was better than most of her sniper days. At least this place had air-conditioning—unlike Afghanistan.

The mic keyed up in her earpiece.

"Thirty seconds to team entry." It was the voice of Katie Matthews, a part owner of the Elite Guardians Agency, an organization that offered specialized protection to those who needed it most.

Christina had joined the Army to protect innocent civilians from evil, but after her retirement it was a struggle to find her place. She found herself in Greece attending bodyguard school where she'd met Olivia Savage, another owner of the Elite Guardians Agency. When Olivia called to offer a permanent position on the team as a bodyguard, Christina didn't have any other offers that intrigued her, so she accepted.

At least with this job, her skills in concealed surveillance and reconnaissance wouldn't go to waste. Staying back and protecting her clients from a distance was a dream job. Like tonight, from her position over the stadium, she studied every face for plausible threats. Yeah, she was in her wheelhouse, all right.

Her smartwatch said only ten minutes until their client,

Governor Barry Winston, would kick off the Wounded Warrior Games Wheelchair Basketball season. During their briefing, his staff said the governor's appearance at the public event would send a powerful message to the sender of the threatening letters —he would not be intimidated. In her opinion, it was an obvious political move designed to secure a nomination as a vice presidential candidate in the upcoming election.

The music picked up and Christina shifted her gaze to the wide opening where a group of men in specialized wheelchairs poured from the tunnel. The crowd erupted with cheers and applause. A man wearing a black and gold Team Army uniform sped up and down the court with an American flag. Several of the Team Air Force players wheeled along the fans in the floor seats, smacking outstretched hands. Christina noticed a few service dogs running beside their owners. One of them wore a custom Army jersey. How cute.

She pulled her eyes from the show below and began her strategic search of the audience, scanning section by section. A partial photographic memory came in handy for these assignments. Memorizing countless faces and their locations to keep track of anyone who looked suspicious. She'd already added two men to her mental spreadsheet and filed them under *Suspicious*. No need to call them in yet. That could wait until they found themselves in her *Threat* column.

The first suspect, a man in a blue hat, was sitting low at her 12 o'clock about mid-court. A long bushy beard and ball cap pulled low concealed most of his face and the Air Force T-shirt seemed a bit too tight over his bulging belly. His bulk was sandwiched between a teenage boy in need of a haircut and an excited grandmotherly woman decked out in Air Force gear. There was something odd about the man who sat ramrod straight, hands laced together in his lap, staring straight ahead. Even when Grandma sprang to her feet and cheered, Blue Hat Guy never moved.

Christina had no concerns about Grandma. The greatest danger the older woman presented was taking someone's eye out with the tiny flag she was brandishing. She was about to continue scanning the next row when Grandma pointed to the court and placed her hand on Blue Hat Guy's shoulder and looked into his eyes with something like love and pride, mixed with pity and regret. She ran her hand down his arm and squeezed his bicep. His focus never shifted.

Christina slid Blue Hat Guy into the *Safe* column.

"One minute until Winston is on the court," said Chief Webb, head of the South Carolina Law Enforcement Division.

Security for the governor fell under the jurisdiction of SLED. Chief Webb had requested additional support from the Columbia Police Department and the mayor had insisted he use the Elite Guardians as extra manpower—or, in this case, womanpower. He'd balked at the suggestion, but Katie and Christina took the assignment despite his complaints about using "so-called bodyguards" instead of trained law enforcement.

The radio in her ear keyed up, but no one spoke. Great.

She shook it off and continued inspecting the crowd. In the darkened section above the VIP box seats was the second man she'd marked *Suspicious*. The highest level of the four-tiered arena was technically closed, but SLED said veterans with PTSD might slip into the closed off areas to escape the crowd and noise.

Ah, there you are. Why are you sitting up there all alone?

A man so tall he appeared to be standing at first glance sat in the dim seating area. She pegged him to be at least six foot seven, and the way his shoulders blended into his neck said he was solid muscle. The shadows darkened his face, but she could tell his head was shaved close and he wore all black. She dialed in her scope and examined the image of a bulldog baring its teeth tattooed on his left forearm. It was a Russian mafia tattoo known to stand for hatred of government authority. This Bulldog guy could be harmless, but best to check him out.

"I've got eyes on a suspicious male sitting alone, upper level, section 223. Big and scary with a bulldog tattoo on his forearm. Need someone to check him out." The radio crackled, and Christina waited for a reply, but, again, no one responded.

Thundering applause erupted from the crowd, drawing her attention to Governor Winston's appearance at the East tunnel. Bleached teeth glimmered behind a picture-perfect smile, and not a single gray hair dared move. He walked onto the court, bestowing presidential waves upon his constituents, and maximizing the media attention.

Christina returned her attention to the suspicious man she called Bulldog and tried her radio again. "Anyone got eyes on my potential threat?"

The response came as static in her ear. Perfect. A nearby radio signal was overpowering their lower frequency channel. She might have better luck on the alternate. "Getting static up here in the rafters. Switching to secondary channel."

She identified herself on the new channel and waited for a response, but none came. Why couldn't she get an answer? She frowned. This is what they got for using SLED's radio communications instead of the military grade gear provided by the mayor. When Katie had recommended using their coms, Chief Webb dismissed the idea with a wave of his hand and said he wasn't about to change protocol after seven years of providing security detail for the governor.

Governor Winston made his way to center court, where each team of ten players and their coaches waited in formation. Team Army lined up on his right, and team Air Force on his left.

Winston stepped into the wide opening between the two teams and greeted the arena. "Good evening! We are here tonight to celebrate and support our wounded, ill, and injured military heroes." Winston paused, and the crowd filled the planned silence with cheers.

She checked the time. Everything was moving like clockwork. A six-minute speech, then the governor would call for the Air Force veteran with the dog for the presentation of an award. Winston's team orchestrated things so the veteran was in line farthest from Winston to maximize the photo ops when the man brought his dog to Winston for the award. The presentation of the award came after a short speech, then tip off.

Christina raised her scope and began her surveillance check from the beginning, sweeping across the crowd in her usual pattern, ticking off every marker by the nickname she'd given them. So far everyone was accounted for. She swept back up to Bulldog.

Wait.

Bulldog was gone.

It had been less than thirty seconds since she'd last checked on him, and now he was missing. The familiar icy touch of adrenaline crept through her veins.

She tried the radio. "My suspicious target is on the move. I've lost eyes, need backup. Possible threat."

The radio responded with the crackle of static.

Christina gripped her scope and scoured the sea of faces for the potential threat who'd vanished into thin air. The man she called Bulldog could have left his seat for the restroom or to get a snack, but a nagging suspicion deep in her gut meant he wasn't here to watch a basketball game.

This was a fine time for her radio to act up. Was this intentional interference? She prayed that her radio was transmitting even if she couldn't receive it. "Be on the lookout for a white male, approximately six-seven, dressed in all black, close-cut hair and a bulldog tattoo on his left forearm." If they heard her, they should be able to locate him. A man like that stuck out like a sore thumb.

The radio was silent. She verified her channel and the battery, but everything checked out. They needed eyes on the suspect and her coms were down. Perfect. She'd love to throw the thing against a wall and watch it burst into a thousand pieces. Of course, where she lay in the maze of rafters and suspension bridges, there wasn't a wall to absorb her frustration.

She rubbed a hand on the side of her pants. Sweat from her palm made the grip on the spotting scope feel like grasping butter. She fought the urge to swing it wildly back and forth, sweeping the crowd as fast as possible, but forced herself to follow her previous search pattern knowing it would yield better results.

"Where are you, where are you, where are you?" she whispered.

What if this Bulldog guy was a harmless veteran overwhelmed with PTSD who had decided to leave before the game started? Possible, but the idea didn't sit right. The way he dressed, his size, the prison tattoo—everything about him threw up red flags.

She clenched her teeth. There was no telling what he was up to. She had to find Bulldog. Now. Moving as fast as she dared, she skimmed the spectators one at a time looking for the big man. The crosshairs slipped past a pock-marked face and her heart stopped a beat. Was that him? She exhaled and slipped the scope a fraction of an inch at a time until it landed on its target.

Bingo.

Colossal shoulders and thick neck. It was him. Now she could see his face. A wide flat nose that looked as if it were pressed to a glass window and sunken dark eyes. The pock marks weren't the only scars covering his face. A long pink scar followed the curve of his cheekbone. And were those burn scars that accompanied it?

The man sat staring ahead while spectators took photos of

LYNETTE EASON & KATE ANGELO

Governor Winston and the players lined up. She lowered her scope and saw the same bulldog tattoo on his left forearm. His hands dug inside a black bag in his lap.

"No, no, no," she murmured. "This is all wrong."

Reporting over her coms at this point seemed futile, but she tried anyway. "Eyes on the threat in section 105, second row from the top. Possible concealed weapon."

She slipped her phone out of her pocket and risked taking her eyes off Bulldog long enough to text her team. A split second after she hit send, a message in red letters appeared under her text: *Not Delivered.*

Something was blocking the radio and cell signals, and she feared it had something to do with Bulldog. He could easily conceal a signal jammer in the bag on his lap.

Training said she should never leave her position, especially without backup. But what if she was the only person who had identified this man as a potential threat? Someone had to check him out. If she didn't act, then she risked not stopping a genuine threat. Leaving to investigate also meant losing her vantage point. He could slip away again unnoticed.

One thing she knew for certain—she couldn't lie here on the grate and do nothing. He could have a gun hidden in his bag. Or a bomb. She growled her frustration and smacked her hand on the metal floor.

A quick glance at the SLED agents closest to the target told her they weren't aware of Bulldog. Winston was still delivering his speech and he would only be in the open a few more minutes. Bulldog hadn't moved, but his hands still fumbled inside the bag in his lap.

Time to move.

She tapped out a message in Morse Code using her piece of junk radio.

On the move. Coms out. Suspect in section 105. Send backup.

She pulled herself into a low crouch to avoid being seen

from below. If a spectator saw her moving around, they might blow her cover. Earlier today she'd viewed the catwalk from the seats below and had chosen her position with maximum concealment in mind. She'd mapped out every entrance and exit and knew the quickest route to take. Another benefit of her partial photographic memory.

She also knew exactly which access ladder would get her to the stairwell near section 105. Unfortunately, it was on the opposite side of the arena, which meant either taking the long way around, or risk being spotted making her way across the footbridge. The black tactical clothes would help her blend with the shadows, and she said a silent prayer that she could pass overhead without being seen.

Now or never, Christina.

Being the center of attention was normal for Grey, but sitting center court with his dog at his side made him uncomfortable. Sure, he enjoyed being the funny guy in a room full of friends, making everyone laugh, and encouraging a good time, but this? No, this was too much. It was bad enough all the military veterans here to play wheelchair basketball were lined up with their injuries on display for the three thousand fans to gawk at —but in a few minutes, they expected Grey to push his wheelchair to the spot next to Governor Winston and pose for a publicity photo with the man he disliked.

"I feel like a moron," Grey murmured.

Wally stood at the end of the line holding his coach's clipboard with his good hand, his right arm hanging limp at his side. "Oh, you're definitely a moron, but it has nothing to do with this," he said out of the corner of his mouth. Even after their medical discharge from the Air Force, Wally looked Special Forces. Daily workouts and a regimented diet earned him a well-toned physique. A smooth jaw and a slicked-back, military-regulation haircut replaced Wally's former beard and shaggy hair.

"Wow, thanks for the vote of confidence," Grey said. "How'd I let you talk me into this anyway?" He glanced up at his friend. Two years ago, he'd stood three inches taller than Wally, but from his wheelchair, he was barely chest height.

Wally looked down and frowned. "What are you talkin' about? You love basketball. We've been shootin' hoops together for years."

"Not from a wheelchair," he muttered.

"Aw man, you've got nothing to worry about. You got the best coach on two legs."

"Why doesn't that make me feel better?"

"You're gonna be fine. Besides, the ladies love athletes. Especially wounded ones. Just look at the hot mama over there making eyes at you."

Grey looked in the direction Wally gestured. The beautiful older woman sitting in the front row was indeed a hot mama. It was his mother, Emma Parker, sitting in the front row, her wide smile as radiant as ever. She'd pulled her silver-streaked blonde hair into a loose chignon that fell at the nape of her neck.

When their eyes locked, she crooked her index finger in a small wave. It had been their secret wave to each other since he was a boy, something only the two of them shared. Grey elbowed Wally in the thigh. "You keep your eyes off my mama, or I'll send my dog after you."

Wally laughed and showed Grey a palm in mock defense. "Oh, I'm so scared. He won't bite me. I'll feed him hot dogs while he hangs out with me during the game."

"Don't feed my dog hot dogs. He's a national asset. At least give him steak."

Grey flashed a grin at his mother and crooked his finger back at her, remembering a similar look of pride on her face and the tiny finger wave as his bus had pulled out for Air Force Basic Training over ten years ago. His father, Rhett Parker, sat with his arm around her shoulder, wearing a familiar brush-popper work shirt and black leather vest. The edges of a smile peeked beneath his salt and pepper mustache. He tipped his Stetson to Grey and gave him a strong thumbs up.

It was too bad Ruby wasn't here to keep them company during the game. His older sister was at a conference speaking on equine therapeutics, but had called earlier to give him a wonderful pep-talk and ease his hesitation about tonight's game. Thank goodness for his supportive family, because he still couldn't believe he'd let Wally talk him into signing up for wheelchair basketball.

Grey rolled his head back and stared at the metal catwalk. He exhaled an exasperated breath. A fleeting movement caught his eye, and he snapped his attention to a shadowy figure slinking from the outer rim of the catwalk to the footbridge spanning the entire arena. A tingling sensation spread through him and his breath caught in his chest. Who was up there? Grey stole a glance at the men around him. They hadn't noticed.

He squinted at the figure creeping along the darkened footbridge. When the figure stood, Grey saw the shapely form of a woman, tall and lean in black tactical clothes and hair pulled back into some sort of ponytail. With long strides, the woman continued crossing the width of the basketball court with careful foot placement. She hugged the railing with her back, avoiding the open areas, clearly trying to conceal her movements.

Halfway across the footbridge, she paused and looked through the metal floor grate. Their eyes locked for a beat and she held a finger to her lips, then looked away and picked up the pace, moving with stealth and speed. In seconds, she'd crossed the basketball court and disappeared down a metal ladder.

Overwatch. The woman must be on the protective detail and

stationed on overwatch duty. What had made her leave her position?

An elbow to his shoulder made him wince. "Ow." He rubbed his arm.

"What are you looking at?" Wally whispered. "Pay attention, man."

Grey half listened to Winston's speech on the history of the Warrior Games while scanning the faces of the undercover SLED agents stationed around the arena. They were impassive. Nothing seemed out of the ordinary. But that woman. She'd moved with a tactical precision that meant something was up.

Winston held his arms wide and invited the audience to cheer for the players lined up on either side of him. "Which is why it is my extreme honor to support these great heroes."

Hero? Grey was no hero, and he knew his teammates didn't see themselves as heroes either. They were shells of the men they used to be, fighting to find a place in the world—a world where people didn't know what to do with a wounded soldier who still struggled with nightmares and depression. No, the last time these men had felt like heroes was that moment just before they'd lost their ability to walk.

If the governor really cared, he'd make an enormous investment toward wounded warrior programs. Set up grants to ease the burden of raising funds to purchase the specialized wheelchairs required to play. If not for a generous donation from local charity Chelsea's Hope, there wouldn't be a team in the Columbia area.

And didn't the governor realize his planned pauses encouraged the crowd to get loud, something that could trigger PTSD? Of course not. He didn't care about this basketball game or who won. All he cared about was making his statement, getting his photo-op, and scoring some political points for himself.

Grey turned his head to look at the long line of wheelchairs. So many men who'd given so much. He let his gaze drift over the arena. So many faces. Genuine threats all over the world were held at bay by men just like these, but was there a threat lurking right here, somewhere among them? Where was that overwatch woman?

"Earth to Grey." Wally patted his shoulder. "What's with you? You're up. Go."

Winston had just mentioned the military working dogs as one of the many warriors deserving honors, which was Grey's cue to take his dog to be presented with a plaque celebrating his continued service to the people of South Carolina through their government contract. Grey was so lost in thought he'd almost missed it.

He exhaled and looked down at his partner, the tan Belgian Malinois who'd been with him through countless near-death experiences including the one that had landed them here. Boss deserved this award and Grey was proud to be by his side.

With the leash draped over his lap, he pushed his wheelchair out of the line and toward his mark next to Winston.

"Okay, boy. This is your big moment. Let's meet the governor."

3

THURSDAY, 3:54 P.M.

A familiar thrill coursed through Christina's veins and her pulse thrummed in her ears. It heightened her senses and propelled her toward her target with a determination she hadn't experienced since her Army days. The threat was genuine, she could sense it, but a niggling doubt still hung in the back of her mind. To abandon her post meant breaking operational security protocols and leaving the rest of the team vulnerable. But this wasn't the battlefield, and she wasn't in the Army any longer. She needed to rely on her instincts and trust herself.

One last ladder and she'd be on ground level, but not out of the woods. This was the worst part. The part where she'd be running blind, unable to see Bulldog or what he was doing. She reached the second ladder, gripped it, and placed her feet on the outside rails. The black combat boots squealed on the way down, the sound echoing into the service room below. She hit the ground with a satisfying thunk and spun on her heel. A red exit sign glowed over the doorway and in three strides she shouldered through the door. The harsh fluorescent lights forced her eyes to adjust a moment. The arena map she'd memorized appeared in her mind and she was in the service tunnel. She knew where to go.

Arms pumping, she raced to the end of the corridor and rounded the corner. As she burst through the exit into the public area, the muffled noise of the spectators came to life in a cacophony of voices and overhead announcements. Clusters of people moved through the lobby or stood in lines at the concession stands. Christina bolted through the crowds, weaving her way around them.

A semi-circle of teenagers posed for a photo in the center of the hall, blocking the entire corridor.

"Move! Get out of the way!" She hated to yell at innocent civilians, but it was the best way to get their attention.

The group looked up with wide eyes and scattered. She darted straight through, checking the overhead signs for her next turn. A shoulder collided with hers, knocking her off balance. She stumbled, regained her footing, and picked up the pace.

"Sorry!" Her yell drifted behind her.

Another left and she would be at the ramp leading to the spectator seating area. Should she make a beeline for her suspect, or hop the rail and throw herself in front of Governor Winston? She didn't want to make a scene if her instincts were wrong about the threat, but what if she was right?

Disastrous thoughts ran through her head, everything from a bomb to a mass shooting with thousands of targets sitting like helpless ducks in stadium seating. She used the images to drive her on even harder.

A woman stepped into Christina's path as she rounded the corner and they slammed into each other. Christina grabbed the woman's shoulders and felt strong hands slip around her waist. Each steadied the other until they regained their footing.

"I'm so sorry—" Christina did a double take and stared at

Katie Matthews. Her sleek black hair was pulled into a tight ponytail that accentuated her high cheekbones and olive complexion.

"Christina?" Katie's dark eyes went wide with recognition. "What are you doing?"

"No time to explain. There's a suspicious male, section 105, second row from the top. Possible concealed weapon. My coms are out."

Katie nodded. "Mine too."

"Grab an agent and go after him. I'm going for the governor."

"I'm on it." Katie turned and raced off.

Christina dashed up the aisle toward the basketball court. She'd never been so relieved to work for a team that had her back and trusted her judgment. She crested the top of the ramp and scanned the faces of the players for any signs of awareness. The way the players waited on the court looked like a firing line to Christina, and Winston was front and center.

Wait. Something was different. The player next to Winston had moved from the end of the line. It was the basketball player with the dog who had made eye contact with her when she was on the catwalk. Winston was still speaking, and he held a wooden plaque between himself and the man. The gold plate in the shape of South Carolina mounted in the center of the award glinted in the light.

How should she get their attention? She glanced at Bulldog, saw him looking down and screwing something together.

The choice was made.

Christina ran as fast as she could toward the black handrail at the top of the ramp. She grabbed the rail with both hands, planted a boot, and vaulted over. Landing with a roll, she then sprang to her feet and came up running. A twinge of pain shot through her ankle, but she ignored it and focused on her objective. She locked eyes with the governor of South Carolina and charged him at full speed.

All around her, bursts of camera flashes illuminated the ruddy face of Governor Winston. His mouth fell open and Christina launched herself at him, arms extended to tackle. Her hands connected with his bony shoulders as she crashed into him. They went down hard.

Winston wheezed and coughed a minty breath in Christina's ear. She'd knocked the wind out of him. He writhed and tried to push her off.

"Stay down." She brought her elbows up and pinned his head in place. "I think someone's trying to—"

The sharp pop of a single gunshot severed the roar of confusion in the audience.

The plaque in Grey's hand exploded. A white hot pain seared his left temple and shards of wood and metal fragments sliced his face. The impact blew his wheelchair backward, but the anti-tip casters kept him upright. A woman held Winston to the ground while bullets popped around them.

Grey dropped what was left of the wooden plaque and let his training kick in. "Boss, behind," he commanded.

Boss moved behind Grey's wheelchair and tucked himself close, where he'd stay until Grey released him. A bullet would have to go through Grey to get to his dog.

Grey grabbed his wheels and pushed himself close to Winston, shouting, "Protect the governor!"

The players used their wheelchairs to form a protective circle around Grey and the governor, still willing to put their own lives on the line for another long after their official service had ended.

Warm blood dripped from somewhere near Grey's scalp and rolled down his face like hot tears. A gunshot wound? He lifted the hem of his jersey and blotted his temple, even as he scanned the crowd for a gunman. Where was the shooter?

The crowd was in chaos. People screamed and shoved each other, all trying to escape. One woman stood frozen, tears streaming down her face, holding an infant tight to her chest, unsure of where to go. His eyes flew to his parents' empty seats and a flood of relief washed over him. Dad knew what to do and Mom was on her way to safety.

Another round of gunfire broke through the noise. Grey flinched, expecting the impact center mass but exhaled when he realized he wasn't hit. Shouts and a scuffle came from near the upper deck and Grey watched a man in a blue shirt take aim at a hulking figure who was slipping through the exit door. The man in the blue shirt took a shot, the gun report kicking the volume of the screaming up a notch. A female in black tactical clothes and a black ponytail hit the exit door just behind Blue Shirt in pursuit of the gunman.

Was there more than one gunman?

The blood was rolling down Grey's forehead and into his eyes. He blinked and wiped his face with the back of his hand. When he looked again, the agents were gone, and several other officers were rushing through the same door.

"Grey! Grey, are you okay?" Wally shouted. His head bobbed over the swarm of agents approaching.

"Wally, I'm here. I'm fine!" Grey shouted over the crowd.

"Get back!" The swarthy man Grey recognized as Chief Webb waded past the players with his weapon up. "Get these players outta here and get this area secured."

"I'll get Boss and take him somewhere safe," Wally said.

A plainclothes agent stepped in front of Wally and put a hand on his chest. "Sir, you need to evacuate."

"Hey, man. I'm the coach," Wally said. "My player looks like he needs medical attention. Why don't you take him to get some help and I'll take his dog out of this mess before he gets trampled."

The agent squared his shoulders. "We'll take it from here. Please make your way to the exit."

"It's okay, Wally," Grey said. "I'll keep Boss with me. He'll be fine."

Wally looked like he was about to argue but nodded. His eyes lingered over the scene for a moment before he turned to go.

Grey turned to see what Wally was staring at. The woman sprawled over Winston hadn't moved and still protected the governor with her body. It was the woman Grey had seen creeping along the catwalk a few minutes ago. Whoa, how'd she get down here so fast? She'd moved like lightning, certainly capable of protecting the governor. And the way she'd hit Winston like a freight train—well, she must be one tough woman.

She turned her head toward the officers and undercover agents surrounding her with guns drawn. "My name is Christina Sherman," she said. "I'm with the protection detail. I'm going to get up." Her voice was calm and firm.

"Perfect." Chief Webb snorted. He holstered his weapon and grabbed Christina under her arms and yanked her to her feet.

She didn't object to his rough handedness but held Webb's gaze with penetrating eyes, noses nearly touching. Strands of her blonde hair escaped from her braid. "Thank you, Chief Webb."

Grey wanted to intervene and put Chief Webb in his place, but Christina stood her ground. It was clear the woman knew how to handle herself. She may be part of the protective detail, but the way she'd detected the threat and protected Governor Winston said her training went beyond the police academy. This woman was strong and fast, and carried herself with confidence. Perhaps former military?

Christina turned to help Governor Winston stand. "I'm sorry, Governor. How are you? You hit the floor pretty hard." Her eyes scanned his face.

"I'm fine," Winston said. "Just had the wind knocked out of me." He dusted the wood fragments from his suit and gave Christina a thin smile. "I have a feeling I should be thanking you, young lady."

Chief Webb angled his bulk in her personal space and pointed a sausage finger at her chest. "Why didn't you radio for backup?"

"You're right, Chief. Calling for backup *is* priority. I attempted multiple times, but my coms and phone were jammed." Her voice was calm and even.

"*Jammed?* How could our coms be jammed?" He shook his head and put his hands on his waist, flicking the sides of his navy off-the-rack suit jacket.

"I understand your frustration, Chief. I was frustrated with my coms too. It's unfortunate they weren't working when we needed to communicate."

Grey admired her smooth handling of the difficult circumstances. She repeated Chief Webb's words back to him like a hostage negotiator convincing a madman to surrender. Did she have experience in hostage negotiations? Grey was all around impressed with this woman who seemed to think fast on her feet.

Chief Webb spun to face Governor Winston. "Do you believe this nonsense?" He threw his hands up.

"Calm down, Webb," Winston said. "Shouldn't you be concerned that your own men didn't see this guy until he'd nearly blown my head off?"

A patch of crimson crawled up Chief Webb's neck and spread onto his face. His eyes flicked to Grey's for a moment before they shifted back to Winston. He slicked his thick black mustache with two fingers and cleared his throat. "I'm sorry, sir. I'll do a thorough investigation and report back to you."

"Meanwhile, where's the shooter? Is he in custody?"

Chief Webb shifted his weight. "No, sir. He opened fire on my team and escaped."

Winston shook his head.

Webb pointed at Christina. "Get her statement. The rest of you secure the crime scene. You know what to do."

Agents led Governor Winston toward the East tunnel. Chief Webb whirled and pointed at Grey. "Make sure he's taken care of."

Strong hands seized Grey's shoulders and pushed him from behind. He dropped Boss's leash and grabbed his wheels, forcing his chair to a stop. "Hey, what are you doing? Don't touch me."

"You need to let go. We're getting you to a medic," a voice said beside his ear. With no other option for steering the specialized wheelchair, the man strengthened his grip on his shoulders and pushed.

Grey's palms burned with the effort to stop his wheels from moving. Anger knotted his stomach. This guy had no manners. Didn't he know better than to touch someone in a wheelchair without permission? It added to the feeling of helplessness, like a toddler plucked from the playground and carried off without his favorite toy.

He wanted to put this guy in his place and tell him he had more important things to do, like find his parents, but he bit his tongue. "Fine, just let me push myself."

Grey reached for Boss's leash, but the man stepped around and grabbed it.

"Is this your service dog?"

"No, he's a working dog," Grey answered. "It says so right on his vest."

"What do you mean, working dog? Isn't that what a service dog is?"

"No. He's a military multi-purpose canine. Trained to sniff out bombs and other terrorist materials."

"So, he doesn't provide any specific tasks or assist you with your disability?"

"I don't need any assistance," he spat. His blood boiled at this agent's insensitivity. "My dog was receiving an accommodation for his years of service to this city, keeping you safe from terrorists."

"If he's not a service dog providing you with specific service tasks, he can't go." The agent walked away, tugging Boss along.

"You can't touch him." He gave his wheels several strong shoves. The modified wheelchair was built for speed on the basketball court and Grey was able to pass him, spin around, and cut him off. "Stop. This is a matter of national security. And way above your pay grade."

The agent glared down at Grey, sidestepped him, and offered the leash to the agent standing close to Christina, jotting down her statement. "Only service animals are allowed during medical transport."

Grey didn't want to leave Boss. Despite what had happened here tonight, he knew SLED was capable and trained in protection, but Boss was too important to leave in the hands of just anyone. He looked for Wally, but the arena was nearly empty.

Christina stepped forward. "I can watch him. I served with military dogs in the Army."

Grey studied her.

"It's okay," she said. "You can trust me."

Minutes had passed since she'd prevented an assassination attempt, one that the rest of the protection detail hadn't seen coming. Grey looked at Boss. The dog glanced up, then strained against his leash until he was next to Christina. Boss ducked his head behind her leg as if telling Grey she'd protect him. Well,

Boss had made up his mind. And if Boss thought he'd be in good hands with Christina, who was Grey to argue?

"Okay. But I'm just going to give my statement and see a medic. My injury isn't even that bad," Grey said. "It's not like it's a peek-a-boo injury."

Christina blinked. "Excuse me?"

"Yeah." He chuckled. "I mean, it's not like I'm going to the *eye see you.*"

A smile played on her lips.

"Oh brother," groaned the agent behind Grey.

Grey cleared his throat. Oh brother was right. Where had that come from? He rubbed the back of his neck. "Can you, um, bring him to the back when you're done here?"

Christina nodded and reached for the leash. She locked her brown eyes with his. "Don't worry. I'll protect him."

The agent put his hand on Grey's shoulder. "Let's go then."

Grey rolled his shoulder and gave him a look of irritation. He mouthed *thank you* to Christina. She nodded, her eyes curious and warm.

The agent led Grey down a ramp to an enclosed passageway with empty white walls. The officer's footsteps echoed until they reached a double doorway with two uniformed SLED agents standing like centurions at the doors. A young agent with red hair and acne scars covering his face blanched when he looked at Grey's bloody face. He averted his eyes and his Adam's apple rolled.

"Looks worse than it is," Grey said.

A dark-haired paramedic pushed through the door with a gust of icy wind chasing her. A chill zipped straight through Grey and he rubbed his bare arms. His sleeveless basketball jersey was a poor barrier to the icy touch of February. The door banged closed behind the paramedic who stopped short when she saw Grey.

"Well, you're looking like you've been in a bingle, mate." She tilted her head. "Mind if I take a look, yeah?"

The Australian accent coming from the woman with dark-rimmed glasses took Grey by surprise. He'd planned to brush the injury off as a scratch in need of a Band-Aid so he could get Boss and find his parents, but the wound was hot and angry. It continued to trickle blood that rolled into his eyes. He'd been using his jersey to wipe it away. "Sure, but can we be quick? I've got to check on my family."

"All right, let's get you over here out of the doorway at least. Name's Narelle by the way." She carried her orange medical tool bag several yards away from the door and dropped it with a clatter.

"Narelle? That's a great name." He stopped his chair a few feet away and folded his hands in his lap.

She squatted next to his wheelchair and unlatched the lid on her kit, found gloves, and pulled a clean pair over her current pair. "Thanks, love. Had it all my life." She winked, tore open several gauze packs, and dumped antiseptic on the white squares.

Then she paused with the gauze poised in one hand and met his eyes. "This might hurt a little."

He nodded and closed his eyes, bracing himself for the inevitable. A flash of cold, then an explosion of pain took his breath away. He clenched his teeth to fight the scream threatening to escape. He'd poked a hornet's nest with a stick when he was a boy, and the stinging sensation spreading across his body brought the memory surging forward.

"Sorry, mate. That gash is a mite worse than it looks." She applied pressure to the cut with one hand and taped the gauze in place with the other. "Looks like you've been nicked by a bullet. We've gotta get you to hospital."

The rude SLED agent stood with his notepad and pen poised. "He can't go anywhere until I get his statement."

Narelle cast an annoyed look over her shoulder.

"Unless it's life threatening, I mean."

Grey never thought he'd side with this guy, but he was relieved. It was a mistake to leave Boss with a stranger and he needed to find him. "I'm fine. Close it with butterfly strips and I'll get it checked later."

Narelle shook her head. "You've got no choice. You're a liability and they'll need a doctor's release for you." She stood and pulled the top pair of gloves inside out and slipped them into her kit.

"Can't I sign a waiver?"

Narelle placed a hand on Grey's shoulder. "Listen, love. I know you're a big strong soldier, but this isn't the battlefield. I can't just patch you up and send you back into the fight. You've got a head injury. If you have a seizure and cark it, that's on me."

She didn't deserve to lose her job because of his stubbornness. Still, his dog was with a stranger.

"I'm not going anywhere without my dog."

4

Christina's adrenaline drained from her system, and with it her
energy. The throbbing in her ankle intensified, but she ignored
it and tried to focus on giving her statement to Agent Mitchell.
They'd moved from the center of the basketball court to the
East tunnel leading to the locker rooms. From that position,
they were protected but still had a clear view.

The arena continued to buzz with activity despite being
cleared of the players and spectators. She looked at the seat
where she'd last seen Bulldog. A crime scene photographer
squatted in the aisle and took photos of what the yellow
evidence markers indicated.

The night hadn't gone as planned, and even though she'd
saved Governor Winston, the sniper had managed to escape.
Not something she was used to. During her sniper days, Bulldog
would have had a bullet between his eyes before he'd changed
seats. But she supposed in her new role as a bodyguard, she'd
performed her job flawlessly. The governor was safe.

She silently thanked God for helping her reach Winston in

time. There was a time when she didn't believe in God, but after watching so many targets die, she was forced to rethink things. To rethink God. Even behind battle lines, her spotter always had an unshakable sense of peace that she'd craved. And like a good spotter, he'd given her the coordinates that pointed her right to God.

Agent Mitchell cleared his throat. "And, uh, what made you decide to run for Winston instead of the shooter?"

"I calculated the risks. Winston was the obvious choice."

Mitchell scratched a note in his pocket-sized notebook. Every few seconds, he paused to wipe the sweat from his brow with his sleeve. Scribble, wipe. Scribble, wipe. The pattern had continued for the last ten minutes. The excessive sweating didn't affect his top-notch interview tactics. He brought up everything she would have asked and a few things she hadn't thought of. She kept her answers brief, giving him only the information he asked for.

The dog sitting by her side let out a sigh and nudged her fingers with his nose. He was growing tired of the endless questions too. Christina ran her hand over the dog's pointy black ears, and he looked up at her with watery brown eyes. He was a beautiful Belgian Malinois with a short tan coat and a black mask around his eyes and nose. This dog reminded her of a military war dog she'd served with in Afghanistan, except his color was lighter.

Of course, this was no ordinary military dog. In the security briefing, the team was informed the dog was considered a national asset and was receiving an award for his civil service. Not only had this dog served the country, putting his life at risk to save soldiers, he was continuing to serve after retirement. She wasn't sure what his role was, but as far as she was concerned, a dog this valuable to the nation deserved more than honor. He deserved respect.

Was that what had possessed her to step up and take the

dog? Or was it the dog's owner? She'd been appalled by the rude agent shoving Grey out of the way like a child. How could an officer treat a victim that way?

But, in truth, he didn't seem like a *victim.* The man was strong and the thick muscled biceps that rippled as he pushed his chair didn't escape her notice. But it was his eyes that drew her. Even under the nasty cuts on his face and dried blood in his sandy blond hair, he had a warrior's eyes. And he'd trusted her with his dog, a national asset—and even if that SLED agent betrayed him, she wasn't about to let him down.

If the owner came back to find they'd moved, he would panic. As soon as she finished here, she would find the man and get his dog back to him.

Agent Mitchell opened his mouth to ask another question, but she interrupted him. "Your interview techniques are great, Agent. I'm sure you've outdone yourself." She smiled. "I suppose I'm free to return this dog to his owner?"

"One more question, Miss Sherman. How many times did you attempt to call for backup?"

"Eight, including the text and Morse Code message."

He put the tip of the pen to his lips and tapped. "And no response of any kind?"

Katie walked up behind Christina and gave her a reassuring pat on the shoulder. "I was having radio trouble too."

A man in jeans and a collared navy blue shirt nodded his greeting. "If it wasn't for this woman's quick thinking, we may not have identified the suspect before he fired again," he said.

Katie nodded. "Agent Moon pursued the suspect, but the guy was already on the move after he fired the first gunshot."

"We cornered him," Moon said, "and chased him to the upper deck, away from the crowd. Right before he went through the exit door, he turned and fired at me. I returned fire, but the guy still slipped away."

"Was anyone hurt?" Christina asked.

Katie glanced at Agent Moon.

"The bullet went high and struck a woman in the shoulder," he said. "The woman will be fine. It was a through and through."

Katie crossed her arms. "Agent Moon hit our suspect. Clipped his shoulder we think."

Moon scowled. "He never should've had the chance to fire. We were all over him." He shook his head. "I have no idea how a man the size of a grizzly bear could move so fast."

"Don't beat yourself up," Christina said. "You did what you could. Without our coms, everyone was in the dark, not just you."

Katie nodded in agreement. "At least he was nice enough to leave a blood sample you can run through CODIS."

Christina chewed her lower lip. A blood sample was a huge break in the case but getting the DNA sample into CODIS—or the Combined DNA Index System—would take time. A lot of time. Bulldog could flee the country. Or worse, he could make another attempt on Governor Winston.

"Has anyone figured out why we couldn't communicate?" asked Mitchell.

"This might have something to do with it," a voice said behind her.

Christina turned to see a man holding a military tactical transceiver in one hand and a black backpack in the other. The backpack looked like the one that Bulldog had held on his lap. "That thing is black ops," she said. "I've seen that kind of equipment before. Even if he wasn't communicating to someone else, it's powerful enough to jam all our coms."

Katie huffed. "He was definitely prepared. If he's a pro, why would he take a shot front and center like that?"

Katie was right. The gunman could have taken the shot from his original seat, but he'd moved to a closer position. A riskier one where he might be seen. "He's more than someone with a grudge. He had a ghost gun, one he assembled on the spot. He had to get close for accuracy."

Everyone agreed and Mitchell made a note.

Katie thrust her chin toward Christina. "Who's your friend? He's pretty cute."

Christina looked at the dog sitting at her feet. Was he smiling at her? He was so quiet, she'd forgotten she still held the leash. "We're just hanging out, but if Agent Mitchell is done with me, I'll get him back to his owner right now."

"You can go," Mitchell said. "Send me your full statement tomorrow."

"Of course."

"Oh, and you might find that guy in the ambulance," Mitchell said. "Take the East tunnel to the street exit. Show your badge and they'll let you through." Sweat rolled from his temple to his chin and he swiped at it before turning away.

"After you get Mr. Handsome there back to his owner," Katie said, "go home and get some rest. I'll report to Olivia."

"Thanks. Have her call me if she has any questions."

"Will do."

Christina headed toward the tunnel, surprised that the dog followed without a command. He pranced by her side as if he anticipated her every move. "Well, aren't you a sweet guy?" She smiled down at him and picked up the pace. The sooner she got him back to his owner, the sooner she could relax. A hot bath sure sounded good right about now.

She flashed her badge to the uniformed officers at the exit doors then slipped outside to find herself standing below street level on the secret VIP entrance road. A fifteen-foot concrete wall topped off with black wrought iron fencing kept it hidden from traffic. The driveway ran along the length of the arena, with a gentle slope leading up to the street exit. The diesel engine of an idling ambulance rumbled a few yards away.

The cold February wind raced up her neck, reminding her

she'd left her coat inside. She hustled to the ambulance and banged her palm against the back door. A moment later, the door cracked open and a paramedic with dark hair and glasses poked her head out the back.

"Ya need somethin'?"

Christina held up the leash and pointed to the dog with her head. "This guy wanted to check on his owner. I think he's in there with you."

The paramedic spoke to someone over her shoulder then opened the door a bit wider. "He wants a word, but you'll have to hurry as we're about to shove off. Just lend us the leash, will you?"

She handed the leash to the woman and the dog hopped up and onto the gurney. Christina stepped closer and peered inside. The soles of two giant tennis shoes pointed skyward, but a squirming dog trying to lick his owner's face blocked her view.

"Okay, okay. I love you too," said the man. "Move so I can thank her." He sat up and peered around the dog. Steri-Strips held a cut on his cheek closed, and a white bandage was wrapped around his head like a turban. "Thank you for bringing him to me. Really, I can't thank you enough."

He wrapped his arms around his furry friend and kissed the dog on the snout. The dog returned his kiss and the man laughed. Christina couldn't help but smile at the sweet reunion.

"It was no problem. My pleasure really. He was good company." She was talking fast and it occurred to her she didn't know either of their names. "I should go. Or rather, I should let you go. To the hospital, that is. But I never caught your—"

Shouts rose behind her. "Hey! Hey, over here!" the voices called.

Christina spun to see a crowd of reporters running toward the ambulance. Without thinking, she grabbed the door and swung it closed, positioning herself between the ambulance and the oncoming crowd. She banged on the door with a closed fist, signaling the driver to leave.

A man pointed his shoulder-mounted camera in her face and began recording. She should've hopped in the back of the ambulance when she had the chance.

"No comment." She turned her back on the reporters and headed for the arena doors.

Reporters always seemed to have the worst timing. As a former sniper, the last thing she needed was her face plastered all over the internet for her enemies to find. And the worst thing of all? She *still* didn't know the name of the warrior basketball player with the adorable dog.

THURSDAY, 9:12 P.M.

Grey laced his fingers behind his head and stared at the stark white ceiling tiles, listening to the sounds of the busy emergency room. A clock on the wall ticked the seconds off one click at a time. Doctors and nurses relayed critical patient information to each other in the hall outside his room. The constant pulsing and beeping of medical equipment invaded his thoughts. When would they get in here and stitch up his wound? It had been hours already. How much longer would he be stuck here?

Boss snorted and repositioned himself between Grey's legs.

"Yeah, me too buddy," Grey muttered. He reached down and caressed the dog's head, pushing his pointy black ears back and letting them pop up again with each stroke.

Thank goodness for the paramedic who'd paved the way for Boss to stay with him. He wasn't about to let the dog out of his sight again. No way. He'd rolled too easily with that overbearing SLED agent, and if the heroine of the night hadn't stepped up and offered to help, Grey would have refused treatment altogether.

Boss was draped over him like a seventy-five-pound weighted blanket. He twirled a finger around the dog's ear and tried to block out the distracting sounds of the hospital. No telling how much longer he'd be here, so he may as well try to get some rest. He exhaled a long breath and turned his head to the other side, the paper-like pillow crinkling under his head. His eyes fell on the basketball wheelchair folded on the floor in the corner.

Great. He'd have to exit the hospital in that thing, the vibrant Air Force blue frame drawing the attention of everyone in the hospital. He blew out a breath and squeezed his eyes shut. The sooner he saw the doctor, the sooner he could get out of here. He hated hospitals.

"Hello, Mr. Parker. I'm Dr. Ayers." The doctor walked with his head down, reading a medical chart. "Looks like your CT scan is clean, no concussion." He glanced up and frowned. "Oh, no. We can't have your dog with you. It's not sanitary—"

"He's not going anywhere." This was non-negotiable. Boss was staying with Grey where he knew he'd be safe.

"Wait, you misunderstand me." He reached a hand toward Boss, then hesitated. "May I?"

Grey nodded his agreement and eyed the doctor. Something about the way he carried himself was familiar. Did he know this guy? Grey studied his blue eyes and military buzz cut. They were about the same age, early thirties. Respectful with a calm demeanor that relaxed Grey's taut nerves. Had they served together? It didn't matter. If this guy wanted Boss to leave, no amount of kindness—or rudeness, for that matter—would get Grey to back down. Not this time.

Dr. Ayers stroked Boss along the length of his back, and the dog's muscles quivered with delight. "I love dogs. Served with several in Afghanistan. He can stay in the room, but not on your lap during my examination." He glanced up at Grey and flashed a grin. A small dimple formed in his left cheek. "It's not sanitary."

Grey looked closer at the slight shadow in the man's eyes. "You were in the Army?"

"I did two tours in Afghanistan as a medic before I got out. I worked on many canine handlers." Dr. Ayers looked thoughtful for a moment then shook his head and exhaled. "Anyway, I know better than anyone that military working dogs save lives."

Boss swished his tail at the praise.

"How'd you know Boss is a military working dog, and not my service dog?"

"The tattoo in his left ear. And..." Dr. Ayers shifted his weight. "And I went to the game tonight with some friends. Rooting for the Army, of course." He smiled and tipped his head at Grey's Air Force jersey.

Grey's eyes widened. The movement sent a twinge of pain shooting through his temple and he winced. "I can't believe you were there."

Dr. Ayers nodded and moved to the sink. Boss lifted his head to see why the petting had stopped, then flopped his head back down on Grey's legs, chest heaving with a sigh.

The doctor scrubbed his hands. "I have a private practice, but I also take ER on-call shifts. After the shooting, well, I figured I'd better get to the hospital ASAP." He glanced back at Grey. "Just in case."

They both knew what *just in case* meant. Mass casualties. "Were there any other injuries?"

"I tended a GSW. Nothing too serious." He cut the water, pulled a few paper towels from the dispenser, and crumpled them, drying his hands. "That's why it took me so long to get to you."

Grey uncurled the bottom of his bloodied jersey and smoothed it. The musty smell of the dried blood made his stomach roll. "Well, sorry we had to meet like this," he said. "But, hey, thanks for coming to the game. The guys and I appreciate your support."

Dr. Ayers tugged a pair of gloves from a box mounted on the wall and wiggled his hands into them. "I'm a big supporter of all veterans and the causes that support them. Chelsea's Hope, Wounded Warriors, the Warrior games. All of them."

Grey smiled and his respect for the man grew. They shared a mutual understanding of what it was like to serve on the front lines. "Chelsea's Hope donated all our equipment." He tipped his head toward his wheelchair on the floor.

"Nice. I was admiring the chairs on the court." Dr. Ayers looked at Boss and cleared his throat.

"Oh yeah. Sorry, Doc," Grey said. "Boss, off."

Boss jumped off the bed and shook out his fur, sending his dog tags jingling. He stretched one hind leg, then the other and yawned.

"At ease, Boss."

Boss walked to the corner of the room and plopped down on the floor, disinterested in the doctor since it was clear he wouldn't get any more affection. Well, it wouldn't be the first time he'd slept through Grey being stitched up.

A nurse pushed a rolling tray table into the room and pulled the curtain closed behind her. "Are we ready in here?"

Grey recognized the suture setup and let out a breath. He dropped his head back onto the pillow and closed his eyes against the harsh surgical lights overhead.

"All set," Dr. Ayers said.

The longer Dr. Ayers removed wood and metal shards from the cuts on his face, the less Grey liked the man. The numbing medicine took the edge off, but it wasn't a complete pain blocker. He wasn't about to let another soldier see him acting like a wimp about it, so he bit back his desire to suck air between his teeth each time the needle pierced his skin.

To take his mind off it, he thought about the events of the evening and tried to make sense of them. Governor Winston had an enemy, a dangerous one. But who? Christina had spotted the gunman from her overwatch position, but somehow Grey had missed seeing a sniper right in front of his face. Was he losing his touch?

"That about does it," Dr. Ayers said. He pulled his gloves off and tossed them in the trash. He offered a hand to Grey and helped him sit up.

"You did great," the nurse said. "Can I get you any water?"

Grey started to say no, but then realized Boss could probably use a drink. "Sure, that'd be great."

Dr. Ayers picked up his chart and began scratching notes. "I closed the smaller cuts with tissue adhesive, and ten sutures to close the laceration on your right temple." He paused and tapped his own temple to indicate the spot. "Everything should heal on its own, but I'm prescribing some antibiotics to stave off infection. I'm assuming it's not your first time with stitches?"

Grey snorted. "Not exactly."

They both chuckled and the nurse pushed the suture tray piled with the bloody gauze toward the door. "I'll tell his family he's done."

Relief flooded him. "My parents are here? When can I see them?"

"Go ahead and send them back," Dr. Ayers told her then turned back to Grey. "Okay, so the rest of your tests look good. No concussions or broken bones." Dr. Ayers trailed off. He closed the chart and tucked it to his chest. "Got a big surgery coming up in a few days?"

Grey nodded. "These cuts shouldn't be an issue, right?" His eyes roamed to his wheelchair. The surgery was experimental, but if it worked, it would be the first step in putting himself back together. A chance at a real life again.

Dr. Ayers tapped Grey's foot with the file folder. "Nah, the cuts won't be an issue unless there's an infection. But I think it would be wise for you to lay low. Get some rest and stay out of trouble, you hear?"

Grey gave Dr. Ayers a salute and watched him leave. Boss jumped to his feet and inclined his head, listening with interest. He moved closer to the door, but Grey didn't stop him. Boss knew to stay close and rarely broke behavior. Sounds of rushing footsteps echoed in the hall. The doctor was speaking to someone in the hallway, but Grey couldn't make out the words.

"Oh, thank You, Lord!" His mother rounded the corner and rushed into the tiny room with outstretched arms. Her soft hands found Grey's cheeks and she planted a kiss on his forehead.

"Ow!" Grey flinched. "Mom, my head."

"Oh," she gasped. "I'm sorry, honey. We're just glad to see you. I was so worried." Her gray-blue eyes roamed over his face, taking in the tiny cuts and bandage on his forehead.

Grey's heart swelled at the sight of his parents. He reached out and took his mother's hand and ran his thumb over her cold fingers. The skin was thinner than he remembered, and her hand trembled under his touch. He cleared his throat, trying to dislodge the lump that had formed there.

His father clapped a sun-weathered hand onto Grey's shoulder. "How you doin', son?" At just under six foot tall, Grey's father never towered over him physically, but his father had a presence, a quiet confidence that overshadowed every other person in the room. His deep gravelly voice had put the fear of God into him when he was a boy, but as an adult he'd found the strength in the man's voice reassuring.

"I'm good, Dad. Thanks for asking. What about you guys?"

Boss squeezed his way between Grey's parents and nudged Rhett's hand with his nose.

"There's my boy." Rhett reached down and scratched Boss behind the ears then fixed his steely blue eyes onto Grey. "Your

LYNETTE EASON & KATE ANGELO

mother has been trying to call you for hours. She's been beside herself with worry."

"I know, I know. I'm sorry," Grey said. Why did his father's words feel like a chastisement? "I didn't have time to get my phone before—"

"I have it." Emma dug in her purse until she found Grey's phone and handed it to him.

Grey swiped the screen and sighed. "Thirty-eight missed calls. You weren't kidding."

Emma gave Boss a pat on the back. "Some of those are from Ruby. We told her you were okay, but you should call her."

"Right now?"

Emma pulled herself onto the edge of his bed and sat with her feet dangling. "You know how she worries."

Yeah, he knew. The wheelchair had changed everything, including the way his family and friends saw him. In their eyes, the chair meant he needed their help. That he was *less than*. And his sister Ruby was the worst of all. She hovered, keeping tabs on his schedule, his physical therapy, and even droned on and on with medical research about his condition.

Unfortunately, they'd never seen him in action. They hadn't been around during missions, when he'd jumped from helicopters and walked up to IEDs with nothing but Boss and a flak jacket. And protesting wouldn't help. The wheelchair spoke louder than his words ever could.

Rhett moved to the recliner in the corner of the room and Boss followed him to sit between the man's legs. Boss placed his chin on a knee and Rhett stroked his head absently while the dog sighed with pleasure.

Grey dialed Ruby's number and waited for her to answer. "Hey, sis!" He forced himself to sound upbeat.

"Grey, oh! I am so glad you're safe. Mom called and said there was a *shooting* at the basketball game. I can't believe it! Why didn't you call me? Are you okay? Was anyone hurt? Who

46

was shot? My heavens, I can't believe it." Her words were coming fast and shaky.

"Hey, slow down. You're gonna hyperventilate. Besides, you already said that."

A silence stretched between them for a beat. "Said what?"

Grey looked at his mom and rolled his eyes. He put the phone on speaker. "You already said you can't believe it."

"Well." She hesitated. "I can't."

"And to think, people actually paid to come hear your keynote at the conference tonight. You're a regular Shakespeare with words, you know that?" Grey flashed a grin at his mom.

"Grrreeey." Ruby drew his name out with a long whine. "You know I worry about you. Why didn't you call me?"

"I don't need a mother, Ruby. I already have one. In fact, she's sitting right here with Dad. You're on speaker."

"Hi, Mom and Dad," she said. "Grey, you know I didn't mean... It's just...your job. It's dangerous. I worry about my little brother. Especially after what happened. Can you blame me?"

Was she talking about tonight, or two years ago when his parents received *that call*? The one every military family member dreads. He glanced at Emma's blonde hair threaded with silver streaks. The dark circles and soft lines around her eyes seemed more pronounced. What had that call cost them?

"I know, I know." He wanted to change the subject. It was a discussion they'd had numerous times. At forty-two, his big sister was ten years older than him, and with her training and years working as a child psychiatrist, he was outmatched. "They took me to the hospital before I could grab my phone. They just now let Mom and Dad come back here."

"Hey, baby," Emma called toward the phone. "We're all here and we're fine. Don't you worry, we'll take care of him."

Emma patted Grey's thigh and he resisted the urge to roll his eyes like a teenager. "There's nothing to take care of, you guys. I wasn't shot. The bullet hit the wood plaque, and a few splinters lodged in my head. The doc cleaned me up and he's sending me home with nothing but ibuprofen. It's no big deal."

"No big deal? Grey, there was gunfire! At a basketball game with hundreds of people. Our parents included. You nearly..." Ruby paused and cleared her throat.

He probably shouldn't bring up the number of times a bullet graze or other injury had to be field patched by a combat medic with less than a year of training. "I meant no one was seriously hurt. In fact, there was this woman—"

Ruby cut him off. "A woman? What woman?"

Emma raised her eyebrows and cocked her head. Grey knew that look. It was the look of curiosity mingled with hope that her still-single son had met a woman.

Grey averted his eyes. "All I know is one minute Governor Winston was handing me an award and the next minute a woman was tackling him like a football player." There. The image of a football player should reign in their wild imaginations.

"Oh yes," Ruby said with enthusiasm. "I saw her on the news. Incredible. Is she a Secret Service agent?"

"The Secret Service protects the president, not the governor," he said. "She wasn't in a uniform, but she said she was a part of the protection detail, so I guess she was an undercover SLED agent."

Emma leaned toward the phone. "The news said the man trying to kill the governor got away."

He really needed to watch the news and figure out what happened.

"Well, I'm glad you're all right," Ruby said. "Unfortunately, the story of Boss's award will get buried under this one in the news tonight. Hang on a second." She covered the phone and spoke to someone nearby.

"So when can we take you home?" Emma patted his knee.

Ruby came back. "What?"

"I was talking to your brother, honey."

"Oh, okay. Give him and Boss a kiss from me. I've gotta go. Some colleagues invited me to a late dinner, and I said I'd join them."

"Sounds like fun," Grey said.

"Yes, dear. Have a good time. We'll see you Sunday," Emma said.

Rhett stood and moved next to Grey. "We love you, hon," he said.

"I love you too, Daddy." Ruby disconnected after another round of goodbyes.

Rhett helped Emma to her feet. "I need to visit the ladies," she said.

"I'll escort you and see if we can get our boy discharged." Rhett put his hand on the small of Emma's back and guided her out the door.

Grey smiled to himself. The love his parents shared after forty years of marriage gave him hope. Would he ever find the kind of love his parents shared? At one time, he thought he would, but then...

No, he wasn't going there. Not tonight. He plucked his phone from his chest and tapped a search for tonight's events into the browser. A cold wet nose nudged his elbow. Boss stood beside the bed, staring at him with hopeful eyes.

Grey laughed and patted the bed. "Okay. Okay. Boss, hup!"

Boss sprang forward and landed on the bed. After walking in a circle, he dropped into position between Grey's legs.

"Good boy," Grey said, smoothing his coat.

The first search result looked promising, and he tapped the link. It was the local news channel and as he suspected, the top story was the attempt on Governor Winston's life at the basketball game. The news article included a video and he tapped play.

"Tonight's Wounded Warrior Games garnered more excitement than most spectators bargained for when authorities foiled an assassination attempt," the reporter said.

The broadcast cut to cell phone footage of Winston and Grey posing for a photo when Christina ran for Winston and took him to the ground.

"South Carolina Law Enforcement confirmed the attack on Governor Winston's life was averted by Christina Sherman, an undercover agent on the protection detail."

The TV cut from the video clip to a photo of Christina looking over her shoulder. Grey paused the video. It was her. The same woman he'd entrusted Boss with. Her full lips turned up in a slight smile. A sharp angular jaw highlighted high cheekbones. Agent, huh?

Grey pressed play and the anchor continued. "Our sources tell us the suspect attempted to assassinate Governor Winston when Sherman intervened, putting herself between the governor and the bullet. The male suspect opened fire on two agents, injuring an innocent bystander in the process. Police returned fire, injuring the suspect. The man evaded police capture, but surveillance cameras revealed the gunman to be Viktor Sokolovich, a known hitman in the Russian criminal underworld."

Grey's heart seized. He knew that name.

Dr. Ayers entered and Grey turned his phone off.

"These are your discharge papers and your script for antibiotics," Dr. Ayers said. He handed Grey a stack of papers. "Directions on how to care for your wounds. Not that you need those." He laughed.

"So, I'm free to go?"

"Yep. Good luck on your surgery by the way. What's the recovery like?"

"The surgeon says the operation is about eleven hours long, and I'll need a few days in the hospital followed by months of physical therapy." Grey commanded Boss to hop down. He was still reeling from the image of Sokolovich and didn't feel like small talk. "Hey, Doc, do you mind?" He pointed at his chair.

Dr. Ayers unfolded the chair and parked it beside the bed. "You know, those surgeons won't be as nice as I am." He stroked Boss's head. "They won't let this guy near the operating room."

"I know."

"It was nice meeting you. I'll root for you at the next game."

Grey thanked the doctor and waited until he left to settle into his wheelchair. Boss stood beside him, and the doctor's words came back to him. *They won't let this guy near the operating room.*

It was an issue that had plagued him for weeks and now he was going to have to make a decision one way or the other. His parents and Ruby didn't have the security clearance the government required. Wally had clearance, but with his long hours at the laboratory, Boss would be a distraction. He refused to do that to his friend no matter how willing he was to take on the responsibility.

Grey returned to the news article and stared at the image of Viktor Sokolovich filling the phone screen. It was him. The same dead eyes. The same brawler nose and boxer ears. A face covered in scars and looking like it'd been run through a meat grinder. Yeah, it was him all right. There was only one reason Viktor Sokolovich would be in the city, and it had nothing to do with killing the governor.

Grey let out a breath and dropped his gaze to Boss. The dog stared up at him with questioning eyes. "I know, boy. We need to keep you safe." He planted a kiss on the top of the dog's head. "I'll protect you. Even if it means postponing the surgery."

5

FRIDAY, 6:40 A.M.

Christina parked her car and cut the engine. She checked the time. Over an hour early for work, same as always. The Elite Guardians headquarters was empty this time of the morning and twilight was just beginning to chase the darkness from the sky. Safety lights illuminated the modern concrete office building. High-tech security cameras mounted to the eaves captured every angle of the parking lot.

So far, she'd completed more tasks this morning than some people did all day. A six-mile run. Check. Morning hygiene routine. Check. A healthy breakfast and a hot cup of decaf tea. Check. An hour of prayer and devotion. Another satisfying check.

Her older brother, Will, had once teased her about spending too much time reading her Bible and praying every day. But it was important that she prepare herself for spiritual battle more fiercely than she prepared for physical battle.

She climbed out of her car and stepped back to admire her new Kia Stinger. The HiChroma Red paint job contrasted with the dark tinted windows and chrome accents that gleamed in the pre-dawn morning. Even though the deep red color garnered far more attention than she was used to, she loved every inch of her car. She didn't usually get attached to material things but had allowed herself this one luxury.

Once inside the office, she punched in the code to disable the security alarm and headed for her desk. Typing up her statement regarding the events from last night would take some time, but she had about an hour of quiet before the rest of the team began arriving.

A creak from the back of the office sent Christina's body rigid. She held her breath and listened, eyes scanning for anything out of place. No one else should be here.

Silence.

Seconds ticked by. She stood frozen, allowing air to trickle from her nostrils. It was possible the noise had come from outside, but doubtful. Perhaps she had imagined it. She relaxed, convinced she was still on edge from last night.

Rustling of fabric and another creak sent tension threading back through her. Okay, she hadn't imagined that. Someone was here. A friend of Bulldog? Had they seen her photo on the news last night and sent someone after her? The reporters may as well have put a bullseye on her back by giving the whole world access to her information.

She pressed her hand on the butt of her pistol, slid it from the holster, and pressed it to her thigh. On the balls of her feet, she crept toward the sound.

A shadow under the door leading to Olivia's office caught her eye. She side-stepped away and watched the shadow dance beneath the threshold. Her hand tightened on the grip of her gun.

The shadow disappeared and another creak came from the office. Crackles and pops rose behind the door. She leaned her ear toward the sound but couldn't place it. It reminded her of frying bacon in a hot skillet. Was the room on fire?

She inched forward and tested the handle. Not locked, and not hot. She added pressure, pushing down until the latch released. In one quick movement, she flung the door open and stepped into the doorway, gun raised. "Don't move!"

The blonde woman standing behind the desk raised her hands, eyes wide. "What in the world—Christina?"

"Olivia?" She lowered her gun. "What are you doing here?"

"I think the real question is, why are you slinking around the office with your gun? You scared me out of my mind." Olivia eyed the weapon.

Christina slid it into her holster and clasped both hands behind her back, standing at ease. "I'm sorry. I didn't mean to scare you. I thought—I thought you were an intruder. Your car isn't in the lot and it's early."

"My car had an issue last night, so I dropped it off with the mechanic this morning. I took an Uber instead of getting Wade and the girls out of bed so early." She shrugged. "I just wanted to get in here and catch up on some paperwork."

"The alarm was set when I arrived."

"Oh, I put it in Stay Mode."

Christina pointed to the speaker on Olivia's desk. "You're listening to a thunderstorm, but from out there, I thought I heard bacon frying."

They both smiled. "I wish it were bacon," Olivia said. "I'm starving! By the way, why are you here so early?"

Christina laughed. "I'm always early."

"Well, I'm glad. There was something I wanted to talk to you about if you don't mind." She seated herself and gestured toward the empty chair across from her desk.

Christina sat and crossed her legs. She piled her hands on her knee. "Okay, shoot."

"Are you happy working here?"

Christina's right eyebrow dipped while the other one raised. "Absolutely. Why do you ask?"

"You've done amazing work, Christina." Olivia placed her arms on her desk and leaned forward. "I don't doubt your skills or your abilities. You've more than proved yourself. Your work with Haley last year was invaluable. Your hostage negotiation skills saved lives."

"Not all of them," she mumbled.

"That wasn't your fault. Belinda was shot by accident, and God used her death to save Micah's life."

Christina thought about that tragic day often. Belinda had sacrificed her life to save her son's. God had allowed a mother to die so her heart could be given to her dying son. "I know. It still bothers me sometimes, thinking I could have done more." She locked eyes with Olivia. "What makes you think I'm not happy working here?"

"It's just..." Olivia paused, searching for the words. "Well, you know here at Elite Guardians we are very close. Like family. But you seem...standoffish."

"Is this about last night? I tried to call for backup—"

"No, no, nothing like that." Olivia dismissed her question with a wave of her hand. "It's just a personal observation."

Christina considered Olivia's words for several seconds. "I *love* my job here, and I love the people I work with. I trust them with my life. If I seem detached, I'm sorry. I'm an introvert. I guess with my past, I'm used to working alone and listening while others speak." There was more she could say—much more —but she decided to leave it at that.

"We love you too, Christina." Olivia's blue eyes filled with compassion. "As I said, it has nothing to do with your performance. I just wanted to make sure you don't regret working here."

She offered her boss a half smile. "I have many regrets, but joining the Elite Guardians is definitely not one of them."

Olivia's features relaxed. "I can't tell you how glad I am to hear that."

"If there's nothing else, I need to get that report done before the meeting."

"Of course."

Christina headed to her office, her mind spinning Olivia's words round and round. Then she sighed. She'd try to be less "standoffish," but she wasn't holding her breath she'd succeed. And what did it matter anyway? People would always come and go from her life, and nothing good ever came from getting attached. And now she had work to do, so the thoughts about her personal life had to cease. She was fine with that.

An hour later, Christina entered the conference room ahead of the weekly staff meeting. Colleagues Lizzie Tremaine and Laila Rabbinowitz sat at the conference table staring at a tablet. Lizzie had worked off and on with the team for the last few years and hadn't lost her athletic police officer build since she'd quit the force. She smiled at Christina, her brown eyes gleaming with delight. "Heard you had an exciting night," she said, tucking a brown curl behind her ear.

"We already watched most of it on the news," Laila said. As a former Mossad agent, she worked undercover, but kept her past a secret. Behind her chocolate brown eyes and shy smile was a deadly assassin with a razor-sharp mind that Christina had immense respect for.

She started to speak, but clamped her mouth shut when she saw Charlie Lee, Olivia's tall, dark, and handsome brother, gliding into the room with two white baker's boxes held high. He whistled a tune and attempted a clumsy pirouette, sliding the boxes onto the conference table. "Enjoy, ladies." Charlie gave a dramatic bow.

Lizzie rolled her eyes. "Nice beard."

Charlie scratched his scruff and a slow smile spread across his chiseled face. His dark brown hair was looking shaggy around the ears, but it added to his rugged good looks. "Yeah, it's my new look. What do you think?" Charlie worked with the Elite Guardians on a contract basis. The last Christina heard, he was undercover on a special project for Mayor Eliza Baker to infiltrate a local drug ring and was rarely at the team meetings anymore.

Lizzie popped the top on the first box. Her face lit up. "Your new look is nothing compared to these beauties."

Laila opened the second box and spun it around to show Christina. Pastries, muffins, and sausage rolls from the Divine Street Bakery filled the box. The fragrance of sugar and cinnamon mingled with fresh baked bread and sausage made her mouth water. Her stomach rumbled. The thought of releasing her rule against eating sugar blipped across her mind, but she pushed it away.

"Thanks, but I already ate." She took a chair near the door, adding some distance between her and the treats.

Laila hefted a massive chocolate muffin the size of her hand. "What's the occasion?"

Charlie hip checked Lizzie and grinned down at her. "Can't a guy do something nice?"

"Not in my opinion," said Laila.

Charlie arched his thick eyebrows and looked like he wanted to respond to her comment but thought better of it. "We have a client coming in—"

"And I skipped breakfast, so I asked Charlie to bring us something," Olivia said. She walked into the room and dropped a stack of files in front of her chair. She pulled a box toward her and grabbed a sausage roll. "They smell amazing."

Christina let her eyes roam over the team. Did they share Olivia's opinion that she was too distant? Lizzie and Charlie were close. They'd worked with Elite Guardians for several years and had a give-and-take flirtation that everyone noticed, but for some reason they refused to acknowledge. Laila had

LYNETTE EASON & KATE ANGELO

started the same day as Christina, but one would never know it. Laila seemed to fit right in, and even ran marathons with Maddy Holcombe and her husband, Quinn.

"Where's Katie this morning?" she asked, noticing the missing guardian.

Olivia chewed and swallowed. "She's on her new assignment. SLED called this morning and asked us to continue our service after what happened last night. Katie will work with SLED, and Governor Winston has requested private protection for his son, Barry Jr. He's a student at USC and I'll need one of you to cover him."

Laila quirked an eyebrow. "His son? Is he the frat boy I keep hearing about?"

"Yeah, and a perpetual college student," Charlie said.

Olivia opened a file and ran a finger over a document. "Okay, Barry Jr. He might be a handful. Whoever covers him will need to be covert. SLED doesn't want him to know he's under protection."

Lizzie held up a finger. "I can take that one."

"Sounds good. Thank you. We also have a new client coming in today." Olivia shuffled the folders. "Captain Grey Parker, former Air Commando, has a special request and should be here any moment. In fact, Christina, do you mind waiting for him while we discuss backup schedules?"

"Sure." The door chimed. "That must be him."

"Go ahead and bring him in, please," Olivia said.

Christina made her way to the front but stopped short when she saw the man waiting near the front door. He grinned when their eyes met.

Recognition flared. It was the man from last night. His wheelchair looked different, smaller and more compact. She didn't even see any handles on the back like she saw on most wheelchairs.

He stuck out his hand to greet her. "Hiya, I'm Grey." Tiny

specks of red dotted his face, and some areas glistened with a translucent glue she knew all too well. A white strip of gauze was taped to his left temple. Probably covering a few stitches from that nasty gash she saw last night.

His eyes were bright and crystal gray, like storm clouds illuminated by the sun. Why hadn't she noticed them last night? She slid her hand into his and allowed him to pump her limp grasp.

Grey...with gray eyes.

He cleared his throat. "Ahem."

She snapped her head and blinked, her thoughts faster than she could get them in order. "Oh! Yes, you, um. You were waiting here in the—" She jerked her thumb over her shoulder. "The back is where I... It's where I waited when you—" She pressed her lips together before more gibberish spilled out without her permission.

Deep smile lines formed like parentheses around his ever-widening grin. The tiny crinkles in the corners of his eyes were endearing, but his chin dimple made her knees go soft.

I'm staring. Stop staring. She dropped her eyes only to land on the T-shirt that stretched across his broad chest accentuating his pectoral muscles. She gulped.

He folded his arms and squinted. "Are you okay?"

She closed her eyes and told her brain to engage. He probably thought she was staring at his disability instead of the adorable cowlick that made his short blond hair swoop in an effortless wave.

I'm a professional. I can do this. Just treat him like the soldier he is. She leveled him with a steady gaze. "Hello, Captain Parker. I'm Christina Sherman, one of the bodyguards."

He pointed a crooked index finger toward her. "You're a...bodyguard?"

And just like that, the spell was broken. This wasn't her first encounter with men like him. Men who seemed to think her gender or her looks meant she was fragile or incompetent. Little did he know, the job of bodyguard was far beneath her skill level, as it was with all the Elite Guardians.

She dropped her hand and squared her shoulders. "Captain Parker, are you trying to insinuate something about women—"

"No! No, no, no." He held up a hand to stop her. "I just meant that you're so...*hot*."

A snort of laughter escaped before she could stop it. "Thank you, I think."

He bit his lower lip and closed one eye. "That came out before I could filter it. The term *bodyguard* threw me. It's just that when they said you were on the protection detail, I thought you were a SLED agent. Sorry."

"Don't worry about it. I think we've met our cap on introductions anyway. We should join the rest of the team." She whirled to go but turned back. "And if you think I'm hot, wait until you meet Laila."

He flashed another heart-stopping grin and held his hands to his heart. "Oy. We'd better go then."

The dog Grey had asked her to watch last night hopped up beside his wheelchair. He was in a vest with a Velcro label that read *Working Dog*. She wanted to greet the dog, but knew petting was off limits when the vest was on.

"Follow me," she said. Grey's thick biceps bulged when he pushed his chair, and she forced herself to avert her gaze.

Grey entered the conference room behind her. "This is... um..." Her mind clouded over. What was his name? Her eyes darted around the room, searching for words but only seeing Laila. A knowing smile spread across the woman's face.

Great. Now she looked unprofessional in front of the client and the team. Why did she babble like an idiot around this man?

Olivia stood and stretched out her hand. "Captain Parker, I assume? I'm Olivia Savage. We spoke on the phone."

"Please, call me Grey."

Christina admired the way Grey seemed at ease. A casual smile and a strong handshake, as if the person he spoke to was the only person in the room. Meanwhile, she couldn't stop making a fool of herself in front of him and now her team.

Get a grip. You're being unprofessional. And if there was anything she prided herself on, it was professionalism.

The room was crowded with the team around the conference table. She shoved a chair aside to make an opening for Grey's chair but must have used more force than she'd intended because it crashed into Charlie.

"Ow!" He rubbed his elbow. "My funny bone."

She mumbled an apology. The handsome gray-eyed man was throwing her off her game and she didn't like it. She squeezed behind Olivia. Before she could take her seat, Laila stood from her chair and slid into the one Christina was about to take. What in the world?

Christina eyed the remaining seat at the table then flicked an "I'm going to kill you" look at Laila. The only empty chair was directly across from Grey. Great, now she'd have to avoid staring at the man for the entire meeting.

Laila lifted her eyebrows at Christina. "You're welcome," she whispered.

Grey wheeled himself up to the conference table and sat with his hands folded, watching Christina. His eyes sparked with amusement and seemed to reach across the wooden ocean between them and seize hers.

Stop looking at him!

Grey's dog stood at his side. He patted his back and said, "Boss, down." The dog let out a long yawn and plopped down at Grey's feet.

"I'd like to introduce Lizzie, Charlie, Laila, and you've met Christina." Olivia gestured to each team member.

Grey nodded at each, letting his gaze linger on Laila. He gave Christina a subtle so-so hand gesture. Heat flooded her cheeks.

Olivia leaned her forearms on the table. "Well, Captain—I mean, Grey. What can we do for you?"

"Thank you for indulging my need for secrecy," he said. "I'm here to inquire about your protection services for my partner, Major Maxwell."

"Oh? You mean the protection is not for yourself?" The question was out of Christina's mouth before she could stop it.

A smile played on his lips. "Why, Miss Sherman, are you trying to insinuate something about *men* in wheelchairs?"

The room went still. Christina darted her eyes to Olivia, whose own eyes grew so wide that Christina thought they might pop out and roll across the table.

Grey let the moment hang as everyone shifted in their seats. After a moment, he burst out laughing. "Don't worry, it's just an inside joke between us. I'm not offended."

Christina shook her head and tried to hide her smile.

"Well, um. Okay then." Olivia stacked her papers and tapped them on the desk to straighten them.

"I'm sorry," he said. "Let me begin again. As I said, I am interested in hiring your agency to provide protection for my partner while I undergo an experimental surgery that could restore my ability to walk."

Charlie and Lizzie looked at each other. Christina folded her arms on the table and leaned forward. She wasn't sure how his partner played a role in this, but she was intrigued. Not only was Grey willing to undergo an experimental operation, but he wanted to make sure his friend was in good hands first.

Grey explained that his surgery would take several hours, followed by a few days of recovery in the hospital and weeks of physical therapy. "The procedure uses Nanorobotic technology to repair the neural pathways that prevent me from walking."

Christina wanted to ask more about his condition, but she couldn't trust herself to speak with coherence when he was around. She didn't want to embarrass herself in front of her team any more than she already had.

"The thing is"—Grey scratched his chin—"whoever is assigned must have TSC and SCC creds."

"Top Secret *and* Sensitive Compartmented Clearance? That's CIA stuff," Lizzie said.

Grey bobbed his head. Silence hung in the air as everyone considered what Grey's partner could be involved in and why he needed a bodyguard. A high-value target or asset who needed that level of security was usually assigned protection by the military or government, not a private agency.

Charlie was the first to break the silence. "Well, I'm out. I'm already on assignment, and besides, I barely had enough clearance to buy these muffins." He picked up his muffin and toasted the room before taking a giant bite. Bits of blueberry and muffin crumbs tumbled from his mouth.

Lizzie rolled her eyes. "Really, Charlie? You're dropping so many crumbs over there that Hansel and Gretel will be showing up any minute."

He grabbed a napkin and wiped his face and the table. With a clean napkin, he dusted off his chest and pants. "Sorry," he mumbled around a mouthful of muffin. He looked at Grey. "We really are professionals, I promise."

Grey chuckled. "I have no doubts," he said. "I saw Christina in action. She was brilliant. I first caught sight of her moving along the catwalk, and in seconds she somehow appeared right in front of me and pushed Winston out of the way. I mean, if the job is to protect then I'd say she's more than capable." He fixed his eyes on her, the look penetrating.

Christina's stomach flip-flopped at his praises. She ignored the sensation and risked speaking. "So, this partner—why does he need private protection?"

"The details are classified, but the bodyguard will be briefed after clearing security. For now, I need to know if you have someone with the proper qualifications who can focus on this for a month or more."

Olivia let out a breath. "We're a little tapped for the next two weeks, but I think we can swing it. Will your partner need twenty-four-hour protection?"

"Yes, but not for the first week or two. We'll use the time for training."

Olivia's brow creased. "Training?"

"Yes, the assigned bodyguard will need to continue training. We'll have to work together. I mean, I assume none of you has experience with handling sniffer dogs?"

Eyes darted around the room.

Lizzie furrowed her eyebrows. "Sniffer dogs? Major Maxwell is a...*dog?*"

Grey rubbed a hand over his face, pulling his lip and releasing it while he thought. He was walking a fine line between breaching Top Secret protocol and confusing the entire situation. "I guess I wasn't very clear. I'm here because I need protection for my working dog."

Olivia leaned over and looked at Boss sleeping on the floor at Grey's feet. She sat up and tapped her index finger on the table. "Are you talking about protecting *this* dog?"

He nodded and gave the command for Boss to join them. Boss jumped to his feet and rested his paws on the conference table. One pointy black ear turned to listen.

"This is Major *Boss* Maxwell." Grey patted his back. "He's a Belgian Malinois and we've been partners for six years. I use his formal name in all official situations, but during missions, the guys started referring to him as *The Boss* and the nickname just stuck." He shrugged. "Boss is a very special detection canine. The details of his current mission are Top Secret."

"Hence the need for TSC and SCC," said Laila.

Grey nodded. "After clearance is confirmed, the bodyguard will be read in. Boss will need around-the-clock protection during my surgery and recovery. We can't lose ground on his training, so I'll need a few weeks for onboarding, and someone willing and capable of facilitating his current training."

"I have TSC, but I've never even applied for SCC." Lizzie looked at Olivia.

"Well, Charlie and Katie are both on assignment, Haley is out of town, and I'm on call with SLED. I guess that leaves Christina and Laila."

Grey watched Laila fix a steely gaze on Christina with a slight twitch at the corner of her mouth. "I'd love to, but I'm allergic to dogs."

Christina snapped her head to look at Laila. "Since when? You've never mentioned it before."

Laila gave her a one-sided shoulder shrug. "It never came up.'"

Grey bit back a smile and had to admit he was enjoying this.

Christina pointed at Boss who was still standing on his hind legs, eyes fixed on the pastry box on the table. "He's been here for twenty minutes and he hasn't seemed to bother you."

On cue, Laila tucked her nose into her elbow and sneezed. She used a napkin to wipe her nose. "Excuse me."

Christina kicked Laila under the table. It was a subtle movement, but Grey caught it. He stifled a laugh and ran his hand over Boss's head and whispered the *at ease* command so Boss could go back to his nap. This was one battle Boss didn't need to fight.

Charlie and Lizzie mumbled a *bless you* to Laila. They seemed to want no part of the situation either.

"Guys, please." Olivia looked mortified, but she needn't worry. He could tell the team was professional in spite of the banter. He was pleased he'd decided to come to the Elite

Guardians. Even better, it sounded like he might have a chance to work with Christina, a woman brave enough to risk her life getting between Governor Winston and a bullet. As far as he was concerned, she had more than proven herself.

"I'm sure Boss would be in great hands with any of you, but he had great things to say about Christina after she saved lives last night," he said.

Christina glanced from Laila to Olivia, searching their faces. There was a hidden communication that passed between them, but he couldn't decipher it. Christina straightened. "You know, it sounds like a great opportunity. I'd be delighted to take this assignment."

Her eyes found his and he saw determination behind them. Why did she have to be so pretty? Maybe this wasn't a good idea after all. He found her intriguing, but he couldn't get involved with her, or any woman for that matter. Getting involved meant things had the potential to develop into more than something casual. And more wasn't an option for him. What kind of husband or father would he be stuck in a wheelchair?

No, he wouldn't let himself even consider a relationship until he knew the outcome of the surgery. He would have to treat Christina like any other soldier under his command.

He gave her a thin smile. "Thank you, Miss Sherman. I look forward to working together."

"Thank you, Christina," Olivia said. "Laila and Lizzie will be on standby for anything that comes up."

"Wow, I can't believe you'll be guarding a dog," Charlie said. He gave a short laugh. "Aren't dogs supposed to be guarding *us*?"

Olivia popped to her feet, startling Grey. "Okay, then. I think that will do it for the rest of you. Let Christina and Grey have the room to discuss the assignment." She gathered up her papers and shook his hand. "Thank you, Captain. Have Christina bring you by my office to sign some papers before you leave."

"Yes, ma'am."

Laila scooted behind Christina's chair and gave him a wave. "Nice meeting you, Grey."

He gave her a half-hearted salute. She was petite with dark eyes and dark hair that fell in waves around her face that made her seem mysterious. Christina was right when she said Laila was attractive. He just didn't find her as beautiful as Christina.

Christina. All he could think about this morning was the confident and strong woman who had stepped up to take care of Boss. But should he work so close with her? It was one thing to have a female soldier fight side by side with him, but inviting this woman into his life twenty-four-seven? That was a whole other ball game. She would need complete access to his home, his partner, his story. Could Grey do that?

The image of Christina hitting Governor Winston like a linebacker last night flashed in his mind. She could keep Boss safe. There was no doubt about it. And that was the reason he was here.

Wasn't it?

6

FRIDAY, 11:00 A.M.

Boss pranced beside Grey, and they followed Christina out of the Elite Guardian headquarters into the bright morning sun. Grey loved late February weather in Columbia. The chilly wind from last night blew the clouds out to sea and the morning brought clear skies and a warm, sunny day.

Grey slipped his Ray-Bans on and turned to Christina. "After we get your credentials at the lab, I can fill you in on why it's so important to keep Boss safe."

Christina nodded. "Sounds good. I'll drive."

She marched to a red sports car and unlocked it with a beep. The side mirrors whirred and unfolded into position. That was her car? He'd had his eye on the sleek Kia Stinger known to be a sleeper, a high-performance car in the form of a sedan with a zero to sixty in four seconds. So underneath the calm exterior was a woman who craved speed. Interesting.

Christina pulled the door handle and paused with the door half open. She looked over the roof to where he sat waiting on the sidewalk. "What's wrong?"

He rolled forward, then tipped his chair back and balanced on the rear wheels. "Forgetting something?" He let his chair down with a clank and grinned up at her.

Her face fell and she blinked at him, then pressed the car door closed. "Captain Parker, I'm so—"

"Call me Grey, remember?"

A strand of golden blonde hair escaped from her braid and fell on her forehead. She swept it behind her ear. "I'm sorry. I wasn't thinking—"

"No worries, Agent." He held up his own key fob, waggled it, and pressed the call button. "I've got a pretty sweet ride."

The fact she'd forgotten his wheelchair had him suppressing a fist pump. She was probably the first person to see *him* and not *him in a wheelchair* since he'd started using it. Something about that made his heart soar.

A black Tesla Model X backed out of a parking spot and drove toward them. She edged around her car and moved to stand beside him, gaping as the car came to a stop in front of them. Her eyes went wide when she realized there wasn't a driver.

She pointed at the doors that opened upward like a bird spreading its wings before flight. "Now *that* is cool."

Grey wheeled to the driver's side and peeked through the open back doors. "They're called Falcon Wing doors. Pretty awesome, right?"

Grey clicked his tongue. Boss jumped into the car and lay down in his dog compartment.

"He has his own space built right in?" she asked.

"Yep. It's even air conditioned in case I need to leave him. I rarely do, but it's there if I need it. And if you like that, you'll love this."

A button on the steering wheel made the car lower itself two inches. "Suspension controls. Now I don't have to lift myself quite as high."

He grabbed the handles and pulled himself into the driver's seat in one quick motion. Leaning down, he pulled his chair and positioned it against the back door. A robotic arm extended from the back seat and in fewer than ten seconds, the wheelchair was tilted on its back and pulled into the car. The Falcon doors closed with a soft click and the car rose to its original height.

Christina's mouth hung open.

It was a satisfying response, and he never got tired of it. "Well, are you coming?"

Christina hopped into the passenger seat and reached to close the door, but it was already closing on its own. She shook her head. "I've seen some amazing technology, but this... This is just...genius."

Grey ran his hand along the sleek dashboard with pride. This car was amazing. Everyone seemed to boast the countless unique features of the Tesla, but it was beyond his imagination. So much technology put to good use.

"No way I could afford this on my own. There's a foundation called Chelsea's Hope. I think the founder has investments in all kinds of businesses with interest in helping others. They've been really gracious about donating to disabled veterans."

Eager to show off his ability to go zero to sixty in less than four seconds, he punched the gas and zipped out of the parking lot.

"Where are all the knobs and buttons?" she asked, pointing to the smart screen that took up most of the console.

"There aren't any," he said. "That is one reason I chose the Tesla. The fewer knobs I have to fumble while driving, the better." He glanced at her and smiled.

"How...how are you using the gas and brake?"

He nodded to a small hand control on the steering wheel. "This device allows me to control them. I've got a few buttons on the turn signal here, but everything else is on the screen. I use voice commands for the most part."

She nodded. "I bet this makes life a lot easier for you."

"Oh, yeah! I mean, the gadgets and self-driving features were a big selling point, but the best part is not going to a gas station. Do you realize what a pain it is to get in and out of a car in a wheelchair?" He shook his head. "What a nightmare."

"The process must be tedious, not to mention tiresome, with a standard vehicle. I never considered how technology could help with something as mundane as getting in and out of a car."

"Neither did I...before I had to do it."

Christina was quiet for a while. Did his remark make her think she couldn't talk to him like a real person now? He didn't want her to pity him. He liked the feeling of being treated normal for once.

He decided to change the subject. "What were you doing at the game last night?"

"I'm not sure what you mean."

"Well, SLED was all over the place, so why did they hire the Elite Guardians?"

She turned and angled herself toward him. "As I understand it, Governor Winston received some death threats and Chief Webb was shorthanded."

"Doesn't every governor get death threats?"

"I suppose, but Webb seemed to take these particular notes very seriously."

"So, what happened last night?" Grey asked.

"What do you mean?"

He flicked his eyes to hers, then back to the road. "I *mean*, how did someone get a gun past security? And why were you the only one who saw him?"

"The man looked suspicious."

"And?"

"And what?"

"Wow, talking to you is like talking to my sister." A headache was forming, and he wasn't sure if it was the conversation or the cut on his forehead. Either way, he needed to take something for it.

"Is your sister older or younger?"

He grinned and waved a finger at her. "Oh no, you don't. Don't flip the conversation around to me."

"What do you mean?"

He laughed. "Oh, I'm onto that trick as well. You can't pretend like you didn't understand the question. You're way too smart for that."

She looked out the passenger window. "How do you know how smart I am? We barely know each other."

"Listen, anyone who's been around you for more than a minute can tell how smart you are, so just tell me. Why were you the only one who saw the suspect?"

"I don't want to speak ill of SLED. They are fine agents, and their security protocol was thorough. They did everything by the book." She seemed to choose her next words carefully. "I was on overwatch and pinpointed a few potential threats. I kept my eyes on them, and in the end, only one felt wrong. I attempted to radio for backup, but the suspect had a device to overpower our coms and we couldn't communicate."

The wheels in his mind were turning. "What about the gun?" he asked. "How did he get it through?"

She sighed. "You know how arenas are. Security officers have hundreds of people to check in a short amount of time. Two seconds to glance in your bag and on to the next. I don't like to think about it, but without metal detectors at the college arena, anyone can conceal a weapon on their person and slip through undetected."

"And metal detectors don't mean much to enemies with a plan."

How would Christina react when he disclosed the real

reason why he'd hired her to protect Boss? She had no idea she'd committed herself to protect a national asset who was their only hope for finding and uncovering a terrorist threat that made 9/11 pale in comparison to the destruction it could cause.

Twenty minutes later, Grey pulled his Tesla onto the University of South Carolina School of Medicine campus and wound past countless identical red brick buildings. The campus centerpiece broke the design pattern with its expansive white brick and limestone pillars that stretched tall to brace the portico.

A landscaper added fresh mulch to the flowering pansies wrapping the ornate sign that read *Veteran Affairs*. He doubted the workers realized every move was monitored by hundreds of surveillance cameras covering every inch of the school grounds.

Patriot Lane was a narrow, tree-lined drive that wound away from the main road and ended in front of an unmarked brick building. Grey pulled into a spot marked RESERVED and tapped a button to open all the doors, including Boss's compartment. Boss stretched his hind legs and waited while the wheelchair lowered, and Christina stood near the back of the car, scanning the area.

Grey maneuvered himself into his chair, trying to suppress his usual grunts and groans in front of Christina. He grabbed Boss's leash, clipped it to the service vest, and with a tongue click, released the dog from the vehicle.

Sunlight beamed down onto Christina's blonde hair, creating a soft golden glow that reminded Grey of a morning sunrise. Warmth ran through him and settled in his stomach. He cleared his throat. "All right, Agent. Time to rock and roll."

She cocked her head. "I'm not an agent."

"Oh, yeah, I know." He handed her the leash and wheeled up the ramp to the building.

At the door, he scanned his security badge and the large

metal door inched open. "All this technology and no one can take a week out of their lives to make accessible doors open faster." He shook his head.

The outer doors opened to a small, empty foyer with a set of blacked-out glass riot doors, impenetrable to most explosives and requiring biometric verification for entry. Grey went to the keypad near the wall and punched in a code. He placed his thumb on a small screen and a click signaled they were approved to enter. Both doors opened into a long narrow corridor.

"Biometrics are captured as we move to the end of this tunnel. We need about two yards between us. I'll take Boss, and you can go first."

She handed him the leash and they locked eyes for a beat before she turned and began the twenty-five-yard walk. The way Christina surveyed her surroundings intrigued him. Watchful, but not obvious. Cautious, but confident. Subtle flicks of her eyes and a tilt of her chin were the only signs she was curious.

"The beige walls bring back memories of the Army barracks," she said.

Ah, so she knew this was a military facility. "They used the same color in the Air Force. The government must have their own line with Sherman-Williams. Hey, are you related to those Shermans?"

She cast a smile over her shoulder. "I think you mean *Sherwin*-Williams. And do you know how many times I've heard that one?"

"Sorry, it's hard to resist." The way she smiled cranked up his pulse. Not a wide, toothy smile like most women. Hers was enigmatic. Like the Mona Lisa.

At the end of the tunnel, Grey and Christina stopped at another set of double doors. Instead of blacked-out riot glass, these were painted the same blah beige as the walls. No door handles or hinges on this side. The thick metal doors were heavy and able to withstand an explosion.

Christina studied Grey's face. Was she searching for answers to questions she hadn't asked? She looked to Boss, then back to Grey. She must be wondering what kind of training required this level of security and protection.

Grey looked up at the corner camera that loomed overhead watching their every move. He wondered if the guards stationed inside would refuse entry because his heart raced twice as fast as his normal readings. The first time he'd entered the building, he was jarred by the technology. The long corridor served to capture muscle movements using the millions of infrared light emitting diodes embedded in the walls. Minute gestures, shapes of the body, information about gait, heart rate, and body temperature were collected and stored to compare with each entry and exit.

At these double doors, more IR LEDs and cameras scanned and captured a 3D image map of the face and used microscopic muscle movements for a second identity verification through facial recognition. The equipment was so sophisticated even Boss had a biometric profile, and he was verified with each entry. No other dog could pose and slip in.

The massive doors swung outward, signaling they'd been approved for entry with Christina. "We're in."

"What is this place?" Christina finally asked.

It was nice to know her curiosity had limits. "I wouldn't want to ruin the surprise now that you've made it this far. Just hang tight a few more minutes and you'll see."

She eyed him with suspicion but folded her hands behind her back and stood at ease beside him. The doors shut, enclosing them in a ten-by-ten room. Grey grabbed the wheels of his chair and braced himself.

"Another man-trap?" she asked.

"Something like that. Keep your balance when the floor

moves." He was impressed by her ability to keep calm and not be thrown by all of the secrecy. She didn't ask questions, simply followed and took in every detail with a keen eye. A sure sign this wasn't the first time she'd walked into the unknown.

Her footing wavered as the room lurched and began to move, but she was quick to regain her balance as he'd instructed. She looked at the ceiling. "I didn't expect an elevator. Are we going up or down?"

"I'd tell you, but then I'd have to kill you."

She snorted. "Funny."

"We're going down. This building has upper floors, but I've never been on any of them." He pondered it for a moment. "You know, now that you mention it, I'm not even sure how to get to the upper floors."

The elevator came to a stop and the doors opened. Two military police armed with assault rifles stood guard as they exited the elevator and approached the reception desk where two men in Army fatigues were sitting behind computers.

"Hey, Johnson," Grey said. "How's it going? Isn't it your lunch break?"

"Not for another ten minutes. Who's this?" He pointed a ballpoint pen at Christina.

"This is Christina Sherman. She'll be taking over as a handler for Boss while I'm having surgery."

"Ah, yes. Nice to meet you, ma'am. I believe I have some paperwork here." Johnson searched his desk, shuffling papers before he pulled a file folder out and clipped a pen to it. "Here we are. We've completed your security clearance and just need you to sign a few of these." He handed them to her then looked at Grey. "Take her to conference room two and go ahead and brief her."

"Thanks. We'll stop by and drop them on our way out."

Johnson saluted and both Grey and Christina did as well.

A loud buzzer sounded, and the metal door unlocked with a

loud click. Grey grabbed the door and held it open for Christina. "After you."

"Thank you, Captain," she said. She slipped through the door and waited for him.

Boss gently tugged on his leash and let his pink tongue hang out, excited to be at his home away from home where most of his training happened. For Boss, the extensive training and reinforcement wasn't work. It was play time. A time to get showered with praise and affection for doing something he loved.

"Not yet, boy." Grey rubbed the dog's side vigorously, ending with a hardy scratch behind the ears. "We've gotta do some paperwork. Then we'll show Christina what you can do."

Conference room two looked like an interrogation room in size and shape. It certainly wasn't designed for comfort. Most of the padding was missing from the metal chair, and it creaked with Christina's slightest move. Under the stark fluorescent lighting, the beige walls had a greenish tint, reminding her of a hospital.

Watching Grey interact with his dog was intriguing. There was a special bond there, a mutual trust. During her sniper days, she'd never traveled alone, but she'd also never had a partner she could trust completely. Sometimes her spotters had ended up bailing out, asking for a reassignment due to the inevitable remorse and trauma from killing target after target. But that was the job. A job that meant locking personal attachments in a compartment where they couldn't interfere with the mission.

But even after Grey was injured, he'd kept Boss and they'd continued to work together. The fact that he used a wheelchair didn't seem to stop him from serving his country. And now he was paying big bucks to hire personal protection for the dog he called "partner."

Her gaze drifted from the papers spread on the table in front of her and landed on Grey. He was sitting across from her with Boss's head in his lap, stroking the dog's pointy black ears. She remembered when Grey had mistaken the name Sherman for Sherwin and the way his eyes had lit up when she'd corrected him.

"What's so amusing?" Grey asked.

She pressed her lips together. The first tactic in avoiding a question was to pretend she hadn't heard it. "Hmm?"

"You were grinning."

She was? No, she wasn't. In fact, she'd intentionally suppressed the smile that threatened to take over her entire face. "Perhaps I enjoy signing my name more than I realized."

A burst of laughter escaped Grey. "Oh, I like you." A flicker of teasing filled his cool gray eyes.

Her pen halted mid stroke. He *liked* her? What did that mean? A lump formed in her throat, and she worried she would revert to fumbling her words if she dared speak. She squared her shoulders, refusing to make a fool of herself in front of this man again. She was a professional. All she had to do was sign this stack of Access Debriefing forms and the Non-Disclosure Agreement and get on with her job.

She took up the pen again and saw she'd left off signing her name after the T. The word *Christ* jumped off the page and hit her square in the heart, confirming why she was here. God was her rock, the one who trained her hands for war and her fingers for battle. She refused to let her training fail her now. Finishing her name with a flourish, Christina pushed the stack of papers toward Grey.

"Okay," he said. "I think you're officially cleared. Sorry to put you through this."

She crossed her arms and leaned back. The chair groaned. "What's a military operation without a mountain of paperwork?"

He grinned. "So, you picked up on that, did ya?"

"I noticed the CBRN uniforms, yes, but I'm unclear on your role here." The government had integrated all military branches of actions into a single installation Chemical, Biological, Radiological, and Nuclear Defense Program with the goal to protect the country against weapons of mass destruction. Top Secret facilities were installed worldwide, but she didn't realize one was in her backyard.

"See, I knew you were smart." He wagged his index finger. "As you know, Air Force scientists and engineers play a big role in combating CBRN weapons. Boss and I are working as civilians under the South Carolina Army National Guard's 218th Maneuver Enhancement Brigade. At this facility, I have been training Boss to track a new chemical weapon called X-VX."

"I haven't heard of it."

"It's classified, of course," he said. "So far, Boss is the only K9 in the world to successfully detect X-VX and we've been using him to track Dr. Kalashnik, the Russian scientist who created it."

Grey pushed away from the table and gestured to his legs. "X-VX is why I'm in this wheelchair."

Christina caught the flash of anger that crossed his face. A thousand questions sprang to her mind, but none of them seemed as important as empathy for what Grey had lost. "I'm sorry, Grey. That must be awful."

"It is. I'm adjusting, but I shouldn't have to." He paused. "You know, I have someone I'd like you to meet." He rolled toward the door.

Christina blinked at the abrupt change. She followed him from the conference room through a wide steel door. Several safety signs were posted on doors, but the white triangle with a skull and crossbones caught her eye.

Grey held the door open, and she stepped into what she assumed was the research laboratory. Rows of white cabinets on wheels with ash-colored tops were covered with various lab equipment and machines, all of it foreign to Christina except the glass beakers and Bunsen burners she recognized from high school chemistry class. The outer walls were lined with biosafety cabinets and wash stations.

Boss trotted off to a glass-enclosed office and plopped down on a fluffy round pillow.

"I guess Boss knows where to hang out," she said.

Grey chuckled. "Yeah, he knows to stay out of the way. This lab doesn't handle chemical weapons—there's a secure lab for that—but we do have some dangerous chemicals here. You should be aware of the eyewash and contamination wash stations here, over there, and there." He pointed to each area, and she hoped she'd never need to use them.

They headed toward the only other person in the lab, a rugged looking man with a short beard and dark brown hair cropped short. He used a long eyedropper to transfer honey-colored liquid into a small vial. The name *Dr. Wallace* was embroidered on his white lab coat.

The man flashed a smile when he saw Grey heading toward him. "There you are, man. I was wondering if you'd make it in today. How's your head?"

"Eh, it's just a scratch. I stopped by to introduce my new friend, Christina Sherman. This fine specimen of a man is Dr. Marshall Wallace."

"You can call me Wally." He extended his left hand to shake. His right arm hung unnaturally limp at his side. His dark brown eyes scanned her face. "You tackled the Governor last night, didn't you?" he asked.

"I did," she said. Heat rose in her cheeks. "It's a pleasure to meet you."

"Same here."

"Christina's taking over training for Boss while I have my surgery," Grey said.

Wally raised a brow. "Aw, dude. I said I'd do it. Why can't he stay with me?"

"We've been over this," Grey said. "You need to focus. Time is of the essence, and you don't need the distraction."

Wally drew in a breath. "Well, at least we'll have a pretty face to look at around here for once."

Grey gave Wally's kidney a playful punch. "Hey now, you're gonna hurt Boss's feelings."

Boss lifted his head from his napping spot in the office and tilted it to the side. The men chuckled and Christina smiled at Boss. He really was quite adorable.

"I thought you could tell her a little about X-VX and what else you've been working on," Grey said.

Wally propped his lean muscular frame against the counter and breathed in as if preparing for a long speech. "It's nasty stuff. A synthetic chemical weapon that can be created in a lab, without the need to access tightly controlled precursor chemicals required to make VX. But what makes it different from other chemical weapons is the ability to choose how slow it works. Take the two of us for example." He nodded toward Grey. "We were ambushed with the stuff, told we were rescuing a scientist, when really we were his human test subjects. He dosed us with a small amount of X-VX, which slowly attacked our neural pathways, but in different ways."

"The scientist who ambushed you was Dr. Kalashnik?"

"Yep, he developed X-VX while in America and offered to sell it to the Russian government. Told them he'd figured out a formula that could be used for anything from incapacitating or killing a victim with a delay that would give plenty of time for the killer to escape before being detected. We were fortunate he chose the low dose stuff, or we wouldn't be talkin' right now."

"How does Boss play a role?" Christina asked.

At the sound of his name, Boss jumped up and came to

Christina. He sat beside her leg and nosed her hand. She looked to Grey for permission.

Grey smiled and nodded. "You can pet him. He's an extraordinary dog. Without being trained, he tried to warn me of the danger. I just didn't realize..." Grey dropped his gaze and rubbed the back of his neck.

"How *could* you have known?" she said, stroking Boss. "It sounds like the military wasn't even aware of the new weapon."

Wally sniffed. "Well, we have the formula for X-VX and Grey is using our sample to reinforce his detection training. I'm developing a nanoparticle-based organophosphate degrading enzyme as a protection against X-VX and other toxic nerve agents."

"In English, please." Grey sighed.

Wally chuckled. "The ODE is a medicine for soldiers to take before they go into battle. If a soldier encounters a chemical weapon, the ODE will break down the nerve agents before it can affect the body. Highly experimental."

"My unit was given the experimental vaccine, but it didn't seem to work. At least not fully," Grey said. "Through government funding, Wally has been working to perfect the formula for the vaccine."

"Yeah," Wally said. "Except I'm experimenting on lab rats, not soldiers."

Currently, soldiers were given Atropine, but only after they were exposed, and it rarely worked. Wally's enzyme could mean the difference between life and death for soldiers battling chemical warfare. "It sounds like you're actively searching for Dr. Kalashnik and using Boss to track him?"

Grey's face brightened. "By George, I think she's got it!"

She couldn't help smiling at Grey's attempt to lighten the mood. "One thing I need you to clarify, though. Does this have anything to do with last night?"

Wally exchanged a knowing glance with Grey and tilted his head for Grey to take this one.

"Dr. Kalashnik claimed he'd been kidnapped and forced to work for the Russian mafia," Grey said. "We later discovered his family is connected to the Petrov Bratva, and with the help of Dr. Kalashnik, they plan to attack the United States. We don't have enough details to stop them, but they don't know that. And we think someone was sent to make sure Boss and I can't get in the way of this attack."

"So, you're telling me a chemical weapon will be unleashed on the United States, and the only thing standing in the way is that dog?"

"That's *exactly* what I'm saying."

7

FRIDAY, 6:16 P.M.

The Scavenger slammed his fist on the hotel desk. Items jumped and clattered back into place. The force sent pain shooting through his wrist, but he embraced it. What had happened last night? A professional hitman had a perfect shot and he failed? How was that possible?

Unbelievable.

The stray bullet had missed its mark and nearly killed the dog. He slammed his fist on the desk again. "I *need* that dog."

A new plan began to form. An even better one. One that came with a contingency if things went wrong again.

Focus. Focus on the plan.

He laced his gloved fingers behind his head and rocked back in the desk chair, looking at the ceiling. Sometimes rethinking things resulted in a better strategy. One that was sure to benefit his bank balance. Risky, and quite dangerous, but more rewarding.

The brown leather messenger bag lay open at his feet. The

silver cap of a small vial peeked out of an inner pocket. He plucked it out of his bag and held it to the light.

A clear plastic case in his bag held two hypodermic needles. He clicked the lid open and chose one of the needles and set the case on the desk. Then he pierced the rubber cap of the vial with the sharp tip of the needle and held it upside down as he drew the liquid into the syringe.

The pinch of the needle lasted a second in the muscle of his upper arm before the cold liquid began to burn. He sucked air between his teeth and withdrew the needle. The pain now should pay off big in the next few hours. He returned the used needle to the case and tucked it with the empty vial into his bag.

The laptop screen glowed in the dark room. His bank balance was growing, and he was more than halfway to his goal. Well on the way to retirement. If his new plan worked, he'd have his money...and his revenge. Then he'd simply sell his product to the highest bidder and disappear.

A chime signaled an incoming transfer of two million dollars. Dropped into his bank account just like that. He leaned forward and ran his finger over the screen, counting the zeros. Funny—zero was fast becoming his favorite number.

He closed the bank account window and used a keyboard shortcut to open the cell phone emulator on his laptop. Stupid criminals used real cell phones. Smart criminals used emulators. Even burner phones could be traced these days, but with the modified phone emulator he'd created, users could mimic a cell phone on the computer while secretly sending and receiving secure communication.

He'd named his secure network *Atom* and it had started as a side project, a way to protect himself, but now criminals were paying big bucks to use it. Messages went through end-to-end-encryption and were routed around the world more than ten thousand times with masked IP addresses. Even if a hacker managed to trace his communication, it would take a lifetime to decrypt the messages. Nearly impossible. It would be easier to toss a glass jar into the Grand Canyon from a helicopter, find the pieces, and reconstruct it than it was to track someone who used *Atom*.

He smiled to himself. The so-called best and brightest would be scratching their heads while he spent the rest of his life sailing around the world.

An image of a smartphone centered itself on his screen. He opened the messaging program and typed a response. *Received. Project will commence in 48 hours.*

He rolled his stiff shoulders and cracked his neck before stabbing the enter key with his index finger. The message was sent. He had 48 hours to deliver the dog to the buyer. Easy money.

Now for a little fun.

The cursor flashed on the screen. He rested his hands on the keyboard and considered what to say. A silly rhyme popped into his head, a little immature perhaps, but he went with it.

I know what you did, and you will pay. You escaped your fate last night, but you've only got a few more days. — The Scavenger

With a single keystroke, the message sent. He checked his watch. It was getting late, and he needed to get going or he'd miss the meeting. He closed *Atom* and opened a terminal window. The keys clacked as his fingers flew over the keyboard. With a few strokes, he hacked into the hotel scheduling software. When would businesses make network security a priority? It was effortless to hack into most business networks. Any wannabe hacker could tap into this hotel system with a few basic skills.

He found his room reservation under his alias and erased the record. Next, he logged into the security cameras and paused all recordings for the next half hour just as he'd done before he arrived. The security monitors would display a live feed from every surveillance camera, but wouldn't save the recordings.

When he finished, he powered down his laptop, closed the lid, and flipped it upside down. With a screwdriver, he removed six tiny screws from the bottom casing. A gentle tug separated the aluminum casing and exposed the internal hardware. He used his finger to dislodge the hard drive and seated a new one in the slot with a click. Then he replaced the back cover, careful to tighten every screw.

Shrugging into his black overcoat, he pulled a watch cap down low and tugged driving gloves over his latex gloves. He dropped the old hard drive into his pocket and returned everything to his bag. After a thorough wipe down of every surface, he ducked under the strap of the messenger bag and adjusted it across his chest. With a critical eye, he looked around the hotel room. It was exactly as it was when he arrived. No one would know he'd been here.

In the lobby, he pulled out the phone he'd lifted from a tourist earlier. A nice iPhone, locked by facial recognition. It didn't matter—his plans didn't involve using the phone. Headlights swept through the glass entry, catching his attention. A large black SUV was pulling into the circle drive.

Perfect timing.

Head down, eyes on the phone, he exited the hotel through the revolving door. Voices came from the now parked SUV. A driver hopped out and ran around to open the back door. A woman stretched her long legs to the ground.

"Thank you, Tony," she said. "I'll be an hour."

"Yes ma'am."

The woman searched for something inside her purse, paying no attention to her surroundings, and before he could move, she collided with his broad shoulder. The phone slipped from his hand, he made a move to grab it, but fumbled and it landed on the ground with a cringe-worthy crack.

"Oh! I'm so sorry." She snatched his phone from the pavement, flipped it over, and looked at the screen. "Looks okay," she said, holding it out for his inspection. "What do you think?"

He didn't bother looking at the phone after she handed it to him. Instead, he stared into her dark blue eyes. "Aren't you Gayle Mooney?"

A strand of dark hair fell over her forehead, and she tucked it behind her ear. "I am." She searched his face for recognition. "Do we know each other?"

"No." He waved the phone at her. "I was just reading an article about you. Congratulations on your promotion to director."

"Oh," she said, seeming to realize the stranger wasn't someone she should know, but whose face she'd forgotten. "Thank you. I didn't expect to run into anyone who would know me by name."

"All I know is you've had a *huge* impact on my life," he said with a forced chuckle.

She nodded but got distracted by her phone buzzing. "Well, it was a pleasure bumping into you. I'm late for a meeting."

"Yes," he said, eyes lingering over her face. "It was...*serendipitous.*"

8

FRIDAY, 7:25 P.M.

What had he done? Why had he asked Christina to come over to his house tonight? She didn't need to stay with Boss for at least a week, but when Grey pulled up to her office to drop her off, something deep inside didn't want their time to end. Before he knew it, the words were out of his mouth, and she was agreeing to dinner and a walk around his house to see where she and Boss would stay while he was in the hospital.

She was beautiful and intelligent, and Boss liked her already. If Grey was honest, he liked her too. She didn't say much, but when she did it was clear she took time to choose her words and spoke with purpose. More than once, he realized she was observing the people around her as much as her surroundings. She had a keen eye and something about being in the same room with Christina brought him more clarity. He wanted to know her more and deepen their connection.

But with her fast paced job, could he keep up with her? Being in a wheelchair brought challenges to his life and those around him. Everything took longer and required forethought.

He had to find creative solutions to everyday tasks he used to take for granted. The car was a perfect example. Sure, it was cool now, but the novelty would wear off.

Why was he even thinking about this? Building a relationship with any woman was out of the question until he found out if he would walk again.

Yet here she was, standing in his kitchen, examining his house with those watchful eyes. "You have a very nice home, Captain Parker."

"Thanks." Was she taking in all the accessible features in the house? His kitchen was the most obvious. The white marble countertops were lower than average, and the base cabinets had open areas to accommodate his wheelchair. Good thing he'd let his mother and Ruby have their way with the design. The white upper cabinets contrasted nicely with the navy lowers, and with the furnishings, the place didn't look like a complete bachelor pad.

He dropped his keys on the T-shaped island that separated the kitchen from the living and dining rooms and with his back turned, stole a touch to the bandage on his temple. The ibuprofen was wearing off and he felt the fiery bite of the cuts stretching against the surgical glue and stitches when his facial muscles moved. He wasn't sure if it was the stitches or the position he'd gotten himself into that was causing the throbbing in his head.

It wasn't like she'd come over to hang out. She was here to survey where Boss lived. The dog followed Christina, nails clicking on the hardwoods. When she paused, his tail wagged and he nosed her hand, asking for a head scratch. This wasn't normal for him. Normal was sticking close to Grey, scrutinizing anyone who came near as a possible threat. But with Christina...

Christina obliged the dog's request, absently rubbing his head and ears. Boss closed his eyes and let his tongue dangle.

Grey wondered if he'd start drooling, the traitor. Was that a flare of jealousy? He needed to get a grip.

She moved into the open living room and regarded the brown leather couch and two deep armchairs his mother said "tied the whole place together."

"Very nice." Christina ran her hands over the leather.

Grey tipped his wheelchair back and balanced for a moment before dropping his chair with a clink. "Thanks. I like it."

Christina stood as though restless. She moved back to the kitchen and placed her hands on the island. Boss and Grey followed. "Did you build this home?" she asked. "It feels comfortable. It suits you."

It suits *you*. Again, she seemed to notice him, and not his wheelchair as his identity. "Yep, I just moved in a few months ago." He grabbed two bottles of water from the fridge and nudged the door closed with his foot. He slid a bottle across the countertop and Christina caught it.

"And before you moved here?" She uncapped the water and took a sip.

He picked at the label of his water bottle. "I um… I lived with my parents."

There was the Mona Lisa smile again. "Do your parents live nearby?"

"They have a horse ranch about thirty minutes from here," he said. "My father has been training horses since he was a kid. My sister works with him, but she trains horses for therapy. She's a child psychiatrist and has about fifteen clients who come to the ranch for equine therapy." Grey snapped his fingers. "Hey, I'm starving, how about I make us some dinner? I make a mean chicken Pad Thai."

"Can you make it spicy?" Christina slid onto a stool and folded her hands on the counter.

He grinned. "I can make it as hot as you can take it." Grey wanted to snatch the words back as soon as they left his mouth.

Christina was a hired professional here to observe, not have him flirt with her.

"Okay, I'm game." She didn't seem to be bothered by his remark and reached for her water bottle for another sip. "Can I help you with anything?"

"No thanks. Too many chefs in the kitchen and all that," he said. "It's spacious, but I have my routines." He moved to the pantry, plucked items from the shelf, and piled them in his lap.

"Do you enjoy cooking?"

He transferred the items from his lap to the counter and turned to the fridge for the chicken and fresh vegetables. "Over the last year I've learned that I love cooking. I even took a culinary class a few months ago."

"Impressive," she said. "Tell me how you ended up with Boss."

Grey washed his hands in the sink on the island and dried them. He flung the hand towel over his shoulder. "Are you asking in general, or after I was discharged?"

"Both. I know not all dogs retire when their handlers leave the military. Was he injured?"

The skillet clanged as he set it on the stove to preheat while he sliced vegetables. The ambush in Siberia was still fresh in his mind even after two years. His team could have been killed or injured far worse than what he'd experienced. "Boss had minor injuries and my commander doubted his ability to detect after what happened. They chalked it up to canine PTSD and gave Boss an honorable discharge. Wally applied for him in case, well...before we knew what my injuries would be. But I was able to adopt him."

"What was your plan with Boss before you decided to hire the Elite Guardians?"

Always with the questions and changing the subject when she saw he was uncomfortable. Was that for his benefit, or hers? "I'd prefer to have him stay with my family, but they don't have clearance. Wally continues to offer, but..." He lifted a shoulder. "I guess I didn't have another plan before I met you."

He glanced up and saw she was watching him with a sharp eye. Heat crept up his neck and he spun away, tossing the chicken into the frying pan. It hissed and steam rose from the pan.

When he turned back around to grab the vegetables, Christina was chewing her bottom lip. "I've been thinking about this business with Dr. Kalashnik. With his ties to the Russian mafia, is it possible the gunman at the arena was sent to take you out? The police say he's a hitman from Russia."

"Viktor Sokolovich. Yeah, I thought about that too," Grey said. "I would be inclined to think Dr. K sent him to assassinate Governor Winston, but it seems too coincidental, and I don't believe in coincidences."

"Neither do I," she said. "I know a few detectives at the Columbia Police Department. I could ask if they have any other information."

"If you think they'd give us access, it would be great." Grey added garlic and vegetables to the pan and stirred it. He mixed the sauce and drizzled it over everything in the pan.

"Our agency works closely with the Columbia PD. I'll put a call in tomorrow. That smells delicious, by the way. I didn't realize how hungry I was."

"Gimme about five minutes and it will be ready. You mind setting the table?"

"Sure."

"Everything you'll need is in one of those drawers there."

Boss hopped to his feet when Christina stood and trailed her to the kitchen. "Great idea putting everything in the drawers instead of upper cabinets, and right next to the dishwasher. Very convenient. I should do this too."

Christina made several trips during the process of setting

the table. Each time, Boss followed close behind as if he might lose her.

Grey used the opportunity to steal a glance at Christina as often as he could. She was taller than most women, probably five-eleven. He'd never seen her without her golden blonde hair in that fancy braid, but liked the way it fell over her shoulder when she bent over the table to adjust the silverware onto a linen napkin. Without being instructed, she'd set a place at the table where the dining room chair had been removed—the spot where he usually pulled his chair up to eat. She really did see the details in even the smallest things. She asked a lot of questions but talked very little about herself. He'd have to change that.

"So how did you end up in the Army?" He brought the food to the table and offered for her to take a seat. Boss sat next to Christina like a sentinel.

"My parents were both in the Army. I spent most of my life around the military." She shrugged. "It felt right."

"What about your siblings?"

She folded her hands and rested them on the edge of the table. "I'm sorry, but do you mind if I pray before we eat?"

At the word *pray*, Boss moved over to his food bowl and laid his face between his paws. He stared up, eyebrows dancing in anticipation. Grey was glad for the distraction. Teaching Boss to *pray* before he ate was just a tool to reinforce his obedience. Something to prevent him from being food obsessed. It had been a long time since Grey had talked to God for himself, and he wasn't about to start now.

A spark of amusement flickered in her eyes. "What's he doing? Is he really going to pray?"

"Here, let me show you." He filled the food dish and brought it back to the dining room. "Boss, pray." Grey did this trick almost every night, but for some reason his nerves were on edge. "Dear Jesus, we thank You for the great day You've given us, and for our new friend Christina. Please bless this food to our bodies today. Amen."

On cue, Boss sprang to his feet and crunched his dog food.

"That's incredible, Grey. How long did it take to teach him to do that?"

"Only a day. He's a quick learner."

Grey's phone buzzed on the counter, and he glanced at the island to see the screen light up with a phone call. Evening phone calls were usually from his mom or Ruby, and after the shooting last night, they would ramp up the helicoptering. He didn't feel like talking to them. Instead, he wanted to have a nice dinner with Christina and get to know her.

"Excuse me." Grey wheeled to the counter and grabbed his phone. He was about to dismiss the call when he saw the number.

Alarm bells clanged inside his head and with a swipe he answered. "Parker."

Christina couldn't hear the other side of the conversation, but she could tell it was bad news. Grey's face hardened and muscles in his jaw worked. Curious, but determined not to listen in, she focused inward on her thoughts.

She was impressed with his skills in the kitchen, and he moved with a practiced ease that made her forget he was in a wheelchair. His home was new and clean—not at all the bachelor pad she'd expected. It was a sort of contemporary rustic décor that she might have picked for herself. The open floor plan allowed her a view of the living room, dining room, and kitchen all at once. The stone fireplace on the far wall was the focal point, and like most guys, he had a giant flat-screen television mounted above the mantel.

Grey disconnected the call and let out a long breath. "I'm

sorry, but I have to go. CBRN called. They have a body possibly killed with X-VX. I need to get to the crime scene with Boss ASAP."

She stood and carried their untouched food to the stove and covered the plates. "Okay, where are we headed?"

Grey snapped the last buckle on Boss's service vest. "Oh. You don't have to go. I mean—"

"I'm Boss's bodyguard and soon I'll be his handler. He'll be in the open, and I'll see him in action. I should go." Not much else to it as far as she was concerned. "Isn't that why you hired me?"

"Oh, yes. Of course." Grey swiped his keys from the counter. "I'll drive."

They were quiet on the twenty-minute drive to the Empire Hotel in downtown Columbia where flashing lights from police cruisers bathed the circular drive. An ambulance blocked the main hotel entrance, so Grey parked behind the coroner's van.

Christina waited while Grey seated himself in his wheelchair and clipped a leash to Boss's vest. "Okay, Agent, time to see Boss in action."

What was with this *Agent* thing? She'd already asked him to call her Christina. Maybe he was one of those people who gave everyone a nickname like Buddy or Sport. As long as he wasn't making blonde jokes, she would ignore it for now.

Grey flashed his credentials to the uniform guarding the door. "She's with me," he said, nodding to Christina.

The officer eyed her with skepticism. She showed her own credentials and he nodded his approval. She caught Grey's questioning stare.

"The mayor gives the Elite Guardians special credentials to allow us to be read in on cases, visit crime scenes, and work with law enforcement," she said.

"Well, that's handy." He smacked the metal accessible button on the wall. The automatic door inched open, and he rolled his eyes at Christina. She chuckled.

The hotel lobby was a hum of activity as witnesses with shocked expressions stood in conversation while police officers jotted down statements. Christina let Grey lead the way, noting that Boss kept pace beside Grey's wheelchair. The clusters of people stepped aside to allow Grey more room to move through.

Yellow crime scene tape stretched across the restaurant entrance, and they headed in that direction. Once again, they flashed their credentials and the officer on guard held the tape high so they could duck under.

The restaurant was empty of diners, their tables left in various stages of dinner. Chairs were pushed back or tipped over as if patrons had jumped from their seats and run for the exit. A crime scene technician crouched near a booth in the back corner. Detectives Quinn Holcombe and Bree Standish stood near Wally, watching the photographer snap photos.

The body of an attractive dark-haired woman was lying on the floor with wide, unseeing eyes transfixed skyward. Christina had seen plenty of death in her time, usually at the end of her rifle and magnified by her scope. But every time she saw it up close and personal, she found it raw and unsettling.

"Christina?" Bree asked. Her brown hair was in a loose ponytail, and Christina noted the dark circles under her eyes. "What are you doing here?"

"Working," she said with a head tilt toward Grey and Boss. "Are you filling in for Steven?" Quinn's partner, Steven Rothwell, was married to Elite Guardian Haley Callaghan. They were on an extended honeymoon in Ireland with their two adopted children, Zeke and Micah. Christina liked Steven, and of all the Elite Guardians, she felt closest to Haley—the fiery red-haired Irishwoman—after they'd partnered on a case last year.

Bree nodded. "Yeah, no one else will work with this guy." She nodded at Quinn, an attractive man in his late thirties. Christina noted his deep blue eyes were almost hidden behind long dark lashes.

"Enough with the family reunion," Quinn said. He pinned an annoyed look at Grey. "If you're from CBRN, then let's get this dog sniffing. I'd like to sleep sometime tonight."

"Don't mind him," Bree said. "He's always cranky."

Wally gestured to the man squatting beside the body. "This is Dr. Zamora, the ME."

The doctor rose to his full height. "Call me Francisco. Everybody else does. Good to see you, Christina." A light Hispanic accent teased his words. Black curls fell over his forehead, and he shook them away.

"You too, Francisco."

"Nice to meet you," Grey said. "I'm Grey Parker and this is Boss."

Francisco waved a gloved hand. "My office received a memo to be on the lookout for deaths like this one. I hope we didn't call you people for nothing."

"I guess we'll let Boss be the judge of that."

Francisco pulled a tensioned hand grip from his back pocket and squeezed then released it. "I have what I need. If the detectives are okay with it, she's all yours."

Bree looked at Quinn, who nodded. "Yeah, we're all good here," she said. She lifted her chin to Francisco's hand grip. "You training for another world record?"

"Pull-ups. Gotta work my hand strength." He winked and Bree's face flushed red.

Christina had heard stories about the quirky medical examiner and knew he held the world record for most sit-ups and push-ups. He always seemed to be moving. And the way he eyed Bree said he'd developed a little crush on the female detective.

Grey led Boss away from the body and stopped at the hostess station near the front of the restaurant. Christina followed at a distance, eyes searching every corner for anything out of place.

Grey unclipped the leash. "Boss, seek," he said in a low tone.

The words sent Boss into an excited frenzy. Tail swishing at high speed, he lowered his nose to the ground, sniffing and maneuvering around fallen chairs and abandoned tables, focused on his task. Not even a hesitation at the uneaten steak left on the edge of a table. Apparently, he enjoyed the hunt more than a slab of meat. Boss paused only to snort and move on, heading straight back toward the crime scene.

Christina kept herself a few steps behind Grey, telling herself she didn't want to interfere, but really, she was unsure if Grey expected her to play a part. After all, he'd said he'd train her to become Boss's handler for a few weeks before his surgery. Had the training started?

When Boss reached the body of the woman on the floor, he sniffed her feet up to her head. He put his nose close to hers and snorted, then sat on his bottom and raised his front right paw.

Grey rubbed Boss's head, then unzipped a small pouch on the side of his wheelchair that Christina hadn't noticed before. He withdrew a ball on a rope and offered it to the dog. "Good boy, Boss. Here ya go."

Boss carried the toy to Christina and dropped it at her feet. A flicker of excitement danced in his eyes as he stood with his front legs apart and head lowered, ready to play. With *her*?

She glanced at Grey, and he gave her a tight smile. "It's his reward. Just be warned. He might pull your arm out of the socket if you're not careful."

The rope handle seemed sturdy so she picked up the toy and moved a good distance from the crime scene before offering it to Boss. The dog chomped down on the rubberized ball and yanked hard, nearly pulling her off her feet. A yelp escaped. Grey wasn't kidding about his strength. Her shoulder burned but she tugged back until Grey gave the release command and Boss unhinged his jaw.

Grey offered her a soft smile and she handed him the ball. "It feels weird playing with him in such tragic circumstances."

"I know, but he did his job. And because of that, hopefully, someone can find justice for the poor woman."

"True."

"Sorry to interrupt, but I'll need to get a blood sample then you can remove the body," Wally said. He looked at Francisco. "You'll need to keep her until we give you the all clear."

Francisco nodded.

Wally waved a paramedic over. "You mind?" He nodded at his right arm. "It'll go quicker with two hands."

Quinn moved closer to Christina and stood shoulder to shoulder with her. "What are you doing at my crime scene?" His tone was gruff, but she was used to his ornery disposition.

"Nice to see you too, Quinn. How's Maddy doing?"

At the mention of his wife, Quinn softened. "Perfect. She's a great mother, and Stacy is growing up too fast, getting big."

"It must be difficult to be here instead of at home with them."

He shoved his hands in his pockets and narrowed his eyes at her. "Which brings me back to my original question. What are you doing here?"

Her eyes drifted to Grey. "I'm on the job."

They stood silent, watching Francisco zip the body bag. The sound was somber in its finality.

"Who is she?" Grey asked.

"Gayle Mooney." Bree stepped into the conversation. "She was recently promoted to Director of the CIRG."

"She was with the FBI?" Christina asked. The Critical Incident Response Group responded to crisis incidents, trained undercover FBI agents, and responded to incidents involving weapons of mass destruction. The fact that she was killed with X-VX had to be linked to her new promotion.

"We haven't verified all the facts," Bree said. "But a quick search told us she started her career at the Columbia Field Office. More recently, she worked out of the Washington Field Office."

"What made you think this was a homicide?" Grey asked.

Quinn rubbed the back of his neck. "Ms. Mooney was meeting a colleague for dinner. He reported that shortly after ordering, she appeared out of breath and began sweating. Within a few minutes, she started talking gibberish and having trouble breathing. At that point, she fell out of her seat and began convulsing. By the time EMS arrived, she was dead. At first, they assumed it was an allergic reaction, but their food hadn't arrived. EMS said something about pinpoint pupils and muscle paralysis." Quinn's eyes drifted to Grey, then shifted to Christina. "And there was a poem in her pocket. We're not sure it's related, but it sounds off. We're looking into it."

"We called Francisco for a cursory look, and he called you guys," Bree said. "Is this Sarin or something?"

Grey looked uneasy and Christina could tell he didn't want to give specifics. It was always a careful dance between lying and breaching Top Secret protocol, and she didn't envy his position.

"Excuse me, coming through," Francisco said over the gurney. The wheels rattled as he rolled by on his way to the exit.

"Looks like we should get going and let these guys clear the crime scene," Grey said. "Christina, will you bring Boss?"

"Of course."

Outside the hotel, the temperature had dropped, and a cold wind whipped between the first responder vehicles still parked in the circle drive. Something about the eerie night made Christina's skin crawl. She stepped in front of Boss and scanned the street, wondering if the killer was nearby admiring his handiwork. It was difficult to see through the flashing emergency lights, and she didn't like Grey and Boss being out in the open.

Wally patted Grey on the back. "Sorry to drag you out, brother. Go home and get some rest."

Francisco loaded the body into the coroner's van and slammed the doors. He turned to Wally. "Hey, don't keep her on ice too long, okay?"

Wally nodded. "I'll get you the results as quickly as I—"

Rapid gunfire burst from the night, shattering the glass doors behind Christina's head. In an instant, her boot was on Grey's wheelchair, and a firm shove sent him rolling behind the coroner's van. She pulled her weapon and twisted into a crouch, blocking Boss and Grey with her body. Francisco and Wally hunkered with their backs against the van.

"Shots fired! Shots fired!" Quinn shouted. The ambulance provided cover for the detectives. "Bree, you okay?"

"I'm fine," she said.

Quinn used his phone to call for backup. "10-75. We've got an active shooter north of the Empire Hotel."

Christina poked her head around the van and scanned the rooftops for muzzle flash, but no more bullets came their way. A shadow passed under the light on the roof across the street. "There!" Christina pointed at the building. "On the roof, ten o'clock."

Bree shifted, preparing to give chase. "Set up a perimeter and let's box him in!"

Quinn was on the move and Bree sprinted after him. Tires squealed and two patrol cars peeled away from the hotel in opposite directions. Christina wanted to run toward the battle with every fiber of her being, but she was a bodyguard now. Not a soldier. Her job was to protect, not apprehend. Besides, one look at Grey's reddened face told her to stay put. He looked angry, and she didn't blame him. Two near-death experiences in the last two days and she'd be angry too.

What had she stepped into? Was this another attempt on Grey's life by Viktor Sokolovich? A wet nose nudged her elbow and she turned to see Boss wedged between her and Grey. He might have only hired her to protect Boss, but she was determined to protect Grey too.

***

Grey clenched the wheels of his chair and stared at Christina. What was she thinking, kicking his chair like that? She'd shoved his chair as if he was an invalid incapable of protecting himself. He was a retired Air Commando, and he could take care of himself. Sure, she might have saved his life, but he hadn't hired her as *his* personal protection. Boss was the priority.

He played the events over in his mind. How would he handle the same situation? At the thought of Christina sitting in a wheelchair with bullets flying in her direction, the heat in his face began to subside. He didn't like her methods, but in the moment, she'd done what she had to. He'd let it slide for now.

Distant sirens drowned out his thoughts, and he turned his attention to Wally and Francisco crouched beside him.

"This is *so* not in my job description," Francisco said, rising to his full height.

Wally rubbed his hand over his short-cropped hair. "Tell me about it. I thought I left all the bullet dodging for a nice quiet laboratory."

"We need to stay here," Christina said. "We can't be sure the gunman won't shoot again."

Bree rounded the corner and jogged toward the group. She was slightly out of breath. "It's clear. We missed him," she said. "Looks like he came down the fire escape and had a car waiting."

"Did you get a look at the guy?" Grey asked. It had to be Dr.

Kalashnik or one of his hired muscles. It was too coincidental a gunman would be waiting at the scene where X-VX was suspected of being used to kill Gayle Mooney.

Bree shook her head. "Nope, but I saw the make and model of the car. We put out a BOLO, but this city is a maze. He could be anywhere by now."

"Well, if it's all the same to you"—Wally sighed—"I'm gonna get outta here. Need to get my samples back to the lab."

"Me too," Francisco said. "I've got a late-night date with a beautiful woman."

Bree folded her arms and rubbed the toe of her shoe against the pavement. "Oh... Yes, of course," she stammered.

Francisco's eyes widened, and he banged a flat hand on the side of his van. "Gotta get *this* pretty lady home safe." With a gentle hip bump, he had Bree's attention. "I'll catch *you* later."

While Bree flushed, Francisco climbed into the driver's seat and buckled up. For a moment, Grey watched the coroner's van ease away from the hotel, navigating around the firemen loading into their truck. A police cruiser pulled to a stop in front of them and Quinn unfolded himself from the passenger seat. He slammed the car door and marched over to Grey, hands on his hips. "What is it with you people and getting shot at?"

Grey suppressed a smile. He liked the detective even if he was grumpy and didn't pull his punches. It was refreshing that, much like Christina, Quinn didn't seem to treat him differently because he was in a wheelchair. An image of Quinn yelling at an elderly man with a walker for walking too slow popped to mind and he suppressed a laugh.

"Are you suggesting this has something to do with the Sokolovich shooting last night?" Christina asked.

Quinn's jaw tightened. "I don't know, Christina. Are *you* suggesting this has something to do with Sokolovich?"

Grey cringed. He'd managed to steer Quinn away from the conversation earlier, but the look on the detective's face said it might not work a second time. "There could be a connection," Grey said, "but the details are classified. Wally will need to confirm the bloodwork, then we can read you in."

"Oh, you've got to be kidding me." Quinn turned to his partner. "Are you believing this, Bree? No, you know what? I don't have time for games. If the CBRN wants the case, you can take over the investigation."

Boy, Quinn really had a temper that went from zero to red zone in a flash. Grey looked at Christina. Did it have something to do with her? Was he trying to get the Elite Guardians out of the way?

"Listen," he said, "let's just slow down a minute. There's no need for the government to take over the investigation, but I'd like to partner with you guys and provide whatever resources you need to figure out who killed Ms. Mooney."

"Sounds like you might already know," Quinn muttered.

Christina turned to Bree. "Any leads on Sokolovich or where he could be hiding?"

"Detective Morris has the investigation. He owes me a favor, so I'll see what I can find out." Bree handed Grey her card. "Text me so I've got your contact number. We've got Christina's info."

Quinn threw his hands in the air, shooing them away. "Fine, fine. Now you guys get out of here and let me get started processing *this* crime scene."

9

FRIDAY, 11:00 P.M.

Christina watched the mirror all the way to Grey's house. Keeping an eye out for a tail was difficult from the passenger seat, but so far she didn't see anything out of the ordinary. Grey was quiet and checked his mirrors often. After tonight, he should reconsider his need for personal protection as well as for Boss. He had been in the line of fire twice in the last two days. The man clearly could use someone to watch his back.

Grey pulled his Tesla into his oversized garage and parked beside her car. He'd given her a spare door opener after she'd decided her flashy red sports car in his driveway might draw too much attention. Christina waited until the garage door rattled down before she turned toward Grey, prepared to discuss his need for protection. One look at the seriousness in his eyes and she reconsidered. If he felt like he was in danger, he'd ask. Wouldn't he?

"Do you think we were followed?" she asked.

"I didn't notice anyone but it's possible," Grey said. "Which is why I have this." He reached under his dash and withdrew a

106

small USB drive. He bounced it in his palm, then offered it to Christina.

She held the device between her thumb and forefinger, considering it. "Is this data from your vehicle?"

"Dash cam footage. I have five camera angles we can review. If we were followed, we'll know it." The corner of his mouth tipped into a smile.

She shifted to face him. "Grey, I realize you didn't hire me for twenty-four-hour protection, but you and maybe Boss have been in the line of fire twice in two days. I'd feel much better if I could hang around tonight. What do you think?"

Even in the low light of the garage, she could see his clear eyes searching hers, weighing the idea. The car was getting stuffy, and she suddenly realized how close her face was to his. She adjusted her position, leaning her back against the door. This side of Grey was different from the happy-go-lucky guy she'd seen so far. This was the soldier in him. Serious, focused, and tough.

"I think Boss would appreciate that. He'd probably sleep much better with his bodyguard around. I've got a guest room you can use."

"Oh, that's not necessary. I've got a bag in my trunk with clothes and my laptop, and I'll be up working."

He raised a questioning eyebrow. "You'll stay up all night? That can't be good."

She shrugged. "I was a sniper." There was nothing more she needed to say. He would know she could go without sleep for up to three days if needed. "I'll do a quick check around the house while you head inside with Boss, okay?"

"Sure."

Christina walked the perimeter of Grey's house, searching for anything out of place. She cleared under the front porch, and a small raccoon scurried away as her flashlight swept the crevice under the accessible ramp.

LYNETTE EASON & KATE ANGELO

Good thing Grey didn't question why she wanted to stay the night. In the military, two soldiers were always better than one. With both protecting Boss, their chances of keeping him safe doubled. And if she happened to push Grey out of the line of fire, so be it.

When she was sure the yard was safe, she brought Boss outside to do his business while Grey showered. Christina had never thought of herself as a dog person, but she found herself growing attached to Boss. She had been flattered when he'd brought the ball to her instead of Grey, and she was starting to love the way his muscled body leaned against her leg when he was next to her. Not only was he adorable and intelligent, but he seemed to read the situation and act appropriately. When the shots were fired, he hadn't barked or lunged toward the action. Instead, he'd ducked for cover and protected Grey.

When Boss finished his business and sniffed every blade of grass around the six-foot privacy fence in the backyard, Christina led him inside and filled his water dish.

"Cold out there?" Grey asked from the hallway. Strands of wet hair spiked up as if he'd run a towel over it and left it to dry.

"A little. You off to bed now?"

Mentioning bed made Grey yawn and he chuckled at the tail end of it. "Wow, I didn't realize how tired I am. Make yourself at home. The guest room is available if you change your mind."

She nodded. "I appreciate that. Get some rest."

Grey patted his knee. "C'mon, Boss, bedtime."

Boss looked up at Christina, then back to Grey.

"Go on to bed, Boss. I'll be here in the morning."

Tail low, Boss padded down the hallway behind Grey. The dog stopped to look back at Christina before he slunk into the bedroom.

Did Boss pick up on her halfhearted encouragement? It sure would be nice to have the dog keep her company this evening. Snuggle with her on the couch by the fire. Follow her on security checks. Keep her warm while she worked. Christina sighed. She shouldn't get attached. This assignment would end and Boss would be out of her life. If she let herself bond with him, it would only result in heartache.

She did another quick check of the doors and windows to verify they were secure. Many of the windows were missing motion sensors, and she made a mental note to recommend upgrading his home security system to Grey in the morning. It wasn't a bad system, but they would have to tighten things to have the best protection.

She carried her laptop to the couch and began reading articles about chemical warfare. Several blogs posted conspiracy theories about the government testing chemical weapons at Ft. Leonard Wood, an Army base in Missouri. The CBRN school at Ft. Leonard Wood was common knowledge, but these articles suggested high rates of cancer and other illnesses among the residents living on or near the Army base.

The Scientist News Today website reported that a Japanese businessman had been dosed with VX in the Madrid International Airport. She clicked on the video and watched the surveillance footage of a man who looked like a linebacker plow into the Japanese traveler, knocking him over. The linebacker continued moving, turning his face away from the cameras. The footage cut to the Japanese man as he stumbled around looking for help for fifteen minutes before he collapsed.

The article reported the man had a seizure and died approximately an hour after the linebacker knocked him over. It was speculated he died from VX poisoning but questioned how he could have survived so long when a single drop of VX is powerful enough to kill within a second. They further questioned how the linebacker could have dosed the businessman and not died from contact. Even the medics should have been killed from the contact during treatment.

Wally's vaccine came to mind. Was it possible another

country had developed a similar vaccine already? Christina replayed the video over and over. Something about the linebacker caught her attention and she paused the video. She zoomed in on the image. Was that a tattoo on his forearm?

A thump came from Grey's bedroom and Christina jumped to her feet, pulse racing. It was after three in the morning. Too early for Grey to be awake. The research had drawn her in and she'd been intent on reading. She waited in the stillness of the night, forcing her nerves to settle while she listened.

A muffled grunt came from the other end of the house. Christina put her hand on the butt of her weapon and inched toward his room. More grunting and it was definitely coming from Grey's bedroom. A low rumble sounded like growling. Boss? She pulled her gun from the holster and moved with long strides down the hallway, stopping to listen at Grey's door.

The sounds were louder now. Grunts and heavy breaths, the sounds of straining. Grey was wrestling with someone in his bedroom. An intruder must have slipped in through his bedroom window.

Christina grabbed the doorknob and twisted. Locked. She put her shoulder to the door, hard. The door popped open. The room was dark except for a soft yellow glow from the slightly open bathroom door. Gun raised, she took aim at the man on the floor by the window.

"Don't move!"

Christina took half a step into the room before Boss lunged and snapped. Teeth bared, Boss lowered his head and hunched his shoulders. The snarling growl sent chills down her spine. Boss was ready to attack. He would protect Grey, and for as much as the dog liked her, she wasn't about to test his loyalty. She hit the lights.

"Whoever you are, show me your hands *now!*"

With Boss growling and the sudden bright lights blinding him, adrenaline shot through Grey. What the—

He used his arms to pull himself into a sitting position, the wound on his head throbbing with the movement. His eyes went wide at the sight of Christina standing in his doorway with her gun trained on him. Boss stood between her and the bed, snarling at her.

His hands went up. "What are you doing?"

"Grey? Are you okay? Is someone with you?" She craned her neck, searching the room.

Was someone with him? What in the world was she talking about? "There's no one else in here."

She swept the room with her weapon. "I heard noises," she said. "Is someone else here?"

"No, I'm alone," he grumbled. "Boss, at ease."

Boss went to Christina and leaned against her leg, a form of an apology Grey had come to know well.

Christina holstered her weapon and reached a slow hand toward Boss to pet him. "Good job, Boss," she said. "Sorry about the door, I thought—"

He waved her off. "Yeah, I know. I couldn't sleep. I was doing push-ups." He couldn't believe she'd heard his workout grunts and thought he was being attacked. Great. She probably thought he was some sort of weakling in here struggling for every push-up.

She stroked Boss. "You have insomnia?"

"Not lately. Must be all the excitement." When his mind wouldn't let him sleep, he usually got out of bed and worked off the frustration.

Christina avoided looking in his direction. Was she uncomfortable being in his room? He followed her gaze to the balled up T-shirt on the floor. "Sorry. Um, give me a minute and I'll get cleaned up."

"Oh, that's not necessary." She took a step back. "It's after three in the morning. You should go back to sleep."

He laughed. "No way. My adrenaline is pumping, and the only cure is greasy breakfast food."

"You mean the only cure *besides* a midnight workout?" Her lips twitched with the hint of a smile. "Breakfast sounds great. Take your time."

And just like that, she was gone with Boss trotting close on her heels.

What was it with that dog? It's not like she was the one who'd raised him from a pup. Maybe Boss had a crush on Christina? He smiled. Well, he couldn't blame the dog for that. There was something about the woman that drew him in too.

The arm crutches leaning in the corner caught his eye. Should he risk trying to use them long enough to make breakfast for Christina? He wanted to stand next to her so she could see he wasn't completely helpless. But if his legs gave out and he fell in front of her, his humiliation would be complete. He'd redeem himself with more of his culinary skills, and maybe this time they would get to eat their meal.

Grey snatched the T-shirt from the floor and sniffed it. He cringed at the sweaty smell and tossed it toward his bathroom. He pulled himself into his wheelchair then retrieved a clean T-shirt from the dresser and yanked it over his head. A jolt of pain sliced through his temple and he sucked air through his teeth. The stitches. He needed to be more careful or he'd be right back in the ER having them close him up again.

When he entered the kitchen, he found Christina at the island with her laptop open, a video playing on the screen. He moved to the opposite side of the counter. "How does a frittata sound? Maybe with spinach, artichoke, and feta cheese?"

Christina's face brightened. "Wow, that actually sounds delicious."

"It's a favorite for late-night meals. Not much prep and makes great leftovers."

Christina rested an elbow on the counter and propped her chin in the palm of her hand. "Can I ask you a question?"

"Of course, ask anything." He grabbed food from the refrigerator.

"I don't want to be insensitive, but I also like to have all the information I can get on a client." She paused for a beat. "I noticed you were able to move your legs in the, um, in the bedroom just now. And earlier you even put weight on one leg when you got into your car."

She hadn't asked a question, but Grey knew what she was getting at. He washed his hands and dried them on a hand towel. "My condition isn't as simple as paraplegia from a brain or spinal cord injury," he said. "It's diagnosed as Acquired Ataxia, meaning parts of my spinal cord are damaged and it affects balance and coordination. It doesn't affect the feeling in my legs."

"Can you stand and bear weight on your legs if you wanted?"

He waffled his hands in a so-so gesture. "Technically, yes. Some days are better than others. I have forearm crutches, but I finally got tired of falling when my legs randomly gave out, so I don't use them much anymore."

Christina nodded. "It must be frustrating to have your body fully capable of walking, but unable to control when and where it happens. Most of us take for granted the ability to move with little thought."

One side of his mouth turned up. "You're really smart, do you know that?"

She straightened. "Thank you." A small patch of pink crept to her cheeks.

He lifted his chin toward her laptop. "What were you watching?"

"Have you heard of Akio Nagamori?"

The name made him pause with an egg poised on the edge of the bowl. He looked at her. "You mean the Akio Nagamori killed in the Madrid airport?"

"So, you *have* heard about him. I was researching and found several conspiracy blogs and a scientific journal, all claiming he couldn't have been killed with VX."

He tapped the egg on the edge of the bowl and separated it with one hand. "And the video?"

"Surveillance footage. It shows Nagamori stumbling around the airport looking for help." She paused and lowered her voice. "It also shows Sokolovich dosing him with the toxin."

Grey's blood ran cold. Had she just said Sokolovich had been captured on video dosing Nagamori? He forgot about cracking eggs. "You've got to be joking. Show me."

She slid the laptop around to face him and pointed at the screen where she'd paused the video. "Look right here. The man who ran into Nagamori is the same build as Sokolovich. And it's very subtle, but he has a bulldog tattoo right here."

"Are you sure it's the same tattoo?"

"Positive. I got a good look at it through my scope and..." She hesitated. "Well, I remember things."

He tilted his head. "You *remember* things?"

"Once I see something, I remember it. Words, numbers, images, faces." She lifted a shoulder. "It's been like that since I was a kid."

"Eidetic memory?

"Maybe, but I know I've seen this tattoo." She tapped the screen. "It's Sokolovich."

How had everyone else missed this? Every law enforcement agency in the world had a file four inches thick with information on the Russian hitman and knew everything about him, tattoos and all. Once CBRN confirmed Nagamori had been killed with X-VX, the government had used disinformation to let the media think VX was the cause of death. If they had this video, why han't Sokolovich been charged with the crime? Grey's thoughts were racing, and he needed to get them lined up.

The scent of burning oil brought him back to the moment. He lowered the flame on the skillet and went back to work. "First things first," he said. "We need to eat. I think better with food in my stomach." He cracked the rest of the eggs and began whisking them.

"Absolutely. We should eat first." Christina closed the laptop and pushed it aside. "Tell me how you ended up on the Air Force basketball team."

It didn't escape his notice how carefully Christina chose her words. Even now she'd left out the word *wheelchair* from his basketball team. For some reason he found it easy to talk to her.

"Wally and I used to shoot hoops together in our downtime. We started as two kids serving in special ops. Basketball was something to take our mind off things. When this foundation offered money to start a wheelchair basketball team, Wally jumped at the chance to coach the Air Force team."

"And you were eager to join in?"

He laughed. "Um, no. The last thing I wanted was to play basketball like…like *this*." He gestured to his chair. "Wally pestered me until I caved. I guess I felt like I owed him since, you know, he couldn't play for the team himself." And it was his fault that Wally's arm was paralyzed.

Christina nodded. "That's a nice thing to do for your friend."

The pan sizzled as he sautéed a mixture of spinach, artichoke, and garlic. He poured half the scrambled eggs over the vegetables, added crumbled feta cheese, then topped it off with the rest of the eggs and slid the cast iron skillet into the oven.

"We'll be eating in about 20 minutes," he said. He maneuvered his chair to sit opposite Christina at his T-shaped kitchen island. "What about you? Do you play sports?"

"Not really. I like to run. I go for a long jog every morning. It helps me clear my head."

"Got a lot of stuff clogging up your head, do ya?"

She smiled and he thought he saw a bit of teeth in it. She was a tough one, keeping her smiles reserved as if she had a limited number to hand out. But seeing this one made him light up inside. He swallowed hard and opened his mouth to coax another one of those heart-fluttering smiles when he noticed Boss jump to his feet.

Boss's ears twitched and he stared at the front window.

Christina bolted to her feet beside Boss. She pressed a finger to her lips. "Someone's out there," she mouthed.

The window blinds were all closed. Christina had made sure of it during her security check, but she was hyper focused on the front window. Whatever put Boss on alert had come from the front yard. Her muscles were tight, and her hand itched to pull her gun.

Boss took a cautious step toward the front door, one foot positioned in front of the other. His hackles went up and his tail was low and unmoving. He waited, ready to attack whoever was on the other side of the front door.

Seconds ticked by and Christina started to feel silly for standing there like a sentry all because the dog heard what could be the raccoon returning to its home under the porch. But she couldn't ignore the burning sensation in her chest, the one that rose each time danger was present—just like when she'd spotted Sokolovich at the arena. She took a measured step toward the door and inclined her ear. A scrape then a bump of the doorknob. Her heart knocked inside her chest. An intruder was trying to bypass the deadbolt.

The noise sent Boss into a frenzy. He lunged at the door, barking.

Heavy footsteps thudded on the wooden porch, retreating at the sound of the vicious dog. Christina ran to the door and flipped the lock. She yanked open the door and burst out into the night. Placing both hands on the porch rail, she hurled herself over, landed in the soft grass, and sprang to her feet, searching the area for movement through a cloud of frozen breath.

A shadow slipped around the corner of the house across the street and Christina bolted after it. The streetlight cast a glow on the front yard, but it didn't quite reach the side of the house where the figure had run. She slipped her gun from the holster and kept it low, moving with long, careful strides.

The familiar sound of a dog barking caught her attention. Boss sprinted past. His body brushed her leg as he chased the shadow.

Oh no! She'd left the door open!

Could she be more stupid?

Now Boss was on the loose and in danger. Whoever was running away might have a weapon and she had to get Boss before he was hurt or killed.

Sounds of barking and the rattle of a chain link fence to her left sent her running in that direction. Maybe Boss had cornered the guy and she could get there before he jumped the fence. She raced toward the back of the yard and saw a dark figure dropping to the other side of the fence. He landed in a half crouch and paused to catch his breath, then looked over his shoulder for a split second before sprinting away. The hood of his sweatshirt obscured his face. Christina couldn't make out any distinguishing features, but the guy was too small to be Sokolovich. The intruder was already out of breath after running a block, which meant she could outrun him.

Christina grabbed the fence with both hands and wedged

her boot into the small hole for leverage. She was about to hop the fence when she looked down at Boss. He was searching for a way through the thick shrubbery planted at the base of the fence. He panted and paced, pausing to poke his nose in an opening only to pull back and continue pacing, frustrated.

No way she could leave him here. She took one last look at the darkness on the other side of the fence and grunted.

"Boss, here." She patted her thigh, and he came right to her. He looked up, tongue lolling as she scratched his chin. "Good boy, Boss. You got that bad guy, didn't you? Let's go home."

Grey's voice carried across the street from his porch as they rounded the corner. What was he doing sitting out in the open yelling? He may as well be shouting for the killers to come take him out. She jogged across the street and patted the air with both hands. "Shhh, you're drawing too much attention."

"I can't believe you let Boss out like that!" The veins in his neck corded. "What were you thinking? I hired you to guard my *dog*, not chase after strangers. That's a job for the police, not a bodyguard. I can't believe you!"

Christina looked up and down the street, expecting to see the neighbors flipping on porch lights and coming outside in bathrobes to complain about the noise. "I've got Boss right here, and he's safe."

"No thanks to you! He could have been killed. C'mon, Boss. Here."

Boss perked his ears and darted up the steps after Grey. They disappeared into the house and Grey slammed the front door. Christina flinched.

Now what? Should she knock on the door, or barge in and collect her things to leave? Her car was parked in the garage, and her keys were in her laptop bag inside.

She huffed a breath and marched up the steps. Before she knocked on the door, she used the flashlight on her phone to inspect the area. Sure enough, there were scrape marks and the trim was splintered near the deadbolt. Looked like the guy had used a screwdriver or knife to try and break in.

An ear-piercing screech came from inside. She didn't bother knocking, just flung the door open and rushed in. At least she remembered to close and lock it behind her this time. The smoke detector in the kitchen screamed while Grey worked to fan it with a towel. Boss was at his side, cocking his head from side to side at the noise.

She rushed over and grabbed another towel from near the sink. "Here, let me."

"I've got it." With one hand, he turned his chair, ramming his knees into hers.

"Ow! Grey, let me do this while you turn the oven off."

"Fine." He threw his towel in his lap and wheeled around with more force than was necessary. After he turned the burner knob, he pressed a few buttons and a small vent rose from the back of the stove and sucked the smoke from the room.

With a few strong waves of the towel in front of the smoke alarm, it finally silenced. Christina folded the hand towel and stared at Grey slumped in his chair, his back to her. She wanted to make this better, but what could she say? He was right. She should have paid closer attention to Boss and never let him out the door. By the time she'd realized what she'd done, it was too late.

"I'm sorry, Grey. I know I disappointed you. I made a mistake." She waited a painfully long minute, but Grey didn't respond. He wouldn't even look at her.

Boss tilted his head trying to understand. Christina was confused too. Why was he taking it so hard? She wanted to go to Grey and force him to look her in the eyes and tell her why he was so angry, but he was rigid. Too upset right now. There was something under the surface to cause this outburst, and she wanted to understand.

Grey didn't bother removing the skillet from the oven

before he turned his chair and rolled to the opposite side of the counter. "The eggs are burnt and I think we should both get some sleep. Boss, here."

Christina didn't try to stop him. She watched his back as he disappeared down the hall with Boss trotting behind him. From the moment she'd met the man, he'd rattled her. She had to get her head back in the job and stop letting herself get distracted before she made an even bigger mistake.

10

Christina's feet pounded the asphalt in time with her breaths. She relished the burn in her lungs from the crisp February air and having a front row seat to the sunrise. Running always helped clear her mind and ease the stress from her job, but so far it hadn't worked. Even the worship music pumping through her AirPods couldn't push thoughts of Grey out of her head.

Boss jogged alongside Christina as if they'd been running buddies for years. Unlike most dogs, he didn't pause to sniff every tree or investigate wildlife. He kept pace and she found she enjoyed having him with her. She'd been reading her Bible this morning when Grey got up to let Boss outside. At first, he was reluctant to accept her offer to bring Boss along on her morning run but relented when she pointed out he could go back to bed for a while.

His words this morning echoed in her head. *"As long as Boss will be safe with you."*

She supposed that was a well-deserved dig about her leaving the door open last night. But he'd handed her the running leash and showed her how to adjust it to fit around her waist so she could run hands free and keep Boss tethered to her body.

Boss was indeed a highly skilled, highly trained canine—she could see that from his work at the restaurant. A valuable asset to the American government. But what was really going on? Why would the killer use a chemical weapon to kill Gayle Mooney then turn around and shoot at Grey? She couldn't wrap her head around the idea. Switching MOs like that didn't make sense. Unless there were two killers.

She let the thought settle as the song in her AirPods picked up speed. The singer sang her favorite lines, and she had to agree—there was nothing that was going to steal her joy.

When the song concluded, Christina asked Siri to call the only person she knew she could talk to. Her best friend, the one who was always there for her. Unfortunately, this time she just happened to be an ocean away.

Christina began speaking as soon as Haley answered. "You know how you like to make lists and try to piece things together? I need that right now," Christina said. "But I feel bad for calling you on your honeymoon."

"Never you mind. The boys went exploring this morning and won't be back until lunch. Your timing is perfect." Haley's Irish accent sounded thicker than Christina remembered. "And you know I'm always here for you. Call me anytime, night or day."

"Thank you, I appreciate it." Christina slowed her pace to a light jog. "First off, my client is a Belgian Malinois."

"Pardon, did you say your client is a Belgian?"

"Belgian *Malinois*. He's a dog, Haley."

Laughter rolled across the line. "We've had some unusual clients in the past, but this is a new one."

Christina smiled despite herself. "His owner is Captain Grey Parker, a former Air Commando who hired us to protect his dog, Boss. Most of the details are classified so I'll share what

I can, but doesn't it seem odd that someone would kill for a dog?"

"Hmm, it does sound unusual," Haley said. "What do they want with...Boss, did you say?"

"That's right. Boss is an incredibly special cross-trained detection canine. Of course, the details of his job are classified."

Boss snuffed.

"Well, it does sound like the dog would be a valuable asset to many a bad guy."

Christina nodded though she knew Haley couldn't see her. "But is the dog so valuable that someone would kill his owner? What would that accomplish?"

Haley was quiet and Christina wondered if the call had dropped. Haley finally spoke. "I don't know, Christina. Do you trust this Captain Parker?"

The question pricked Christina's heart and she felt the need to defend Grey. "Absolutely. He hired a bodyguard to protect his dog, Haley. He's left the military and works as a civilian in search of this new chemical weapon. And he's about to undergo a risky surgery to restore his ability to walk. Everything about him checks out."

"Wait, your client can't walk?"

"Not my client. The dog is my client, remember?"

"Okay, so you're working with this Grey guy to what? Learn how to handle Boss during the surgery and recovery?"

"Exactly. The problem is Grey is also a target, but he won't let me protect him."

"Stubborn, is he? I know all about stubborn men."

"I guess you do." Christina laughed. "He's been shot at twice, and last night someone tried to break into his house. I pursued the suspect, but in my haste, I let Boss get out. I let the guy go and brought the dog back, but Grey was angry with me. I don't understand how he could be mad at me for chasing a suspect."

"Did you consider his anger stems from something else?"

At Haley's words, Christina stopped running and pressed her hands to her temples. Boss stopped and looked up at her, waiting for her cues. "How could I be so thoughtless?" She groaned.

Haley laughed. "You have an uncanny ability to see things from everyone's point of view, Christina. It's a gift, and one of the reasons Olivia was so keen on hiring you. Maybe you just like this guy too much to see his disability?"

"Like him? No, no. I don't like him. I mean, yes, I like him and he's cute... I mean he's nice, but—" She was getting flustered again. It was so annoying how Grey could do that to her and he wasn't even in the vicinity. "I'm a professional, Haley. I can't let my emotions get in the way of the job. That's how people get hurt."

"This isn't Afghanistan, Christina. It's not the same. Our emotions are more than subjective reactions to situations we encounter. God gave us emotions for a purpose, and you can't keep them bottled up forever or one day you'll explode. It's okay to feel something for him."

In her experience, emotions had only led to failure or pain. But Grey seemed to make her smile like no one else. What would happen if she opened up to him a little?

She shook her head. Impossible. If she let herself get involved, it would only lead to more devastation. "Listen, Haley, I'm about to finish my run and get my client back home. Thanks for taking the time to talk it out with me. See you in a few weeks?"

"Okay, but think about what I said, yeah?"

"I promise." She disconnected the call with a tap to her AirPod and eased back into her running pace with Boss. With only two more miles to go, she opted to pray instead of listening to worship music.

God, I don't know what You're doing or what Your plan is, but please keep us safe. Help me to help Grey find this evil doctor before it's too late. Show me the way.

The sound of an engine revving broke into her prayer. A black sedan rounded the corner half a mile in front of her and picked up speed. This was one of her favorite running trails because the wide asphalt sidewalk ran alongside the Broad River offering great views of the water. The curbed street was on her right, and ten yards to her left was the sheer drop leading to the narrow river.

At this time of day, the streets were quiet, but it wasn't unusual for cars to be out. However, this car was approaching faster than the speed limit. She hugged the left edge of the pavement, forcing Boss to run in the grass beside her. The car sped toward them. She looked for a license plate, but didn't see one anywhere on the front bumper.

The black sedan was about twenty-five yards ahead when it jumped the curb, skidded across the grass, and headed straight for them. She grabbed the leash and pulled Boss toward the river. Her foot slipped on the wet grass, and she slid down the steep embankment, falling toward the icy water below.

She let go of the leash and grappled for something to hold onto. Boss stiffened his legs, bracing himself for the downhill slide, not bothering to stop his descent. His weight pulled at the leash connected to her waist and dragged her down the hill.

She dug her hands into the wet grass, trying to stop before they hit the freezing water. Her shoe hit something hard, jarring her to a stop at the edge of the water. She winced as pain shot through her ankle and radiated to her knee.

Boss gained his footing a few feet below where she'd come to a stop. He belly crawled up the hill and stopped beside her. They were both breathing hard. Another five yards and they'd be taking the polar bear plunge.

The car engine revved again from somewhere above their heads. She pressed herself flat on the side of the hill and scanned the area around her. The top of the ridge was about ten steep yards above her head. It would be a difficult climb back up.

Lights appeared at the edge of the embankment, and she pulled Boss to her side. The sun had come up during her run, but she prayed the side of the hill would still be dark enough to keep them concealed. A shadow passed in front of the lights and she could hear the car idling nearby. She held her breath and wished she'd brought her gun.

A long minute slipped by before the shadow passed in front of the lights again. She heard a car door close and tires spinning, trying to gain traction on the wet grass. A metallic clank echoed down the ridge as the car went over the curb and pulled back onto the road.

She waited until the engine noise disappeared and blew out a breath. "It's okay, Boss. We're okay."

Her smart watch buzzed. The SOS feature had detected a hard fall and asked if she was okay. She considered the two options and with a slight tremble in her hand, she swiped *I'm okay*. She wouldn't call the police. Not yet anyway. First, she needed to get Boss back home where he was safe.

"Siri, call Laila," she said to her watch. The ring sounded in one ear. Ugh, she'd lost her left AirPod. Great.

The call connected and Laila's groggy voice answered.

"Hey, can you come get me? Someone just tried to run me over."

SATURDAY, 7:21 A.M.

Coffee. He needed coffee. The coffee maker sputtered and gurgled the blessed brew into the clear carafe while Grey watched. The smell made him feel more awake—and guilty. He never should've lost his temper last night. It wasn't like him. The stress of being shot at, learning a woman was killed with X-VX in *his* town, and the intruder trying to break in last night… well, it was too much to handle all at once.

It was no excuse for being so sensitive, but he couldn't let Christina distract him from finding Dr. Kalashnik before his Russian mafia goons unleashed X-VX on the nation. Boss could have been taken last night—and without his dog, the CBRN team would pat Grey on the back and say, "Thank you for your service."

Never mind it was *his* ability in dog training that had brought out Boss's natural gift for guarding and scent tracking. As a soldier, Grey was useless to his country in his current condition, but with Boss they took him seriously and he had a real chance of tracking Dr. Kalashnik even from a wheelchair.

The coffee pot beeped, and Grey poured his first cup. The clock said he had two hours before basketball practice. Maybe he should text Wally and tell him he couldn't make it. His head was throbbing, and his entire body ached.

He carried his cup to the kitchen island and picked up his phone to text Wally. Before he could press send, the doorbell chimed. His heart froze for a beat. She was back from her run. He would man up and face her in person.

Grey took a deep breath and prepared himself to apologize to Christina. After a quick hand over the back of his head to push down any unruly hairs, he opened the door.

"Mistake number one. You didn't bother checking the peephole. I could have been a murderer." The woman marched inside and whirled on him. "A guy like you needs a video doorbell. Check it from your phone."

A guy like him? What was that supposed to mean? He recognized Lizzie from the meeting at the Elite Guardians, but she hadn't seemed quite so bossy yesterday. Was Christina so upset she'd asked for a new assignment?

"What are you—"

"And a better security system." Lizzie pointed at the keypad on the wall. "You're worried about your dog's safety, and you have this low-level security system?" She shook her head.

"Please, come in. Lizzie, is it?" He hoped she'd pick up on his sarcasm. "Can I get you some coffee?"

"Coffee would be great, but I can get it." She moved through the house as if she'd been here a hundred times before. After she poured a fresh cup of coffee, she leaned against the counter and eyed him. One dark eyebrow rose as if she expected him to respond to a question she hadn't asked.

A rock settled in the pit of his stomach. Christina must have given up on him after the way he'd exploded last night. Lizzie was here to take over as soon as Christina returned with Boss.

Lizzie was nice, but he didn't want to hash out his guilty feelings with her. He wanted to talk to Christina. "Did I—I mean, did Christina ask for a new assignment?"

She narrowed her eyes. "No, why would she ask to be reassigned?"

He rubbed the back of his neck. "Well, I sorta lost my temper with her last night and she left."

"Does Christina strike you as someone with thin skin?" She took a sip, staring at him over the edge of the cup.

Grey smiled. "No, not at all." He sighed and reached for his own coffee cup to refill it. "What's up with that by the way? I spent most of the day with her yesterday and I still don't know anything about her—other than she's an expert at redirecting the conversation."

"Yeah, she tends to do that. It has something to do with her time in the service and why she retired."

"Why did she retire?"

"I think you should ask her about it," Lizzie said. "It's not my story to tell."

Grey appreciated Lizzie's willingness to protect her friend's confidence. It spoke volumes about Christina and the respect she carried. From the brief interactions with the Elite Guardians, Grey saw a special bond.

"Don't you think Christina will avoid the conversation?"

"Well, you'll never know unless you try. One thing I do know is trust is a two-way street, my friend." She toasted him with her coffee mug and took another sip. "So, what got you so hot last night?"

Grey took a deep breath and stared into his cup. "Someone tried to break in, and Christina went after him, but she left the door open and Boss escaped. He could have been taken...or worse."

"Boss didn't obey you when you told him to come back?"

"It all happened so fast. I don't think he heard me."

"Did she catch the guy?"

Grey shook his head. "I don't think so. I didn't even ask. She's supposed to protect Boss, but she let him run right out of the house."

Lizzie put her coffee cup down and leaned over the counter. "You have to realize that you're asking Christina to put an animal life over a human life. That's hard for anyone, but for a former special ops soldier?" Lizzie flattened her lips. "It's tough."

"Yeah well, imagine how hard it is for me to sit here and watch while they run toward danger." He gestured to his wheelchair.

Lizzie's eyes softened. "I think you're going to have to trust her to help you, as well as Boss."

He grunted. "Is that why you're here? To protect me?"

"Maybe." Lizzie lifted a shoulder. "She asked for a little backup, so here I am."

He wasn't sure what to make of that but decided to leave it for now. He checked the time. "Where are Christina and Boss? Shouldn't they be back by now?"

"Not sure. I'll check their ETA while you get ready."

"Sure. I'll be back in a few. Make yourself at home." He paused. "Oh, wait. You already have."

Her laughter followed him down the hallway.

Twenty minutes later, Grey was in his workout clothes with his gym bag packed. Going to basketball practice was the last thing he wanted to do today, but when he'd called Wally to bail out, Wally said the team was counting on him. They were looking forward to the rescheduled game and needed to practice.

Lizzie appeared in his doorway. "Christina just pulled up. Hang tight while I search your vehicle."

"My car has been in the garage all night," he muttered. The lack of sleep was making him cranky. He needed to pull it together. If he didn't want people to treat him like a toddler, he shouldn't act like one in desperate need of a nap.

He followed Lizzie to his garage and watched her circle both vehicles with a small explosive detection mirror mounted on a telescopic arm. The same kind he carried.

"All clear," she said.

Grey reached to unplug his car from the wall outlet but paused when the unmistakable sound of the garage door motor kicking into gear sent his heart racing.

He glanced at Lizzie, but she didn't seem concerned. The garage door continued to rise, exposing thin hands resting on hips and the dog leash dangling from her hand. Her hair was a mess of blonde frizz and...was that a leaf in her hair? Her brown eyes seemed darker, more intense, and her jaw was set tight. A fresh scrape on the side of her face was a deep pink that only enhanced her high cheekbones.

"Christina?"

Christina held up a palm and headed straight for him. With the spare garage remote he'd given her, she sent the garage door rattling back down.

"Listen, I made a mistake last night," she said. "One I won't repeat."

Boss nuzzled Grey's elbow and he rubbed his ears. There was a distinct wet dog smell coming from him, but he felt dry.

He furrowed his brows. "What happened? Are you okay?"

"Clearly you have a target on your back, and now it seems your enemies aren't very happy with me either," Christina said.

"Did they catch whoever tried to run you down?" Lizzie asked.

Christina shook her head.

Grey pushed his chair closer to Christina, his pulse pounding in his ears. "Someone tried to run you down?"

"While I was on my morning run, a vehicle jumped the curb and came after us. Thankfully, I saw it coming and while I got a good look at the car, I couldn't see the driver."

His hands tightened on the wheels of his chair until they ached. He wanted to…wanted to what? What could he do about it? Nothing now that she was back.

"The gall to come right at you instead of from behind." Lizzie snorted. "Amateurs. Did you get a plate number?"

Christina shook her head. "No, they'd removed the plates."

"Probably someone trying to scare you off," Lizzie said.

"Either way, whoever is behind this means serious business." Christina dipped her chin and stared into Grey's eyes. "Listen, if you *really* want me to protect Boss, I'll do it. But we do things my way. We follow my rules."

Her rules? This was starting to sound more like he'd hired a babysitter than a bodyguard. He glanced at Lizzie, and she raised her eyebrows at him. Her words from earlier reminded him to trust Christina. She was a highly trained professional and had already saved his life more than once—and Boss's, too, apparently.

Grey looked at Christina and nodded. "Okay, but before I agree, I've got a few rules of my own."

Christina folded her arms and gave him a sidelong stare. "Okay. Let's hear them."

The stare made him uneasy, but he could see behind the tough-as-nails exterior that the incident this morning had rattled her.

He cleared his throat. "Well, I need you to agree to protect Boss first and foremost. He's the priority even if there's a gun to my head. You choose Boss over me every time."

Christina dropped her arms, eyes darting between Boss, Grey, and Lizzie. It was a difficult ask and Grey knew it. But he hadn't been so blunt about it when he hired her, and he needed to make sure she understood.

Christina's shoulders rose and fell with a deep breath. "And?"

"And," he continued, "understand that I'm still on call. If someone needs Boss, we'll have to go out like we did last night. It might be dangerous, but that's why I hired you."

"I hear what you're saying," Christina said. "Anything else?"

He shook his head. If Christina could keep Boss safe while Grey tracked down Dr. Kalashnik, there wasn't much else he cared about. Boss was their only hope to stop an all-out attack on America.

"Okay, I agree to protect Boss first, *but* I will also protect you." Her hand flew up to hold back any objection. "I'm not about to stand by and watch someone kill you. I'll stop it if I can."

Lizzie chuckled. "You can't really argue with that logic, now, can you?"

Grey snorted. "I guess not."

"Things are getting serious, and I think you"—she paused to correct herself—"*Boss* needs twenty-four-hour protection. We're going to move you to a safe house."

"A safe house!" His voice was louder than he'd intended, and he forced himself to rein it in. "If you guys haven't noticed, I'm not exactly mobile. I can't just pick up and go anywhere."

"He's right," Lizzie said. "Our usual place is kind of cramped."

Christina chewed her lower lip. "Okay, I get it. I'll have Charlie turn this place into a safe house. He's an expert at security systems and let's face it, yours could use an upgrade."

Lizzie snorted. "That's what I told him."

A smile played on Christina's lips. "Well, it won't be an issue once Charlie is done. We'll lay low here until we find this Dr. Kalashnik who's after you."

Grey's phone vibrated and he checked the screen. "This is my sister. I haven't responded to her texts from this morning and if I don't answer, she'll be here in the next ten minutes."

Lizzie and Christina exchanged a look.

He answered his phone, forcing cheer into his voice. "Hey, sis. What's up?"

"You haven't read my texts, or Mom's for that matter. Are you coming to lunch today?"

"Lunch? Today?" He searched his memory for the plans he'd made and grimaced. That's right, he'd planned to meet Ruby and his mother for lunch after basketball practice.

Ruby sighed. "Yes, Grey. Lunch. The lunch we've had planned for weeks. The one where we're going to discuss our parents' fortieth wedding anniversary? Are you sure you don't have a concussion from that plaque hitting your head?"

He pinched the bridge of his nose. "Oh, yes, that lunch. Um, I don't know if I can make it today, Ruby."

Christina and Lizzie looked at each other with raised eyebrows.

Grey switched his phone to speaker. Maybe if they heard Ruby begging, they could figure out a way to make it happen.

"You have to come," Ruby said. "This is a big event, and we have to finalize all the plans. It's not fair to ask Mom and Dad to do all the work for their own fortieth anniversary party. This is *our* responsibility, Grey." Her pleas echoed through the garage.

Christina flattened her lips and gave a decided head shake. "Reschedule," she mouthed.

"Listen." He sighed. "Because of the shooting, some things have come up. But don't worry, I'm not about to leave you holding the bag. You know I wouldn't. I'll call you back and reschedule."

There was a long silence and Grey looked to see if the call had disconnected. Ruby hadn't hung up, which meant she was processing.

"I do trust you, Grey. I'm disappointed, but I understand. Call me tonight, okay?"

"I will, promise. Give Mom and Dad my love, will ya?"

"I will. I love you, baby brother," Ruby said.

"I love you too, big sis." The call disconnected and he glanced at Christina.

She was smiling and it was beautiful. A warmth spread through his chest and he forced himself to look away. Boss sat beside Christina, tongue lolling to one side in a doggy smile. The sight made the warmth spread deeper, and he couldn't stop the grin forcing itself to his lips. Even in this difficult situation he'd found himself in, he was glad he had Christina watching their backs.

11

SATURDAY, 8:32 A.M.

Christina stood in the bathroom with her hands braced on the counter and examined the pink scrape on her cheek. It wasn't too bad and probably wouldn't bruise, but the entire incident shook her more than she wanted to admit. She splashed her face with cold water and closed her eyes, seeing behind them the black sedan jumping the curb and careening toward her.

All in all, she'd come out relatively unscathed considering what could have happened. Boss could have been run over or seriously injured when they'd fallen down the hill. What was the driver trying to accomplish by running into her? Did he want Boss dead? And how did he know where they were? The intruder who tried to break in last night must have been watching Grey's house and followed her when she'd left this morning. And she hadn't noticed.

With one last look at herself in the mirror, she pushed off the counter and loosened her braided hair. She was being too hard on herself. The car had caught her attention as soon as it rounded the corner, and because of her alertness, she'd had enough time to get out of the way. Grey might not have been so lucky.

In the kitchen, Grey was giving Boss a thorough brushing.

"Whew, he stinks. Smells like he rolled on a dead animal or something." Grey wrinkled his brows. "He needs a bath."

"Well, no time for a bath if you plan to make it to practice on time," Lizzie said from the couch.

"Okay, let me just spray some deodorant on him. I don't think we want to be trapped in the car with him smelling like this."

Christina smiled to herself, watching Boss trot down the hall behind Grey. She liked seeing Grey interact with Boss, and his family for that matter. Earlier when he was on the phone with Ruby, she thought it was brave to show his love for his sister in front of two women who were strangers. Christina's own brother, Will, was five years older and while they had a fine relationship, they'd never been super close. There was only one person she'd been that close to, but that person had long since left her life.

"You okay?" Lizzie asked.

Christina plopped onto the couch beside her. "I don't know. I'm thinking Grey should still skip basketball. Just lay low for a bit."

"I planned to stay and help Charlie set up the security system, but I can go with you if you need extra backup."

"We'll be fine. We'll only be gone a few hours, and I doubt the person who tried to run me over this morning would try something again so soon." Although, really, she wasn't all that sure.

"Did you tell him about Bertha?"

She gave Lizzie a knowing glance. "Not yet."

Lizzie giggled. "Oh, he's going to love this."

"Love what?" Grey asked as he came back with Boss.

Lizzie clapped her hands together and sprang to her feet.

"You'll see. Go ahead and get going. I'll clear the perimeter and meet you out front."

"Okay, but I need to let Boss out first," Grey said.

"Let me do it while you grab some water bottles for the road," Christina said.

"Sure."

Boss followed Christina to the backyard to do his business. Lizzie moved around the yard searching for anything out of the ordinary. Christina eyed the trees for movement.

Grey had his gym bag in his lap. "Ready when you are. Can't wait to show you my moves on the court." He tipped his wheelchair back and spun in a circle.

She searched Grey's eyes, but she found no humor there. The cheerful demeanor was an act, and she sensed the events over these last few days had pushed him outside his comfort zone.

"I bet this is difficult for you," she said. "Having people come into your home and sort of...take over. I want you to know I would never ask you to do this if it wasn't the best option."

Grey shrugged. "What's life without a little adventure?" Again, his words said one thing, but his humorless smile proved her instincts correct. He pushed his chair toward her, stopping when his knees touched hers. A jolt of electricity buzzed through her.

"Adventure, you think?" She stumbled over the words and realized she was on the edge of babbling again. Why did she have difficulty talking when he was close? She took a half step back and cleared her throat. "Well, um. I'm glad to hear you say you're up for an adventure because I've got one more thing to tell you."

"One more thing? Oooh boy." He blew out a breath. "Okay, then. Let's hear it, Agent."

The nickname made her hesitate and she shot him a curious look. "I'm not an agent, remember?"

He rested his hands on his gym bag and his broad smile sent her pulse racing. She didn't fight the smile that consumed her face. When Grey was around, she always seemed to smile more. And bigger. His casual teasing drew her out of her shell. He was a sweet and fun guy. Someone she could relax with, maybe even open up to. Maybe.

She shook away the thought and focused her attention on Grey. "You see... It's about Bertha."

"*That's* Bertha?"

Grey's mouth hung slightly open at the sight of a late 1970s model Lincoln Continental parked in the street at the end of his driveway. It was almost twenty feet long with wide doors. Trying to see over the hood must be like gazing across an ocean. No way Christina could drive this black-and-chrome monstrosity. It wasn't a car. It was a *boat*.

Grey threw his head back and laughed. "Okay, okay. I get it. You're pranking me, right? This is some sort of joke to ease the mood?"

Christina and Lizzie exchanged a look.

No way. Were they serious? They wanted him to ride in something that looked like a throwback to a 1970s gangster movie?

His smile faded and he held both hands out toward the car. "You can't possibly think this hideous thing is less conspicuous than my Tesla. Just look at it!"

"Hey," Christina chided. "Don't call her hideous."

Grey gaped at her. "I don't know what's worse, the fact you *own* this behemoth or that you called it a *her*."

"It belonged to my dad. He named her Bertha," said Christina.

Lizzie ran her hand over the hood. "I think she's beautiful."

"How am I supposed to get in and out of this thing?" As soon as the words came out of his mouth, he knew it was a flimsy excuse. With one look, he knew his wheelchair would fit on the floorboard of the front seat. He could probably squeeze two or three wheelchairs in there.

And he couldn't claim that he couldn't get in and out of the car. The doors were almost as wide as his entire trunk. And the car looked low to the ground. Perfect to lift himself in and out with ease.

Grey just didn't want to tell Christina that.

She opened the passenger door. It groaned like an eighty-year-old man trying to stand up from his easy chair. She waved an arm inside. "Look! It's huge in there. Plenty of room. If you can squeeze into your tiny Tesla, you can get in here."

He crossed his arms. "What about my chair?"

"The trunk is *huge*. There's enough room for three dead bodies in there!"

"And the shovels," Lizzie said with a laugh.

"I do *not* want to know how you two know that," he deadpanned.

Peals of laughter burst from Lizzie and Christina, and he was so distracted by the sound of Christina's laughter he didn't care that they might be laughing at a real memory of hauling dead bodies in Bertha's trunk. Their laughter was contagious, and he found himself laughing along with them.

Boss smiled and wagged his tail. He hopped from one foot to another, joining in with an excited dance. Grey patted the dog's head.

"The only thing I don't have figured out is Boss," Christina said. "Can he ride in the back seat?"

"As long as he wears a seat belt. Wait, this thing has seat belts, right?" The image of Boss sitting with a seat belt across his chest made him chuckle.

"Of course, it has seat belts."

"Okay, okay," Lizzie said. "We've been out in the open too long."

Christina sobered. "She's right. We need to move. You'll be late for practice."

"I'm waiting for Charlie to help him install the surveillance equipment," Lizzie said. "I'd like to be done before you get back so we don't keep him from his undercover job any longer than we have to."

"Thanks, Lizzie. You've been a huge help today." And in more ways than one. She might have burst into his house this morning and taken over while Christina was gone, but the woman had helped him see things from Christina's perspective.

Christina opened the back door of the car and waited for Boss to get in. He looked at her, then the back seat, questioning.

"He's waiting for permission," Grey said.

Christina patted Boss. "It's okay, boy. Get in."

Boss didn't move. He looked to Grey, then back to Christina, eyebrows bobbing.

"Tell him H-U-P," he said, spelling the command. "Or click your tongue like I did yesterday. He won't get in without permission."

"Oh, I see. What a gentleman." Christina clicked her tongue twice and Boss jumped into the back seat.

The dog sniffed around the expansive back seat, snorted, then plopped down and licked his paw.

As Grey suspected, it was relatively easy to pull himself into the Lincoln. The car only had one accessibility handle, which was unfortunately located on the door. He grabbed the headrest and briefly stood on his right leg to give himself the extra push he needed to slide into the car.

Christina waited until he'd settled and took his wheelchair to the trunk. A slight pang of embarrassment hit his stomach as he watched her collapse his chair and cart it away. The woman hadn't signed up for this. She must feel more like a nurse than a bodyguard.

The entire car jolted when Christina slammed the trunk and the humor of the situation hit him again. Was he about to ride around in this colossal car? It was some getaway vehicle. He rubbed his eyes. What had his life become?

Christina slid into the driver's seat and cranked the engine. To Grey's surprise, it roared to life right away. He expected the whirring of an almost dead starter, but the car sounded like it had just rolled off the production line.

She pulled a mini iPad from beneath the seat and attached it to a mount on the dash. The iPad scanned her fingerprint and came to life, displaying a similar camera feed as his Tesla with four angles showing a 360-degree view of the exterior.

"Okay, you're starting to worry me. Does this thing have a machine gun under the license plate?" He twisted and looked through the back window. "Is there an oil slick we can spew out the back?"

"No, but now that I've been around you, I'm considering installing bullet-resistant windows."

Grey laughed. "Perhaps you should consider the ejection seat too."

Christina pulled the massive car away from the curb with a slight smile on her face. This was a new side to the woman he hadn't seen before, and it made his heart happy. Was he breaking through that hard exterior to see through the cracks to a funny, quirky Christina? Well, if he had to ride around in Bertha to see more of this side of her, then sign him up.

12

The Scavenger sat among the students at the University of South Carolina Carver Auditorium to hear Cathy Wright's lecture, "Empowering Women to Rise Above." The pamphlet said the woman had "pushed through the glass ceiling," a phrase he doubted the college students knew the meaning of. So she'd graduated college and become a chemist. Big deal. He knew who she really was.

It was risky being here in the open, but he was careful. Countless precautions had been taken to ensure he blended in with the crowd. Dressed in skinny jeans with a white T-shirt under a plaid dress shirt, he looked like every other guy here albeit a tad older. He kept his short beard but added a wig, as well as facial prosthetics and skin tint to make his skin appear darker.

Laughter and loud conversation drew his attention to a group of students walking down the aisle behind him searching for enough seats to fit their group. A perfect time to test his disguise.

He stood and waved his hand. "You guys looking for seats? I've got five right here."

A cute blonde girl who seemed to be leading the group spoke up first. "Really? Are you sure?"

"Oh, yeah. I may not stay the whole time anyway." He lifted his shoulder. "I mean, I'm just here for the extra credit."

"I hear ya, bro," said a sandy-haired guy. The Scavenger looked him up and down, happy to see the guy's clothes were almost identical to his own.

The cute blonde gave Sandy a playful punch. "It wouldn't hurt for you to learn a little something while you're here. Maybe something about appreciating smart and powerful women." She slid past The Scavenger and took her seat.

The three girls who followed wore looks of disgust. To The Scavenger, the girls looked like clones. Same long hair highlighted, singed, and flattened within an inch of its life. Same overly done makeup and perfectly straight teeth. Sandy was in over his head.

The Scavenger took his seat, pleased that his disguise worked. Inches apart and they were none the wiser. Later, he would destroy everything, including the prosthetics, and no one would ever see *this* face again.

The overhead lights dimmed, and a hush fell over the crowd. A small round woman entered from the side stage and waddled toward the podium. One of her orthopedic shoes squeaked with each step. Squeak. Step. Squeak. Step. Squeak. The Scavenger clenched his teeth.

The round woman reached the podium and the blessed squeaking ceased. She reached up and adjusted the microphone, sending an ear-piercing shriek through the speakers. The entire crowd winced in unison. She pulled the microphone lower and lower, causing more feedback until she settled it into place. The Scavenger could barely see the top of her head over the lectern, and her roundness protruded from each side.

Someone should bring her a box to stand on.

"Good morning, students." Her voice was almost as squeaky as her shoes. "It is my extreme pleasure to introduce to you a woman who has taken a dream and turned it into a very successful career. As a student at our Honors College, she earned her master's in chemistry in under five years. She landed an internship with the United States Army Research Laboratory and worked her way to assistant director of a research laboratory in White Sands while working on her doctoral thesis. Our guest is an inspiration to women everywhere, and a true testament to what you can do with hard work and dedication. Please give a warm U of SC welcome to Ms. Cathy Wright."

To his surprise, the crowd jumped to their feet with applause. The small crowd seemed to make more noise than an entire stadium. The sandy-haired guy put two fingers in the corners of his mouth and screeched a long whistle. These students thought Wright was some sort of celebrity.

Cathy Wright strolled onto the stage in a white pantsuit, waving to the audience like a politician. Silky black hair swished gently at her waist. The round woman gave Wright a brief hug then tottered offstage.

The Scavenger worked to keep the scowl off his face. He stood with the crowd but refused to applaud the woman. No, he was thinking about the show he'd so artfully planned. It should begin any moment. He realized those around him were seated and plopped down. He needed to pay attention. Not forget to blend in.

Wright, a practiced public speaker, clicked the microphone off before she raised it closer to her mouth. A soft click indicated she had switched it on. She grasped the edge of the podium and surveyed the crowd. The smile she beamed was utter confidence and it infuriated him. Did she plan to deliver a memorized speech, or did she have note cards waiting? He would know once she got beyond the beginning of her speech.

If she got to speak at all.

He laced his hands in his lap and resisted the urge to lean forward. It would happen. It had been planned. The time, the day, the location. It was inevitable. The knowledge made him giddy.

"Ladies and gentlemen," Wright began. The milky smooth voice dripped with kindness while still exuding confidence and authority. "It is my honor to address this fine educational establishment with high hopes of broadening your understanding and..." Wright's eyelids drooped, and she shook her head as if she was trying to wake up.

A warm vibration filled The Scavenger's stomach. His facial muscles wanted to turn up in a smile, but he fought against it. He slid the front of his teeth together with a slight movement of the jaw instead.

"I'm sorry," she said. "I...I seemed to have lost my words for a moment. Excuse me." She lifted the glass of water from under the lectern and drank from the straw. She let out a breath, readying herself to begin again. "I was saying, I hope to broaden your understanding and help you take your passion and turn it into a future. A future where—"

The Scavenger put his hand over his mouth. It was happening.

Wright's glassy eyes stared sightlessly into the audience as if entranced. Murmurs rippled through the stadium. Students whispered and lifted their phones to capture the moment. Yes, he would relish seeing these clips later. Seconds ago, Cathy Wright had appeared to be a leader, someone to look up to. Now she stood statue still and mute, looking like she had stage fright.

He caught a glimpse of her nearly black eyes rolling back into her head just before her body crumpled to the floor with a satisfyingly sickening thud. The audience gasped and sprang to their feet, craning their necks to see around the lectern. The

Scavenger happily stood with them, putting his excited energy to good use.

People ran onstage and rushed to Wright's side. She thrashed on the floor, her shoulders and head banging against the hardwood floor. Legs kicked involuntarily.

The Scavenger jumped the short distance to the stage, unbuckled his belt, and whipped it free of the loops. "Here! Put this between her teeth," he said.

A man took the belt and forced it in her mouth. He cupped her chin and closed her mouth.

The Scavenger stood transfixed, watching the life drain from Cathy Wright's body.

SATURDAY, 2:22 P.M.

At basketball practice, Christina caught a glimpse of the soldier and leader inside of Grey, one she thoroughly enjoyed. All the veterans on his team looked up to him, and she could see why. Watching them maneuver a wheelchair while dribbling a basketball gave her a newfound respect for the men and the sport. It took talent and coordination, and she wondered if she could manage it.

They returned home to find Charlie adding the finishing touches to the high-tech security system he'd installed in Grey's house. He tossed a drill gun into his tool bag and wiped a hand on his shirt. "Well, that about does it. Doors and windows are wired, and you've got surveillance on any device you need. Phones, tablets, even the TV."

Charlie stretched his neck and stifled a yawn.

"Thanks, Charlie," Christina said. "I'm sorry to pull you off the job. I appreciate your willingness to come do this for us."

"Are you kidding? I'd do anything for you guys. Besides, this is late for me. Drug dealers don't exactly keep normal working hours."

Each time Charlie interacted with the Elite Guardians, he risked blowing his cover, but he was always cautious and ready to help when they needed him.

"Sounds like you're off to bed then?"

"Bed sounds great right about now, but first let me show you the few blind spots on the video feeds." Charlie pointed the remote at the television mounted over the fireplace mantel.

Twelve video feeds gave them a clear view of the perimeter of the house, roof, the street, interior hallways, main living area, and the front door. Christina was impressed. This was far more than she had expected him to do.

"See that? A tree branch is covering a six-foot area in the backyard," Charlie said. "You'll have to get someone to come and cut that down. And right here a large vehicle could park on the street and create a blind spot, so keep an eye out."

Grey moved his wheelchair in front of the television. "Wow, Charlie. This is incredible. I should have you install this at my parents' ranch."

"Just say the word and I'll put the order in."

"Something to think about, if we don't catch whoever is after me," Grey said.

Christina stared at the TV and watched a small video square capturing an elderly woman walking to her car. "Did you say we have remote access to view the camera feeds?"

"Let me show you." Charlie held his hand out for her phone and tapped the screen a few times before handing it back. "There you go. And if you tap the squares, they will expand so you can see them better."

All twelve video feeds showed on her phone, and she nodded. Grey angled his wheelchair and moved in for a closer look. When his arm brushed hers, she jumped and fumbled her phone, snatching it before it hit the ground.

The smile that spread over Charlie's face didn't escape Christina's notice. "You okay there, Christina?"

"Don't even think about starting up with me, Charlie." Christina had a feeling she'd be fighting a losing battle if she engaged with Charlie's teasing.

Charlie held his palms up. "I wouldn't dream of it."

She ignored his teasing. "I suspect whoever tried to break into Grey's house last night might be back. With this, we could catch them in the act."

Charlie nodded. "I started recording the feeds in case they come back any time soon. All the footage will be saved to the cloud."

"Perfect. Can you set it up for Grey's phone as well?" Her phone buzzed and an alert said it was a text from Bree asking to call her. "Excuse me, I need to make a call. Thanks again, Charlie."

"No problem," he said, tapping Grey's phone. "I'm going to head out. Text if you have any problems."

Christina nodded then went into Grey's guest room. Boss followed and waited until she sat on the edge of the bed before lying down by her feet. She dialed Bree and the call connected after the first ring.

"Sorry to bother you on a Saturday," Bree said. "I thought y'all would want to know that the blood from the arena confirmed the gunman is that Russian hitman, Viktor Sokolovich."

"Do you have any idea where he is?"

"We found a burner phone with his prints on it and think he dropped it outside of the arena. I have a mountain of Russian text messages and voicemail translations to slog through, but we should know something in the next few days. Unless you speak Russian, that is." The detective laughed.

"A little, but I'm not fluent."

Bree was still on the other end of the line for a beat. "Are you serious?"

"I scored high in linguistics. I learned Arabic, Pashto, Dari, and Russian." Just to name a few. The truth was, she had an ability to decode anything she worked at long enough.

"Huh, how about that," Bree said. "Well, if you don't mind taking a look, I can email everything over to you as soon as I clear it with the captain."

"Sure, anything to help. I plan to lie low with Grey at his place, so this will give us something to do."

"I heard about the near hit and run today. Have you filled out a police report yet?"

Christina breathed a sigh. "No, not yet but I'll do it online."

"Good, it will help in case all this is tied to Sokolovich," Bree said.

"I'll have Grey fill out a report about the intruder last night as well."

"What are you talking about?" An edge of panic laced her words. "Did something happen to Grey?"

"No, not exactly. He wasn't hurt, but someone tried to break into his house last night. I chased after the guy, but he gave me the slip."

"This is all too coincidental." Bree sighed.

"I agree, and I don't believe in coincidences that big. I've secured Grey's house for his protection, so if the alarm company dispatches to his address, you'll want to be notified." She gave Bree the address and thanked her before disconnecting.

Christina returned to the living room, and her eyes fell on the empty wheelchair in the corner. Grey was on the floor, face down with his arms underneath him, straining to push up. His veined biceps quivered as he held his weight on two hands. The image was jarring since she'd never seen him out of his wheelchair, except the other night when he was sitting on the floor, bare chested and glistening with the exertion of exercise. The image sent heat flooding to her cheeks, and she chastised herself.

A client. He was nothing more than a client.

"Are you okay? What happened?" She squatted beside him and touched his back. His shirt was damp to the touch.

Grey released his hold, crashing his chest to the floor with a laugh. He turned his head to look at her. "Don't make me laugh when I'm planking! I almost fell on my face!"

"Planking? You mean like yoga?"

Grey turned over on his back and dropped his hands on his chest. "You mean the yoga mat didn't give me away?"

Only then did she notice the blue mat underneath. Talk about rushing to judgment. She'd thought he'd fallen out of his chair and was struggling to get up. "Oh, um. I didn't mean to interrupt." She started to stand but he grabbed her hand and pulled her to the floor beside him.

"What was the call about?" he asked.

"That was, um, Bree." She cleared her throat. "The blood sample taken from the arena confirmed it was Sokolovich. They also found his burner phone, but everything is in Russian. Bree said she'll email me what she has and we can go through it."

"Wow, that's great." Grey worked himself back into his chair and she settled on the couch. "So, tell me about your time in the Army. You said you were a sniper. Why did you retire?"

She swallowed hard. "Hmm." She was finally feeling relaxed, and he wanted to talk about one of the darkest moments of her life.

"You don't have to be closed off from the world, Christina." His voice grew softer, and his gray eyes seemed to penetrate her defenses. "I might be a client, but I'm also a human and was special ops as well. I can listen. Tell me what keeps you so closed off."

She let out a breath. "God must be trying to tell me something because someone else said the same thing. I've been praying about it."

Grey shifted and averted his eyes at the mention of God, and she was quick to pick up on it. "Are you not on speaking terms with God?" she asked.

"Put it to you this way," he sighed. "When it comes to me talking to God, there's nothing left to say."

Well, he'd walked right into that one. Grey knew Christina was a master at turning the conversation around, but he'd tried anyway. Instead of talking about her time in the Army, she'd somehow managed to bring the whole thing back to his relationship with God. Or his lack of one.

Christina leaned forward and touched his arm. "Even when you don't have words to say, God's still there," she said. "All you have to do is talk to Him."

A familiar bitterness rose inside and he forced himself to control his words. No need to spew his anger onto Christina. "Really? Well, He's done listening to me as far as I can tell. Has been for a long time."

Christina frowned. "What makes you say that?" Her question was asked delicately, and he could feel a deep desire to understand behind her words.

There was something about Christina he found disarming. Around her, he didn't feel the need to hide himself or pretend he was fine with his current condition. Without words, she somehow understood his frustrations and the difficulties of living with his limitations. She neither made excuses for him, nor coddled him for it. The compassionate side of her didn't try to fix or take over for him.

"You know, you sound like my mom," he said.

She arched an eyebrow. "Is that a bad thing?"

"No, not at all." He chuckled. "My mom is a prayer warrior, the most faithful Christian I've ever known. I remember walking by her bedroom every morning and seeing her on her knees, leaning over this old leather ottoman in the corner with her hands folded in prayer. Day after day she would kneel there and talk to God. Laughing, weeping, and sometimes even crying out in anger."

Christina smiled. "What about your dad?"

"Right there with her most of the time. When he left for morning chores, she usually stayed with God for a while."

"I like that, 'stayed with God'."

"That's what she called it. When I was four or five years old, I thought God was sitting in the armchair and that's why she always prayed at the ottoman." The memory fell over him like a veil. His mother with her wild blonde hair gathered in hair clips, kneeling at the feet of God as the morning sunrise streamed through the bedroom window.

"You mentioned your parents are celebrating their fortieth wedding anniversary. Is that right?"

He blew out a long breath. "Yes, it's next Friday. I haven't helped with the planning like I promised."

"You've been preoccupied," she said. "It must be difficult to keep your family in the dark about this Top Secret stuff. How do they handle it?"

"My sister, Ruby, is always trying to see behind the curtain so to speak. I think that has more to do with being a big sister than her psychiatry degree. My parents, on the other hand, are the most understanding people in the world. They deserve the best party we can give them."

"Forty years is a long time."

"And you know what? It's been a happy forty years. In my whole entire life, I only remember one big argument. I've always wanted a marriage just like theirs." And he thought he'd found love once, but it had slipped right through his fingers.

Christina shifted and propped her elbow on the couch cushion. "What was the argument about?"

"Oh, you know, just a disagreement over their boneheaded son." Grey really didn't want to talk about it. Why bring up the bad stuff and ruin their great conversation? He'd much rather see if he could make her smile again.

Christina nodded and tried another angle. "What made you join the Air Force?"

"The short answer? A recruiter came to my high school."

"And the long answer?"

Grey shrugged. Here they were, back to the tough stuff again. He'd have to choose his words the way Christina did. "I always knew my parents wanted me to go to college and eventually take over their business, but my grades weren't exactly scholarship worthy. I didn't want my parents in debt over my college, and the recruiter said I could go to school free with the GI Bill. Couple that with the stories of adventure the recruiter told me, and I signed up on the spot."

"Adventure? In the Air Force? Are you kidding me?" she teased.

He gave her a playful whack with a throw pillow. She caught it and clutched it to her chest. "I'll have you know, Air Commandos arguably have the most dangerous job. We're the ones who roll in and clear the battlefield for the rest of you. Remember 'Kilroy was here'?" Most soldiers knew of the phrase graffitied on battlefields to tell World War II soldiers that the area had been cleared of enemy mines.

"Yeah, I know. But then you go back to your base and have a nice steak dinner while the rest of us eat MREs for the next six months." She swatted him with the pillow.

They both laughed and his heart pounded hard at her wide smile. Grey noted the flecks of gold speckling her brown eyes. Was it his imagination or did they brighten when she laughed?

"I've eaten plenty of MREs and I hope I never eat another

one," he said. "When I enlisted, I thought the Security Forces would see the most action. My recruiter glorified the position, but little did I know the other Airmen saw me as not much more than a mall cop." He chuckled. "I applied to be a K9 handler, hoping I would see the battlefield. Once I got in, they sent me to Lackland where I met Boss as a puppy. Eventually we finished training and qualified for Special Operation Forces."

Boss twitched an ear at the sound of his name but didn't bother to lift his head.

"How did you meet Wally?"

"We were in the same SOF unit right from the start. We both took college courses online and ended up studying together. Of course, Wally is an overachiever. He did an accelerated bachelor's degree in chemistry and used all his leave time to complete the required lab courses back in the States."

"That's amazing. It sounds like he was motivated and dedicated."

"Truly. I've always been impressed by Wally's determination and drive. It's the main reason why I feel so bad about walking him right into a trap."

The guilt sat in his stomach like a bowling ball. He looked away from Christina and stared at Boss stretched out in front of the couch, as close to Christina as he could get without sitting on her lap. It hadn't escaped his notice earlier when Boss followed Christina to the bedroom during her call. Even his dog found comfort in Christina. Grey figured he'd all but lost Boss's loyalty when she was in the room, and wasn't sure if he should feel happy or jealous.

Christina shifted her body to sit on both feet. "What do you mean?"

"Siberia," he said. "It's really my fault..." He let his words hang, unsure if he wanted to talk about it.

Christina placed her hand on his arm. The simple touch

grounded him, dragging him back to the moment. Concern filled her eyes. "Tell me what you mean."

"The attack in Siberia." He hesitated. "If I'd read Boss correctly, it never would have happened. He was trying to tell me something and I was too thick to get it." It wasn't the first time his failure to read an animal had gotten someone hurt.

Grey shook his head. "If I had listened to Boss that day, we would have captured Dr. Kalashnik and none of this would have happened."

He stared into the distance and put his head in his hand, brushing the stitches on his temple. The gesture made them itch and he fought the urge to scratch. The memories were too vivid, and he didn't want to think about them. He wanted to enjoy this moment of closeness with Christina.

"You seem to read Boss like no other person I've ever seen with a dog," she said, her voice soft. "And he's obviously in tune with you or he wouldn't be so well trained."

"If I was so in tune with him, I wouldn't be sitting here. Or there." He nudged his wheelchair. Maybe he'd still be jumping from airplanes and clearing mines with Boss. Panic seized him as memories of explosions flooded his mind like rapid gunfire.

"Grey, listen to me." She reached out and stroked his arm, her firm words grounding him in the present. "You can't live in the past. A thousand things could have changed the outcome of the attack in Siberia, and you only failed at one. You had bad intel. It happens. You and I both know we can follow every order according to protocol, take every precaution, and still end up with collateral damage. You both put your lives on the line that day and walked away with them. Don't let your emotions stand in the way of your goal. You have to try and move past it."

Grey noticed her lower lip trembling, but she covered it with her hand. The gold flecks in her dark expressive eyes shimmered with unshed tears.

There was personal pain behind her words. She was

speaking from experience. What secret did she keep hidden deep in her heart? What collateral damage did she have buried? And how hard would he have to dig to uncover it?

Christina withdrew her hand from Grey's arm where she'd let it linger far too long. For reasons she didn't understand, the man saw down to the real person she kept hidden from most people. There were things she wanted to tell him that she hadn't allowed herself to tell anyone else. Things to make him understand how emotions could get in the way of doing the job.

When Grey finally spoke again, his voice was gentle. Small lines of concern formed around his mouth. "What is it, Christina?"

She hesitated. Grey had opened himself up to her without a second thought. It couldn't be easy for him to let a stranger disrupt his life and force him out of his routine. Not only had he willingly let her turn his home into a safe house, but he'd answered her prying questions. If nothing else, he'd earned the right to know what living by emotions could do to a life.

Before she could speak, Grey tilted his head toward her. "Okay, if you don't want to tell me, that's fine. How about this? While we're on the subject of our military careers, tell me why you retired."

Another part of Christina's story she avoided talking about. Her partners at the Elite Guardians Agency knew she'd chosen to retire after a failed mission, but what they didn't know was that *she* was the cause of the failed mission.

Christina blew out a breath. "I've never told anyone this before, Grey. I'm only telling you now because I think it might help you. Do you understand?"

She lifted her eyes long enough to see Grey nodding his

agreement. If she didn't look at him while she spoke, she might get through her story before she lost her nerve.

"I was in the Army, a special ops group." Her pulse quickened with each word.

"A sniper, right?"

"Yes, up until a few years ago. I was on a joint task force with a Marine unit in Musa Qala fighting the Taliban. My job was mostly neutralizing high-value targets and recon."

"Wow, that sounds fun."

"I guess if you find lying in dirt in the scorching sun for hours on end *fun*, then okay."

He snorted. "Okay, maybe not fun, but it's exciting work. You were truly making a difference."

Christina closed her eyes and took a calming breath. How much could she let out without breaking the bottle where she'd stuffed so many emotions? "I'd like to think so. We often eliminated hostiles before they could execute their plans."

Her words came quicker, eager to get through the story now. "We had some intel come down the line saying a suicide bomber planned to attack the market and take control of the city. We didn't have much else to go on at first, but within a day we intercepted enough communication to provide a target. We knew it would be a young female and instead of wearing the customary black niqab, she would try to blend in by wearing a hijab, but in Taliban flag colors. I waited for twenty-eight hours before I saw her. A nervous girl about twelve or thirteen, younger than I'd ever targeted."

Christina could still feel the sweat pooling on her back as the sun beat down on her that day. "I saw her before my spotter, and he radioed our unit to prepare for the aftermath after I made the shot. At only seven hundred meters and no wind, it was a simple shot for any marksman. When the girl reached the mark, I received confirmation to execute. Before I squeezed the trigger, the girl looked over her shoulder. Her headscarf slipped and I saw her face..."

The face of the girl was as clear as if she stood right in front of Christina. No matter how hard she tried, Christina couldn't erase the memory of the girl's face. "It was a girl...a girl who looked like..."

She shook her head to clear the image from her mind and stared down as she fingered the hem of her shirt. "I hesitated. By the time my brain made sense of what I was seeing, the target slipped into a building. It was too late. She detonated the bomb."

Her eyes brimmed with tears that threatened to spill over. Tears she'd never allowed herself to shed. Crying was not an option. If she let the tears fall, there would be no stopping them.

She wanted, no *needed* Grey to know it was her emotions that had killed sixty-three people that day. There was nothing she could do about it except put the memory in a box and shove it in the back corner of her mind. Take her thoughts captive and move past the feelings and her mistake.

There was more to the story, but no matter how hard she tried to speak, she couldn't push the words past the lump in her throat.

Grey wrapped his arms around her and pulled her toward him. She resisted, stiffening at his touch. Getting close to a client was dangerous, and this had the potential for utter disaster.

But she was embarrassed her tears were so close to falling. She gave in and let him guide her closer. He held her tighter, and she relaxed into his warm embrace. With her face buried in his chest she prayed silently, asking God to help her get control so she could help Grey.

The lump in her throat finally gave way and she swallowed. She pushed herself away and looked into his eyes. "Do you see now? See how letting your emotions and regret take over your life can hurt others?" Her voice was firm, and the tears were gone. "My emotions got in the way of my target and ended the lives of sixty-three innocent people. That's why I retired." She let her head hang, avoiding eye contact.

He brushed a stray hair out of her face, his hand warm and tender. "I do see," he whispered. "I see a strong and capable woman who trusts God with everything in her life."

The comment was gentle but hit her like a slap in the face. God had healed her, hadn't He? Or had she merely put the feelings in a box and ignored the bleeding wound? Trusting God meant trusting Him with all areas of her life, but was there a piece of her that hadn't fully surrendered? "There are some things I haven't trusted God with yet, and I guess I should start talking to Him about it."

Grey traced her jaw with his thumb. "You could talk to me too, you know."

"I will," she said. "Right after *you* start talking to God." She poked his chest with her index finger.

"Oh, I see how it is." He grinned. "You know blackmail is illegal, right?"

A smile played on her lips. "Technically this falls under extortion." She grabbed a pillow and aimed to thump his head with it. Grey caught it mid-air and wrestled it from her grip.

They were laughing when the sound of a cell phone vibrating on the counter drew her attention. "I'd better check that."

She crossed the room, disappointed their moment had been interrupted. When she saw both phones lit up, her gut clenched. She handed Grey's phone to him then checked her messages. Their eyes locked.

They had the same message.

There was another body—and they needed Boss.

14

On the short drive to the University of South Carolina, Grey's mind buzzed with thoughts about the disaster that might await them in the main auditorium. There could be mass casualties.

Taking a deep breath, he led Boss and Christina into Carver Auditorium using the main entrance. They flashed their credentials to the officer guarding the door.

A wide aisle divided the rows of seats that led to a small stage with stairs on either side. Grey spotted Bree and Wally standing near Francisco, the medical examiner he'd met at the Empire Hotel. Quinn crouched near the edge of the stage, his body blocking Grey's view of the body. By now, they'd all received the proper security clearance and had been read in on the details regarding X-VX, so he could discuss the chemical weapon with the detectives and Francisco without breaching protocol.

Bree bounced down the stage stairs and met them in the aisle. "Hey, thanks for coming." She turned and pointed to the back corner of the room. "There's a ramp to the stage this way."

"Thanks, I wasn't sure if I could convince Christina to carry me up the steps."

Bree gave a quick laugh and headed in the direction she'd pointed.

Grey glanced over his shoulder but Christina either hadn't heard him or didn't find his joke very funny. She'd been quiet on the car ride over despite his attempts to make small talk. Before they were interrupted, she'd seemed playful. But now? Now she was keeping him at a distance.

Grey followed Bree through a side door in the corner of the room. A U-shaped ramp led to the backstage area. Grey was happy Christina chose to walk beside him instead of walking up the steps in front of the stage. She didn't have to do that. She could have left him with Bree.

"Who's the victim?" Christina asked.

"Cathy Wright, a chemist here to give a lecture to inspire more women in STEM fields."

A chemist? If she was killed with X-VX, it could be a solid connection to Dr. Kalashnik. Grey exited the ramp and saw the body of a woman in her late forties lying on the floor next to the lectern—her eyes frozen open, her head turned away as if taking one last look at the audience.

"What's in her mouth?" Grey asked.

Quinn spun to look over his shoulder then frowned. "Oh great, it's you." The detective patted his chest. "And to think, I didn't wear my bulletproof vest. You didn't bring your Russian friends, did you?"

"Don't listen to him," Bree said. "He missed his nap today."

Francisco squatted next to the body and gestured to the dead woman's mouth. "Someone gave her a belt to bite down on during the convulsions. Symptoms matched the other victim, Gayle Mooney. I called you guys before I removed the belt in case it's contaminated."

"Let's see what Boss says." Grey put Boss into work mode and dropped the leash.

The dog sniffed the ground and moved to the body, working his way from her feet to her head. He lingered near her hands before moving on to her torso and mouth. Boss did his work without touching the woman. When he finished, he sat beside the body and held one paw in the air.

"That's a good boy, Boss." Grey patted his head and offered the dog his toy as a reward.

Boss didn't seem interested in the toy. He sniffed Francisco's shoes, then Wally's.

Wally rubbed the dog's head and showered Boss with praise. "Yes, that's a good boy. You did a good job. Who's the Boss? You are. Yes, you're the Boss."

Francisco pointed at Boss. "Do you think he can come to my office and tell me the cause of death for the rest of the unknowns?"

Grey chuckled. "I'm not sure, but I think you have your answer on this one." Grey turned his wheelchair around to face Christina. "Would you walk Boss around the seating areas? If the killer was in the audience, Boss might be able to detect where he was sitting."

"I don't know, man. If the suspect had X-VX on his body, he'd be dead too," Wally said.

"Not if he had it in a container," Grey said.

Wally nodded. "Yeah, I guess the Boss dog has been tracking the stuff in an enclosed container."

Grey lowered his voice and inched closer to Christina. "Do you mind? I would do it, but I don't think my chair will fit between the rows."

Christina picked up Boss's leash. "Of course." She paused and scanned the room. "Keep an eye out, will you?"

Grey bit his lip to hide a smile and nodded. Christina was worried about him, but she kept her word and stayed with Boss.

Her concern was endearing, unlike when his family worried over him, which was sometimes annoying.

Christina walked the area of the stage, allowing Boss to lead as Grey had done. He really needed to show her how to handle Boss. It was becoming evident Boss would be needed more and more until they located Dr. Kalashnik. Should he cancel his surgery? The waiting list for the experimental procedure was over a year long. Would he have to wait another year if he cancelled?

Christina and Boss backtracked the way they'd come and he returned his attention to Francisco. The ME knelt beside the victim, collecting blood samples.

Wally patted Grey on the shoulder. "Sorry to call you again. This is the last thing you need to think about before your surgery. You want me to take Boss for a few days?"

"Thanks, man. I'd rather you focus on your lab work." Grey sighed.

Wally ran a hand over his close-shaved hair. "I'm working on it. X-VX wouldn't be as dangerous if there was a preventative."

"I don't think that would have saved this woman," Grey said.

"Here you go, my friend." Francisco offered three vials of blood to Wally. "Now, let's get this belt out of her mouth."

Bree crouched beside Francisco and held a large evidence bag open with her gloved hands. Francisco snapped a clean glove on and slid his index finger between the dead woman's lips. He wiggled the belt from between her teeth. Once it was free, he dropped it into the evidence bag. Bree stood and sealed the bag with an evidence sticker and signed her name.

"Wait, what's that?" Grey squinted and moved closer. "Bree, it looks like there's writing on the back of the belt."

She twisted the evidence bag and examined it closer.

"What's it say?" Quinn asked.

"I can't tell." She jostled the bag then moved the belt so she could see. "It says, 'This is one of many marks. I will kill more until you bring to light what you've done in the dark.'"

Quinn snatched the bag. "Well, that's the dumbest poem I've ever heard. At least the last time a serial killer left me a note, it didn't sound like Dr. Seuss."

"He may not be a poet," Wally said, "but he's clearly trying to tell you something."

"Why this woman?" Grey asked. "Why here?"

Bree stared at Quinn a beat. Grey saw how their eyes connected in a silent exchange. They were holding something back.

"It's obvious this guy wants an audience to watch his victims die. First the restaurant, and now this." Bree gestured to the empty seats.

"Grey?" Christina called his name from the rear of the auditorium

Boss sat near an aisle seat with one paw on the arm of the chair.

"Looks like Boss found something," Grey said. "Did Ms. Wright ever sit there?"

Quinn shook his head. "She was in a private room until she walked onstage."

"You think it's a false positive?" Wally asked.

"He's never given a false positive." The memory of Boss whining at the cabin door made Grey's pulse quicken.

Quinn turned to a uniformed officer and waved him over. "Find out who was sitting there." He jabbed his finger at the officer's chest. "I want every millisecond of video taken tonight. Locate every cell phone that was here and find every video uploaded to the internet. I want it yesterday." He paused. "Please."

Was it Grey's imagination or did the officer's lip quiver as he turned to leave? If there was one thing Grey had learned in the past few days, it was that he did *not* want to be on Quinn's bad side.

Wally picked up his kit. "I'll get these samples to my lab and get back to you." He started to leave but turned back to Grey. "Hey, man, I'm looking forward to your parents' anniversary party next Friday. Thanks for the invite."

Oh no. Grey blew out a long breath. The party. He'd promised to call Ruby back but had forgotten all about it. She was going to kill him.

SATURDAY, 8:20 P.M.

Christina wasn't surprised the video of Cathy Wright's death was all over social media within minutes of the incident. The students attending the lecture had recorded and posted videos capturing the horrific scene. There was so much available online the lack of official surveillance footage wasn't a huge loss. Christina sat at Grey's kitchen table and searched for an angle that had captured the audience, but came up empty. After hours of scouring social media, she hadn't found anyone who'd captured the seat where the killer was presumed to be sitting.

Grey turned his iPad toward Christina. "Look here." He paused the video and zoomed in. "Right here, a man pulls his belt off and hands it to the guy next to Wright." Grey tapped the screen with a finger.

Christina took the offered iPad and stared at an image of a man with long black hair. "So, the man takes the belt from a stranger and puts it in her mouth to keep her from biting her tongue. This is the man who wrote the message on the belt."

She rewound the video and played it from the beginning, watching as the stranger rushed to the stage from somewhere out of frame. The suspect unbuckled his belt and whipped it from his belt loops in one long motion. "I think the suspect is speaking to the man kneeling beside Wright," she said.

Grey leaned over Christina's shoulder and watched the screen Christina held in her hands. She caught the smell of sandalwood and black cardamom. Was that his aftershave, or was he wearing cologne? Whatever it was, it sent a zing down her spine, and she had to force herself not to turn her head toward his neck and breathe in more of the scent.

"I think you're right. He takes the belt from the suspect. Do we know who the helpful guy is?"

"Ross Davidson, a chemistry major at USC."

Grey raised his eyebrows at her. "How'd you know?"

"He's tagged in several videos." She gave him a slight smile. "I'm sure Quinn and Bree are questioning him as we speak. Maybe he can give them a sketch."

"That would be helpful. The suspect is smart. He kept his back to the cameras so we couldn't see his face, but someone else must have seen him."

Christina tried to ignore the heat from Grey's body sitting inches away. It was difficult to concentrate. "How, um." She cleared her throat. "How high would you say the stage is? Three and a half or four feet?"

"That sounds about right."

"How tall are you?"

Grey laughed. "Do you mean in my chair or standing like a real person?"

She gave him a sidelong glance. "I'm going to ignore that. How tall are you standing?"

"Six foot four."

"I'm five eleven, and the stage came to right about here on me." She held her hand at her waist. "It's not very scientific but based on these basic measurements, I believe our suspect is under six feet tall, my height, give or take an inch."

"So, what do we know? Our suspect is approximately five

eleven with long black hair, and he's a student at the university?"

"I doubt he's a student. Look at this." She pulled her laptop closer and found the video she was looking for. The video began in slow motion, and she angled the screen toward Grey so he could see. "The way the suspect walks is more like an older man. Maybe in his thirties."

Grey drew back. "What? How can you tell his age from how he walks?"

She lifted a shoulder. "I spent years in reconnaissance. I can tell."

He pointed at the screen. "I see he's wearing gloves."

"Really? I didn't notice."

His lips turned up in a grin. "Oh, really?"

She ignored his gloating and followed his finger where he tapped the screen and paused the video. "Right here. You can't see fingernails," he said.

Sure enough, the suspect wore flesh-colored gloves. "Impressive. We'll have to make sure the detectives see this."

"I agree," Grey said. "And I think he's wearing a wig."

Christina looked closer, but she wasn't so sure. "How can you tell from all the grainy photos and videos?"

Grey pulled his iPad closer and flicked the screen a few times. He turned it toward her. "This person used a camera flash. See where the light reflects on his hair? That's unnaturally shiny. It looks synthetic to me."

He was right again. Was she losing her touch? She'd looked at the same images but hadn't picked up on those small details. Well, this was more proof that two soldiers were always better than one.

Grey rolled his chair away from the table and stretched his arms over his head. "My eyes are bleary. I think I need a break."

"Okay, I think I'll work a little longer. We've got to find a picture of this guy."

"Isn't this a job for your detective friends? You should take a break too."

"I will. In a bit."

"Your call."

Christina bit her lower lip. It wasn't her job, so why was she obsessed with finding this guy? She'd like to think it was because all threats to Americans needed to be neutralized, but was there more to it? Yeah. There was.

And it was all about the guy who'd started to make an impact on her heart.

15

A door chime startled Grey awake. It was the new security system alerting that a door had opened. He bolted upright on the couch and saw Christina coming through the back door. It was dark out already. How long had he been asleep?

Christina turned the deadbolt and saw him. "Oh sorry, I didn't mean to wake you. I wanted to clear the backyard before Boss goes out."

He ran a hand over his gritty eyes. "Thanks. I didn't even hear the door the first time."

"You were tired." Christina peeked through the blinds into the front yard. Why didn't she check the cameras on the TV? Maybe she trusted her eyes more than the technology.

"I didn't plan on falling asleep." After staring at the computer, his eyes had needed the rest. And now the cut on his temple throbbed. When he touched a finger to the stitches, the wound felt hot. A little more antibiotic cream would help stave off infection.

"Are you doing okay?" Her eyes scanned his face.

Grey waved a dismissive hand at her. "Oh, yeah. A little sore and these stitches itch like crazy."

"Been there," she said.

Their conversation from earlier left him with questions and he wanted to know more about the suicide bomber in Afghanistan. How could he get her to open up again?

There was something that had caused her to hesitate that day. Some reason why she hadn't squeezed the trigger. Had she recognized the target? It was clear Christina struggled with guilt about that day, but she chose to bottle her feelings up instead of sharing. He'd try to respect that. For now.

Grey's stomach rumbled and he pressed his hand to his belly. "I'm starving. How about I order some dinner? Chinese?"

"Sounds lovely." She was still watching through the window and her words sounded distant.

He tried again. "What would you like?"

"Anything is fine."

Okay, so small talk wasn't going to get her to open up. Had he done something wrong? "I know this great place that delivers. I'll order one of everything. It's good to have options, don't you think?"

"Mmhmm." She released the blinds. "I'll take Boss out. Bree sent over the texts and voicemails from Sokolovich's phone. We can listen to the messages over dinner."

"Romantic."

One eyebrow shot up in surprise.

Great. The word had slipped out as a joke, but he wanted to yank it back. The last thing he wanted to do was scare her away.

Christina clipped Boss's leash to his collar and left without a word.

"Smooth," he said. "Real smooth."

With a suppressed grunt, he moved into his wheelchair and found his cell phone in the kitchen. He used an app to order way more Chinese food than the two of them could eat in a week. Movement on the television caught his eye and he turned his wheelchair for a closer look.

A camera captured Christina and Boss walking around the backyard. The infrared lights illuminated them in black and white as they paced the grassy area, pausing every few moments for Boss to sniff something interesting.

It felt invasive to stare, but no matter how hard he tried to look away, his gaze drifted back to the screen. He needed a better distraction.

He went to the kitchen and filled Boss's food and water dishes. When he finished, he glanced at the television again. Christina knelt in front of Boss, her fingers weaving in and out of her hair as she plaited the long strands into a braid. All the while her mouth moved as if she was talking to Boss. A slow smile spread over his face. Sometimes he talked to Boss too. The dog was a great listener.

Boss watched Christina and cocked his head side to side at her words. He was interested in the conversation. So was Grey. It was a good thing the surveillance didn't have sound, or he'd have had trouble not eavesdropping. It was difficult enough not to stare at her.

Which was why he was staring.

Enough. Grey grabbed his iPad and checked his email. Bree had sent a secure link to an online storage drive full of text and voice recording files from Sokolovich's burner phone. He wanted to dig in, but decided it was best to wait for Christina. If it was in Russian, he'd be lost anyway.

When she returned almost thirty minutes later, she double-checked the deadbolt. Boss shook out his coat and pranced over to Grey for a head scratch. Oh, so his dog hadn't completely abandoned him for Christina. He gave Boss a vigorous head rub and heard the water in the kitchen turn on. The sight of Christina washing her hands spiked his pulse. How could something so casually domestic ignite such longing in him? She glanced up and caught him watching.

Amusement played at her lips and she tipped her chin in his direction. "The delivery driver is here."

Grey swung his head toward the television. A teenage boy with saggy pants climbed out of a small, dark-colored car. "Awesome, I'm starving. I wasn't sure I could make it much longer." And he might not have been talking about the food.

Christina kept her eyes on the television. "I'd feel safer if you and Boss were in the other room while I open the door."

The comment snapped him back to reality. "Are you kidding?"

The look she threw over her shoulder said she wasn't.

"Fine," he groaned. "C'mon, Boss."

Boss followed Grey through the hall to the bedroom and stared up at him. The big brown eyes always melted Grey's heart, but he was careful not to forget that Boss was a trained killer.

The door chimed and he heard the door open then close again. Christina must have moved to the porch to accept their food. Smart. Always thinking like a soldier.

Again, the door chime rang out as the front door opened and closed. Every time a door opened and closed, the chime sounded and Grey felt like he was in a convenience store. This was going to be a challenge to his nerves.

"It's clear," Christina said.

Grey's stomach rumbled as soon as his eyes landed on the brown paper bags. "Smells great. Should we listen to the voice-mails while we eat?"

"Sure," she said. "I'll bring the plates."

Plates. Right, she probably didn't want to eat out of the carton the way he always did. She set the plates and two water bottles on the table and sat down next to Grey's spot. "I thought we could use the chopsticks."

"Perfect," he said, pulling the oyster pails from the plastic bag. "Did I order this much food or did these things multiply on their way here?"

"I always order too much when I'm hungry," she said. "I'd like to pray and I want you to join me."

Boss went to his food bowl and lowered himself into his praying position. Grey eyed him over Christina's head. Was he ready to talk to God?

The way she offered her long slender hand to him to hold was inviting. If he refused, Christina might be offended, might even close herself off to him. But he wasn't about to fake it. The least he could do was respect her enough to listen as she prayed. He grasped her hand, warm and soft in his. Looking at her soft lips curved into a smile sent his mind swirling for the right words to say, but he didn't have to say anything.

Christina closed her eyes and bowed her head. "Lord, our help comes from You, the Maker of heaven and earth. You will not let our feet slip and You cover us by day and by night. Watch over us, keep us safe from all harm. Watch over our coming and our going both now and forevermore. Amen."

She squeezed his hand and held it a moment longer before releasing it. A sense of peace washed over him. It was unlike anything he'd experienced in a long time. The prayer was a paraphrase from Psalm 121, one of the many psalms his parents had recited with him as a child. Every time he heard the psalm, his courage soared, and like David conquering the giant, Grey knew he could tackle anything. Somewhere along the way he'd forgotten all about that. The way he knew God had his back. He stole a glance at Christina and wondered if God would listen if he recited the psalm.

Christina pulled her laptop toward her and began tapping the keys, unaware of the effect the prayer had on him. His chest swelled with the knowledge that with Christina's help, they would find Sokolovich and he would lead them to Dr. Kalashnik. They would stop him before it was too late. It was only a matter of time.

The first file Christina opened was a mugshot of Viktor Sokolovich.

"He's one ugly dude," Grey said with a mouthful of Mongolian beef.

Christina smirked. "At this point, a few more scars might actually help."

He almost spit rice onto the screen. Christina didn't make very many jokes, so it caught him off guard. "Find the voicemails and I'll pull up the translations they've done so far."

They matched the file names, and Christina played the first voicemail and listened as a man spoke Russian in a gravelly voice.

"I think that's Dr. Kalashnik," Grey said.

"Are you sure?"

"I only heard him speak that one time, but it feels right."

They read the transcript translated from Russian to English while Christina played the voicemail again and agreed it wasn't helpful. There were at least twenty voicemail audio files, and hundreds of texts. This was going to take a while.

After the first few times, they fell into a comfortable rhythm of matching the translated transcripts to the voicemails and text messages. A few times they listened to the same message multiple times, pausing and rewinding so Christina could make notes. By the time they made it through all the files, Grey's eyes were back to the gritty feeling he'd had earlier.

He stretched his arms over his head and glanced at the clock. It was getting late, and the Chinese food was sitting like a rock in his stomach. "Well, what do you think?"

Christina's wheels were turning. Her mouth rested on her laced fingers as she stared at the laptop. "I'm not fluent in Russian, but I think the interpreter made a mistake in translation."

Grey straightened, new energy coursing through him. "What? When?"

"I heard it earlier, but I wasn't sure about my translation until the third time listening." She pulled the laptop closer and scrolled until she found the file she was looking for. "Open the translation file for this."

Grey listened to the Russian voice and stared at the translation on his iPad. "I don't get it. What am I missing?"

"The interpretation reads, 'The bratva sent you not to kill one man, but many.'" She pointed to the line on the iPad. "In the voicemail, the speaker says *bratstvo*, which the interpreter translated to *bratva* in English. I think that was a mistake. Later, the voicemail says *bratstvo tserkov*, and the translation was, 'He was sent by his brother, Tserkov.'"

"And? What does that mean?"

"I don't think Tserkov is a person," she said. "I think it's a place."

SUNDAY, 1:21 A.M.

She had to be insane to agree to this. The moment Christina explained what she suspected the voicemail was really saying, Grey had insisted they scout it out. She wanted to call Quinn and Bree with the information, but Grey persuaded her not to bother them in the middle of the night for what could turn out to be nothing. He said he was too excited to sleep so they may as well go check it out rather than lie awake all night.

So here they were at nearly one thirty in the morning, sitting in Bertha and staring at the small church across the street from a plastics manufacturing plant. An atypical church, it was housed in a rundown building off Shakespeare Road and

Arcadia Lakes Drive. The white sign posted over the door read *Bratstvo Tserkov*—the Brotherhood Chapel.

Christina cut the headlights and parked Bertha between two semi trailers on the gravel lot owned by the manufacturing company. She turned the engine off and checked the back seat. Boss was fast asleep.

Grey sighed. "So, we're just going to sit here? For how long?"

"I don't know. It was your idea to scout the building. I say we watch for anything out of the ordinary and call Bree if we see something."

Recon was one of the many parts of her job that she loved. She could sit alone for hours, observing her surroundings and taking a mental picture of anything and everything. It was the reason she'd caught the phrase *Bratstvo Tserkov*. She'd seen the sign one day and it had stuck in her mind. So long as Grey stayed in the car, she could wait here as long as he wanted.

After half an hour of watching the building and listening to Boss's soft snores from the back seat, Grey broke the silence. "I think we should walk around the building. See if Boss hits on anything."

She shot a look at him. "Are you crazy?"

"We've been sitting here for thirty minutes without so much as a car passing by."

"There are plenty of cars going by." She gestured to the cars speeding down Shakespeare Road, thereby proving her point. "No need to go looking for danger." Danger seemed to find Grey all on its own. Even though he'd made it clear she wasn't *his* bodyguard.

He put his arm on the back of the seat. "Well, I guess we can sit here and talk."

Her body went rigid. She didn't want to talk. "No need to talk," she said. "We can watch a while longer. Maybe someone will come out and we can follow them."

LYNETTE EASON & KATE ANGELO

"You said the face of your target in Musa Qala looked familiar. Who was it?"

"Fine." She sighed. "I'll walk Boss around the perimeter. If he signals anything, I'll come back, and we can call it in."

"I'm going with you," he said, opening the car door.

She grabbed his arm. He looked at her and she yanked her hand back. "Grey, it's not a good idea."

"So what, you're going to leave me here in the car? What if someone sneaks up? I'd be a sitting duck."

This was an impossible situation. On one hand, he couldn't walk off to investigate without some help, but on the other hand she couldn't leave him here alone. The best thing was to go back to the house and wait until morning to call Bree with the information. But what if they were right and this was Dr. Kalashnik's secret laboratory? If they could catch him before he left...

"Okay, a quick walk around the building." She held her finger up. "I'm looking out for my client, remember?"

Grey grinned. "Sure thing, Agent."

She rolled her eyes. The door groaned even though she only cracked it enough to slide out. How had she never realized how loud it was? The back door was somehow even louder and she winced.

She clipped Boss's leash to his vest. With a tongue click, she released him from the car, and Boss began smelling the new ground. She closed the door and was rounding the front end of the car when she heard Grey clear his throat.

"Ahem." Grey cocked his head, clearly trying to communicate something.

It took her a beat to realize he meant his wheelchair. "Sorry, I keep forgetting."

"Yeah, I like that about you."

She brought his chair to the passenger side. "You do? I thought you would be annoyed."

"Are you kidding? Finally, someone who doesn't treat me like a child or constantly try to help because I use a wheelchair. As if that somehow makes me less able to think for myself."

She smiled. "I can see where that would be frustrating. I never considered your chair an issue."

The gravel crunched under his wheels. "Since we don't have Boss's long lead, I'll have you handle him. Otherwise, he might pull me if he gets a scent. He's trained to go as far as thirty meters on his own."

"Are you sure he'll work for me?"

Grey chuckled. "I think he'd do anything for you. Haven't you noticed? He's got a little crush. Just make sure he's looking at you then tell him to go to work using this gesture." He held up two fingers, then pointed forward. "We'll want to use signals and stay silent. Look at me and I'll show you what signal he might need."

Christina walked beside Grey and stayed on alert for any movement or sound. They stopped beside the church building and Grey nodded to put Boss into work mode. She tapped Boss to get his attention. When he made eye contact, she gave him the signal. Boss dropped his nose and went to work, tail wagging. His muscles rippled beneath his coat.

The three of them worked their way around the entire building to a smaller parking lot behind the church. Yellow light from the streetlamp cast an eerie glow over a white cargo van and a black sedan. Christina's heart picked up speed. Was this the car that had tried to run her over? Boss sniffed his way around the black sedan as she checked for any indication that it was the same car.

She was looking under the front fender when she realized the sound of gravel grinding under Grey's wheels had disappeared. She jumped to her feet and brushed the dirt off her hands, searching the parking lot for signs of him. A movement near the back door of the church caught her eye. The door was wide open, but it was too dark to see whoever was inside.

She wanted to call out to Grey, but held her breath and crept toward the opening. As her eyes adjusted to the darkness, she saw the outline of his wheelchair deep inside the church. What was he thinking? He couldn't just waltz into a church in the middle of the night, especially without her.

The door inched itself closed, but she slipped inside with Boss and stilled. She withdrew her gun and pulled the slide back to verify a round was chambered. At the sight of her gun, Boss moved between her legs. In the Army, they'd called this behavior *tactical heeling*, but Christina wasn't aware Boss was trained for it. Even better. She dropped his leash and fisted her mini-Maglite, clicking it on with her thumb.

She swept the dark hallway with the flashlight, stepping with wide strides. Boss anticipated every move, keeping between her legs. The click of his nails on the tiled floor was a cacophony of sound in the quiet church.

The hallway branched off in two directions. Which way should she go? Left, or right? She flicked her light down each, but both were empty. The soft click of a door sounded on her left. Well, that was one way to decide. The left hallway ended in the foyer of the church and she realized the other hallway led here as well. A set of double doors opened into what she assumed would be the sanctuary. She opened the door a crack and peered through the slight opening. What she saw made her stomach drop to the floor. The church sanctuary was empty of pews and filled with lab equipment.

She slipped inside and switched off her Maglite, letting her eyes adjust to the dim light emitted by the equipment. Boss remained in his tactical heeling position between her legs and glanced up with a look of worry. Yeah, she sensed something ominous too. Christina dropped the Maglite into her pocket and caught hold of the leash. With Boss's leash in one hand and her gun in the other, she surveyed the room.

From what she could tell, the setup was similar to the CBRN lab where Wally worked. It had the same rolling counters covered in chemistry experiments and equipment. What was going on here? Was this where Dr. Kalashnik made X-VX?

A clink of glass followed by a soft grunt came from the far left corner of the laboratory. She rose on her toes, searching for a glimpse of Grey over the counters and biting back the urge to call out to him. Even whispering was out of the question unless she wanted to risk broadcasting her location and getting caught. She didn't see Grey—or anyone else, for that matter.

Boss strained against the leash, pulling toward the sound. She followed him to a wall of metal shelves. Rows and rows of clear plastic containers housed squeaking rodents. This must be the source of the sound she'd heard. She lowered her weapon and looked closer at the white lab rats skittering inside their confined space. Beady red eyes stared back at her and Christina shivered.

Boss rose on his hind legs, placing his front paws on the highest shelf he could reach and sniffing the boxes. After a few moments, he sat down and lifted a paw.

Her skin prickled. X-VX, here? In these boxes? They must be using these rats for testing.

Christina rewarded Boss for his work with a head scratch and he sighed with pleasure. When she'd finished, he went back to sniffing. There was something he found interesting on the shelf and he stuck his nose between two boxes to investigate. The dog used his nose to nudge his way further between the containers and accidentally knocked a box off balance. It teetered off the edge, and Christina managed to snatch it just before it fell to the ground.

The sound of rustling fabric caught her attention and she whirled, bringing her gun up.

A short man with wire-framed glasses and wild gray hair, wearing a lab coat, waved the barrel of a revolver in her direction. "Drop your weapon," he said in Russian-accented English.

"I don't think so. You drop yours." She lifted the tip of her gun to encourage him and kept Boss's leash fisted tight. She wasn't about to let anything happen to the dog, especially now that she knew X-VX was here. She shifted her stance and Boss resumed tactical heeling.

"Stop moving. Who are you? What are you doing in my lab?" The barrel of the man's gun wobbled.

"You must be Dr. Kalashnik. Put the gun down, and we can talk about your work." With a nod, she gestured to the shelves of rats.

"How about I shoot your dog instead, hmm?" He lowered his aim at Boss.

Christina tensed. "Listen, I don't want to hurt you and I'm pretty sure you don't want to shoot an innocent dog."

He used a shaking thumb to cock the revolver. The familiar clicking sound triggered a rumbling growl from Boss. "Drop it now, or I shoot."

"Whoa, okay. Look, there's no need to—"

The doctor took a step forward. "Now!"

One look at the sweat beading his temples and the slight quiver in his hands told Christina this man lacked experience with a weapon. If she could close the distance, she could take him down. "Look, I'm going to holster my weapon." It was a small concession, one she didn't want to make, but she couldn't risk Boss's life. She slid her gun into the holster. "Okay, now put yours down and let's talk."

"No, I have a better idea," he said. "Gregor!"

Footsteps came from behind. She looked over her shoulder to see a stout man in a black suit striding toward her, his gun aimed at her chest. His bald head shone with perspiration. Great, now she had two lunatics to deal with. Gregor stopped a few feet behind her and grunted. The smell of stale cigarettes and gasoline tickled her nostrils. This man was confident with his weapon, and his stance was solid, but he was too round to be the suspect she had chased over the fence the other night.

Boss bared his teeth and snarled. He didn't like this any more than she did.

"Easy, boy," she whispered, hoping Gregor would also respond to the soothing words.

They were trapped. Pinned between the counters on either side and the two Russians aiming guns at her. Where was Grey? Had Gregor already found him and...?

Red hot anger flared up and she calculated how quickly she could disarm Dr. Kalashnik and turn the gun on Gregor. Not fast enough. Even if she attacked Gregor first, Dr. Kalashnik might shoot and she couldn't risk Boss getting hurt in the fight.

"Listen guys, I don't know what this is all about—"

A crash came from behind them. Gregor's gaze shifted and Christina used the split-second distraction to spin into a hook kick and knock the semi-automatic from his hand. It clattered to the ground and slid under the lab bench.

Boss lunged forward, ripping the leash from her hand. The dog knocked Dr. Kalashnik to the ground and clamped down on his forearm with two hundred pounds of bite pressure per square inch. Snarling, Boss whipped his head side to side.

The man wailed painfully in broken English. "Get off! Get dog off!"

Gregor came at her, but she managed to pull her gun and point it at his chest. "Don't do it, Gregor."

The fireplug of a man stopped dead in his tracks, palms up. His face twisted into a sneer.

From behind, she heard a tangle of vicious grunting and growling. Boss sounded like he wanted to tear the doctor's arm off. She stepped to the side, keeping her gun trained on Gregor on her left. From her right side periphery, she could make out the figure of Boss tugging on Dr. Kalashnik. The doctor brought his revolver up and waved it near Boss, trying to take aim with his free hand while Boss pulled and tugged his other arm.

Christina's blood turned to ice at the sight of the gun. He was going to shoot Boss. Her eyes darted from Gregor to Boss and back to Gregor. If she could only get to Dr. Kalashnik and keep Gregor from attacking her. Her eyes bore into Gregor as she sidestepped toward the doctor.

Gregor's eyes flicked toward the floor then back to Christina. When he dropped his weapon, it couldn't have gone far. The man was weighing his options like Christina.

"Don't move," she said. "I'll send my dog after you."

Gregor smirked and charged forward. A gunshot went off and she froze. Wide eyed, she stared at the black hole in the center of Gregor's forehead. Blood poured from the wound and trickled down his shocked face before he crumpled to the floor face first. She stared at the gaping exit wound exposing skull fragments and brain matter as blood pooled on the tile.

The bullet had missed her by inches. Another adrenaline dump sent blood surging into every muscle and her nerves danced like fire. Where had the shot come from?

Christina spun on her heel and trained her gun on Dr. Kalashnik. A look of horror clouded his face from what he'd done to Gregor. Boss held his bite on the man's arm, but Dr. Kalashnik held the gun firmly in his free hand. The sleeve of Dr. Kalashnik's white lab coat was red with blood.

"Drop your weapon and I'll call my dog off." Grey's commanding voice came from behind Dr. Kalashnik.

Christina's eyes snapped to Grey. Relief flooded her.

"Okay, okay. Do not shoot. Get dog off." Dr. Kalashnik released his gun and it clattered to the floor.

With the toe of her boot, Christina pulled the gun closer and used the sleeve of her shirt to pick it up and tuck it into her waistband. She kept her weapon trained on the doctor and nodded to Grey.

"Boss, out," he commanded.

Boss unhinged his teeth from Dr. Kalashnik's arm and backed up until he was pressed to Christina's thigh. He barked and snapped a warning to the doctor that he was ready for another bite.

Dr. Kalashnik sat up and cradled his bleeding arm. "Ow, my arm," he moaned. With fast, jerky movements he rocked back and forth, whimpering about his injuries.

Grey fixed his weary eyes on Christina. "Are you okay?"

"Yeah, we're good." She blew out a breath and flicked her gaze to Grey. She had questions and things to tell him, but those would have to wait until they were out of this mess. "Call it in."

"Already done."

Out of the corner of her eye, Christina saw Dr. Kalashnik rock himself forward and reach for Gregor's gun under the lab table. She lowered her weapon and rushed for the gun, but he was too fast. He turned and raised the weapon on her.

In a flash, Christina took aim. They were in a standoff only a few feet apart. She tightened her grip around her gun. "Drop the gun, Dr. Kalashnik."

The gun weaved between Boss and Christina, his shaky finger on the trigger. One false move and he might shoot one of them on purpose or by accident. This man didn't seem like a killer, just a nervous lab geek in over his head.

"I will kill you, then your stupid dog," Dr. Kalashnik spat.

"No need to kill anyone," she said. "No one else needs to get hurt."

Behind him, Grey snaked closer. If he could distract the doctor, she could get the gun.

"I'm going to put my gun away, Dr. Kalashnik. You can put yours away too, and no one else dies here today."

Gradually she opened her stabilizing hand and showed both

palms with her gun held by the trigger guard. Putting her weapon away was risky, but he needed some assurances. Besides, if he lowered his guard a fraction, she could take him down.

Dr. Kalashnik watched her slide her gun into the holster and nodded, oblivious to Grey's movements over his shoulder. "You keep your dog away from me?" he asked.

"Yes, he won't attack if you put your gun down," Christina said.

The doctor hesitated, scanning her face for any hint of deception. Somewhere along the way he'd lost his glasses and Christina realized his eyes looked like small black circles set deep into his eye sockets.

"No! You lie to me! I see it in your eye." The doctor thrust the gun in her direction and she took half a step back.

Boss barked and lowered his head. With one word the dog would attack, but Christina worried he'd get shot in the process. She prayed he'd stay put at least until the doctor put his gun down.

When Christina glanced at Grey, he was on his feet, standing at his full height. The look on her face must have broadcast her surprise to Dr. Kalashnik and the man swiveled to see what had her attention.

Grey stepped forward and reached for the gun. Before he could get his hands on the weapon, Dr. Kalashnik jumped back, bumping into Christina. She reached for his gun hand and missed but managed to force him to lower his arm. Grey had his hands in the fight, prying Dr. Kalashnik's fingers loose. The doctor twisted and turned, trying his best to wrench himself free. The gun went off beside her ear.

All at once, the fight went out of Dr. Kalashnik.

16

Christina tore the gun from Dr. Kalashnik's hand and twisted his uninjured arm behind his back, shoving him against the lab counter. Blood droplets stained his pant leg and she groaned. This guy had the worst aim. First, he'd accidentally shot Gregor right between the eyes, and now he'd managed to shoot himself in the leg? No wonder the doctor was so nervous around guns— he had no idea how to handle them.

The doctor continued to struggle and tried to free himself from her grip so she wrenched his hand higher. A sound that was something between a shriek and a gasp escaped from the man as his shoulder threatened to pop out of its socket.

"Stop fighting me," she said. "I don't want to break your arm."

"Christina?" Grey said.

"One second." With one hand holding Dr. Kalashnik in place, she tucked his gun in her waistband and pulled a pair of Flexi-Cuffs from her back pocket. After she secured the doctor's hands, she looked him over. His leg didn't seem to be bleeding enough for a gunshot wound. "Where are you shot?"

"Christina…"

Sirens wailed from somewhere outside. The sound mingled with Boss's growling.

Dr. Kalashnik snorted. "You stupid girl." He lowered his head and ran at her.

Was he kidding? It was too easy. She side-stepped and grabbed his shoulder, redirecting his momentum into the counter. With his hands cuffed behind his back, he fell face first into a tray full of flasks. Glass shattered and rained down as he stumbled and tried to regain his balance. "Ahh!" He cried out in pain.

"Christina, if you have a minute, I could use some help."

"Just a little busy here," she said over her shoulder.

She grabbed Dr. Kalashnik and righted him. She spun him to face her. A shard of glass protruded from his eye and she cringed. Cuts freckled his face and blood spilled down his cheek. Could this night get any worse?

"Here, sit down." She forced him to the ground. "Stay put or we'll send the dog after you."

"No, no dog!"

"Whenever you're ready, Christina," Grey said through clenched teeth.

She looked up and saw Grey was in his wheelchair and had both hands pressed on the side of his leg. Blood seeped between his fingers.

"Grey! You're shot!" She raced to him and covered his hand with her own, adding pressure to the wound.

"Just a flesh wound." He gave a pained chuckle. "Besides, I wasn't really using this leg anyway."

She shook her head. "Too soon, Captain. Too soon."

Police officers burst through the doors and swarmed the laboratory.

"We need a few medics!" she shouted. The blood wasn't spurting from Grey's wound, so it most likely had missed the artery.

"And call CBRN," Grey said. "We think this laboratory is manufacturing chemical weapons."

A uniformed officer held his hands up, afraid to touch anything. "Okay, let's get these people out of here. Take them out the back while the guys get the fire under control."

"Fire? What fire?" Christina asked.

"Some vandals set fire to a car across the street. We've got a crew over there trying to keep it contained."

Her eyes went wide. "The car, was it a black Lincoln?"

"Possibly," the officer said. "C'mon, we gotta clear out."

Great. That was why Gregor had smelled like gasoline when he'd come in. He'd killed Bertha. "Hang on a sec, officer. I've got the gunman's weapons in my waistband."

The officer handed her a latex glove and she used it to remove Gregor's gun and drop it in the evidence bag. "This belonged to the dead man, but both our prints will be on it. We've got prints on file." She gave him Dr. Kalashnik's revolver. "This belonged to the other suspect. You'll find our prints on this one too."

The officer nodded and made a note before heading out the door.

Grey cleared his throat. "Christina, can you...I mean..." He hesitated. "I—I can't push my chair and hold pressure on the wound."

It cost Grey a lot to ask for help and she knew it. "I've got you." She moved behind him and slid her hand between the small backrest and his muscular shoulders.

He shifted. "Hello? Are you trying to tickle a guy while he's got a gunshot wound?"

"Well, it'd be a lot easier if your wheelchair had some handles on it." She gave him Boss's leash and turned the wheelchair around, careful not to bump him into anything. "Or would you rather have Boss push you?"

Grey laughed, then winced.

She followed the officer, pushing Grey while he held pressure on his wound. Leaning in, she spoke into Grey's ear. "Are you sure you're all right?"

"I'll be fine. I'm just glad we found Dr. Kalashnik and his lab."

"I can't believe you risked your life for us and ended up getting shot."

Grey chuckled. "It's a good thing the doctor wasn't trained to use a gun because he was pretty deadly by accident."

"Quinn is going to blow his stack when he hears about this. We should have called as soon as we suspected anything."

"I still think we did the right thing," Grey said. "It might be a little messy, but we've stopped him."

"I saw Boss lift his paw at the rats. That means he smelled X-VX, right?"

"Yeah, Dr. Kalashnik must have been testing it on them."

"Is there any chance we were exposed?"

Grey shook his head. "No, he's evil but not suicidal. He wouldn't keep it out in the open like that."

"So now what?" Would Grey still want her to guard Boss? Maybe now that they'd shut down Dr. Kalashnik's lab, he wouldn't need her anymore. There was a twinge of regret at the thought.

A paramedic jogged toward them. "I can take it from here," he said.

"She's got it," Grey snapped.

"I'll take him to the ambulance then he's all yours." Christina pushed Grey to the EMS vehicle and watched the two paramedics lift him onto a gurney.

Before they loaded him into the ambulance Grey pointed to Christina. "She's coming with me. My dog, too."

The paramedics looked at each other.

"I'm a bodyguard with the Elite Guardians Agency." She flashed her credentials. "I have law enforcement privileges. I'll escort him to the hospital."

The driver hopped down. "Sure, just let me confirm with the officer."

Christina and Boss climbed into the ambulance. The driver hurried back and put his hands on the door to close it. "The officer said to stay at the hospital and a detective will be there to question you."

Christina sighed. Yep, Quinn was going to blow his top.

SUNDAY, 8:21 A.M.

Grey fought against the heavy blanket of sleep weighing him down. The remnants of a nightmare clawed at his mind. Dr. Kalashnik with his hands on the edge of a wire-framed cot pushing himself up. Grey's hand reaching out to stop him. Wally's wide eyes bulging behind a gas mask.

Grey's eyes snapped open. The pinch in his left hand snagged his attention and he lifted it to see clear tubes and tape that held an IV in place. Faint beeping noises registered. What was he doing in a hospital bed? He shifted and a sharp pain shot through his leg.

Oh, right. The gunshot that had gone wild, grazing his thigh. An early morning surgery to clean debris from the wound. Soft snores came from his right and he rolled his head in the direction of the sound. Christina slept on a small recliner angled in the corner of the hospital room, but she wasn't snoring. The snores came from Boss. He'd managed to wedge himself into the chair with Christina, his head draped over her shoulder and one paw on her waist. Grey's heart filled to bursting at the sight of them asleep together.

LYNETTE EASON & KATE ANGELO

Christina's braid had come loose, and messy ringlets of blonde hair fell down around her shoulders and over her forehead. Eye movements beneath her lids made her long dark eyelashes quiver. He nestled his head into his pillow and watched her sleep. It made him happy to see her get some good rest after how hard she pushed herself each day.

If things were different, he could see himself falling hard for Christina, but what would that mean for her? The X-VX had ravaged his body, forcing him to rearrange his life to accommodate his physical issues. The experimental surgery gave him hope of getting back to something normal, but what if it didn't work? Christina lived a dynamic life. She wouldn't want a man who'd slow her down. No, he couldn't do that to her.

But if the surgery worked...if he could walk again...

Longing flared deep within his heart—not at the thought of walking, but of a life with Christina. She challenged him and overlooked his disability, yet somehow still accounted for his wheelchair. She'd risked her life for him and Boss and helped him find Dr. Kalashnik. But...could she ever be happy with a man in a wheelchair?

One look at her and Boss snuggled on the recliner made him think *yes*. She didn't have to stay here with him. She could have taken Boss to his house and waited for him, but she was right here by his side.

Christina's head snapped up, startling Boss. They were nose to nose for a moment before she petted his head and he lay back down. She saw Grey and smiled. "Hey, how are you feeling?"

"I'm fine. You can go back to sleep. I might do the same."

She rubbed her face and untangled herself from Boss to stand. "I can't believe I slept so hard. And with Boss."

"He's not just the best sniffer dog in the world—he's also the best cuddler."

"I'm sorry, Grey." She held the bed rail with both hands. "You shouldn't have been shot. I should have—"

"No, you did what you should have. You protected Boss." Grey took her hand in his and squeezed. "We make a pretty good team, don't we?"

"Yeah, we do." With her free hand, she ran a thumb over his hair near the cut. "The doctor said your stitches are healing well."

"I was hoping you'd say they removed them. They've been itching like crazy."

"Really? Here, let me try to ease it a bit." She leaned forward and lightly rubbed the area around his cut. "Better?"

"You have no idea. My fingers are too big to do that without hurting myself."

She continued to caress his forehead and hairline, a gentle smile playing on her lips. Her Mona Lisa smile enraptured him and he suddenly realized how close they were. Their faces were mere inches apart. Christina's brown eyes dilated, drawing him in. Her gaze roamed from his forehead to his eyes then lingered on his mouth. It took every ounce of restraint he possessed to not wrap his arms around her and pull her close to feel her lips against his. Instead, he relaxed and waited as she slowly lowered her mouth to his—so close he could feel her soft breath.

The door opened and Christina jumped away from the bed. A look of shock fell over her face, and she blinked it away, thrusting both hands behind her back as if putting them as far away from Grey as possible.

Boss jumped from the chair and positioned himself between Christina and the door.

"What are you, some kind of bullet magnet?" Quinn marched over to Grey's bed and lifted a chin. "You two ever consider wearing your flak jackets 24/7?"

Grey grinned. Christina had said he'd be grumpy, and she wasn't kidding. The guy had a way of commanding a room. If anyone should be irritable, it should be Grey. The man had barged in and interrupted their almost kiss. "Hello, Detective," Grey said. "Thanks for dropping by."

"Don't get smart with me. I should arrest you both and let the DA sort it out."

"We appreciate your willingness to hear our side of the story," Christina said. "Where's Bree?"

"Getting coffee," he huffed. "Some of us aren't exactly morning people. You two are really okay?"

"I could go for some coffee," Grey said.

Christina shook her head. "We're fine, Quinn. Thank you for asking."

Quinn let out a breath. "There's military and suits crawling all over this hospital. This Russian doctor you found is pretty hot stuff."

"The doctor is here?" Grey asked.

"Yeah, a few rooms down. We've got a uniform by the door. The Feds won't let us question him until he's off some of the pain meds."

Grey and Christina stared at each other for a beat. Christina grabbed Boss's leash and clipped it to his collar. "I know you'd like to question us separately, so I'll take Boss for a walk and let you get Grey's statement. Back in fifteen minutes?"

Quinn waved a dismissive hand at her. "Fine, fine. Just stay out of trouble, will ya?"

17

SUNDAY, 8:38 A.M.

Christina let the hospital door click shut behind her before
bending at the waist and sucking in a few breaths to still her
pounding heart. She'd never been so grateful for a Quinn interruption in her life. Had she really been about to kiss Grey? This
was not like her. He was her *client*. She was still working for
Grey even though Dr. Kalashnik had been arrested, right? They
hadn't found Sokolovich at the laboratory last night, so as far as
she was concerned, Boss was still in danger.

She glanced at Boss. "You could have stopped me, you
know."

He tilted his head in response.

"You won't tell anyone what you saw back there, will you?"

Boss whined then nudged her hand with his nose.

"Good boy." She rubbed his ears and Boss panted, letting his
tongue fall to the side of his mouth.

Bree stood near the nurse's station with a cup of coffee in
each hand. She was talking to a man in a suit that looked as if
he'd picked it up off the floor this morning. Quinn had said the

hospital was crawling with government and military, and she wondered if the man was FBI. Would the FBI take over so Grey could get his life back?

Bree noticed Christina and lifted her cup of coffee in greeting. Christina held up the leash and pointed to the elevator. Bree nodded her understanding.

Christina headed toward the elevator. Three rooms down from Grey's was a uniformed police officer sitting in a chair in the hall. It must be Dr. Kalashnik's room. The officer on guard had a magazine on one knee, his chin resting on his chest. Was he sleeping?

Christina glanced at Bree, who was still speaking with the Suit. How could the officer guard the room if he couldn't stay awake? Quinn would bite this guy's head off if he found him sleeping on the job. She'd save him some humiliation and wake him before Bree or Quinn saw the guy sleeping.

Boss sniffed the ground and strained against the leash, tugging Christina's arm as he had last night when he'd pulled her toward the wall of rats. He was onto something. She loosened her grip on the leash and gave him more room to explore.

The dog headed straight for the officer who didn't seem to notice them. When Boss reached the man, he smelled his shoe and sniffed up his leg. The magazine slid from the man's knee and fluttered to the floor. Boss sat down and held his front paw in the air.

What in the world? Had Boss found X-VX, or was it some other drug or chemical he was trained to sniff out?

She reached down and touched the officer on his shoulder. "Sir?"

The man slumped over in slow motion, and she dropped the leash to grab him before he fell onto the floor.

"Bree!" she called over her shoulder.

Christina heard feet running toward her. She pressed her

fingers against his neck but didn't feel a pulse. "I think he's dead."

Nurses swarmed the officer and Christina backed into the hospital room, pulling Boss away from the crowd of doctors and nurses. The room was still. Her fist clenched Boss's leash and she stared at the privacy curtain hiding the hospital bed. She stepped farther into the room and saw a man in a dark navy suit slumped in a chair in the corner. Boss strained toward him, and Christina released his leash. The dog went straight for the man in the chair and began sniffing the man's pant legs. He smelled his way up to the man's chest, then put two paws on his knees and stuck his nose in the man's face.

Oh no.

Christina didn't need a signal from Boss. This man was dead too. "Bree, in here." She felt his neck for a pulse. Nothing. Bree rushed into the room and grabbed the curtain. She yanked it back, exposing the bed where the Russian prisoner was recovering. The head of Dr. Kalashnik's bed was positioned at a forty-five-degree angle. Bandages covered most of his face. An oxygen mask covered his mouth and nose, and his eyes were closed.

"Doctor! We need a doctor in here," Bree yelled. She pressed her fingers to his neck and shook her head. "I think he's dead." Bree looked at Christina with confusion.

Christina wasn't sure why the man needed oxygen. Hadn't his cuts been treated in triage? She noticed the screen on his monitor was blank and her eyes followed the cable. She pointed at the floor near Bree's feet. "Look, his monitor was unplugged."

"Don't touch anything," Bree said. "Stand by the door and don't let anyone in here except the doctor."

Christina nodded. Her heart pounded and her breaths came in abrupt pants. She clamped her mouth shut and grabbed Boss's leash. "Good work, Boss."

Bree pulled her phone from her pocket and dialed. "Quinn? You better come to Dr. Kalashnik's room. He's dead."

The phone call that interrupted Quinn's line of questioning was welcomed as far as Grey was concerned. The man peppered him with questions, sometimes repeating them and treating Grey like a suspect instead of a witness. But the longer Grey spent with Quinn, the more he respected the man underneath the cranky exterior. He was a solid detective and his take-charge attitude yielded results. What would have happened if the detective hadn't barged in and interrupted his moment with Christina? The woman was complicated and he might never get another moment like that with her.

Grey watched the blood drain from Quinn's face from whatever he heard on the other end of the call. He disconnected and pointed his phone at Grey. "Don't go anywhere, Parker."

Grey gestured to his legs. "Where am I gonna go?"

Quinn seemed to ignore him and stormed across the room, phone still clutched in one hand. The door opened and Grey heard Quinn brush past someone on his way out.

"Hey, what's with him?" Travis Briggs, the baby-faced soldier from Grey's past, walked into the room with Wally on his heels.

Grey's face brightened. "Briggs! Hey man, I haven't seen you in forever!" Not since two years ago at the man's wedding, if Grey remembered correctly.

Briggs crossed the room and gave Grey a fist bump. His clothes were threadbare and he smelled of stale cigarette smoke. The man's bloodshot eyes darted around the room. "Oh, yeah. Well, I heard about the basketball game and called Wally to check in. He said you were shot last night and dragged me here to see you." Briggs ran a hand over his chin and shifted his weight.

Wally stepped beside Grey and offered his left hand for an awkward handshake. "What's with you lately? Everywhere you go bullets seem to be flying. You'd think you were back in uniform."

Grey laughed. "Just doing my job, I guess. Did you go to Dr. Kalashnik's lab last night?"

Wally nodded. "I'm heading back there after I catch a few hours of sleep. I came to see you and to duck into the lab to drop off a formal request for blood samples from Dr. Kalashnik." He stared at Grey and shook his head. "Man, I can't believe you found that crazy Russian scientist right here in our own backyard."

"What are they going to do with him?" Briggs asked.

"Pump him for information to start," Grey said. "The Chemical Weapons Convention will want the X-VX formula."

Wally snorted. "Since when has Russia ever played nice with the CWC?"

He was right. Evidence proved Russia continued to create and deploy chemical weapons on a small scale despite signing the CWC treaty. They denied the formulas used to create nerve agents known to originate from their own country, thereby skirting the treaty. And with Russia's ability to synthetically create the heavily regulated chemical compounds needed to make nerve agents, there was no way to stop them.

"They might not get Dr. Kalashnik to talk, but we've got his lab. I'm sure you'll have a team of researchers helping you," Grey said.

"Just what I need." Wally sighed. "More government suits looking over my shoulder. By the way, where's Boss?"

Good question. Christina had left a while ago, and the way Quinn had run out of here didn't look good. What if something had happened to Christina? Even though Dr. Kalashnik was under arrest and Gregor was now in the morgue with a bullet in his forehead, Viktor Sokolovich was still on the loose.

Something was off.

"Christina took Boss for a walk. They should be back soon," Grey said.

Wally wagged his eyebrows and grinned. "Oh, she's still here, huh?"

Grey's face flushed hot, and he fought to suppress a smile.

"Who's Christina?" Briggs asked.

"That would be me." Christina walked in with her shoulders squared and head held high. Boss trotted beside her. The look she cast at Grey told him something had happened. She unclipped the leash and folded it in her hand. "He's been a good boy today."

Boss hurried to stand between Wally and Briggs. Both men leaned over and gave the dog a hearty scratch. Grey's heart swelled with pride for his beloved partner who had once saved Briggs from stepping on an IED by pulling on his pants until Briggs got the message.

"Hey boy, it's been a while," Briggs said.

Boss skirted around Briggs, sniffing up and down his pant leg. He paused at his shoe and began pawing at his laces. Briggs jumped away and moved to stand in the doorway.

Wally held Boss by the collar. "Hey, give the guy a break." He knelt and let Boss lick his chin while he spoke in doggy talk. "I heard you caught a bad guy last night. Yes, you did. You got that bad guy, didn't you?"

Boss sat and waved his paw. Wally laughed. "Oh you wanna shake, do you, boy?"

Boss jumped on Wally, knocking him off balance. Wally tried to break his fall with his right arm but ended up on his rear.

"Hey, Boss. Get off," Grey said with a laugh. "He's excited to see you, I guess."

"Sorry, Wally. He didn't get his walk," Christina said. "Boss, heel." The dog snapped to her side and joined her on the opposite side of the room where Christina sat in the recliner.

Boss sat on the floor at her feet and whimpered. Christina smoothed his ears. "It's okay, Boss."

Wally stood and dusted his pants. "Don't worry, I'm used to it. Boss is a little more relaxed around me since we've worked together so long." He turned to Grey. "Say, man, if you need me to take him, I can."

"Naw, man. You'll be way too busy and besides," Grey said, "I've got Christina."

Wally flicked his eyes to Christina and nodded.

The door opened and a young nurse in blue scrubs came in pushing a laptop on a rolling cart. "Mr. Parker? Looks like we've got your discharge papers. Are you about ready to get out of here?"

"You have no idea."

The nurse smiled. "Okay, I need to go over some things."

"That's our cue. I'm glad you're safe, brother. Stay that way." Wally gave Grey a fist bump.

"Okay, okay. Get outta here," said Grey. "Good to see you, Briggs. Let's stay in touch."

Briggs jutted his chin in response and hurried out ahead of Wally.

"He sure left in a hurry," the nurse said.

"Who? Briggs?" Grey was thinking the same thing. "I think he's afraid of hospitals. Never liked them."

"Me either." The nurse laughed.

For the next few minutes, she explained his discharge papers and how to clean and dress his wound. More prescriptions for antibiotics and one for a pain medicine that he wouldn't take, and a number he should call for a follow-up appointment.

On her way out, the nurse said he should press the call button when he was dressed and ready to go.

When he glanced at Christina, she was chewing her lip, lost in thought.

"You okay?" By now he'd seen that look enough to know something was on her mind.

"Mm? Sorry, I was thinking."

"I know." He laughed. "What about? Did it have anything to do with why Quinn bolted out of here and hasn't come back?"

"That's part of it, but..." She hesitated. "Listen, you should get dressed. There's a lot to tell you, but if I were you, I'd want to get out of this place." Christina stood and Boss jumped to his feet by her side.

Good point. If there was something going on in the hospital, getting out of bed and getting dressed were the first steps to finding out. "Wait. I, um, I don't have any pants. I think they cut my jeans off."

Christina pressed her lips together, suppressing a smile. "I asked Charlie to swing by your house for a change of clothes since he can bypass the security system. They're in the bathroom. He's waiting to give us a ride when we're ready to go."

"Oh, that's right. Bertha." Grey ran a hand over his mouth. "I'm sorry, Christina. That's my fault. I never should have—"

"Stop." She held up her hand. "We might not have found Dr. Kalashnik if you hadn't pestered me to take you."

The elation of catching Dr. Kalashnik hadn't worn off. Two years of hunting him and now the man would finally face consequences. Too bad the Department of Justice would take it from here and Grey would be sidelined for a while. But at least Americans would never even know how close they'd come to a chemical attack.

"Christina, I can't thank you enough. It's really because of you that we found Dr. Kalashnik last night—"

"Grey, listen." She cut him off. "We need to talk."

Christina sat on the edge of Grey's hospital bed and stared down at her hands, unsure where to begin. She wasn't great at handling emotions and the news that Dr. Kalashnik had been murdered in this very hospital was sure to be a gut punch for Grey. Best to blurt it out. Rip the Band-Aid off, so to speak.

She opened her mouth to speak but quickly pressed her lips together. One look at the concern on Grey's face and she knew it was the wrong approach. They'd been through a lot together and he deserved more than a military-style debriefing. They'd started down this path of finding Dr. Kalashnik together, and she'd stay the course. Until Grey decided it was time to leave, anyway.

"Christina, what is it?" He bunched the blanket in his fist and released it.

Oh, how she wanted more time to process all that she'd seen tonight, but she'd be delicate. Start with Briggs and go from there. Something didn't sit right with that guy. "It was nice of your friends to come visit you. I hadn't met Briggs before. How do you know him?"

"Uh, okay. First Lieutenant Travis Briggs. We served together. He was with us in Siberia. What about him?" Grey sounded suspicious.

"I didn't notice any physical injuries from the attack," she said.

"He was outside on guard." His tone was harsh, and he sighed. "Look, Christina, what's going on? You can't say, 'we need to talk' and then leave me hanging. Is this about the kiss?"

A flutter rippled through her stomach and sent heat rushing to her cheeks. "Kiss? There was no kiss. I wasn't—we didn't kiss."

"Yeah, I know, but we were about to, before Quinn barged in and you flew out of the room like your hair was on fire." The corner of his mouth turned up in a grin and he took her hand.

"No, I—" He'd thrown her for a loop by bringing up their

near kiss and now she was flustered. She had to get it together. "It's not about that at all, Grey. Dr. Kalashnik is *dead.*"

Grey stilled. "What?" He blinked and shook his head as if to clear the confusion. "Did you say he's...dead?"

Christina nodded. "I decided to pass by Dr. Kalashnik's room on my way to the elevator with Boss. When we reached the officer on guard, Boss started pulling on his leash, trying to get to him. Grey, the officer was dead. I took Boss into Dr. Kalashnik's room and both the agent and Dr. Kalashnik were dead. Boss sat down and lifted his paw. His reaction means they were killed with X-VX, right?"

"Yes but..." Grey's grip tightened on her hand and his nostrils flared. "How could this happen? We're in a hospital swarming with agents and...I just—I just don't get it."

"I know, I don't get it either. They're checking security cameras for anyone who entered or exited the room, but what are the chances they'll find anything?"

"Maybe whoever Dr. Kalashnik was working for decided to silence him." Grey pinched the bridge of his nose. "I can't believe this. I thought it was over. Wait, why were you asking about Briggs?"

Maybe bringing his friend up had been a bad idea. "Do you guys stay in touch?"

"Not really. He left the Air Force and started a construction business, got married, and had a baby in less than two years. I've tried to connect, but his business is very successful and he doesn't have much free time."

"Yes, it can be difficult to keep in touch," she said.

"Tell me what you're thinking, Agent."

"He looked nervous and jumpy. His eyes were all bloodshot and Boss acted strange around him."

"Yeah, I saw that."

"Do you think Briggs could have killed Dr. Kalashnik?"

Grey ran his thumb over her hand, still holding her firm. "I don't see how. Where would he get X-VX? And even if he did find it, how could he kill Dr. Kalashnik and—what did you say, two guards?"

Christina nodded.

"How could he manage that in a busy hospital, under surveillance, and not have a trace on him?" Grey shook his head. "Besides, the way Boss pawed at his shoe? That's the signal for narcotics, not X-VX."

"We might want to check into Briggs's background a bit more." She stood and smoothed the wrinkles she'd made in the bed. "I think I should step out so you can get dressed. Let's go back to your house and regroup, okay?"

"Sounds great," he said. "But can we stop for food along the way?"

Christina smiled. "Absolutely. I think Boss and I are hungry too."

Boss hopped up and stretched his front legs, then his back legs. A long yawn exposed the sharp teeth he'd used to bite into Dr. Kalashnik's arm. Christina did *not* want to ever be the target of those powerful jaws.

She unfolded Grey's wheelchair and positioned it next to the bed. "With a gunshot wound in your leg, will you be able to manage your chair? I can…well, I can help or get a nurse."

"I'm fine, thanks. Still pumped up with pain meds. Just…" He scratched his head. "Just hurry back, okay?"

"Absolutely. Five minutes." She gave him a half smile. "I'll take Boss with me."

In the hallway, Christina pulled her cell phone out and texted Olivia. *I need a full background check on 1LT Travis Briggs. He served with Grey in the Air Force.*

Olivia's text response came right away. *You got it. How's Grey doing?*

Being discharged. Dr. K was killed. I'll fill you in later. Christina tucked her phone in her back pocket and saw Bree standing with her arms folded in front of Dr. Kalashnik's hospital room. The body of the dead police officer was gone.

Bree nodded at Christina.

"Hey, I'm about to take Grey and Boss back to the safe house. We're going to regroup there and decide if Grey still needs protection."

Bree sighed and unfolded her arms. "I don't know what to think at this point." She looked up and down the hall then lowered her voice. "Christina, there was a note in Dr. Kalashnik's hand."

Christina flinched. "A note? What did it say?"

Bree laughed a humorless laugh. "It was another stupid poem. I snapped a picture. Here." She pulled up the photo and handed her phone to Christina.

A photograph of a tiny slip of paper filled the screen. Typed words read:

All bad men will have to pay.

But the Governor only has a few more days.

Christina read the text twice. "It's signed The Scavenger, just like the others. Any idea who it is?"

Bree took her phone from Christina and pocketed it. "It's safe to say it's not Dr. Kalashnik. Governor Winston has been receiving notes like these for a month, but we're just now learning about the signature from SLED."

Christina wondered if they had it wrong and Viktor Sokolovich really was aiming to kill the governor. "Did you see who went into the room?"

"We checked and other than doctors and nurses, no one else went in or out. We've pulled them for questioning."

"I thought it was strange Dr. Kalashnik had an oxygen mask on when his only injury was the glass in his eye and a dog bite."

"The glass was removed by a plastic surgeon and Dr. Kalashnik was put on oxygen until he woke up from the surgery. We think the killer planted the X-VX in the medical gas system. It can be accessed from a different area of the hospital, and each room has its own system."

"So," Christina said, "the killer has access to the hospital, and he has a vendetta against Governor Winston? How are the other deaths connected?"

"Quinn is convinced it's the Russian mafia, but I'm not so sure."

"Dr. Kalashnik has ties to the Petrov Bratva. If they thought he might turn on them, they could send a hitman to get rid of him," Christina said. "It makes sense to me, but what has got you doubting?"

"The notes. The Russian mafia doesn't play games like this." Bree waved her phone for emphasis. "Why would a hitman use X-VX instead of a gun? Doesn't sit right with me. No, this is personal."

Christina nodded. "It does seem personal. Now the question is whether or not the killer has more victims in mind besides the governor of South Carolina."

Either way, she still needed to protect Grey and Boss from an unnamed killer using an invisible weapon that only Boss could detect.

MONDAY, 5:10 P.M.

Christina peeked over her laptop and stole a look at Grey sleeping on the couch. A throw pillow and the arm of the couch kept his wounded leg elevated. Seeing him try to get comfortable on the sofa was amusing. At six four, he struggled to find a place where his head and feet didn't dangle off the ends. One arm shielded his eyes, and his broad chest rose and fell in rhythmic breaths. The news about Dr. Kalashnik's death had hit the man hard, though he tried to hide it.

Grey was attractive, she'd give him that. Years of serving in a male-dominated military had given her plenty of opportunity to observe men of all types. Athletic, thin, toned, muscles that rippled—she'd seen it all. Yet something about Captain Grey Parker gave her butterflies in her stomach, and it was more than just his rugged good looks and adorable smile. It required more recon to figure out what it all meant.

Boss sighed from the floor beside the couch. His long black snout nestled between his paws. From the moment that Grey had handed Boss's leash to her at the arena, her entire world had been turned upside down. Her precious routine was out the window, and while a small part of her craved a return to normalcy, she knew she wasn't ready to leave this assignment.

Was this still just a job, or had they moved past *assignment*?

Her cell phone vibrated on the table and she snatched it up before the buzzing woke Grey. It was Olivia calling. She waited to answer the call until she was in the guest bedroom. "Hey, did you get eyes on Briggs?"

Olivia had emailed a complete background check on Travis Briggs yesterday, and what Grey had said about the man was not all true. Briggs had left the Air Force after his first tour and returned home to work on a construction crew. He was fired after a work injury sent him to the hospital and a blood test in the emergency room revealed narcotics in his system. Multiple citations for driving under the influence. And one police report told a horrific story of Briggs attempting to kidnap his three-month-old daughter from his wife at gunpoint. It was no wonder she'd received full custody of their daughter and moved in with her parents. Travis Briggs was a dangerous man.

Rock music blared from Olivia's end of the call. "I'm looking at him right now. Holed up in this nasty biker hangout, Dirty Dogs. He's been sitting at the bar drinking for the last two hours. I get the feeling he's waiting for someone."

"Hmm." Christina wondered if he was waiting for a drug dealer, or a Russian hitman. "I appreciate you helping out, Olivia. I don't know what's going on here, but someone is killing people with X-VX, and Boss acted weird around Briggs."

"Not a problem," Olivia said. "I'll let you know if anything changes."

Christina disconnected the call and looked at Boss sitting at her feet. Poor guy had been stuck in the house, and to keep him from going stir crazy, Grey had showed Christina how he was training Boss to fetch items by name to qualify for the service dog program. Grey wasn't exaggerating about Boss's ability to learn. Boss was able to retrieve her cell phone, the TV remote, and his own leash.

She patted his head. "Are you bored? You've already had your dinner and a walk. What else can we do without waking Grey?"

The dog's head tilted side to side at the words *dinner* and *walk*. Every time Boss cocked his head like that, she found it endearing. She was falling in love with this dog. And if she would allow herself, she could fall in love with Boss's owner too.

A rustling of movement on the couch caught Boss's attention. He nosed the door open and trotted to the living room to check on Grey. Christina followed Boss and saw Grey tossing his head.

Nightmares again. She knelt beside the couch and touched his shoulder. He flinched and his eyes flickered open with a blank stare.

"You okay?" she asked.

He rubbed his eyes and let out a breath. "Was I talking in my sleep again?"

"Just tossing a little. Bad dream?"

"Not this time. I was dreaming about something other than war for once." He pulled himself into a sitting position and pain flashed across his face at the movement.

"Easy, no sudden moves." She pulled an ottoman closer and helped Grey prop up his injured leg, tucking a pillow under his knee. "Let me get you a drink of water."

"Wait." He patted the couch. "Sit with me for a while."

The cushion sank with her weight and caused Grey to dip toward her shoulder. She hadn't meant to plop down so close to him. Christina tucked both legs under her and adjusted to put a little distance between them. "What were you dreaming about?"

"Horses." He chuckled.

"Horses? That sounds better than explosions."

"I guess so," he said. "Have you been around horses much?"

"My best friend, Haley Rothwell, has three horses on her property, and my brother has a barn in Kentucky, so I ride every now and again. You said your parents own a ranch. You must ride often."

"No, I'm not exactly comfortable around horses." He frowned.

That surprised Christina. Grey seemed to be great with animals if Boss was any indication. "I never would have guessed. Did something happen?"

"You could say that." He looked past her and stared at Boss lying on the armchair.

Seeing Grey so defeated hurt her heart. She covered his hand with hers and dipped her head to catch his gaze. "Will you tell me about it?"

His chest rose and fell with a heavy sigh. "It's no big deal. I mean, what's life without a little childhood drama?" He laughed.

Grey diffused heavy situations with humor, but there was pain behind his eyes and it went deeper than his jokes.

"Really, Grey. Will you please tell me?" She squeezed his hand. "I'd like to know about it."

———

Grey blew out a breath. He couldn't believe he was going to tell Christina about his childhood. But she was unlike any other woman he'd ever met, and somehow he knew she was a safe place.

"Ever since I was a little boy, I wanted to be like my dad. He's this rugged cowboy horse trainer. The best horse trainer in fact. People bring the most difficult horses from all around the world to our ranch. Within a few days, the horses learn to trust and listen to him. Every night I prayed I could be just like my dad, but..." He trailed off, losing sight of what he'd meant to say as a memory surfaced.

"But..." Christina encouraged him to continue.

He needed to back up. He shifted to situate his aching leg better. "There's this one time I remember. I used to sit on the fence and watch my dad work the horses, and he would explain how he could earn trust by leading them through their fears. My father was working with a two-year-old gelding. It seemed like the animal was afraid of everything. Sticks on the ground, dogs, a strong gust of wind, and especially children. His name was Blue. A beautiful white Dutch Warmblood destined to be a champion jumper, if only he could get over his fears."

"Hmm..."

He shot her a sideways glance, noting her rapt attention. "After a few weeks of working with Blue, my father had changed him into a confident horse able to handle small jumps with a rider. Blue even let me brush him a few times, a huge feat considering he used to freak out when I got near. Everything was going great. Until it wasn't."

"What happened?" Christina scooted closer.

"My dad thought it was time for me to work Blue on my own. I was nervous, but I hopped off the fence and took the lead like he'd taught me. Dad stood in the center while I walked Blue around the edge of the round pen, stopping every few minutes to praise the horse. I was petting his neck when he got nervous and reared up. I let go of the lead and Blue went haywire, bucking and kicking. I froze. I didn't know what to do. Before I knew what was happening, my dad shoved me out of the way, and Blue came down on top of my dad. Our ranch hand, Jim, helped me get on the other side of the fence." Grey gulped the knot in his throat. "Blue trampled my dad until Jim got the horse under control."

Christina's free hand flew to her mouth to cover a gasp. "I

can't believe you had to see that. I can imagine how helpless you would have felt."

"Yep and been feeling that way ever since," he muttered.

She dropped her hand from her mouth and placed it on his shoulder with a comforting squeeze. "Grey, you're not helpless, but sometimes things happen right in front of us and there isn't anything we can do." With a final caress of his shoulder, she dropped her hand. "What happened to your dad?"

Grey rubbed the back of his neck. "Dad knew how to protect himself, but Blue's attack caused a broken hip. He still walks with a limp." Grey felt guilty each time he saw the hitch in his dad's step.

"It was good he got out of the way," she said. "Things could have been much worse."

"Yeah, he was in the hospital for a while. Remember that fight I said my parents had? The only one I'd ever seen? I was at the hospital and waiting in the hall when I overheard their fight. Mom was angry that Dad let me around such a dangerous horse. My father laughed it off and said it was no big deal, everyone was afraid from time to time. Mom thought it was a very big deal, but Dad really took it in stride."

"Well at least your dad didn't blame you."

"Yeah, but after that I was terrified of that horse. Most horses in fact." Grey chuckled. "I thought I could hide my fear, but Blue saw right through me. My dad always imagined I'd work with him. Side by side, father and son, until one day I would take over the ranch. At one time, it was my dream too. But no matter how hard I prayed, I could never be comfortable around horses."

He'd also learned to stop asking God for things. His prayers went unanswered and his dreams of growing up to be like his father had gone out the window. If God wouldn't answer prayers that were noble and honorable to his parents, then what prayers *would* He answer?

"So you grew up on a horse ranch and held a secret fear of horses the entire time?" she asked.

"Yep. From then on, I avoided working with the horses and opted for other chores instead. Ruby was a natural with them, but I knew I needed to go another direction. So as soon as I was old enough, I joined the Air Force."

"And became a dog trainer instead of a horse trainer."

"Imagine my surprise when I scored high on the aptitude tests in that area." He laughed. "Sometimes I worry I still can't read animals."

"Grey, animals aren't humans. They can't communicate with words, and just because you didn't understand Boss once doesn't mean you don't understand animals. Boss loves you and he's always trying to make you proud."

"I think Boss is ready to leave me for you," Grey said with a smile. "But then again, who can blame him?" He bumped his shoulder into hers.

"I think you're both pretty amazing," she said. A soft pink color spread over her cheeks.

Grey released her hand and pulled his injured leg off the ottoman. He shifted until he was facing Christina. "I've always struggled with trusting people, Christina. So, when someone comes along who's honest and loyal like you are...well, I know that you're one of the few people in this world I can trust." He searched her eyes. "And I dream of a day when you can trust me too."

A gentle nudge deep in her spirit told her to trust Grey with more of her story. He'd opened his past to her, and she wanted him to have a piece of her past too. Maybe not the whole story, not just yet, but a piece.

"Do you remember when I said I was an Army brat?"

Grey nodded.

"My parents were career military and we moved every two or three years until I was twelve. It's not easy for me to make friends." She smiled. "I'm sure you've noticed I'm a bit reserved."

"No! Seriously?"

Christina gave him a playful shove. "We can't all be as charming as you are. Anyway, it took me a while to make friends, and it seemed by the time I finally would, we'd move. I begged my parents to stay but we never did. My mother tried to ease the pain of losing friends by reminding me that we had a duty to serve our country and it was more important than our feelings. She said friends come and go, and we should prepare our hearts for it."

Her mother had first given her this talk when Christina was in first grade. They were moving from Oklahoma to Germany and Christina was sad to leave the neighbor boy she played with every day after school. Her mother had held her hands and kissed the tears from her cheeks. *"Crying doesn't change a thing."*

"Each time we moved it was the same thing. I would get settled and make a few friends and we'd move. My brother Will is five years older than I am. In a way, you remind me of him. You know, the kind of guy who can walk into a room and everyone loves him?" She twisted the end of her braid and avoided looking directly at Grey. The image of the first day they'd met at the Elite Guardians Agency and the wide smile that had reached his eyes still made her blush.

"Well, let's just say that with our personalities and age difference, Will and I weren't very close. He was the protective big brother, of course, but we didn't play together. When my parents finally retired, we settled here in Columbia and became a home for foster kids. Usually, the children placed with us were infants and toddlers, and they didn't stay long. But one day my parents took in a teenage girl close to my age as an emergency placement."

"Wow."

Christina nodded and ran her thumb over the seam of the couch cushion. "Alana was supposed to stay for a few weeks while arrangements were made to transport her to a relative in California. A few days before she was to move, Alana's caseworker asked my parents if she could stay longer. Apparently, they couldn't find a relative with the right qualifications. The days turned into months and we became best friends. We were like sisters, really. They stopped talking about finding another placement, and after about six months, my parents sat us down and asked if they could adopt Alana. It was the best news and we were both overjoyed."

"That day must have been so amazing for your whole family, especially you and Alana."

Christina smiled at the memory, but the smile faded fast. "Yes, but like every other person I grew close to, she was ripped away."

"Oh no, Christina…"

Grey's soft voice, full of sympathy, registered, but she kept her focus on her story. If she didn't get the words out now, she might not ever be able to. "We were counting down the days to her adoption date, planning a special party with a photographer and everything. Then one day the social worker told my parents an aunt and uncle in California had been located and Alana would be going to live with them. She moved just before my fifteenth birthday."

Christina stared at her palms. The day Alana left, a new kind of pain and anger had ripped through her at the feeling of betrayal. At the adults who took her away. Why had the caseworker let their family get attached to Alana if she would just be torn away? It never made sense to Christina how they could do that to a family. Because that's what they were, a *family*.

Grey reached out and took her hands in his. A calloused

thumb caressed her knuckles. "Christina, I'm so sorry. Were you at least able to keep in touch with her?"

"The caseworker said we couldn't contact her, but I don't remember why. It didn't matter because I enlisted in the Army as soon as I finished high school. I was deployed to Afghanistan right away."

"Have you tried to look for her now that you're both adults?"

She shook her head. "No."

"I'm sure with your skills and connections you could locate her."

"I could."

"So why haven't you tried?"

Christina stared at Grey's hands holding hers and lifted a shoulder. "I'm not sure it would change anything."

Grey was silent for a long minute. He tipped her chin so they were looking at each other. "The suicide bomber looked like Alana, didn't she?"

His words triggered the memory. The heat, the smells, the pure focus on getting the job done. "From my spot on the roof, I saw the girl. It was like she looked directly at me and I saw Alana's face underneath the hijab. I hesitated and she turned and walked into the market. A second later, it exploded."

A flood of emotions rolled over Christina like a wave. She grasped at them, trying to push them into the box where she could hold them captive. "It was my fault. I...I didn't pull the trigger, and all those innocent lives..."

She couldn't finish the sentence. Like a dam breaking, the tears bubbled up and spilled over, running down her cheeks. No matter how hard she fought against it, she couldn't control them. Embarrassed, she pressed her head to Grey's chest and cried. Tears dripped like rain from her nose and chin, leaving dark spots on his pants.

Grey wrapped his arms around her shoulders and held her tight. "It's okay," he whispered into her hair.

Each sob forced her to gulp air until her body shuddered with each breath. The last time she'd really cried was the day Alana left. On that day, there was no one to comfort her. Her mom was sad, and her father told them both not to cry. *"What's done is done."*

Christina was forced to hide in her closet where no one could see her crying. Now, enveloped in the safety of Grey's arms, Christina was free to let it all out once and for all.

Tears fell endlessly and she wondered when her body would dry up. "I don't know why I'm still crying." She hiccupped and sniffed.

"I would cry too." Grey ran a hand over her hair and down her back with a gentle caress while holding her tight with both arms. "It's okay to let it out, Christina. I'm not going anywhere."

Christina decided she wouldn't fight the tears. She'd been holding them back all her life, and now she would let them flow. It was more than his strong arms holding her as she cried that made her feel safe. It was Grey. The man had peeked inside her heart, and he was still here.

For the first time in her life, she knew that if she wanted it, she had someone who would always be here.

19

"I don't understand why this is so difficult," The Scavenger growled into his phone through clenched teeth. "Get rid of him once and for all."

"Why you do not poison him with X-VX?" The Russian's broken English grated on his nerves.

"He's immune, you idiot." He spat the words, growing tired of talking to the muscle whose IQ was that of a potato. "I've told you a thousand times. Now listen, it's all set up. He will be here in a few hours. Can you kill Grey Parker or not?"

"Yes, of course."

He disconnected the call and restrained the urge to snap the phone in half. Instead, he slipped it into his pocket and turned the collar of his coat up. The frigid February wind cut through to the bone, but the pain was nothing compared to the sting of losing his laboratory.

Millions of dollars in equipment, gone in a matter of minutes. The loss would delay his pay off, but not his plan.

While the police and FBI chased their tails trying to find the source of the X-VX, he would get his message across. It was only a matter of time before they linked the victims together.

The Scavenger would see that Governor Winston's evil deeds didn't go unnoticed. He wouldn't get away with the cover-up. Judgment was coming and no amount of protective detail could stop it.

In fact, the only thing that could stop what he had planned was still in his lab. His secret weapon. How had Parker even found it?

Sokolovich.

The Russian meathead had gotten himself shot and had blown his easy opportunity to steal Boss. And then he'd given up the location of the laboratory by losing his burner phone. The Scavenger gritted his teeth. As soon as he dealt with Grey and Bodyguard Barbie, he would take care of Sokolovich. He paced the sidewalk across the street from the bar, glancing now and again toward the door when he heard someone exit. The Atom Network was up and running on his phone and he saw a text from his buyer.

Buyer: *You have your money. Now where is my product?*

He scratched his chin, considering how to respond.

The Scavenger: *Small delay. Delivery will be arranged by Saturday.*

Buyer: *This is very important to me. If you disappoint me again, I will start killing those who are important to you.*

The Scavenger snorted. It was obvious the buyer had no idea who he was dealing with. Everything important to The Scavenger had been taken from him in one catastrophic moment. Yes, thanks to Governor Winston, he had nothing left.

He tapped out a one-word reply. *Understood.*

The destruction of his lab and the death of Dr. Kalashnik would slow him down. He needed the doctor to continue manufacturing X-VX while he was preoccupied with other things, but killing Dr. Kalashnik had been an unfortunate necessity. The nervous old scientist could *not* be trusted under the stress of an interrogation.

For every mission, there was always collateral damage.

The formula had been tested and it was ready to sell, but he still needed the dog. Grey's dog, Boss, would indeed fetch a pretty penny.

Fetch.

He chuckled to himself at the pun. Oh yes, that dog was the equivalent of a winning lottery ticket and he wasn't about to pass it up. He would get the dog, cash in, and then disappear.

The Scavenger's phone buzzed. The GPS indicator said his mark was on the move. Show time.

The harsh thump of techno music rose and fell as the bar door opened and closed. A man wearing jeans and a button-down shirt with the sleeves rolled up to his elbows stumbled, then righted himself. He leaned against a lamppost and lit a cigarette. The red glow of the cherry flared as he inhaled. The Scavenger wrinkled his nose at the sight. He hoped the man enjoyed his night of smoking and drinking—because it would be his last.

The man walked half a block to his small white sedan parked at the curb and climbed behind the wheel. The Scavenger waited until the car had pulled into traffic before remotely activating the tiny device he'd left in the back seat.

He watched the taillights as the car pulled away, gaining speed. The car drifted toward the center line then pulled back into his lane. A second later the car swerved and cut across the oncoming headlights. Car horns blared but the driver did not attempt to correct.

The car picked up speed and crashed into the curb with a metallic *thunk* and plowed into a telephone pole. The front end of the car completely crumpled on impact. Sounds of twisting metal and tires squealing rose against the otherwise quiet night.

The Scavenger slipped his phone from his pocket and dialed. The call connected and he spoke first. "It's done. They will be here in two hours. Be ready."

20

TUESDAY, 3:17 A.M.

Grey wasn't sure how long he'd been holding Christina when she'd finally drifted off to sleep in his arms. Little by little her sobs had turned into sniffles, and the sniffles had morphed into a slow rhythmic breathing. Crying had exhausted her emotionally and physically, so he decided to let her sleep. Once he was sure she wouldn't wake up easily, he shifted so she was tucked under his arm with her head resting on his shoulder. He'd leaned his head back and closed his eyes, listening to her steady breathing and thinking how crazy he was for this woman. If only he could have her by his side forever. His special *Agent*.

Grey stirred and opened his eyes. He'd drifted off with Christina still sleeping on his shoulder. He slipped his phone from his pocket to check the time. After three in the morning and he'd missed several calls and texts. He tensed as he read through them.

"Christina," he whispered. "Christina, wake up. We need to go."

She lifted her head, and her eyes went wide at the sight of

him. When she realized she'd been sleeping on his shoulder, she pushed herself away faster than if he'd been a stranger on an airplane. Not exactly the reaction he'd hoped for.

"We've got another body," Grey said.

She checked her watch and let out a soft groan. "This Scavenger guy is really starting to frustrate me."

"I know what you mean." He pulled himself into his wheelchair and clicked his tongue at Boss. "C'mon, boy. Another late night for us."

Grey's leg was throbbing from a combination of sleeping sitting up and not taking any pain medications. Nights like this were the reason he refused narcotics at the hospital and opted for something over the counter instead. If his head was fuzzy, it was because it was filled with thoughts of Christina.

They were back in his Tesla, and it felt good to be behind the wheel—though he had to admit, Bertha's smooth ride had grown on him. The fifteen-minute drive to the small night club near the University of South Carolina campus took almost twice the time. Traffic was backed up as vehicles merged from the four-lane road down to using two with the help of a traffic cop. The flashing lights from the emergency vehicles could be seen from a mile away.

They pulled to a stop in front of an officer standing with his thumbs hooked in his duty belt. He tried to wave them on, but Grey held his credentials out for the officer to examine.

"Park over there. We're trying to keep the cars moving."

Grey followed the man's finger to a parking lot across a wide patch of grass. No way did he want to attempt to traverse the distance in his wheelchair.

"Listen, officer." He leaned on his elbow out the open window. "I don't think my wheelchair can make it that far. Can you make an exception?"

The officer groaned and looked around. "Fine. Park over there out of the way."

Grey parked close to the medical examiner's van, allowing enough room to get his wheelchair out. Christina clipped Boss's leash to his service vest, leaving Grey free to maneuver through the vehicles with both hands. Officers and first responder vehicles parked close to form a barrier around the scene of a car accident. Grey squeezed his chair between two police cruisers and scraped his knuckles on a tire. Cold intensified the minor pain in his frozen fingers.

Rounding the front of the ambulance, Grey saw the crumpled remains of a car. The scene took his breath away. A small sedan had driven straight through a telephone pole, leaving it wedged into the engine compartment mere inches from the passenger side windshield. The front tire was turned sideways, and the bumper lay shattered in thousands of pieces on the ground. A white airbag blocked the view of the driver.

Grey moved behind the car where Wally stood with Francisco. The medical examiner tucked his hand grip into his back pocket and reached to shake Grey's hand. "Feels like we're becoming old friends."

He glanced from Francisco to Wally then back to the medical examiner. "This is a car accident. I'm not sure why you need us for a car accident."

Francisco let out a sigh. "I know the damage to the car looks bad, but this accident did not kill the man behind the wheel. His injuries are quite minor thanks to his seat belt and the airbag. I'll know more when I get him on the table, but from everything I see and a few witness accounts, it sounds like he was dead before he crashed."

"And they found a note in the car," Wally said.

"A note?" Christina sounded surprised. "From The Scavenger?"

Bree slipped beside Christina and stifled a yawn. "I'm really getting tired of this guy. Literally. I'm exhausted." She looked at her notes. "The driver was Matthew Dennison. He spent most of the night at the bar across the street. A note from The Scavenger was found in the back seat. We wanted Boss to confirm X-VX was involved."

"Any leads?" Wally asked.

"A few. Let's just get this over with so we can clean up this scene. I'd like to get back to my warm bed before I lose a toe to frostbite." Bree looked at Grey then shifted her weight and looked at the ground. "Sorry, Grey."

"What? I've got all my toes. Some of them even work." Grey wagged his eyebrows at Bree. "You're starting to sound a little cranky like your partner. Where is Quinn, by the way?"

Bree nodded behind her. "I lost the coin toss so he's questioning witnesses over in the nice warm bar."

Grey laughed. "Well, I better get started."

Christina placed a hand on his shoulder. She leaned in, placing her lips so close to his ear he felt her warm breath. "Is it safe for Boss? There's glass and metal everywhere."

He ignored the zing that sent warmth spreading through his chest. "He's got thick skin. It shouldn't be a problem. Thanks for keeping an eye out," he said. "And looking out for both of us."

She squeezed his shoulder and smiled, handing him the lead.

Grey turned his attention to the serious task ahead. "Boss, seek."

Boss lowered his head and swished his tail side to side. They started with a search of the exterior, the dog sniffing the edge of the car and working his way back to the starting point. The driver's side door was jammed and they couldn't get it to open so Boss stood on his hind legs and tried to sniff the driver through the broken window. The dog dropped back down and looked at Grey.

"I think he needs in the car," Grey said.

Bree opened the back door. "Go ahead."

Boss hopped into the back seat and sniffed. He turned his head, smelled the dead man in the front seat, then shifted his focus back to something in the back seat. The dog appeared to be confused. With his front paws on the seat, Boss craned his neck to thoroughly smell the man's face. Boss plopped down on the back seat and held his paw up.

Grey nodded to Bree, and she put her phone to her ear.

"Someone get me the blood samples," Wally said.

Before Grey could release Boss from the car, the dog began sniffing near the floor in the back seat.

"Wait." Grey watched Boss move to the floorboard and sniff the air vent. "What's that?"

Bree pushed herself between Grey and the car. "Don't let him touch it."

Grey commanded Boss to come out of the car. The dog glanced at Grey then back to the air vent before obeying. "Good boy, Boss."

Grey moved his wheelchair out of the way and Bree used her glove to remove a small square air freshener from the vent near the floor in the backseat.

She dropped it into an evidence bag. "Is there any way Boss can confirm X-VX without touching it?"

"Yes, hold the evidence bag to his nose," Grey said.

Bree followed Grey's instruction and Boss sniffed, then sat and lifted a paw.

"That's a good boy." Grey held Boss's head between two hands and scratched with vigor. He gave him his toy and Boss chomped down on it.

"I think we can rule out someone dosing him in the bar." Quinn appeared behind Grey.

"You sure?" Bree asked.

"An hour of questioning and nothing."

Bree held the evidence bag and scrutinized it. "That's okay. I'm fairly certain we have our X-VX delivery system right here."

Christina stared at the evidence bag in Bree's hand and a spark ignited deep within her gut. Finally, they had physical evidence and a possibility of fingerprints or other forensic evidence. Would the evidence lead to Sokolovich?

A distinctive high-pitched squeak of wet brakes bringing a car to a stop caught Christina's attention. It hadn't come from the slow-moving traffic on her right. Boss noticed the sound too, his pointy ears turning and his muscles tensing. She followed the dog's gaze to the university building parking lot. The expansive grassy area that separated the parking lot from the street was dark. No signs of a car's headlights or brake lights.

The sound of a van door sliding open sent her pulse racing.

Christina crouched and with one hand grabbed Boss's collar and tugged. Grey saw her movement and put a hand on her back and shoved. She stumbled and fell to the asphalt, catching herself on her right palm and dragging Boss down with her. The side mirror of the police cruiser where her head had been a second ago exploded into a million pieces and rained down on her back. The echo of rapid gunfire rang out and sparks lit up the night as a spray of bullets pelted the vehicles. Christina scrambled behind the ambulance where Grey was taking cover with Boss. The dog barked as bullets sank into the thick ambulance doors.

"Keep your head down!" Christina put herself between the gunman and Grey and took a moment to scan him for injury.

"I'm fine. Just stay down."

"The shooter is in the parking lot. Ten o'clock," Christina said. The exact spot where Grey was instructed to park earlier.

"Yeah, I see him." Quinn took aim, using the police cruiser door for cover and shouting orders. All at once, the officers returned fire.

Bree used the wrecked sedan as cover and radioed for back up. "10-75, shots fired!"

Christina searched for Wally and Francisco. Had they taken cover or were they caught in the crossfire? Christina risked a peek around the ambulance door and saw Francisco on the ground with his arms covering his head. Apparently, he'd dropped right where was standing.

Wally wasn't on the ground and he hadn't taken cover. He was standing still, like a statue, eyes locked on the ambulance with an unblinking stare. What was he doing? He was a former soldier—he knew what to do. Why was he just standing there staring? He was going to get shot.

"Wally!" Christina yelled his name over the chaos of gunfire.

He didn't flinch, but his eyes drifted to hers.

"Wally!" she roared. "Get down!"

His eyelids fluttered and it took another beat for him to snap into action. The bullets continued to fly, but Wally dropped to the ground so fast Christina worried he'd been shot. She wanted to rush to him and drag him out of the way, but the gunman was laying down fire on the ambulance and Wally was a good distance away.

He lifted his chin from the pavement and looked in her direction. Good, he wasn't hit. The man was probably in shock. PTSD or something.

Christina crouched with one hand on Grey's knee and her gun in the other. Keeping herself between Grey and the gunman, she scanned the field for the muzzle flash.

"Bree, stay here and secure the scene," Quinn shouted over the gunfire.

Bree nodded to Quinn. "He's not giving up easily, so be careful."

Before Quinn had a chance to move, the gunfire from the parking lot ceased. Quinn took off for his car with two officers right behind him. Quinn's tires squealed as he pulled away from the scene.

Christina scanned the shadowy parking lot, but from her

position fifty yards away in the darkest hours of the night, visibility was low. A glint of light under a large oak tree caught her eye and she saw a dark-colored panel van with the side door open camouflaged beneath the thick hanging Spanish moss. The side door of the van slammed shut and red taillights signaled the sniper was on the move.

Christina hit record on her cell phone's camera app, attempting to zoom in on the driver. "Bree—"

"I see him." Bree spoke into her radio. "Black panel van, heading north from the parking lot. I can't see his plates. Head him off. Don't let him get away."

"I didn't get the plate either, but I took a video," Christina said. "I'll send it to you. Maybe it'll help."

Christina turned to check on Grey. His chest heaved and his gray eyes appeared dark and wild. She patted his shoulder. "Are you okay?"

"I feel like my heart is about to burst from my chest. That was way too close. You almost got hit."

Christina let out a breath. The bullet had missed her head by inches. "Well, I'm thankful you had my back, Captain."

Grey took her hand. "Always, Agent."

Christina ran a hand over Boss, checking for wounds. "Boss is okay."

Grey turned his wheelchair to see Wally and Francisco. "What about you guys? Anyone hurt?"

"I'm fine," Francisco said. He offered a hand and helped Wally up. "You okay, man?"

"Yeah, I'm fine." Wally flicked a glance at Christina then averted his eyes.

Francisco dusted gravel from Bree's sleeve. He held her elbow and looked into her eyes. "Are you all right?"

Bree nodded.

Francisco whirled on Grey. "What is it with you two? Whenever you and Wally show up, people start shooting."

"I think we need to get you guys somewhere safe for questioning," Bree said.

Christina glanced at the bullet holes freckling the police car and pressed her pinky finger into one of the entrance holes. A high-powered rifle had made them. A 7.62 caliber round similar to what she'd used as a sniper, if she had to guess. One thing she knew for certain, this wasn't a random drive-by shooting with a pistol.

This was the work of a professional.

21

WEDNESDAY, 11:40 A.M.

The dining room table was somewhere underneath Christina's piles of papers. Added to the heap were her laptop, tablet, Bible, and journal. Tracking The Scavenger was more difficult than she'd imagined.

An internet search of the three victims turned up an interesting connection to the Aberdeen Proving Grounds in Maryland, where the Army Medical Research Institute for Chemical Defense was located. All three victims—the woman in the restaurant, the female doctor, and Night Club Guy—worked at the CBRN Command and Control laboratory in one way or another. Unfortunately, that was about as far as she could get. Christina was only able to find a short article posted on a military website stating the research facility was destroyed in an explosion, but the details were vague. Scholarly articles published by Cathy Wright, the chemist who died at the university, required high security government login credentials to gain access. The clearance wasn't a problem, but gaining a username and password to this particular system would take some time.

She pinched the bridge of her nose and said a silent prayer, asking God to help her keep Grey and Boss safe and find this Scavenger guy, whoever he was.

Christina saw movement on the surveillance cameras displayed on the television. Bree parked in the driveway and got out of her car with a white paper bag. Christina smiled to herself. After a long night of investigating the car crash, dodging bullets, and gathering statements, Bree was bringing them treats. Bree was a wonderful woman, and she'd mentioned she was considering retirement from the police force. If she did retire, Christina hoped she would consider working as a bodyguard with the Elite Guardians.

Christina opened the door before Bree had a chance to ring the bell. Grey was sleeping and she wanted him to rest. His leg was still healing from the gunshot wound, and despite his efforts to hide it, she knew he was in pain.

"Talk about service." Bree stepped inside and held up the bag. "I heard you don't eat sugar."

"Have you even had a chance to sleep?" Christina took the bag from her and peeked inside. It smelled divine.

Bree ignored the question and pointed to the bag. "Breakfast for you, donuts for Grey, and a little something for Boss in there too."

Christina popped the top of a Styrofoam container and smiled when she saw a golden-brown spinach feta quiche. Boss hopped down from his favorite chair and padded to the kitchen. He sat in front of Christina and licked his lips.

"Did you hear Bree say she brought you a treat?"

"It's in the foil." Bree sat down at the table. "What's all this?"

Christina unwrapped the foil and fed Boss three thick slabs of bacon. "Research. I found the connection between the three victims."

"Aberdeen?"

Christina nodded and took a seat across from Bree. "How are Grey and Boss connected to Aberdeen?"

"I don't know. Have you asked him?"

"Grey says there isn't a connection and believes the X-VX victims are targeted test runs by the Russians leading to something bigger."

"And what do you think?" Bree rested her chin on a fist.

"The notes are too personal." Christina forked a bite of the quiche and ate.

Bree nodded. "Quinn and I agree. The three all had notes signed by The Scavenger and each victim can be traced back to Aberdeen. We've tried to get some help, but the Army is shutting us out. Even their personnel records are sealed."

"Wright was a chemist, and Mooney and Dennison were former Army. Is it possible they were researching X-VX or another chemical weapon and discovered the formula? That would give the Russians a reason to eliminate them."

Bree tilted her head, brow furrowed. "It's possible, but why kill them now? If they discovered the chemical formula, the Army would have it."

The detective was right, but Christina had a feeling the Aberdeen laboratory was the key to finding the killer. "We need a list of everyone who worked with the victims."

"I agree, but as I mentioned, the Army is shutting us out."

Christina checked the hallway for any signs of Grey. Seeing none, she leaned in and lowered her voice, not wanting him to hear her suspicions. "Have you checked into Travis Briggs?"

"We ruled him out. Olivia had eyes on Briggs all night. He was at a bar on the other side of town until closing." Bree shook her head. "Besides, I don't think he's organized enough for this."

Bree was probably right. As much as Christina wanted to believe Briggs was behind the plot to kill Grey, he was too unstable to plan and organize a complex murder spree.

Bree covered her mouth and yawned. "So what are y'all planning to do about the anniversary party?"

Christina took another bite of the quiche and pointed to it with her fork. "This is delicious. Thank you," she said around a mouthful. "Grey is adamant about attending, and I can't blame him. Forty years of marriage is a reason to celebrate, and his parents deserve to have their son present. I've arranged for Lizzie, Charlie, and Laila to be undercover at the party. It's at his parents' ranch, so we can set up tight security before the guests arrive. I don't think we will have anything to worry about."

"Sounds like you're doing all you can for your client."

"What about you and Quinn? Are you any closer to finding this Scavenger character?"

Bree leaned back in her chair, folded her arms. "No fingerprints, no DNA, and no leads from the video at the university. Dennison was the only victim who lived in the area, so our guy has done his research. He knew when and where the victims would be." She sighed. "It seems like he's always two steps ahead of us."

"Twice, a gunman has opened fire while we were at the crime scene. Is that a coincidence, or could these X-VX killings be a way to lure Grey and Boss out in the open?"

"That's an interesting thought." Bree tapped her fingers on the tabletop. "But Grey hired you as a bodyguard for Boss, right?"

"That's right. He was very specific. Boss is the asset. National security depends on his survival, and I should protect the dog over Grey if it comes down to it."

"Seems like he needs a bodyguard as much as Boss."

Christina agreed. "In every situation, I calculate for both of them." And apparently, he was doing the same for her. Earlier, he'd shoved her out of the way just in the nick of time.

Bree exhaled. "At this point, I would say the X-VX killings

have very little to do with Grey or Boss. The notes left with the victims are the same notes Governor Winston had been receiving for weeks before the shooting at the basketball game. SLED kept it under wraps until we found the note with Mooney. Besides, if the killer wanted Grey dead, couldn't he simply use X-VX?"

"I guess you're right." Christina wondered if The Scavenger planned to kill Grey with X-VX but was unable to get close enough. She remembered Wally said something about a vaccine to prevent chemical weapons from affecting soldiers. Grey's unit had been involved in testing the new drug, and she made a mental note to ask Grey about it.

"The Scavenger has a message he wants to convey, and once we figure out how the victims are tied to Governor Winston, I think we'll have our answer," Bree said.

Christina nodded. "Then we can stop The Scavenger before he kills anyone else."

WEDNESDAY, 12:31 P.M.

Grey hadn't slept past noon in ages, though he wasn't sure if he'd classify his restless night as "sleep." He headed for the kitchen, but paused in the hallway and watched Christina for a moment. She twirled the tip of her braid and moved her index finger along the smooth pages of her Bible.

"Staring is rude," she said without looking up.

"I didn't want to disturb you," Grey said. "I heard voices and came out to see who you were talking to."

Christina dropped the end of her hair and glanced up at him. "It was Bree. She just left, but she brought treats. Yours is on the counter there."

Grey opened the bag and looked inside. "All right! Donuts!"

There may have been a bit more excitement in his voice than he had intended, but he really needed a sugar fix.

Papers cluttered the tabletop, and a small journal lay next to her Bible, with colorful notes scribbled in blocky handwriting. "I didn't mean to disturb your Bible study."

"No bother. I'm finished." She closed her journal. "I'm sorry if we woke you."

"Nah, I was tossing and turning. I should have gotten up hours ago."

Christina rested her chin on her hand. "More nightmares?"

"Not exactly." He dropped the bag of donuts in his lap and pushed his wheelchair up to the table. "There is something nagging in the back of my mind, and no matter how hard I try, I can't put my finger on it."

Christina laid her pen in the crease of her Bible and leaned forward. "Something about last night?"

Grey shook his head. "I don't think so..." He let his sentence trail off as a hazy image clouded his mind. Dr. Kalashnik sitting on the cot in the cabin. Wally's bulging eyes staring at Grey as he lay on the floor.

"Grey?"

He blinked. Why did he keep thinking about the attack in Siberia? Even when his PTSD was at its worst, his dreams weren't of Siberia. "Sorry, what did you say?"

"I asked if you were excited about your surgery next week."

"I'm excited for the results, but I think I've had about enough of being in hospitals for a while." He flashed a grin and took a bite of his glazed donut. Oh yeah, that's what he needed this morning. Deep-fried sugar.

"I see your point. How long until you see results?"

"Results? Oh, uh, several weeks, I'd imagine. Those nanorobots are slow workers I guess." He gave her a half-hearted chuckle.

Did it matter if the surgery didn't work? If he couldn't walk again? Would she be happy living life with him like this? There were so many things he could never do from a wheelchair, things she loved. Running was important to Christina, but they'd never be able to jog together. Holding hands on a long walk. Impossible because he needed both hands to push his chair. And how could he steer his wheelchair with a baby in his arms?

Wait, what was he thinking? How had he jumped from, *Hey, Grey, are you excited about the surgery?*, all the way to being married with a baby?

"So, uh. What is all this?" He gestured to the table.

Her brown eyes searched his face for a moment. This woman was brilliant, and he had no doubt his clumsy attempt at changing the subject hadn't escaped her notice. Could she see behind his words to his heart?

"Some research on the victims, and a security plan for your parents' anniversary party." She closed her laptop and began stacking papers. "I put together a protection team to attend undercover as guests. Charlie and Lizzie will arrive early and make sure only invited guests are attending."

"Wow, that…that sounds amazing, Christina. Thank you. You don't know how much it means to me."

She averted her eyes and lifted a shoulder. "It's my job."

There was a softness behind her words and he wanted to believe he had become more than a job to her. They'd shared every moment together for the past week, and now he couldn't imagine a future without her. His parents were going to love Christina—Ruby too. Even Boss already loved Christina.

Love? Was he really thinking of the L-word? Nope, he wouldn't go there. Opening that door was too much to unpack.

"I need to pick up my tux," he said. "Think it's safe enough to stop by and grab it later today?"

Christina pinched her lip with her finger for a moment before releasing it. "I can get one of the other Elite Guardians to pick it up. I'm sure we could handle it but—" She stilled. "Wait... did you say *tux?*"

"Yeah, why?"

"This is a *formal* party?"

He winced. "It's black tie. I...um...I probably should have mentioned that sooner, huh?"

"I didn't exactly bring a formal dress to work with me, Grey."

The tips of her ears appeared to be turning red, and he found it endearing. "Is this going to be an issue?"

"I'm sure it won't be a problem. I can figure something out. I should let the rest of the team know."

"If you're sure. I mean—"

She held a hand up. "Really, it's not a problem. We do this all the time. I was about to finish my Bible study with a prayer. I think we could really use God's protection, don't you?"

At the word *prayer*, Boss hopped up and repositioned himself at Christina's feet. He put his head between his paws and waited. The dog flicked his eyes between Christina and Grey.

Grey wadded up the empty donut bag and pushed his wheelchair away from the table. "I'll order some lunch and leave the prayers to you and Boss."

Christina crossed her arms and lifted an eyebrow. "I thought we already discussed this."

"Discussed what?"

"I opened up to you, now you need to open up to God again."

"Christina." He sighed. "I don't see the point. I believe in God. I have since I was a child, but what's the point in praying if He won't listen to me?"

She scooted her chair and positioned herself in front of him. With a gentle tug, she drew his wheelchair closer until their knees touched. "God hears your prayers, Grey. Our world is broken and filled with evil. It's our job as Christians to stand up and fight back the darkness. One way is through prayer."

"Oh, yeah?" he snorted. "What do you call this? We're walking in darkness now, and every time my prayer really mattered to me, it didn't matter to God."

"God isn't some sort of genie, Grey. You can't expect Him to grant your every wish. Prayer is just one of the ways we can have a relationship with God. Just talk to Him." She placed her hand on his knee.

He covered her hand with his and stared into her eyes. Vibrant and assessing, they invited him to see through to her soul within. She trusted God, and so had he...at one time. "I want what I see in you, Christina. I want to trust God and I want to talk to Him. I've been struggling to come to grips with those unanswered prayers."

"Which ones?"

"You know...'Lord, keep us safe from harm,' then an hour later a kid drops a grenade into my pal's Humvee. Days and days of walking in the darkness says God doesn't answer my prayers."

"The darkness is all around us, but as Christians we walk in the Light. We're here to show love and kindness and give grace and mercy to others as God does to us."

"How can you say that when you've taken so many lives?" As soon as the words were out of his mouth, he regretted them. It was thoughtless. When would he learn to think before speaking? The last thing he wanted to do was use her words against her.

Her gaze fell to their hands, and she spoke without looking up. "Before I found God, it was impossible. I saw the faces of my victims every time I closed my eyes. The guilt was overwhelming. But with God, my sins are forgiven and I am made new again. My feelings of guilt aren't from God, so I talk it out with Him. I've found peace and joy, even in the most difficult circumstances. And when I face those trials or make a mistake, I can trust that God is with me. It doesn't take away the pain, but knowing He's there to hear my every thought..." She shrugged. "It helps."

Grey's pulse picked up speed. Why did Christina's words excite him? He knew better than to trust God when God had let him down so many times before, but he wanted what Christina had found. Peace and joy in the trials. But he had so many questions.

"How can you still serve God after He took Alana away from you? After He allowed all those people to die in a senseless bombing, and for what? So some mad men could take over a town by killing innocent citizens?"

Christina's dark brown eyes softened and shined with unshed tears. "God isn't to blame for those things. Evil is to blame. I believe God blessed us with special skills and talents and we can't waste our gifts. We must use them to battle spiritual enemies as well as earthly enemies."

The words made sense, and he wanted to believe he could find peace and joy with God the way Christina had. He wanted to ask God to help him find The Scavenger, to protect Boss, his family...and Christina. But every time Grey asked God for something, the opposite seemed to happen, and he wasn't ready to lose everything.

Again.

22

THURSDAY, 7:30 A.M.

Christina sat on the kitchen floor, brushing Boss after their morning run. Her strict routine had been rocked off its axis over the last week, but she was beginning to enjoy the new routine. After her morning run, she gave Boss his breakfast and showered while he ate. A quick trip to the backyard to relieve himself, and a ten-minute stroke with the dog brush.

Brushing Boss gave her time to think about the conversation with Grey yesterday. How could she help him see past the death and destruction of war, and even what they were facing right now, to the place where she was spiritually? It wasn't that she was okay with death. Quite the opposite. But she knew God's plans were bigger. Well, she wouldn't force God onto Grey. She'd just be there for him when he was ready.

"I think you're spoiling him." Grey pushed his wheelchair up to Boss and rubbed his ears. "He does look good though."

"Well, you know what they say—one hundred strokes to make your hair shine." Christina cleaned up the hairy mess that she had brushed off of Boss and washed her hands while Boss rolled around on his back on the living room rug. "Hey, you're going to mess up your hair."

Boss jumped to his feet and shook out his coat.

Grey laughed and Christina shook her head. That dog was so endearing. It was hard to believe he was the same dog capable of sniffing out bombs and chemical weapons or attacking on command.

Boss went to his favorite chair and hopped up. He settled down with his chin on the armrest and closed his eyes.

Grey joined Christina in the kitchen and poured himself a cup of coffee. "So, how do you feel about a road trip?"

"Road trip?" Well, that caught her by surprise. "What did you have in mind?"

"A day trip to Charleston—well, Folly Beach actually. We can grab some lunch, take a walk on the boardwalk." He raised his eyebrows, hopeful.

"Can Boss go?"

He laughed. "Yes, Boss can go."

She leaned against the counter and studied him. "So, tell me the real reason you want to take this road trip."

Grey nodded. "You know me too well already, Agent."

Her eyebrows furrowed. "You know I'm not an—"

"Okay, okay." He held up a palm. "Listen, all throughout my childhood, my parents talked about the Diamond Blue 1956 Ford Thunderbird convertible they owned. They loved to reminisce about that car and all the dates in it. Beach trips, drive-in movies, evenings of stargazing. The whole nine yards. When Ruby came along, they decided to sell it for a more family-friendly vehicle, but always dreamed of the day when they could afford to buy another one exactly like it."

"It's a beautiful old car. They were probably sad to see it go."

"You don't know the half of it. Whenever my mother would see a fifties model Thunderbird, she would point to it and say, 'We had a car like that once. Oh, how I loved it.' Ruby and I would roll our eyes. She was drawn to trucks, and I loved muscle cars."

Christina slid onto a chair at the island. "I'm partial to sports cars myself."

"You don't say," he teased. "Well, for their anniversary party, Ruby and I plan to surprise our parents with an identical vintage Thunderbird convertible. Here, check it out." He showed her a photo of the car on his phone.

"Wow, Grey, that's beautiful. What an amazing gift."

He looked at the photo and grinned. "I know, it's cool, right? We plan to have the car parked near one of the barns, out of sight of the party, and have a crew set up a drive-in movie, complete with a screen on the side of the barn. All the guests will be directed to park in rows so that when we make the announcement, they can go to their cars and watch the movie. After dinner and dancing, Ruby and I will lead our parents to the car and surprise them. They'll recreate their first date with their new car and a drive-in movie."

"Wow, Grey. Your parents are going to flip out." Excitement for the big reveal had her sitting on the edge of her seat. The gift was not only generous but a truly heartfelt one.

"The movie is *Casablanca*, of course. Mom and Dad's favorite."

"You know, I've never seen it."

Grey laughed. "Me either. I guess we'll get to see it for the first time together."

Just like his parents had. "I'd like that." Christina's pulse quickened and she couldn't suppress a grin. "But what's this have to do with a road trip?"

"The car was supposed to be delivered tomorrow, but the seller called me this morning and said his wife is ill. He can't deliver it." Grey shrugged. "I was hoping you'd go with me to pick it up."

"Of course, I will." The boyish way he said it stirred the

butterflies in her stomach. Part of her wondered if this was his way of asking her on a date, or just a friendly outing. She was working, after all. It didn't matter. If she had a good day with Grey, that would be enough. "When do we leave?"

Boss lifted his head, aware they were talking about leaving. He placed his front paws on the ground and stretched while his hind legs were still in the chair. A yawn ended with a high-pitched whine, and he pulled the rest of himself off the chair to come stand beside Christina.

"Looks like Boss is ready for a road trip too," Grey said.

Half an hour later, they were in Grey's Tesla heading east down I-26 toward the coast of South Carolina. The sun shone in a clear blue sky and Christina was thankful for the warmer weather. It would be a great day to walk around Folly Beach, and she may not even need the jacket she'd brought.

Boss slept in his special compartment and Grey thrummed the steering wheel, his Ray-Bans hiding his eyes. Christina kept her eyes on the traffic around them, mentally tracking each vehicle and watching for anyone who might be suspicious.

A snort of laughter escaped Grey and she snapped her head to look at him. "What's funny?"

"I was thinking about this time in basic training when a guy in our flight misheard the TI." Grey laughed again. "Our first night of basic, our TI comes in and yells at us, 'Go to the latrine and shave off all the hair on your face except your eyebrows! You have one minute!' Less than a minute later, fifty of us are standing at attention behind our beds, cuts all over our faces, but our TI notices one of the guys is missing. So he stomps over to the latrine." Grey paused, breaking into laughter.

Watching him, Christina couldn't stop the smile on her own face.

"The TI says a few curse words and drags this poor guy out of the bathroom. He's standing there with one eyebrow gone and the other all lathered up. Our TI screams at the guy, 'I said all the hair *except* your eyebrows!' The poor kid looks him dead in the face and says, 'Sir, may I shave the other one?'" Grey roared with laughter, trying to get the rest of the story out. "This guy had to spend the next six weeks marching around with only one eyebrow."

Christina dissolved into giggles. "What did the other flights say when they saw him?"

"Oh, they teased him like crazy. Every day someone would tell him, 'I think you missed a spot.'" Grey chuckled.

"That's one thing you can't say to a sniper."

"What?"

"You missed."

Grey snorted. "No, I guess that's one thing you'd never want to hear. What about you? Any funny stories from basic?"

She exhaled, trying to give her lungs a break from all the laughing. Her ribs ached and they were only halfway to Folly Beach. "All I can remember is Mr. Fuzzy."

"What's a Mr. Fuzzy?"

"It was the first week of basic and we were standing for inspection. The woman across from me had this piece of fuzz on her uniform. Our sergeant made her carry the fuzz around and any time she asked to see Mr. Fuzzy, the woman had to produce it."

"Ha. Okay, so what would happen if she didn't have Mr. Fuzzy?"

Christina snickered. "Push-ups. Lots of push-ups."

"Classic."

Christina checked the cars around them. So far, it didn't seem like anyone had followed them. Hearing the stories of their time in basic was good for a laugh, but she was glad to be done with the Army. She loved her job with the Elite Guardians.

"What was it like when you left the Air Force?"

He blew out a slow breath. "Chaotic. My family was all over me with worry. We didn't fully understand my condition for a while, and it brought a lot of anxiety. The girl I was dating said she couldn't stick around. Said she wasn't ready for the long-term hassle and walked away."

She touched his arm. "Oh, Grey, that's terrible."

"I thought so too, but if I'm honest, it was for the best. If she couldn't stick around in the early days, she wouldn't have been able to hang around for the tough stuff. Sometimes people can't handle the cards they're dealt and they fold." He glanced at her with a flat smile, then back to the road. "Living life with someone in a wheelchair is a challenge and not everyone is up for it."

She wanted to see his eyes behind the dark sunglasses. How could someone leave him in his time of need like that? And what had that done to his poor heart? Underneath that easy-going, fun-loving exterior had to be some deep wounds.

"You know, I've never been one to shy away from a challenge."

Grey smiled.

The weather at Folly Beach couldn't have been more perfect for a date if he'd ordered it himself. Blue skies and a warmth that made it feel like spring. Maybe God was listening to him after all. It was a quick prayer last night, a few words to ask for a good day with Christina. One without death and destruction. So far, God had listened, and the day was perfect.

They had lunch outside at a table overlooking the ocean and shared war stories. Some funny, some serious. They teased each other and even talked about military tactics. Through their conversation, Grey saw more of the woman than ever before. Her subtle, witty remarks occasionally caught him off guard. And he had to admit, the woman was brilliant. Far smarter than he was. And instead of finding it intimidating, he found it alluring.

After lunch, they walked Boss to the end of Folly Beach Pier and watched the white caps fold over themselves as the waves made their way to shore. He snapped a few photos of Christina when she wasn't paying attention. His favorite photo was of her crouched beside Boss, with her hand on his side and the sun glinting off her hair.

It was juvenile, but he wanted to hold her hand while they walked. The only thing stopping him was the need to steer his wheelchair. One thing he knew for sure, he wanted more days like this with Christina. Days to explore together, laugh together, and days to deepen his knowledge of the woman who intoxicated his heart.

"How about some ice cream?" she asked.

His eyebrow went up. "I thought you didn't eat sugar?"

"What's a road trip without a little sugar?" She grinned and tugged his hand. "Come on, this way."

Grey let her hold his hand and pull his wheelchair, steering himself with only his left hand. Okay, he'd never thought about having her help steer while they held hands. A few minutes ago, hand-holding seemed like such a mountain to overcome, and just like that, they'd found a way to make it work together.

They brought their ice cream outside to the chairs overlooking the water. Boss sat between them and watched the other dogs play on the beach. Grey didn't care about what was happening anywhere else—he liked the view right here, watching Christina enjoy her double chocolate cone. The ocean wind pulled at the hairs in her braid and her brown eyes glinted in the sunshine.

"I think I finally found your weakness, Agent." He nodded to her ice cream. "Chocolate."

Stray hairs whipped around her face, and she brushed them

away with the back of her hand. "Are you ever going to tell me why you keep calling me Agent?"

"Someday."

"But not today?"

"Not today." He grinned and she rolled her eyes. "We still have an hour before we can pick up the car. Should we browse some of the shops?"

"Ice cream *and* shopping? You really know how to make a girl's day."

Grey chuckled. "Something tells me you do about as much shopping as you do ice cream eating."

They browsed several shops and Christina pointed out corny T-shirts she said he should have. While she was distracted picking out postcards, Grey found a beautiful leather journal and paid for it. He tucked himself away in the corner and inscribed the first page. When he found Christina, she was finishing her purchase.

Grey followed Christina outside across the street to a flat park bench with a view of the ocean. The ocean roared in the background, a sound he always found soothing. He uncapped the bottle of water he'd purchased and filled Boss's collapsible bowl. The dog lapped the water thirstily.

"Look what I found." Christina dug to the bottom of her shopping bag and pulled out a white dog bowl and held it up for him to see. On the side it read *I'm the Boss* in block letters.

"That's perfect," he said. "Boss will love it." And he loved her excitement over the purchase.

Boss swayed his tail and squinted up at Christina.

Grey handed his shopping bag to Christina. "I got you a little something too."

His heart thundered as he watched her take the journal out of the bag and flip to the first page. The wind whipped the pages and she held them down with her palm.

When she saw his inscription, she glanced up and smiled.

She read his handwritten note aloud. "Don't be afraid to take a risk with your heart. Proverbs 3:5." Christina stared at the page. "Proverbs 3:5. 'Trust in the Lord with all your heart and lean not on your own understanding; in all your ways submit to him, and he will make your paths straight.'"

"I thought you might know that one." He stared at his messy handwriting.

Christina ran her thumb over it. When she looked at him again, her face beamed. "This is the most thoughtful gift I've ever received."

Grey fiddled with his hands, suddenly aware of how personal the gift was and hoping it wasn't too much. He shrugged. "It looked like your journal was filling up fast. I thought you could use another."

"I'm not talking about the journal, Grey."

He looked up and saw her beautiful eyes fixed on him. It was a good thing he was already sitting down because his knees went weak. What was this woman doing to him?

Christina closed the journal and swung her leg over to straddle the bench so she was facing him. Before he knew what was happening, she'd wrapped her arms around his neck in a firm hug and whispered, "Thank you."

The hot breath against his ear sent a shiver down his spine. He slipped his arms around her waist and held her body tight against his chest. When she moved, he loosened his grip a fraction. Christina pulled her head back and looked deep into his eyes. Oh, how he wanted to kiss her. They were only inches apart, noses nearly touching.

"Christina." He breathed her name. "I want to kiss you, but I'm your client."

She shook her head slightly, her nose brushing his. "You're not my client. Boss is."

A slow grin spread across his face, and he let his eyes search hers. She bent her head and pressed her lips to his. He held the kiss for a long, delicious moment before deepening it. The world around them stopped as he clutched her to him. He didn't want to let her go, but her kisses were coming hard and fast, shooting through him like a rocket. When he broke their contact, Christina planted one last soft kiss on his lips and smiled at him.

She rested her forehead against his. "I think it's time to get the car."

23

FRIDAY, 3:08 P.M.

Christina's heart was aglow the next morning and all throughout the day. Her first kiss with Grey had been magical, and she couldn't stop smiling. Tonight, she would meet his parents and his sister, and she wanted to make a good impression.

The doorbell rang and Christina glanced at the television surveillance. Perfect timing. When she opened the door, Laila squeezed her way through, carrying garment bags and a large canvas tote.

"Hey, Grey. I've got your tux." Laila held a bag out to him. "Are you excited about the party tonight?"

"If you can believe it, I'm a little nervous." He laid his tux over his lap and turned to leave. "Thank you. I appreciate your help but I'm off to get ready."

"No problem," Laila called after him. She dangled a second garment bag from her index finger and offered it to Christina. "A little surprise for you."

Christina eyed Laila and accepted the bag. "What is it?"

Laila grinned. "You'll see. Olivia said to tell you she wished she could help tonight, but she's already on the job. Governor Winston is having a fundraiser of some sort at the Empire Hotel Convention Center tonight."

Laila marched down the hallway and paused. "Which one's your room?"

Christina pointed to the door on the right and Laila pushed her way in. She plopped herself on the bed and kicked her shoes off. "That's better."

Christina hung the garment bag over the bathroom door and lowered the zipper. A silky, emerald-green dress hung in a clear plastic bag.

"Wow," Christina gasped. "This is gorgeous. It's Olivia's?"

"Yep. She also packed what she called a *beauty bag* and said it would have everything we need. I peeked inside and I'm pretty sure this bag belonged to Mary Poppins. It's stuffed."

Christina slipped the protective plastic off and held the dress up. It was shorter than she thought it would be, falling above her knee. "It's a little short, don't you think?"

Laila rolled her eyes. "At least try it on before you start complaining."

Christina frowned. "Fine." In the bathroom, she slipped into the dress and managed to zip it halfway before she needed Laila's help.

When she stepped out, Laila let out a long whistle. "Whoa, that dress was *made* for you."

Christina moved to the edge of the bed and turned her back to Laila. "It was actually made for Olivia. Zip me up, will you?"

Laila pulled the zipper to the top and patted Christina's back. "There you go."

A full-length mirror hung over the bathroom door and Christina stepped in front of it. A slight smile played on her lips when she saw her reflection. The dress was form fitting, but not tight. The deep green color looked good with her skin tone and

LYNETTE EASON & KATE ANGELO

accentuated curves she didn't know she possessed. The dress wasn't as short as she'd imagined, but the length wasn't her biggest problem.

Christina spun toward Laila and threw her hands up. "How in the world am I supposed to run in this thing?"

"The slit in the front is strategically placed to account for that." Laila checked her manicure.

A modest slit opened over her left knee and traveled up about mid-thigh. Not too revealing, and not too sexy. "And what am I supposed to do about my gun? How am I supposed to conceal it?"

"Olivia thought of that too." Laila rummaged around in the oversized bag. "It's in here somewhere. Aha! Here, use this."

Christina took the small black thigh holster and eyed it. "My gun will never fit in this thing."

Laila groaned. "Well, no. Not that monstrosity you insist on carrying. Don't you have a smaller concealed gun?"

Christina slid her hand into the boots she hadn't bothered to take off and withdrew a subcompact 9 millimeter Sig Sauer. "Of course I have a concealable gun. I *am* a professional."

She fastened the holster to her thigh and situated it until it was snug. Her Sig slipped in nicely and she pulled the dress down over it. Once she'd smoothed the dress, she looked at Laila. "How's that?"

"Girl, you look amazing," she said. "But we're gonna have to do something about your hair."

"What do you mean? What's wrong with my hair?" Christina pulled her braid over her shoulder and played with the end of it. "It's the perfect hairstyle for me. Always out of the way, but a little more feminine than a plain old ponytail."

"Oh, it's cute, but it will never work with the dress."

"I think you've seen the extent of my abilities to do hair and makeup." Christina had taken to wearing blush and a bit of eyeshadow, but nothing more. It always seemed to smear or get on her clothes, so she didn't bother.

"Don't you worry about it. I can handle this." Laila stood and grabbed the desk chair and pulled it to the bathroom in front of the mirror. "Sit." She placed her hands on Christina's shoulders and guided her into the chair. Laila grabbed the Mary Poppins bag and searched inside until she found a curling iron, hair spray, and an oversized hairbrush.

Christina took her braid out and combed through it with her fingers. "Where did you learn how to do hair?"

"Undercover necessity."

"Really?"

Laila shrugged. "I was undercover with the Mossad for so long, I had to learn different ways of applying my makeup and styling my hair."

"Well, it's a skill I never thought I would need as a bodyguard."

"Maybe they should teach a special class at the bodyguard school, huh?" Laila laughed.

"We've never really discussed your background from your time with the Mossad. What kind of undercover work did you do?"

Laila began sectioning Christina's hair and put each section in a hair clip. "Not that different from your job as a special ops sniper. Recon, infiltration, observation." She smiled. "Camouflage."

Christina watched Laila through the mirror. "What made you leave and become a bodyguard with Elite Guardians?"

"Oh, you know, one huge, failed mission."

Christina met Laila's eyes in the mirror and gave her a rueful smile. "Yes, I do know."

Laila wrapped a small section of Christina's long blonde hair around the flat iron and held it for a moment before pulling the iron down and leaving a long bouncy curl in its wake. "Is that what happened to you?"

Christina shifted in her seat. Olivia's words about Christina keeping to herself played in her mind. She had trusted Grey with her story—should she also trust Laila? Christina didn't know if she could tell the story again without crying, and she didn't want to cry in front of her colleague. Especially not now. Not before they went on an assignment together.

"It's not something I normally talk about, but I've recently begun to process the emotions." She took a breath and fidgeted with her hands. "I hesitated when I saw the face of my target—a suicide bomber in Afghanistan. My hesitation caused the death of sixty-three people."

Laila released another bouncy blonde curl from the iron and spritzed it with hair spray. She met Christina's gaze in the mirror. "Wow, I think that would do it for anyone." She scooped up another section of hair and repeated the process.

"My training says otherwise. I'm supposed to chalk the deaths up to collateral damage in a senseless war and move on." She shrugged. "I just couldn't do it that time."

Laila fell quiet while she worked on curling Christina's hair.

Did the woman think less of her for not being able to deal with her emotions? Laila was a former Mossad agent who had likely been in many similar situations. Afghanistan was a difficult place for a woman, and Laila had served much of her time in the chaotic country just like Christina had.

"Christina, I know you are a great soldier." Laila's voice was soft. "I've seen you in action. But you're a human, not a robot. It's perfectly natural to feel guilt or grief over such a loss. You've handled it much better than most, so don't beat yourself up too much."

Christina's eyes moistened and she pressed her lips together to keep them from quivering. An overwhelming sense of relief flooded her. Getting it off her chest was actually helping, and she began to see what she'd been missing by being distant with the people in her life.

FRIDAY, 4:13 P.M.

Grey's heart stopped dead in its tracks when Christina walked out of the bedroom. Boy, was it a good thing he was sitting down because he thought he might pass out at the sight of her. The dress accented her curves in all the right places. In all the days of working with Christina, he had never seen her with makeup. Her hair fell to the middle of her back in long cascading waves of gold.

Grey's throat was thick and when he opened his mouth to speak, a croak escaped. "You—" He cleared his throat. "You look green. Um, I mean, you look great."

A wide smile began to spread across Christina's face, and Grey knew she was remembering the day they'd met in the Elite Guardians office. She'd stammered like he was doing now. His jaw snapped shut.

Christina fiddled with the snap on the small purse in her hands. "Thank you."

"She does look amazing, doesn't she?" Laila asked.

Amazing didn't cover it in Grey's opinion. Christina was downright gorgeous.

"Christina, you are a vision."

"Well, I'd say you were going to be the most handsome dude at this party tonight in your tuxedo, but I think Boss has you beat."

Boss sat next to Grey wearing a dog tuxedo complete with red bow tie. The dog tilted his head at Christina then stood and walked to her side. She ran her hand over his head.

"Hey, don't mess up his hair! I spent forever trying to get it to lay just right," Grey said.

"I think you nailed it." Laila piped up. "I'm gonna go. I need to get my dancing shoes on as well. Charlie and Lizzie should be in place soon."

"Thank you for everything Laila," Christina said. "We'll see you there."

Laila winked at Grey, then hiked the bag over her shoulder and left. The door closed with a soft click.

Grey suddenly wasn't sure where to look. He tugged at the collar of his shirt. Was it getting hot in here?

"Did your package get delivered in time?" Christina asked.

Thankful for the distraction, Grey checked his watch. "I had a text message saying Charlie delivered it about ten minutes ago. I can't wait to reveal it to my parents."

"Your parents are going to cherish this night."

"I really hope you're right."

Grey also hoped everyone would be safe and the night would go off without an incident. He trusted Christina and her team, but he couldn't bear the idea of his parents being in danger even for a moment. He had wrestled with the idea of canceling until after his surgery, using it as an excuse—but in the end, he couldn't take this night away from his parents.

24

The Parker Ranch was breathtaking. Lush green pastures boxed in by black rail fencing captivated Christina and she was instantly in love with the beauty of the property. The driveway was a long gravel road lined with trees on both sides. It must be even more beautiful in the spring when the trees were in full bloom.

Several barns with paddocks attached to them dotted the landscape. Each was painted a matching deep red with white trim, like an old-fashioned barn. Grey pointed out the large barn that hid the drive-in movie set up.

"Where are all the horses?"

"They've been put into their stalls for the night," Grey said. "These are very expensive horses, some of them costing upward of a quarter million dollars. We wouldn't want anything to happen to them."

Christina arched an eyebrow. "That *is* an expensive horse. Do you think I'd have an opportunity to see them?"

"You really want to see the horses?"

"I love horses. There's something about them, their strength, their endurance, their desire to be with humans, the beauty of them. I don't know," she said. "I've just always loved them."

"I'm sure we can slip away at some point. If I don't get you out there, I have no doubt Ruby would love to show you her therapy horses."

Pawning her off on his sister and she hadn't even met her yet. Was it because it would be too difficult for Grey to maneuver his wheelchair into the barn? Or perhaps his fear of horses kept him from the barn altogether. She gave him a sideways glance.

He caught her looking and grinned. "Don't worry, I'll take any opportunity to sneak off to the barn with you later."

Heat flushed her cheeks, and she was glad to get out of the car. "I think it's best if I keep Boss with me tonight. You know, if a situation comes up where we're separated."

"Oh, of course."

In the main house, Christina followed Grey into the kitchen and stopped in the doorway. Boss sat beside her and let his tongue loll out of his mouth. Christina inspected the kitchen, admiring the rustic elegance. Exposed beams, dark hardwood floors, oak cabinets, and miles of brown marble countertops. The entire wall opposite the island was floor-to-ceiling windows overlooking the sprawling backyard lit up with a huge white tent, the kind she'd only seen at weddings.

A woman in her early sixties with silver-streaked hair greeted Grey with a kiss on his cheek. She wore a stunning champagne-colored gown covered in intricate beaded lace, and her hair was pulled back in a graceful chignon. "Grey, it's so good to have you home. How are you feeling?" She lifted his chin and turned his head, examining his face.

"Hi, Mom. I'm fine. Happy anniversary."

"Leave the boy alone." A tall man with salt-and-pepper hair

and a thick mustache walked up and shook Grey's hand. "Looking good, son."

"Thanks, Dad. You too. I've never seen you in a tux. No hat tonight?"

"Not this time. Your mama's one request." He walked across the room and offered his hand to Christina. "Ma'am."

Grey turned his wheelchair around and moved beside Christina. He put his hand on the small of her back and a zip of electricity flew through her veins.

"Mom, Dad. This is my...Christina. I mean Christina Sherman. These are my parents, Rhett and Emma Parker."

Before either parent had a chance to respond, a woman crossed the room, arms extended. Her blonde hair was swept back into a chic bun, exposing a long neck and shapely shoulders, and she was dressed in a stunning black evening gown. "And I'm Ruby, Grey's sister." She wrapped Christina in a deep hug. Ruby pulled away, holding Christina by the arms and enrapturing her with the same stunning gray eyes as Grey's. "We are so pleased you're here. And look at how handsome Boss is tonight!" Ruby stroked Boss then planted a kiss on his head.

"The pleasure is all mine," Christina said. "Happy anniversary, Mr. and Mrs. Parker. You have a beautiful home."

"Thank you," Emma said. "Don't you look lovely this evening? We're so thankful you were able to come. I look forward to getting to know you."

Rhett lifted Christina's hand and kissed the back of it. His mustache tickled. "Thanks for taking care of my boy."

Ruby kissed Grey on the cheek. "The caterers delivered the food, and dinner will be served in an hour. The guests will be arriving in the next thirty minutes." She turned to her parents. "We have taken care of everything tonight. We want you both to mingle with your friends and enjoy your special day."

Ruby hooked an arm with Christina and tugged her forward. "So, Christina. Do you like horses?"

"I love horses. My friend takes in rescue horses at her place, and we ride together sometimes."

"Well, any time you want to come out here, we would *love* to have you."

"I appreciate the offer very much," Christina said. "I might take you up on that. I'd love to learn about the benefits of equine therapy. But for now, I think I'm going to take Boss on a short walk and leave you to have some much needed catch-up time with Grey before the party."

Christina took Boss outside and found Charlie checking the guests and their vehicles as they arrived. Like everyone else, he was dressed in black tie. "You sure clean up nice."

"I'll take that compliment, even though I know it's hard to look bad in a tux."

"Don't be so hard on yourself. I think the beard is a good look on you."

Charlie scratched his chin. When he was undercover, it looked scruffy, but tonight he had touched it up, shaving straight lines around his square jaw. "Thanks. Lizzie seemed to like it. She's on the perimeter, by the way."

"Good, keep an eye out for anyone with an Eastern European accent," Christina said. "I've emailed you photos and—"

"I've got it, I've got it. Go." Charlie shooed her away. "Have fun."

Christina headed to the backyard where the main event awaited. Glowing lanterns formed a lighted walkway leading from the parking lot to the open-air tent. Fairy lights overhead provided an otherworldly feeling. The round tables were covered in white tablecloths, soft candle-light, and china place settings with black and gold accents. A crystal chandelier was suspended over each table. The dreamy scene was beyond anything Christina had ever imagined.

Christina patted Boss's head and watched Grey and his parents greeting the guests.

Ruby slipped up beside her and linked her arm with Christina's again. "I've never seen my brother so happy and relaxed. What's going on between you two? That is, if you don't mind the big sister butting in."

Christina smiled and continued to watch Grey. "I'm not sure what you mean. I'm really here to help with Boss."

Christina eyed Wally as he sauntered toward them, thankful for the incoming interruption. She wasn't sure how to explain her growing relationship with Grey. If she was honest with herself, she was a little worried it was all too good to be true.

Wally smiled. "Well, don't you two look beautiful?"

"Marshall, how have you been?" Ruby asked.

"I'm great, sweetness. How 'bout yourself?" Wally leaned in to give Ruby a hug, awkwardly holding his drink above her shoulder with his good hand.

Ruby held his arm and looked him up and down. "You're as handsome as ever."

"You really do look great," Christina said.

"Why, thanks. It means something special coming from you," he said. "But if you'll excuse me for a moment, I think I'll go congratulate the happy couple. Christina, would you like me to take Boss for a while so you can enjoy the party?"

"That's a very nice offer, Wally, but I'm fine for now. I'll let you know if things change."

Christina smoothed Boss's tuxedo, then watched Wally make his way toward Rhett and Emma. He smiled and lifted his drink in greeting to various people along the way. His movements were casual, and she wondered how difficult life had become for the man with only the use of his left arm. A few times she'd noticed Wally using his right arm to steady himself like when Boss had knocked him over at the hospital. Was his injury similar to Grey's, allowing him occasional use?

"I didn't realize Wally knew your parents and so many guests," Christina said.

"Oh, yes. Wally and Grey were unit brothers. When Wally's wife died, he really leaned on Grey for comfort. I'm a psychiatrist and I mainly focus on children with PTSD, but I'm also contracted by Veteran Affairs. Wally turned to me for grief counseling. Obviously, those conversations are confidential, but we've become friends."

Why hadn't Grey mentioned any of this to her? The news dampened her spirit. Grey claimed to trust her, so why had he withheld this information? "I had no idea Wally was married."

Ruby frowned. "Grey didn't tell you?"

Christina pursed her lips and eyed Wally. He laughed at something Grey said, then put his drink on the table and clapped his friend on the back. "No, neither mentioned Wally had a wife or that she passed away. May I ask what happened?"

"I can tell you what Wally shared freely with our family. Her name was Dr. Michelle Wallace. She was a brilliant chemical engineer who died in a tragic lab accident."

"Grey didn't tell me any of this," she whispered.

"The worst part is that Michelle was eight months pregnant. A little girl. They were ecstatic. I even attended the baby shower with Grey." Ruby glanced at Wally and her lips quivered into a half smile. "The loss was devastating, as you can imagine. Wally was beside himself with grief."

Hundreds of questions poured into her mind all at once. Where was the lab? Did the accident have anything to do with Aberdeen? What about the research Wally was conducting?

Guests crowded the floor in clusters. She scanned the sea of black overcoats, searching for Grey, but she couldn't locate him in the mass of people.

"Ruby, come with me. I need you to tell me more." Christina gripped Ruby's elbow and steered her away from the string quartet playing nearby. She found empty chairs at a table in the corner of the tent and guided Ruby to sit.

Boss poked his nose under the edge of the drapery and sniffed before crawling underneath. He plopped down on the outside of the tent where he could lie in the cool grass rather than the hard tent flooring. Christina lifted the tent curtain and double checked that the leash was clipped to Boss's collar, then secured the leash under the leg of her chair.

She sat and scooted to the edge of her seat. "Listen, Ruby, I need you to tell me everything you know about Wally, Michelle, the accident. All of it."

FRIDAY, 5:23 P.M.

Grey mingled with his parents and the guests near the table of honor at the front of the tent. He was delighted to see so many friends and family members at the party to honor his parents. Former clients had traveled from all over the world to attend and Grey listened as one guest after another approached the happy couple and shared memories. His parents had built a life of love and respect. They treated everyone well, and it showed by the number of people who had come to honor and celebrate them.

His father clapped him on the shoulder and leaned in. "Listen, son, the night's gonna get away from us pretty quick. Come with me into the house for a minute. There's something I've been meaning to give you."

Grey followed his father through the throng of guests, pausing to say hello, shake a hand, or receive a hug on his way to the house. His father led Grey into the master bedroom, pausing to move the ottoman for Grey's wheelchair.

"I can't believe you guys still have that chair." The cognac leather armchair wore well after more than thirty years of use. A small table tucked in the corner beside the chair was piled with books and his mother's worn Bible.

His dad let out a contented sigh. "Your mama and I love this chair." His face softened, and he ran his calloused hand over the cushion. "Not because it's the most comfortable thing, nor because it looks particularly good anymore. We love this chair because it's where God hears our prayers and where He continues to answer them—not because of the chair, of course. We know He hears those regardless of where we pray. But the chair is sentimental and so we keep it."

"I hope to one day have what you and Mom have." Those were all the words he could muster. Somewhere, deep in his heart, Grey heard God saying He heard his prayers, even the ones he didn't verbalize.

His dad searched Grey's eyes. "Son, if you truly want a good life, you'll need to get you a chair just like this one and spend every day on your knees. And when you get married, do the same with your wife."

Grey stared at the chair and ottoman with its veins of creases from years of use. Christina deserved a chair like this. She deserved a man who would stay with her, good times and bad. He looked at the ottoman and imagined Christina on her knees with her Bible open and hands folded in prayer. A fire burned in his stomach at the idea that he could be the man she deserved.

He was starting to fall for her. No, he was already in love with her. With all his heart, he wanted to have a future with Christina. It meant being honest with her about his limitations, but she had shown him that she could handle it. He would be strong for her, and no matter what, he would keep talking to God.

Grey repositioned his chair. "That's great advice, Dad. I've recently started talking to God again, and I plan to keep it up."

"I'm glad to hear it, son. You know we've always been proud of you. I always knew you were strong and brave. I am amazed at your skill to train that dog. It's something I could never do."

Whoa, his dad thought he was a good handler? All his life he'd prayed to be like his dad, and God had answered. He just hadn't realized it. Not a cowboy, but a soldier. Not a horse trainer, but a dog handler. "Wow, Dad. That...that means a lot to me. More than you'll ever know."

His dad's laugh was a deep, throaty sound. "Well, son, I didn't intend to bring any of that up, but the Lord pressed it upon my heart." The man rested his large hand on Grey's shoulder and gave him a firm squeeze and a pat on the back. "Good, now I can do what I came here for. Then we'll be needing to get back to the party."

Rhett moved around the king-size bed and opened the nightstand drawer. "I know this might not be important to you right now, but God told me to give this to you tonight." Rhett turned and walked back to Grey. In his hands he held a thick Bible that looked as well used as the leather chair. Rhett placed the Bible in Grey's hands.

Grey swallowed. This worn Bible, with the tattered edges on the cover, was the one his dad read every day. The one he'd read from after dinner each night while the family was gathered around the table. The one he'd pulled out to read from when he needed to give Grey a lecture on obedience and living a daily life worthy of God.

"Dad, this is your Bible. You've had it all my life. I can't take this. You still need it."

His father placed a hand on Grey's shoulder and looked deep into his eyes. "Son, you need this more than I do." His voice was strong and serious. "Besides, your mom bought me a brand new Bible for our anniversary."

He pointed to the new leather Bible resting on his nightstand. His reading glasses were right on top.

Grey looked at the Bible in his lap and ran his fingers over the gold-embossed letters. Rhett Greyson Parker. Somehow holding the Bible made him feel bigger, stronger. A man worthy of a full life with everything God had in store for him.

Grey eyed his dad's new Bible. It would be well worn in a matter of weeks. Next to it, a clear tube attached to a mask caught his attention. "Hey, Dad, what's that?" Grey pointed to the device.

"Oh, this? It's my new CPAP machine. Apparently, I have sleep apnea. It's why I've been snoring my whole life." Rhett chuckled. "This thing is amazing. I'm finally able to sleep through the night and wake up feeling rested. It goes on like this." Rhett placed the oxygen mask over his nose and mouth in demonstration.

Grey's heart stopped cold. Images flickered through his mind and a dark realization took shape. Wally had had his gas mask on *before* the explosion. He was ready for Dr. Kalashnik to release the X-VX. That was why the doctor had nodded to Wally. And that was why Wally had slipped his gas mask over his face before the explosion.

No! No, it couldn't be true. Could it?

"Grey." His dad snapped his fingers in front of Grey's eyes and waved. "Son, are you okay?"

The room came back into focus, but Grey's heart thundered like the hooves of a thousand horses. "I know what happened."

Grey didn't bother to explain. He spun his chair around and thrust his wheels forward. He had to find Christina. He had to tell her what he remembered.

25

Christina was utterly flabbergasted at the story Ruby was sharing with her, and she had to keep herself from rushing Ruby through it. How had this never come up in all her time with Grey? Now that she thought about it, Grey *had* started to talk about Wally, but she'd redirected the conversation.

"While Wally was deployed, his wife, Michelle, was a chemical engineer at the Aberdeen Proving Grounds in Maryland," Ruby said. "She worked in the CBRN Command and Control laboratory at the Army Medical Research Institute for Chemical Defense."

Christina's eyes went wide. The same laboratory where all three victims worked.

"According to Wally, Michelle developed the formula for a new drug she called The Scavenger, a vaccine that could fight the effects of nerve agents."

The Scavenger. Her blood ran cold at the name. The same name on the poems left with the victims. Part of her wanted to launch to her feet and find Wally right this second, but she couldn't run off without all the intel. Not yet.

Ruby sighed. "Wally said the drug was nowhere near ready, but Michelle's supervisor ordered it to be tested on active duty soldiers. Grey and Wally's unit was one. Michelle thought it was too risky and had too much at stake personally if they tested it on Wally, so she threatened to go public. A few days later, there was an explosion in the lab that killed fourteen employees, including Michelle and her unborn baby girl."

Christina shook her head. "That's tragic." She couldn't tell Ruby that Wally was working on the same vaccine. It was top secret.

Ruby took a sip of water and watched her finger slide around the rim of her glass. "Wally took leave to come home and bury his wife and child." She sighed. "But Wally returned to duty before the investigation about the explosion was completed."

"What did the investigation reveal?"

"This is where things get worse." Ruby looked up and pinned Christina with her clear gray eyes. "They claimed Michelle was a traitor working with the Russians and the explosion wasn't an accident. They blamed Michelle and said she intentionally caused the lab accident but died in the process."

Christina gripped a butter knife in her hand and pressed the bottom of it into the table. It took every ounce of strength to stay seated while Ruby finished her story. "What did Wally do?"

"Well, he was livid, of course. He knew Michelle wasn't working with the Russians, and she certainly would not have killed those people and risked the life of their child. He tried to get someone to listen, but...then six months later Grey and Wally were injured and sent home for good. We always thought it was a strange coincidence that both Grey and Wally were injured in a chemical weapons attack so soon after Michelle had died in a chemical weapons research laboratory."

Christina didn't think it was a coincidence at all. Was it possible Wally was involved in the X-VX killings here in Columbia? Wally was a researcher. He was at every crime scene, caught in the gunfire with Grey and in just as much danger as Grey. And the man at the university who gave his belt to help Cathy Wright could use both arms. Was there someone trying to tie up loose ends by killing everyone involved with the Aberdeen laboratory, including Wally?

"Christina, are you all right?" Ruby asked. "You look flushed, and you're breathing hard. Here, have some water."

"No thank you, I'm fine. You've been a huge help. I'm processing everything you've told me."

"I hope I haven't broken privilege with anything I've said." Ruby's eyes sparked with concern.

"It's okay, Ruby. I do have a question though. I scoured the internet for information on Aberdeen. How come I didn't find any news articles about the accident?"

Ruby bit her lower lip and seemed to consider her words. "I think if you asked Wally, he would tell you the government covered it up because they were the ones who caused the explosion. Several people escaped the lab, and to hear Wally talk about it, they stole Michelle's work."

The poem. *This is one of many marks. I will kill more until you bring to light what you've done in the dark.*

The poem was about a cover-up. The Scavenger was killing people involved in the cover-up.

Christina jumped to her feet. "I've got to find Grey." She whirled around and bumped into Grey, nearly falling onto him. "Where's Wally?"

Grey frowned, his face ruddy and shimmering with perspiration. "I was about to ask you the same thing."

"Ruby just told me Wally's wife was killed at Aberdeen. I think he's The Scavenger and he's killing everyone involved in covering it up." Her words came tumbling out.

Grey ran a hand over his hair. "Yeah, I know. I don't know why I didn't put it together until tonight," he growled. "You know that nagging thing I couldn't put my finger on? Well, I think I've figured it out. Wally is working with the Russians and he set us up for the ambush in Siberia."

"We've got to find him." Christina pulled her phone out and called Lizzie. While she waited for it to connect, she said, "Ruby, I need you to take Boss and lock yourselves somewhere safe." Christina held up a finger and spoke into the phone. "Lizzie, Wally is The Scavenger. I need you to take Ruby and Boss and—"

"I'm right here." Lizzie clutched the end of her long red dress and jogged up, her long brown hair swaying with each step.

Christina disconnected the call. "Take Boss and Ruby and get them someplace safe. Call the others. If they see Wally, detain him."

Lizzie nodded and began dialing.

Ruby lifted the tent curtain and looked underneath. "Where's Boss?"

Christina crouched and looked, but Boss wasn't there. The leash was still looped around the leg of her chair and led to the other side of the tent. She yanked the leash but it was no longer clipped to his collar. A spike of nausea shot through her stomach.

Boss was gone.

"Christina, where's Boss?" Grey's voice was loud and angry. "Where's Boss?"

Christina's chair blocked Grey's path and he knocked it out of his way. It fell against the table, sending glass and silverware to the floor with a crash. He rolled his chair up to Christina's knees and snatched the tent curtain from her hands. With one strong motion, he tore the thick fabric from its metal clips and flung it to the ground. The lights attached to the tent frame came down with the curtain and dangled behind his head. Several guests turned and gaped at them, but with nothing more dramatic to see, they returned to their conversations.

Indignation flashed in Grey's eyes and his nostrils flared. "You were supposed to be guarding him!"

Christina's heart crashed to the bottom of her stomach. She didn't have time to think about the horrible mistake—she had to find Wally. It would be near impossible to pick him out of a sea of black and white tuxedos at night with the dim lighting. "Grey, I'm sorry. I don't see—"

"You *lost* him." Grey's voice was strained. "I trusted you with him and now he's *gone!* I knew I shouldn't have left him with you. I knew—" He snapped his mouth shut and worked his jaw.

Before Christina could respond, he turned his wheelchair around and shoved the wheels hard, leaving her standing there. Her heart thundered in her chest and her mouth hung open. She watched Grey's back disappear into the crowd.

Lizzie took Ruby by the elbow. "C'mon, Ruby, let's go find your parents. Christina, I'll stick with them while the rest of you find Wally and Boss."

Christina nodded and left to locate Grey. Party guests conversed in small crowds. The scene Grey had made by tearing down the curtain went unacknowledged, and she was grateful, because the last thing she needed was a crowd of people getting in the way. She spun in a circle but didn't see him. Then through the tent door she caught a glimpse of his back. He was already in the parking lot.

She ran to catch him before he could disappear into the darkened field of parked cars. Laila had been right—Christina's dress was more than accommodating for running the short distance.

Christina stepped in front of Grey's wheelchair, where he was looking at his phone. "Grey, I'll find Boss. I think he's with Wally and they couldn't have gone far."

Grey looked up from his phone. "Yeah I know, but it's too late, Christina. I trusted you, and now Boss is gone."

The disappointment in his eyes was like a dagger to her heart. He tried to steer around her, but she stepped in his way again.

"It's not too late. We can find him. Trust me."

"I did trust you." His eyes held hers.

She blew out a breath. "Listen, Boss needs us. We have a job to do. Let me help you."

Grey wanted to rage some more against Christina for losing Boss. How could she have been so distracted? The loss was a kick to his stomach and one he didn't expect. Not tonight. How could this happen tonight?

His blood boiled but he could set that aside for Boss's sake. "Fine. I need to find Boss and get him back before Wally does something stupid. As soon as this is over, we need to talk."

Hurt flashed in her eyes, but she nodded. "I'll call Charlie. Can you get the car?"

Grey summoned his Tesla and Christina dialed Charlie while they waited for the car to appear. "Put it on speaker," he said.

"Charlie—" Christina started but the man cut her off.

"Wally left ten minutes ago. I'm sorry, Christina, I didn't think anything about it."

"Did he have Boss with him?" Christina asked.

"I didn't look closely," Charlie said. "I waved him through when I recognized him."

Laila appeared beside Christina. "The family is fine. Lizzie has them secured, and Grey's parents don't know what's going on. One of the servers said she saw a man leaving with Boss. Sounded like Wally."

"Yeah, I've got Charlie saying the same thing."

The Tesla rolled to a stop in front of them. "Boss has a microchip and I can track him. Let's just hope Wally keeps Boss with him."

"Do you think he will..." Christina hesitated. "Would Wally hurt Boss?"

"No, Boss is too valuable. If Wally has a connection with the Russians like I think he does, he will most likely sell Boss to them. Or maybe he already has. For all I know, he's been trying to get Boss for a while now."

Christina nodded. "That would make sense. He's always asking if he can take Boss off your hands."

A pang of guilt stabbed Grey in the stomach. All those times Wally was at the crime scenes, he'd steered clear of Boss. When they were at the hospital, Boss had put his paw up near Wally as if he was trying to tell Grey that something was wrong. It wasn't Boss giving a false read or signals because Wally worked in the laboratory with X-VX.

How could Grey have been so stupid? A knot formed in his stomach. Boss had tried to warn him, but Grey had missed it. *Again.* Not only that, but there were other clues that pointed to Wally's guilt. Like the fact that in the middle of the gunfire, he had stood statue-still instead of taking cover.

His phone beeped and Grey looked at the screen. "I've got him. He's on his way to downtown Columbia."

"I'll call Bree on the way," said Christina. "Charlie, stay with Grey—"

"I'm coming with you."

"This is your parents' anniversary party, Grey. We can take care of this. I can get Boss back for you." Her eyes pleaded with his. "I promise. Just trust me."

Grey shook his head. "I'm going with you. Boss is my partner and my best friend. He's my responsibility."

Christina only hesitated for a moment. "Laila, follow us.

Charlie, make sure nothing happens to Mr. and Mrs. Parker. If they ask, tell them Grey is on call and responding to an issue but he'll be back as soon as he can."

"And tell Ruby to go ahead and give my parents the surprise. I don't want anything to get in the way of their special night." He regretted he would miss seeing their faces the moment they saw their car, but stopping Wally was more important.

Grey wasn't sure what Wally was up to, but he could be planning something big. Much bigger than the minor explosion in Siberia. He lifted himself into the driver's seat of his Tesla then remembered the Bible. He'd tucked it behind his back. He leaned over and grabbed it from his wheelchair. As the robotic arm pulled his wheelchair into the back, Grey laid his hand on the Bible and said a silent prayer.

God, protect my family and help me stop Wally before it's too late. Thank You for sending Christina. I guess You were listening to me even when I wasn't speaking.

When he finished his prayer, he handed the Bible to Christina, who'd slid into the passenger seat. "Please put this somewhere safe. I don't want anything to happen to it."

Christina's puzzled expression didn't escape his notice. She was probably wondering why he'd hidden a Bible in his wheelchair. He hoped he would have the opportunity to explain it to her after this was all over.

26

FRIDAY, 7:01 P.M.

Nerves prickling, Christina stared at Grey's phone as the Tesla sped down the highway toward downtown Columbia. The map with Boss's tracking device indicated he was stopped at the Empire Hotel and she prayed he would stay there until they could reach him.

Christina used her own phone to call Bree and put it on speaker so Grey could listen. As soon as the call connected, Christina blurted it out. "Wally is The Scavenger."

"What? What are you talking about?" Bree asked.

"No time to explain the whole thing, so listen closely. Wally's wife was killed in Aberdeen, and he orchestrated the ambush in Siberia so he could come home and take his revenge. He's the one sending the notes to Governor Winston and killing people with X-VX." Christina glanced at the map on Grey's phone again. "Wally has Boss right now. We're tracking them through Boss's microchip. It looks like he's stopped at the Empire Hotel."

"The Empire Hotel? That's where I am."

"What? What are you doing there?"

"Governor Winston is announcing his run for president to a room packed with a thousand people," Bree said. "The Coroner's Office had a table and Francisco asked me to be his plus one."

Christina shared a look with Grey. "I forgot that event was tonight. Olivia is there on the protection detail and the place should be crawling with SLED agents."

Bree said something that Christina couldn't hear. "I didn't catch that, Bree."

"I was talking to Francisco. He's calling Quinn now. We can take it from here," she said. "Don't you go getting involved."

Grey shook his head, then pointed to the map on his Tesla. They were exiting the highway and would be at the hotel in two minutes.

"Bree, Wally has Boss. We've got to find him before Wally does something stupid. We're pulling in now."

Christina heard Bree talking to Francisco again. She came back to the phone. "Quinn is right behind you. He'll be here in five minutes. Wait for me at the VIP entrance in the back. I'll let SLED know you're here. What are you driving?"

"We're in Grey's black Tesla X. One minute away." Christina disconnected the call before Bree could tell her to stay in the car. She wasn't about to let Wally get away. Once Boss was safe, Christina had every intention of finding Wally.

"I don't understand this," Grey said.

"I think Wally's out for revenge."

"I get that part, but what's this have to do with the guy who tried to break into my house, or whoever was shooting at us?"

Grey had a good point. Was there someone else involved? "Do you think Wally hired muscle to scare you away from the crime scenes? To keep Boss from detecting the X-VX?"

Grey shook his head. "That doesn't make sense. Wally was already at the crime scene. He could have told Francisco that the victims didn't meet the criteria for X-VX poisoning. He didn't have to call me at all."

"So Wally was trying to draw you to the crime scene." Christina chewed her bottom lip. But why? "What happens to Boss if you die?" The question made Christina's stomach roll. She didn't want to think about it.

Grey pulled off the highway and drummed his thumbs on the steering wheel waiting for the red light to change. "I guess if I'd been killed at the basketball game, Wally would have taken Boss home with him and no one would have given it a second thought"

"Just like that?"

He shrugged. "It's not like Wally doesn't have the security clearance."

"I can't believe they'd let him go so easily."

"He has a history with Boss," Grey said. "Wally even applied to take him after Siberia. Back when they weren't sure if I'd want him. But how does Winston factor into all this?"

Christina huffed a laugh. "I read his biography. He was the Commander in Chief of the Army Medical Research Institute for Chemical Defense during the time Michelle would have worked there. He was elected governor two months after the accident."

Grey's eyes darted to Christina then back to the road. "Yeah, I think I remember the news saying his investigation into the so-called traitor at the lab put him over the top." His jaw muscles flexed.

The light turned green, and Grey punched the accelerator, rounding the corner hard.

"At the next road, turn left," Christina said.

Grey sped along the outer road around the hotel and turned into a private parking lot behind the convention center where a sea of black SUVs spanned the darkened lot. He stopped in the aisle and they both looked for signs of Wally.

Grey pointed to a stretch limo parked near a metal door leading into the back of the building. "That must be the VIP entrance."

Christina checked the phone. "According to the tracker, Boss should be there." She pointed over her shoulder at a dark-colored van parked along a row of trees at the edge of the lot. "I think he's in that vehicle."

"That's not Wally's car. It looks like the van from the other night."

Grey pulled the car alongside the limo and parked. The Falcon doors opened and the whir of a motor signaled the robotic arm was lowering his wheelchair to the ground. Sirens wailed in the distance.

"Quinn should be here any minute. Bree alerted SLED, and every agent inside should be looking for Wally."

Through the passenger window, she scanned the top of the nearby buildings and spotted two SLED agents on the roof of the hotel. The parking lot was motionless. So far, no sign of anyone else.

Grey shut the vehicle off. "Go inside and find Wally. I'll find Boss."

Christina put her hand on his arm. "Hold up. Wally could have a sniper waiting for us or rigged the car to explode. Let me get Boss, then we'll *both* go inside." She had already lost Boss— she wouldn't risk losing Grey.

"No way," he said. "It's too dangerous. Wally is off his rocker and there's no telling what he'll do."

"I'm going. Wait here."

"Boss is my dog. I should be the one to get him."

She bristled. Was that a jab at her mistake? She pinched the bridge of her nose. "We don't have time for this."

"Christina, I can handle this. You've got my back, right?"

"Absolutely."

"Then go stop Wally while I get Boss. You'll be much faster, so just *go*."

"Fine." Christina slipped the Sig from the leg holster strapped to her thigh.

Grey's eyebrows went up when he saw her weapon.

"Keep your witty remarks to yourself," she said with a smile. She slide-checked her gun and turned to Grey. "I'll go inside and try to find Wally. You get Boss. We're going to need him to locate the X-VX."

Grey let out a long breath and nodded. "Watch your six."

She narrowed her eyes at him. "I'm the bodyguard here, remember?"

"Yeah, I know—"

The corner of her mouth turned up in a half smile. She gave his hand a quick squeeze. "I'll see you inside."

She slipped out of the car and pressed her back against the door until it clicked shut. A shiver ran down her spine. The short party dress was doing nothing to fight against the chilly February wind that had kicked up in the last hour. She slipped behind the Tesla and watched the darkened parking lot for movement. Nothing.

With one last look at Grey, she said a prayer and sprinted toward the building.

Grey took his time getting into his wheelchair, keeping an eye out for any sign of Wally in the dark parking lot. The transition from his car to his chair was the most vulnerable position he could be in with a potential attacker lurking. There were too many shadows, too many oversized dark cars to hide behind, and he didn't want to take any extra chances.

He headed toward the van, keeping the building on his right and the parked cars on his left. At least this way he had protection on one side. He'd give anything to have a weapon right about now. It didn't even have to be his military-issued M16. At this point, he'd take that tiny little subcompact Christina had hidden under her dress.

An involuntary smile crept to his face at the image of Christina hiking her dress up about six inches above her knee to reveal her leg holster. She'd moved so fast he'd barely had a glimpse, but it had taken him by surprise. Even with danger all around and Boss in the hands of the friend who'd betrayed him, the woman continued to amaze him. When he'd seen Boss's empty leash lying on the ground, he'd almost lost control. But if Wally hadn't taken Boss, would they have been here in time to stop whatever he had planned?

Flashing lights caught his attention as an unmarked sedan screeched to a halt near his Tesla. He spun his chair around at the sound of a familiar voice.

"You gotta get those people outta there," Quinn yelled into his phone. "I'm telling you, we've got a suspect with a chemical weapon." He paused. "No, we can't confirm it, but you've got a detective with the Columbia PD telling you. Isn't that enough? Oh, for crying out loud." Quinn disconnected the call and put his phone in his jacket pocket.

He jogged over to Grey. "They won't evacuate until they confirm the suspect is actually inside."

"By then it could be too late."

Quinn stared at him. "Thanks for that, Captain Obvious. You better pray Christina and Bree get eyes on him fast. Now where's your dog?"

Grey pointed to the van. "I think he's in that vehicle."

"I've got you covered. Go get him." Quinn pulled his gun and nodded for Grey to go.

Grey moved quicker with an armed detective on his heels. The sound of Boss's deep bark reverberated inside the vehicle. He was not happy. The van rocked slightly and Grey imagined

Boss was pacing or walking in a circle trying to figure a way out. Heat flushed through Grey when he saw Wally hadn't bothered to crack a window to give the dog fresh air.

They scanned the area before they crossed to the van parallel parked along the curb at the edge of the lot.

"It's clear," Quinn said.

Grey moved to the back door, but he couldn't see anything through the blacked out windows. "Hang on, Boss. I'm here. I'll get you out of there, buddy."

Quinn reached for the door handle.

"Stop!" Grey yelled. "It could be wired with explosives." At this point, he wouldn't put anything past Wally.

The detective's eyes went wide, and he pulled his hand back.

"I've got a search mirror in my bag," Grey said. "Do you have your Maglite?"

"Yep." Quinn snapped the light on.

"Go to the side with the curb and search the underside. I'll check from here."

Quinn stepped into the grass and crouched beside the van. A beam of light moved from the rear tires toward the front, and Grey followed along using the mirror to check for wires or anything taped to the chassis.

Boss barked louder, this time snarling and growling in frustration.

Grey heard a loud grunt and the metal flashlight clattered to the ground. He swung his mirror toward the sound and watched the light roll to a stop under the van. A beam of light fell on Quinn's face.

Before Grey could move, a strong arm wrapped around his throat and into a headlock.

27

FRIDAY, 7:41 P.M.

After searching through endless supply closets and the employee locker rooms, Christina was losing hope. Wally was nowhere to be found.

She checked her watch. By now Quinn and the rest of the officers should be here for backup. But why wasn't SLED evacuating the building, or at least patrolling these areas? Anyone could sneak in the back door just like she had. This was a serious oversight, but at the moment it worked to her advantage.

Thankful for Olivia's dress and comfortable shoes, she ran down the corridor and slowed at the L-shaped intersection. A round mirror mounted on the ceiling gave her a view of the empty hallway. She rounded the corner and ran to a set of double doors. Through the small circular windows, she could see a bustling kitchen. She lowered her weapon and concealed it against her leg.

The kitchen staff didn't seem to notice her entering. "Hey, did any of you see a man come through here? About five-ten, short brown hair, and a full beard? He may have been dressed in a tuxedo."

A woman chopping vegetables paused and pointed her knife toward the door behind her.

Christina took off and shouldered the swinging door. It stopped short when it hit something on the other side.

"Ow!"

She cringed, hoping she hadn't just knocked a waitress off her feet. She caught the swinging door with one hand as it came back toward her. With her other hand, she tightened her grip on her weapon. She pulled the door toward her and peeked around the edge.

Bree stood on the other side, rubbing her shoulder. What in the world? Christina stepped through the door and for a split second they blinked at each other. She almost didn't recognize Bree in the floor length, silver sequined ball gown, her dark hair curled and falling in waves down her back instead of the usual ponytail. The detective was stunning.

"What are you doing here?" Bree asked. "I thought I told you to wait for me."

"I came to find you. What's going on? Have you found Wally yet?"

Bree shook her head. "There are over a thousand people here. SLED is refusing to evacuate. Winston wants his moment in the spotlight."

"If we don't find Wally, he just might have more spotlight than he bargained for."

Bree looked down the wide hallway. "There are too many doors leading to who knows where. It's going to take forever to check them all."

"Well, we'd better get started." Christina raced to the first door and pressed her back against the wall.

Bree withdrew her compact gun from her clutch and tossed the purse on the floor. She took up position on the opposite side of the doorway and held her weapon up. After a deep breath, she nodded to Christina to open the door.

Christina flung the door open and moved out of the way.

Bree stepped in the entry and cleared the room with her gun raised. "Clear."

They cleared three more rooms before Christina heard muffled sounds of music and voices. "It sounds like it's coming from the main ballroom."

"We should be getting close to a dressing room or the reception room," Bree said. "Wally could be hiding in any of them."

Bree stepped forward and grabbed the next doorknob.

There was a sound of crackling and Bree crumpled to the ground.

"Bree!"

For a second, the detective said nothing, and Christina searched her body for blood. Nothing. She patted her cheek. "Bree!"

The woman roused, coming to with a start, a gasp. "Oh!" She grabbed Christina's hand. "Oh, wow. I forgot what that felt like."

"What—?"

"Taser. He tased the door and now...shoot, I can't move my legs. Leave me here. I'll be okay. But, Christina." She took a breath, her voice low. "Be careful. Who knows what other booby traps are out there."

Right. She'd never missed Boss more in her life. "Call for backup. I'll get him."

Viktor Sokolovich had made a big mistake by engaging Grey in close combat. The arm around his throat was strong, but with a few quick jabs to the man's head, Viktor had released Grey and stepped back to put distance between them. Grey pushed his wheelchair back until he was directly behind the van. His pulse pounded in his ears and his hands gripped the wheels of his chair.

Viktor snarled at Grey. "What are you going to do without your friend, hmm?"

Grey stole a quick glance at the shadowy figure of Quinn, facedown on the grass beside the van. His gun lay on the ground near the back tire. Grey worried he might be dead, but there was no time to check. He didn't dare take his eyes off the Russian for an instant.

"I can take you sitting down," Grey taunted.

Boss's barking grew louder, and the sound of his nails scratching the window told Grey he was ready to fight, if only he could get out.

From out of nowhere, a thick arm lashed out like a viper strike. The Russian threw his entire weight behind the punch. Grey shifted his head to the right and blocked with his left arm. He captured Viktor's hand and twisted his wrist backward until he heard a cracking sound. Viktor let out a scream of pain and stumbled forward. As he moved past the wheelchair, Grey landed a hard hammer strike to his kidney.

He whirled his chair around to face him and backed up. The big man scrambled to his feet and this time ran forward with both arms outstretched. Grey turned his chair and blocked both arms with his left. The sweeping motion turned Viktor's momentum, and Grey thrust the heel of his hand upward into Victor's solar plexus, knocking the wind out of him.

The Russian was on his knees, coughing. He crawled forward and Grey realized he was going for Quinn's gun.

With a thrust of his wheels, Grey nailed him with the sharp edge of his foot plate. Viktor flinched and landed on his stomach with a grunt. He stretched out and wrapped his hand around Quinn's gun.

Grey backed up in a half circle and positioned himself on the passenger side of the van. Viktor surged to his feet, still coughing. Grey would have taken pleasure in the sound, but now the Russian had a gun and things were getting serious.

He saw Viktor's arm first, then the man stepped in front of Grey and leveled the pistol at him. He sneered. "Not so tough now, are you?"

Okay, this was bad. If he didn't get close, Grey couldn't disarm him. If he pushed his chair, Viktor would squeeze the trigger.

Boss lunged at the passenger side window, his lips and teeth pressing against the glass.

"Maybe I shoot your dog first?" Viktor took two steps forward and pointed the gun at Boss.

Grey took the opportunity to strike. He shoved his chair forward and grabbed Viktor's gun hand, lifting it up and away from Boss's head. The gun went off and the sound shattered the night. He ignored the ringing in his ears and slammed the palm of his hand against Viktor's wrist. Once, twice, three times. He couldn't break his grip.

Viktor brought the gun down toward Grey's face, but Grey's upper body strength was far greater, and he put all his muscle behind pushing back against Viktor. When the gun was clear of Grey's head, he curled the tips of his fingers toward his palm and knuckle punched the Russian in the throat with vicious force.

Viktor released the gun and grabbed his throat with both hands. His eyes went wide, and his mouth fell open, gasping for breath. Grey gripped the gun and aimed it at the red-faced man.

Quinn stepped around the van, rubbing the back of his head. "What the—" His eyes narrowed at the Russian now on his knees, still clutching his throat and wheezing with each breath.

"You okay?" Grey asked.

The detective ignored the question. "What did you do to him?" His eyes snapped to Grey. "Is that my gun?"

"Yeah, you dropped it when you took your little nap." Grey

grinned and offered the weapon to Quinn, who snatched it and holstered it.

"Just get your dog. I'll take care of this," Quinn grumbled. He cuffed the Russian and sat him on the curb behind the van.

Grey pulled the door handle. "Locked."

"Locked here too," Quinn said from the driver's side. "Call Boss to your side, and I'll break the window."

"Boss, stay." The dog stopped barking and sat down in the passenger seat, his panting breath fogging up the window.

Quinn used the butt of his gun to shatter the driver's side window and reached a hand inside. Grey heard the click of the locks and yanked the door open. Boss launched himself from the van and landed on Grey's lap, knocking his wheelchair back.

"Okay, okay." Grey laughed. "Boss, you're okay." He patted Boss on his side and scratched behind his ears.

Boss licked Grey's face and neck and nudged him with his wet nose.

Now that Boss was safe, it was time to stop Wally.

A patrol car pulled in hot, lights flashing. Two officers jumped out and took over with Viktor.

Quinn was yelling into his phone again. "I've got the Russian who tried to kill Winston." He paused. "Yeah, he's right here but his partner is inside. You've got to—" Quinn muttered something under his breath and shoved his phone in his pocket.

"Have they evacuated the building?" Grey asked.

Quinn shook his head. "Not yet. They're still searching for Wally."

"C'mon, we've got to get in there."

"What are you talking about? You're not a soldier anymore. We can't just charge in there—" The detective winced at his own words. "I didn't mean it like that, man."

"Did you stop to think, maybe they haven't found him because he dropped a bomb and left? If Wally is planning to detonate a bomb with X-VX, Boss will find it." Grey pushed his

chair in front of Quinn until they were inches apart. "I'm taking Boss inside. Don't you *dare* try and stop me."

Grey didn't give Quinn time to argue. He took off as fast as his arms could propel his chair forward. Quinn still sprinted faster and reached the door in time to open it.

Grey pulled the silly tuxedo off Boss and smoothed out his coat. "Okay, Boss. Let's go to work."

At the word "work," the dog's tail wagged, and he put his nose to the ground. Boss took off running down a hall unleashed, leaving Grey and Quinn to chase after him. Boss pressed his nose to the bottom of a door and looked at Grey.

"I've got this." Quinn looked through the round window. "Kitchen."

As if reading Quinn's mind, a worker pointed to a door, but Boss was already heading in that direction. Grey opened the door for Boss and the dog sprinted down the wide corridor. Boss ran with long strides, his muscles rippling with each step. The carpet slowed Grey and it took more strength to keep up with the galloping dog. If only he had his basketball chair.

Boss stopped halfway through one of the open doors near the end of the hall, his tail swinging. The back half of the dog pranced with excitement. What was he doing?

When Grey reached the door, he sucked in a breath.

Bree sat on the floor with her legs out in front of her. She held up her hands against Boss's licking and nose nudges. "Okay, okay, Boss. Thanks. I'm okay."

Quinn darted to her and dropped to his knees, placing his hand on her shoulder. "What happened? Are you all right?"

"Someone rigged a Taser to the doorknob. I got quite a shock when I touched it. I'm fine and have already called it in. Just needed to catch my breath."

"SLED hasn't evacuated," Quinn said. "When you've got your legs under you, can you get out to the main ballroom and help Olivia?"

She nodded. "I can do that."

"Where's Christina?" Grey asked.

"Through that door." Bree pointed behind her. "She went that way."

Grey frowned. "By herself?"

"Yeah, but—"

Grey didn't wait for Bree to finish. "Boss, seek."

FRIDAY, 8:06 P.M.

Wally stood in a long receiving line, shifting his weight from foot to foot. He'd paid two thousand dollars to have his photo taken with Governor Winston in a private ballroom and the ability to speak with him for a few moments. A *campaign contribution*, they'd said. What a joke.

The special receiving room was a who's who of South Carolina's wealthiest and most powerful people. He looked around the room and recognized an actor from a superhero movie and a former NFL linebacker. Plenty of other actors and actresses local to South Carolina chatted while they waited for their photo op. They thought they were something, but little did they know their riches were nothing compared to the three female billionaires in the room.

He snorted at the irony. Billionaire Zanita Hudson, owner of the world's largest chemical manufacturing company, stood in the corner surrounded by her own personal security team.

But the cost of the photo was nothing compared to the twenty-five thousand dollars the elite had plunked down for a seat at the top tables in the ballroom. Yet another tax-deductible *campaign contribution.*

He was careful to control himself despite how antsy he was. The crowd around him buzzed with conversation, but he easily tuned it out. The thrumming of his pulse kept him on high alert for anyone who might look at him with suspicion. He gripped his leather messenger bag tight in one hand. Inside his bag was a special treat just for Governor Winston.

The explosive detection dog that had checked him on the way in had ignored him. Oh, he had a bomb all right. But it was unlike anything they were expecting. That was another reason he'd gotten Boss out of the way tonight. The dog would have alerted to his bag and blown his entire plan. That bodyguard Grey hired had almost ruined everything. She'd put herself between his muscle and Grey one too many times, but it didn't matter anymore.

As the saying went, if you wanted something done right, you had to do it yourself. There was no need to kill Grey to get to Boss now. All he'd had to do was wait for Bodyguard Barbie to get distracted with her girl talk at the party. Once he'd seen the opportunity, he'd taken it. He'd simply unclipped Boss's leash and attached his own to the dog's collar. Boss was hesitant to come at first, but Wally had told the dog to come, and he'd obeyed. Simple as that.

The line moved up and Wally stepped into the opened space.

With the dog out of the way, Wally would finally make Governor Winston pay. As soon as it was his turn to have his photo taken, he would reach into his bag and release the X-VX. A simple aerosol can would spray with enough force to ensure the X-VX would cover the room and seep into the air vents, poisoning anyone inside the building.

Governor Winston and all of the socialite friends here to flaunt their power and wealth would die within seconds. These "friends" of Winston deserved to die as much as the governor did. Friends who would stop at nothing to get their man into political office. Friends who would lie for him and cover up for him. But tonight, they would all die right here in the ugly world they had created.

Except him, of course. He had the vaccine.

He sighed. Well, maybe the hundreds of guests sitting down to dinner in the massive conference hall would only suffer the same fate as Grey. A little paralysis. It didn't seem to slow Grey down too much. A small price to pay for their support of Winston.

As soon as Wally completed his task here, he would walk out the back door and drive Boss to his new owner. The buyer was planning on cloning Boss and creating an army of highly intelligent canines. They would be capable of protecting the Russian military and their interests against the American version of X-VX.

He didn't care what they did with the dog—he just wanted his paycheck. In truth, the real money would come when he got paid for the Scavenger drug formula. Michelle had been so close to perfecting it before she'd died but never realized it. His beautiful, brilliant wife. It was difficult to think of her without wondering what might have been. Where would he be right now if Winston hadn't killed Michelle? Mia would be two, a sweet chubby toddler. A stabbing pain in his stomach made him clench his teeth and he pushed the thought away.

Thanks to Dr. Kalashnik and his X-VX, this would all end tonight. It had to. The crazy old scientist had gotten himself caught, and Wally had had to get rid of him before anyone could connect the dots.

Wally clenched his fist around the bag with the deadly X-VX bomb inside. The last of the chemical weapon was right here, and now that the Scavenger vaccine was complete, Wally would have buyers clamoring to get their hands on it.

Wally had found Michelle's research hidden in her home

office the day after he'd buried his wife and daughter. The Petrov Bratva had sent Dr. Kalashnik and some disposable goons to test it. Thanks to Grey and his involuntary participation in the trial, they'd realized the vaccine formula was only partially correct.

Two years of development and a few "trial runs" with well-deserving test subjects, and it was perfected. Wally ground his teeth as he remembered watching Wright writhe on the floor. She'd deserved it for what she'd done. So had the others.

Wally took three long strides forward and fixed his eyes on the smiling Winston posing for a photo. It would have been nice to have watched that posed face die from a bullet at the basketball game, but this was better. Now that Wally was immune to the effects of X-VX, he could enjoy watching him die a slow, painful death.

And by this time tomorrow, The Scavenger would be long gone.

This plan could not be stopped.

He'd seen to it himself.

29

Christina moved into the crowded room and spotted Wally standing in a line of women dressed in ball gowns and men decked out in tuxedos. He had attempted to disguise himself with a stylish hat and gold-rimmed spectacles. The only reason she recognized him was because she had expected him to do this very thing.

In the opposite corner, a SLED agent stood with his hands clasped in front of him, scanning the room, but thanks to Wally's simple disguise, the agent's eyes drifted past him several times.

She used her Bluetooth earbud to connect a call to Quinn. "I found Wally. He's in some sort of receiving line for Governor Winston. I only see one agent in the room, but he hasn't spotted the suspect yet."

"Copy that," Quinn said. "Is he armed?"

"I think so. He has a messenger bag. Pretty sure there's nothing but bad news in it."

"Okay, I'll evacuate the main ballroom as quietly as we can. Don't spook him, Christina. He could set off a bomb..."

"I know," Christina said. "He nailed Bree with a Taser. Can you send someone to check on her?"

"We found her. She's fine."

Quinn's words sent her heart racing. "What do you mean *we*, Quinn?" Christina hissed.

"Grey is using Boss to track. It's how we found Bree so fast."

"Quinn, don't let him come in here. It's not safe. If Wally sees Boss, there's no telling what he'll do."

The receiving line moved forward and she watched Governor Winston pose for a photo with an older couple. It reminded her of the night the man had posed with Grey and Boss.

The couple laughed at something Winston said and stood talking with him as if they were old friends. The man put his hand on Winston's elbow and whispered into his ear. Winston nodded, then flicked his eyes toward the crowd. Was the man warning him?

Winston finally smiled, clasped the man on the shoulder, and continued the conversation. Good, they weren't done talking, and she prayed the chatty couple would buy her some more time. She had no idea what Wally had planned, but she knew it wasn't good. Did he have X-VX ready to poison Winston once it was his turn for a photo? She bit her lower lip and eyed the messenger bag. It could be a bomb in there. No way to know. Either way, Wally was about to do something, and it wasn't a question of if—it was when. There had to be a way to stop him before it was too late.

Christina ignored the hammering in her chest and eyed the crowd. She saw an opening and weaved her way toward Wally from behind, dodging elbows and a man who almost spilled his drink on her. She held her gun low in front of her and used her free hand to conceal it. Wally glanced over his shoulder, and she ducked behind a large woman and turned her face away. After a few moments, she stole a peek around the woman. Wally had returned his gaze to the head of the line.

With a few quick steps she weaved her way to stand behind the last remaining couple. She took a deep breath and stepped around them and slipped behind Wally. She leveled her hand and pressed her gun into the small of his back.

Wally's body went rigid.

Christina put her mouth to his ear. "What are you doing, Wally?"

He stood still. Christina knew it was risky to hold a weapon within reach of a trained soldier like Wally, but in the crowded room it was her best option. And since he'd been faking his arm paralysis, she wasn't taking his abilities for granted. She was on alert for any movement, ready to take him down.

"Hello, Christina," Wally whispered. "Fancy meeting you here."

"Drop the bag, Wally. No one needs to get hurt here."

Wally shifted his hands.

"Slowly." Christina pushed the barrel harder against his back.

He lifted both hands in the air, letting the bag dangle from his supposed bad hand.

Christina reached for the bag.

"She's got a gun!" Wally shouted.

The entire crowd made a collective gasp and a woman screamed. The crowd pushed away, running toward the exits and leaving Christina and Wally standing alone in the center of the large room.

"Drop your weapon." A SLED agent trained his gun on Christina. A second later, two other agents appeared, weapons aimed at her.

Christina wrapped her free arm around Wally's chest, using him as a shield. "This man is trying to kill Governor Winston."

"Stand down!" Quinn yelled from behind her. "She's law enforcement." He inched forward.

"Stop! Don't come any closer." Wally pushed himself against Christina, forcing her to take a half step back. "I've got a bomb in my bag, and I'll kill everyone in this building. Don't mess with me!"

"Don't do it, Wally," Grey said. "What will this solve?"

Christina twisted to see Grey with Boss at his side. A sickening knot formed in her stomach. She clenched her teeth and pierced him with her eyes.

Wally squirmed against her grip, but she matched him in height and the adrenaline in her veins added to her strength. She held him firm.

"They have to pay. Don't you understand? I've been warning them. They think just because they have all the power, they can do what they want and then cover it up. But I know what they did and now they will pay!"

They? Who was he talking about? Movement caught Christina's eye and she saw the SLED agents inching Governor Winston toward a hidden exit door.

"Don't you move, Winston!" Wally's voice screeched. "I'll blow this bomb right now if you take another step."

Winston stopped and held his hands up. Sweat glistened on his brow.

The heat radiating off Wally told Christina that he was coming unhinged. Right now, she had to calm him down. If she could keep him talking, it would buy them time to figure this out.

There was no hope of a sniper taking him out. Too risky. No one knew what evil was in his bag or what would happen if he dropped it.

Christina heard Quinn in her ear. She almost forgot she still had the call connected to her Bluetooth. "Keep him talking," he said. "A hostage negotiator and SWAT are on the way."

She forced herself to stay in control despite her heart thundering so hard in her chest that Wally surely felt it slamming against his back. Christina narrowed her eyes and pressed the muzzle of her forty-five even harder into Wally's back.

The last time she'd been in a hostage situation, it had ended with the loss of two lives. That was not an option this time.

Adrenaline surged through Grey's veins and his pulse roared in his ears at the sight of Christina and Wally in the center of the room. She was too close to Wally. Too close. With one swift move, he could snatch the gun and turn it on her. Grey had watched the man do it time and time again in training and in combat. Wally would kill her without a second thought.

There had to be something he could do here. He could not lose Christina. He *wouldn't* lose her.

Think. He had to think.

In a blur, Wally dropped his hands and spun on Christina, lashing a strong arm at her face.

She sidestepped his attack. Whirled and trained her gun at center mass. Her jaw muscle flexed as she pierced Wally with her stare. "Don't move."

Grey clenched the wheels on his chair and rolled forward an inch, ready to...what? What could he do? If he made a move, he could set Wally or these SLED agents off.

A growl rumbled from Boss. Body rigid, hackles raised, the dog locked his eyes on Wally and curled his lip into a snarl. He was ready to attack if Grey gave him the command.

At the far wall, opposite Grey, two undercover SLED agents bookended Governor Winston and pulled him toward the exit door behind them.

"Stop moving," Wally growled. "Winston is going to die here tonight, and there's nothing you can do to stop it." Wally slipped the strap of a brown leather messenger bag over his head and held the bag close to his chest. What was in that bag? What if Wally's bag contained the same explosive used in Siberia? The one that had sent X-VX into the air?

The uniformed agent at Grey's three o'clock planted his feet in a wide stance and adjusted his grip on his weapon. Quinn stood close to Grey with his gun trained on Wally. The three of them formed a triangle around Christina and Wally at the center of the room.

Winston paled and his chest heaved with each breath. "Listen. Let's all take a moment to relax."

"Shut up!" Wally's face reddened. "You don't have a say in this. You've made your choices, and now you and your greedy friends will pay."

"Wally, listen, man. I'm putting my gun away." Quinn lowered his weapon and in a few slow movements, he had it holstered. "Now, if you put the bag down, Christina can put her gun away too."

No way. Grey stared at Christina. She wouldn't dare drop her weapon. She was inches from the bomb-wielding serial killer and her weapon was her only defense.

Boss let out three loud barks and Wally flinched. "Shut that dog up before I do!"

Boss flattened his ears and took half a step toward Wally.

"Boss, out."

The dog snorted a response, but stood alert, muscles twitching and ready to pounce.

Grey knew exactly how the dog felt. He wanted to put his fist through Wally's face. If it wasn't for his stupid wheelchair, he would make Wally wish he'd never been born. Grey balled his fists. How could he have been so blind?

Fury boiled under his skin, but one look at the fire in Christina's eyes, and he *knew* he could trust her. She would keep Wally talking while they evacuated the building.

Christina finally spoke. "Wally, I want to hear what happened." Her voice was firm but kind. "Tell me what they did."

"They killed my *wife and child*." Sweat poured from his temples. "And then they covered it up."

"Who did, Wally?"

"They killed her and Mia and then they *blamed her*." Wally's face twisted into a painful grimace and a single tear slid down his cheek.

What was Wally talking about? Michelle had died in a lab accident. Grey's heart had ached for his friend when he'd heard about the tragic loss. He'd seen a shift in Wally, a sort of crack in his tough exterior. But he never would have thought he'd turn on his country like this.

"What they did to your family is unthinkable. You deserve justice, Wally, but not like this." Christina's voice was rock solid. "You've got a room full of law enforcement right here. Tell us what Winston did."

Boss was growling, emitting a low rumble. The dog's lips were quivering as he fought the urge to attack. "Easy, boy," Grey soothed.

He watched Christina. What would he do in the same circumstance? If he was married to Christina and he lost her and a child, would he turn to God, or would he seek vengeance by his own hands?

"Michelle gave them her whole life. She worked in the research lab for six years to develop the Scavenger drug. Then *he* ordered Cathy Wright to kill her." Wally wasn't screaming as he had done before, but his words had an edge of hatred. "Michelle had proof they were testing the drug on American soldiers before it was ready. Young men and women who were dying because the vaccine didn't work. Michelle went to Gayle Mooney, and Gayle turned her back on her."

"What about Dennison?" Christina asked. "What was his role?"

Wally snorted. "He was a loser. Just some random lab assistant Wright decided to hire to do her dirty work. The dumb kid didn't even know what he was doing. His little *lab accident* killed Michelle and everyone else working that day."

"And you made them pay? Didn't you, Wally?"

He shook his head and patted the bag. "Not everyone. Not yet." Wally glared at Winston.

Grey knew Christina was on the edge of losing him. Wally had nothing to lose, and he could go off at any moment. Quinn's lips were moving, and Grey wondered if he was still speaking to Christina through her earpiece. Did she have a hostage negotiator on the line?

Grey looked around the room. Governor Winston's protection detail had moved in front of him, shielding him with their bodies. As if that would do any good against a chemical weapon. Had the police evacuated the building? Grey wasn't sure if they'd had time, but he started to formulate another plan in case Wally decided to set his bomb. It was risky, but it would be their last resort.

"Wally, tell me what Governor Winston did. I don't understand—help me understand," Christina pleaded.

"Of course, you don't understand!" he yelled. "You blindly follow orders, but did you ever stop to think about who was giving you those orders?"

"Who's giving the orders, Wally?"

"The Commander!" He spun and pointed at Winston. "*He* told them to get rid of her before she could tell the world what they were doing. Killing innocent soldiers with a vaccine that didn't even work! They killed my wife and child, then blamed her for the lab accident." Spittle flew from Wally's mouth and stuck in his beard.

Boss barked and looked at Grey, ready to attack.

Wally had worked himself back into a frenzy and his chest heaved with each breath. They were running out of time.

Grey locked eyes with Quinn and saw him dip his head in a slight nod.

Wally reached down and unbuckled the messenger bag.

"Boss, get 'em," Grey growled.

At the word, Boss went into action. With three long strides, he launched himself at Wally. His teeth sank into his right forearm, trapping Wally's arm between his teeth. Wally yowled and fell to his knees as Boss thrashed his head side to side.

Christina lowered her gun and rushed forward.

"Careful!" Grey shouted. He didn't want Boss to think Christina was a threat and go after her.

Wally fell on his back and writhed in pain. Boss tugged his arm, dragging Wally and keeping his arm outstretched.

"I got it." Christina dropped to her knees and unlatched the bag from the strap over Wally's head. Once she had the bag held tight to her chest, she scurried back.

Quinn and the other agents stood in a circle around Wally with their guns on the man.

"Call him off," Quinn said.

"Boss, out."

Boss released Wally's arm and stood over him growling, prepared to attack again if Grey would let him.

The SWAT team, clad in all black riot gear, burst into the room, pouring in from the door behind Grey and the door behind Winston. They rushed past and formed a circle with Wally in the center.

Grey couldn't see around all the men, but he heard a grunt, and several people ran to Governor Winston.

"Get the EMT in here!" Quinn bellowed. "Winston collapsed. I think he's having a heart attack."

Winston wasn't the only one who needed a medic. Wally rolled on the ground with his knees up in a protective gesture.

He held his bloodied right arm tight against his chest and sucked air between his teeth. Grey knew Boss had done some significant damage. From now on, Wally wouldn't be faking his arm injury.

Christina held the bag out to a SWAT agent who took it and gently lowered it into a bomb box. She wiped the perspiration from her forehead with the back of her hand.

"Boss, heel." Grey watched Boss turn from an attack dog with killer instincts to a proud dog, ready for his reward. Boss pranced over to Grey with his tongue falling out of his open mouth. Grey rubbed Boss's soft coat. "You did so good, Boss. Yes, you did." He gave Boss his toy and let him chomp on it.

Grey glanced up to see Christina watching him, her lips turned up in a smile. He blew out a breath. Now that Wally was in custody and SWAT was clearing the room, his adrenaline was draining and he needed to talk to Christina before they got pulled away for statements.

Grey wheeled his chair to Christina. He rubbed the back of his neck and sighed before looking into her eyes. "We need to talk."

Christina followed Grey down the hall and into the governor's green room. The setup provided Winston and his staff a private place to relax before and after his speech. With all non-essential people evacuated from the convention center, Grey and Christina had the spacious room to themselves.

The leather furniture was arranged to create a comfortable conversation area, and a corner table boasted a fine spread of plated hors d'oeuvres. One look at the smoked salmon canapés and Christina's stomach rumbled. How could she think about food at a time like this? She knew what *we need to talk* meant. Grey had brought her here to tell her it was over.

Tension balled in her shoulders, and she was pretty sure her nerves were more on edge in this moment than when she'd faced Wally and his chemical weapon.

Grey stopped with his back to her and heaved a sigh.

Boss looked at Grey, then back to Christina. She rubbed his ears. "At ease, Boss," she whispered.

Instead of jumping onto one of the couches, Boss circled then plopped down by her feet with a huff. He rested his face on his front paws and closed his eyes.

Grey turned to face her. "I'm so furious I don't even know where to start."

She blinked. Furious? The word seemed extreme. In the car, he had seemed to set aside his anger, and to say now that he was still furious rocked her. "Grey, I—"

"No, listen. I trusted Boss with you and then…and then it all went wrong."

"I know, it was a mistake. A terrible, devastating mistake." She looked at her hands. "I can't even begin to imagine how you feel."

"No, you can't," he snapped. "You can't imagine how it feels at all. I had to hire a *bodyguard* because I'm not capable of taking care of my own dog!"

She stiffened. "That's not true—"

"Yes, it is. I'm always trying to keep up, always trying to make everyone see me as a normal person instead of just some helpless guy in a wheelchair, but you know what? They're right. There are some things I cannot do!" He pushed his chair backward and stared at her, eyes ablaze.

She clamped her mouth shut. Right now, she needed to hear him out. Not interrupt him with excuses or self-deprecating remarks about how she'd let her walls down and it had almost cost them everything.

"There are things I will never be able to do. I can't run with you and Boss. I can't drive a normal car or live in a normal house." He smacked the wheels on the side of his wheelchair. "I'm stuck in this chair because I can't trust my body! I can't even trust my legs to walk! I *am* helpless! I should have protected Boss. Every day I watch bits of my life slip through my fingers, and all I can do is smile and pretend it's all okay. It's like I'm a kid, right back on that rail fence watching the horse trample my father and there's nothing I can do about it!"

Christina bit her lower lip and took a half step toward him. He was pushing his chair forward and back again in a rocking motion. His version of pacing. She wanted to correct him, to help him see the man she saw, but she let him continue.

"I've been so wrapped up in my own self-pity and helplessness, I didn't even notice that my own friend, the man that I work with day in and day out, is a serial killer!" Grey stopped moving and met her gaze.

She stepped in front of him and put a hand on his shoulder. "You are not the only one who missed what was going on with Wally. It probably feels like you're responsible for this, but you're not." She, on the other hand, was entirely responsible for her mistakes. She'd killed those people in the marketplace as sure as if she had detonated the bomb herself.

Grey laced his fingers and stared at his palms. "I'm angry and afraid of what this life will look like if the surgery doesn't work."

"And what if it doesn't work?"

His eyes darted over her face. "Then I guess I'm stuck like this."

"I like you like this, Captain," she said with a small smile. She dropped into a nearby chair so that she could look into his eyes at the same level.

He stilled and the corners of his mouth twitched. "You do?"

She nodded. "And so does Boss."

Boss swished his tail as if in agreement.

Grey pushed his wheelchair forward until his knees touched

hers. "I know you keep that heart of yours walled off, but do you think you'll ever let anyone in?"

Christina shrugged. "I already let one in."

"You did?"

"Yep, and he's a handsome veteran." Her smile spread wider.

Grey took her hand. "You're talking about Boss, aren't you?"

She threw her head back and laughed. Grey laughed with her, and Boss decided to investigate. He wedged his head between them and nuzzled the hand Grey held.

When the laughter died down, Christina sobered. "Grey, I think we make a great team. But I'm...I'm worried that I'll be caught up in my emotions and make a huge mistake. One that could come at a painful price to everyone."

Grey tipped her chin until their eyes met again. His thumb caressed her jawline. "Listen, Agent, if there's one thing you've helped me to understand, it's that God has our back. Did Boss get stolen? Yes. But if Wally hadn't taken Boss, we never could have tracked them and stopped Wally."

"All things work together for good," she said, paraphrasing the Scripture.

Grey nodded. "We do make a pretty good team, don't we?"

A sense of peace fell over Christina, and she realized that Grey was including God in their team. If she let herself fall for Grey completely, then she knew she could trust God to work everything out, even if she got hurt.

"Yes, we make an amazing team," she said. "And for the record, I know you're not helpless. You're the strongest, most capable man I've ever known."

A slow grin spread across his face as he pulled her onto his lap and pinned her with his steely gray eyes. "You bet I am."

She wrapped her arms around his shoulders and he slipped a warm hand behind her neck. Christina's pulse thrummed, but not out of fear or adrenaline. This was a new kind of thrill—one that left her entire body tingling.

Grey pressed his lips to hers and she melted into the kiss. Slow and tender at first, then more firmly as he deepened it.

Boss barked and they broke apart, laughing. Grey brushed her hair out of her face and kissed her forehead.

Christina pulled back and cast a questioning look at Grey. "There's something I've been meaning to ask you."

Grey raised his eyebrows, waiting.

"What's with the Agent thing?"

"Agent Thirteen."

What was he talking about? She'd never heard of Agent Thirteen.

At her blank look, he tried again. "Agent Thirteen? Sharon Carter?"

She lifted her eyebrows and shook her head.

He gave her a dramatic eye roll, putting his whole head into it. "From the comic book! Agent Thirteen was the love of Captain America's life. Not so much in the movies, but in the comics, their love spanned time and space and lasted decades. They worked side by side to fight against evil."

"You're kidding me." She couldn't contain her smile if she tried. All this time, she'd been confused and annoyed by the nickname, and he'd been calling her Agent as a term of endearment.

She threw her arms around him and kissed him again.

"My Captain," she said. "My hero."

30

ONE WEEK LATER

FRIDAY, 9:23 A.M.

Grey opened his eyes to see Christina curled up asleep in a recliner with Boss taking up all of her lap. For a moment, he couldn't remember what had transpired since the last time he'd seen her sitting in the hospital. A rustle of papers near the foot of his bed caught his attention and he lifted his head to see his mother sitting in a recliner reading her Bible. When she saw him awake, a smile spread across her face. She closed the Bible and walked to his bedside.

"You're finally awake, honey." His mother brushed his hair away from his forehead.

"How...how long have you been here?" His throat was scratchy, and he cleared it.

"We've all been here since you went in for your surgery."

His mom lifted a plastic water container with a flexible straw and held it to his lips. He took a long sip, the cold water soothing his dry throat. "How long?" he croaked.

"I think it's been about thirteen hours now. Christina has been napping for about thirty minutes, and your dad and Ruby went down to the cafeteria. I don't think they're hungry. Just wanted to stretch their legs." She smiled at him.

Christina shifted her weight and her eyes popped open. When she saw Grey, she smiled. A full smile, the one he loved so much. "Hey there, sleepyhead."

"I can't believe you stayed here the entire time."

Christina helped Boss off her lap so she could stand and come to his bed. She took his hand in hers and squeezed.

His mom tucked her papers into her Bible. "I think I'm going to go find your dad before he gets lost." She gave Christina a wink and a gentle pat before she turned to go.

"Thank you, Christina," Grey said. "Thank you for staying with me—"

"I promised myself I'd do something the moment you woke up." She leaned in and pressed her lips to his. They were warm and soft, and his entire body shuddered at the sensation. A satisfying weight settled in his chest as Christina brought her hands to his face and pulled him closer, deepening the kiss.

Grey slid his hand behind Christina's neck and pulled her in, needing to feel her closer. The heart monitor beeped faster, but he ignored it while every nerve in his body fired at the same time.

The sound of a throat clearing, then a voice. "Oh, I see. Um, yeah. I'll just…"

Christina broke the kiss, and they turned their heads in unison to see a nurse blushing.

"I'll just leave you two alone." The nurse left and Christina looked into Grey's eyes.

Laughter bubbled from both of them and she kissed him again, smiling through the kiss. "I'd better let your heart rate settle back down before they come rushing in with the paddles." Christina sat on the edge of the bed.

Grey held her hands in both of his. "Christina…I know it's only been a few weeks, but I've fallen in love with you."

But there was so much more that he wanted to say. All the reasons why he thought they shouldn't be together. What if the surgery didn't work? What if she wouldn't trust him to stick around and not leave her? The thoughts were coming at him too fast. Without intending to, he found himself silently reciting a verse from Philippians. *Whatever is true, whatever is noble, whatever is right, whatever is pure, whatever is lovely, whatever is admirable—if anything is excellent or praiseworthy—think about such things.*

"I'm in love with you too." A tear formed in the corner of Christina's eye. "I never thought I could let myself get close to anyone. I thought keeping people out would keep me safe. But you've shown me that with God, I can have the good with the bad." She sniffled. "Wait, I didn't mean that the way it came out."

The tear escaped and rolled down her cheek. He caught it with his thumb and smoothed it away. Those dark eyes that didn't miss a thing captivated him. He prayed that one day soon God would allow him to wake up to those eyes every day for the rest of his life.

"It's okay, Agent. I know what you meant. I'm glad to hear you say it because I have a little surprise for you. Will you hand my phone to me?"

She narrowed her eyes, searching his face for a hint. "What have you got up your sleeve?"

Smiling, he took the phone from her. "Can't have anything up my sleeves in this hospital gown." Grey winked at her. "It's a surprise." The new message icon flashed, and he scrolled through the seemingly endless *Get well soon* messages and found the one he was looking for.

Christina tried to peek at his phone screen, and he held it to his chest. "Hey, no peeking."

"It's okay, I bet I can guess the surprise. It's a puppy, isn't it? I think Boss needs a friend. He's been feeling like the third wheel."

Boss perked his ears and looked confused at being dragged into the conversation.

"We'll talk about a friend for Boss later. This surprise is better than a puppy." He showed her the message.

MONDAY, 10:17 A.M.

Christina paced Grey's hospital room and chewed her thumbnail. Each breath came faster and faster. What had happened to her special ops training? Why couldn't she use it to keep herself calm? This was insane. She never let her nerves get the best of her and she never chewed her nails. It was a disgusting habit she'd been forced to give up when she'd enlisted in the Army. She dropped her hands and clasped them behind her back.

Grey came out of the bathroom and pushed his chair into her path, forcing her to stop pacing. He secured the last two buttons on his shirt. "Are you sure you're okay with this?"

Christina snapped her eyes to his. "I don't know. Should I be...I mean, is this really the best place for this?"

"Why wait one minute longer?" He rolled up one sleeve of his shirt. "I thought you wanted to do this."

"I do." She absolutely wanted to do this.

Didn't she?

"Are you worried about how you look?"

She blinked at him. "What's wrong with the way I look?" She marched into the bathroom and checked her reflection in the mirror. "Is it my hair?" Curls escaped from her braid, but when she'd looked earlier, she thought it looked messy-cute. Did Grey think it was just plain messy? She pulled the braid out and reworked it into a tighter weave. With one last swipe at an errant curl near her ear, she presented herself to Grey. "Is that better?"

A soft laugh escaped. "Yes, but I also thought you looked great before."

"Oh no! Should I go back to the messy braid?" She began tugging at the edges of the braid to loosen it and give it a more natural look.

Grey moved to her side and reached for her hand. "Christina, listen. I know this is a big day, but you've got nothing to worry about. It's all going to be fine. I promise." His tone was gentle and calmed her nerves.

She took his other hand and let out a breath. "I know. You're right. I'm sorry I'm getting so worked up. This is going to be the greatest day of my life." She leaned down and kissed him.

"Yep, and the best is yet to come."

"Knock knock." A soft voice came from the hall.

Christina stood ramrod straight and her eyes widened.

Grey smiled and kissed the top of her hand. "You've got this," he whispered.

The day Christina had thought about for years was here.

She turned and couldn't believe her eyes. Where she expected to see the slight frame of a lanky teenager now stood a beautiful woman. Thick dark hair fell down her shoulders and she pushed her bangs away from her eyes.

"Alana." Christina released the name in a breath.

Alana smiled wide and turned to wave behind her. A boy about seven or eight years old with the same dark hair, dark eyes, and almond skin as Alana stepped into the room. He slipped his arms around her waist and buried his face into her side. Her eyes locked onto Christina's for a beat before she looked at the boy.

"This is my son, Rocco." Alana ran a hand over his hair. "Rocco, this is my sister, Christina."

Tears welled up in Christina's eyes and a spiky lump formed in her throat. Alana had called her *sister*.

Alana whispered something to Rocco, and he released his grip on her waist. "Pleased to meet you, Aunt Christina."

That was it. The dam of emotions broke, and Christina burst into tears. Alana rushed forward and hugged Christina. The embrace was strong, and Christina wasn't sure she wanted to let go.

"I've missed you," Alana said into Christina's hair, her voice trembling. "You're all grown up and so beautiful."

"Hey, buddy." Grey stuck out his hand. "My name is Grey. Nice to meet you."

Christina reluctantly pulled away, but Alana held onto her hand. They turned to see Grey shaking hands with Rocco, who was eying Grey's wheelchair.

"That's a cool wheelchair," Rocco said.

"Yeah, I know. It's really fast too. Maybe I'll let you try it out later." Grey ruffled the boy's hair.

It warmed Christina's heart to see them together and she wondered what Grey would think of becoming a father to a child in foster care someday.

"I'm sorry, I don't know what's come over me." Christina wiped the tears from her eyes and dried her hands on the side of her jeans. "I never get emotional, but in the past few weeks I can't seem to do anything about it."

Alana smiled and nodded toward Grey. "You have a great man there. I don't know how he did it, but he found us. When I heard you were here, I booked us on the next flight to Columbia."

"What about your job? Your family?"

"It's nothing," she said. "I needed a break from my job, didn't I, Rocco?"

The boy nodded but didn't look up. He was running his hand over the wheel of Grey's chair. Christina realized that before she met Grey, she'd never seen a wheelchair up close either. Sure, she'd seen people in wheelchairs, but always from a distance. Rocco appeared shy at first, but Christina could tell that he was brave and curious too.

"You ladies have a lot of catching up to do. What do you say? We head to the cafeteria for some dinner?"

"I'd like that," Alana said.

Christina kissed Grey on the cheek then patted his chest. "You're full of great ideas."

EPILOGUE

SIX MONTHS LATER

THURSDAY, 3:17 P.M.

Alana elbowed Christina and pointed toward the center of the basketball court. "Look! Look!"

Grey dribbled the ball and made his way toward his basket. He took a shot and the ball sailed through the net. Team Army took the ball and Grey winked at Christina as he pushed his wheelchair back toward center court. She didn't fight the smile that spread across her face. Instead, she waved then blew him a kiss.

"Ugh, you're so cute, do you know that?" Haley gave Christina a playful bump with her shoulder.

Steven and Haley had recently returned from their extended honeymoon at her second home in Ireland. She'd only had a few weeks to adjust to Christina's relationship with Grey, but she'd given her approval wholeheartedly.

Rocco sat in the row in front of Christina. He'd made friends with Haley's two adopted sons, Zeke and Micah, and the boys were inseparable. Micah and Rocco were discussing the game and how cool it would be to play in wheelchairs like the men on the court.

"Is Grey upset that the surgery hasn't worked?" Haley asked.

Christina kept her eyes on Grey, watching him block a shot before stealing the ball and passing it to his teammate. "You know, he doesn't seem to care one way or another. We still pray for God to heal him, but I've noticed the prayer isn't as fervent as it was before."

Alana leaned closer, making herself heard over the cheers. "What have the doctors said? Is there still time for it to work?"

"His doctor is optimistic. It was an experimental surgery, and we knew it would take some time. But you know, I never have thought about Grey as different." She lifted a shoulder. "He's just Grey to me."

Haley groaned. "Wow, you sure turned mushy while I was away. What happened to ya?"

Christina laughed and pointed at Grey. "He happened."

The buzzer sounded, signaling halftime.

"That's my cue." Christina stood and scooted past Alana to the aisle.

"Go get 'em, girl!" called Alana.

Having Alana back in her life was a gift. As a single mother and an underwater detective for LAPD SWAT, Alana was in high demand. The moment she'd put out the word that she wanted to relocate to Columbia to be near Christina, the offers had flooded in. Olivia was one of the first to extend a job offer to Alana, and Christina secretly hoped she'd take it.

She jogged down the steps to the basketball court and joined the group of military wives and girlfriends gathered in one corner. They had planned a special event in honor of their men, and Christina couldn't wait to see the look on Grey's face.

"Ladies and gentlemen," the announcer crooned. "May I have your attention, please? For your halftime entertainment, we have six extraordinary guests."

The women took their positions in their wheelchairs. Christina dribbled the basketball and pushed her wheelchair to the free throw line. The five other women lined their wheelchairs up and the referee blew his whistle. She passed the ball to Bev, one of her teammates, and headed to her position under the basket as they'd practiced. Bev passed the ball to Sarah, and she made a basket.

The crowd cheered, but not as loud as the men watching from the sidelines.

Christina caught Grey's open-mouthed stare and winked at him. The look on Grey's face was worth the two months she had spent practicing in secret. She had a newfound respect for the guys who could give their wheelchair a push in between each bounce of the basketball.

They played the half-court basketball game in borrowed wheelchairs until Christina's team scored five points. The announcer declared them the winners and the referee handed Christina a plastic trophy. She grinned and held it high.

A second buzzer signaled the end of halftime and Christina hurried back to her seat to watch the rest of the game.

Alana hugged Christina. "That was amazing!"

"I had no idea you had moves like that." Haley put up her hand for a high five and Christina smacked it.

"Thank you, guys. It's way harder than it looks. I can't imagine playing the whole court like that."

"Can I hold the trophy?" Micah asked.

"Sure." Christina handed it to him.

Micah was enthusiastic and bubbly, a complete change from the sickly child in need of a heart transplant Christina had met a year ago. Looking at him always caused a bittersweet pang of regret for the moment Micah's mother Belinda was killed before Christina could get the gunman to give up his weapon. But seeing him now, so full of life thanks to Belinda's heart beating inside his chest, Christina knew God had worked it out in a way none of them could ever have imagined.

It was a tied game with seconds on the clock. Grey pushed hard to catch up to his opponent headed down court with the ball. The player lifted his arms to shoot from the three-point line and Grey maneuvered beside the man and attempted to block the shot. They watched as the ball sailed through the net at the sound of the buzzer.

"Great shot, man," Grey said.

"Thanks, brother. And I hope your girlfriend doesn't hold her halftime victory over your head too long."

Grey looked at Christina and held up both hands in a *what are you gonna do* gesture.

The two teams lined up to congratulate each other with hand slaps in passing. Grey was glad he'd decided to return to the basketball team. It was a difficult decision since he'd only joined the team for Wally in the first place. But Wally's betrayal made an opening for Grey to talk to the team about forgiveness. He'd made friends with his teammates and had even begun a small Bible study group with them once a week after practice. Each teammate was struggling with his disability in different ways, but there was a common thread that could lead them all back to relying on God instead of their own strength.

Grey gave his chair a push and let it sail toward Christina. He threw up his hands. "What was that, Agent? I had no idea you could shoot hoops, much less in a wheelchair!" At the last second, he grabbed one wheel and stopped his chair before he crashed into her.

"You know, it's much harder than it looks!"

He snorted with laughter. "Oh, really now? I had no idea."

Christina took his offered hand and he tugged her down until she was in his lap. "You're really something, do you know that?"

She slid her arms around his neck and Grey had no doubts that God had been listening to his prayers all along. She was everything he'd prayed for, and everything he had been too embarrassed to ask God for. But God had seen deep into the desires of his heart and known. It had only been a few months, but Grey knew he wanted to spend the rest of his life with Christina.

Most of the spectators had left the arena seating, but a few family members stood in little clusters of conversation.

Grey released his grip on Christina and put his hands on his wheels. "Hold on tight."

He turned them around then gave the wheels a few strong pushes toward center court.

Christina twisted to look over her shoulder. "Where are you taking us?"

Before Grey could answer, there was a loud snap, and the entire stadium went dark.

Christina tensed and jumped off Grey's lap. Her pulse quickened and she spun on her heel, scanning the arena. What was happening? Why had the lights gone out while spectators were still around? Before her eyes had time to adjust to the darkness, overhead a halogen light crackled then snapped to life.

The single light beamed down like a dim spotlight, illuminating only her and Grey. She scanned the seats for her friends, but they were gone. She caught a glimpse of a small flame that sparked to life. Another light came on to her right. Then another to her left. What in the world?

One by one, small yellow flames awakened. They shone like tiny fireflies in the summer night. There must have been fifty specks of light surrounding them in a circle. And they seemed to be moving toward them.

Christina looked to Grey. "What's this?"

He put two fingers in his mouth and whistled. Boss galloped to his side and Christina was relieved to see him. What—why was Boss in the tuxedo from the anniversary party? Realization dawned and she snapped her eyes to Grey.

A wide grin spread across his face. "You're not the only one with a surprise up their sleeve."

Christina turned in a circle. They were surrounded by candlelight. Behind each light was a familiar face. Alana held an LED candle in front of her chest and beamed a smile at Christina. Haley stood next to Steven and Zeke while Katie and her husband, Daniel, stood beside them with their own candles. Micah and Rocco held candles in each hand and waved them around in a mock lightsaber battle. Christina chuckled at the sight.

She saw the faces of Laila, Charlie, and Lizzie. The entire Elite Guardians team was somewhere in the circle. Even Quinn was there with Maddy, holding his infant daughter, Stacy, in one arm and a battery-powered candle in the other.

Christina had no idea how Grey had pulled this off. She turned to see who was standing behind them and spotted Bree and Francisco whispering to each other. Even Rhett, Emma, and Ruby were here.

Her heart soared to bursting and tears began to fill her eyes. Grey took her hand and tugged her toward him. "Hey, Agent," he said softly. "Boss and I have a question to ask you."

Heat crept up her neck, and she covered her mouth with her hands. She was nodding and Grey hadn't even asked anything yet. He leaned over and slipped something from a pocket on Boss's tuxedo. It was a small square velvet box.

Grey pushed himself out of his wheelchair until he was kneeling in front of her.

This was happening.

Grey pulled Christina's hands from her mouth and brought them to his lips. He kissed her fingers one by one, then pulled back and held the box in the palm of his hand.

His jaw worked and he swallowed hard. "Christina, I have trusted you from the first moment I laid eyes on you. I put Boss in your hands that first night because something deep inside told me to. I know now it was the whispers of God. Over the last few months, you've taught me to listen to that voice and now I hear Him loud and clear."

He paused and looked up at the ceiling, then sucked in a deep breath before bringing his eyes back to hers. "I've been praying about this for weeks, and right here, in front of our friends and family—and a few strangers," he teased, "I want to ask you. Will you marry me?"

Christina nodded and forced a single word past the bowling ball in her throat. "Yes." She dropped to her knees and looked him in the eyes. "Oh, yes!"

Grey cupped her face in his hands and kissed her. The crowd cheered and he smiled behind the kiss. He pressed his forehead to hers for a moment then kissed the bridge of her nose. "Okay, well since you said yes, Boss has a little gift for you."

Grey cracked the lid on the ring box to reveal a brilliant round diamond mounted in a Tiffany setting on a plain platinum band. Christina gasped. It was beautiful. Simple yet elegant. Exactly what she would have chosen for herself. He slipped the ring onto her finger and kissed her hand.

"Grey, it's beautiful," she said. "I...I..."

She didn't have a chance to finish her sentence. Grey pressed his lips to hers again. The noise of shouting and clapping faded as Christina gave in to his kiss.

When he released her she sighed. "You're the most amazing man I've ever met, Captain Grey Parker. Is there anything you *can't* do?"

"Um...yeah, actually there is one thing."

She drew her head back and looked at him.

He leaned in and placed his mouth beside her ear. "I, um. Actually, I can't get up. A little help?"

Christina smiled and kissed him again. She silently thanked God for sending her this wonderful man.

And to think—it had all started with Boss.

CONNECT WITH SUNRISE

Thank you so much for reading *Driving Force*. We hope you enjoyed the story. If you did, would you be willing to do us a favor and leave a review? It doesn't have to be long—just a few words to help other readers know what they're getting. (But no spoilers! We don't want to wreck the fun!) Thank you again for reading!

We'd love to hear from you—not only about this story, but about any characters or stories you'd like to read in the future. Contact us at www.sunrisepublishing.com/contact.

We also have a monthly update that contains sneak peeks, reviews, upcoming releases, and fun stuff for our reader friends. Sign up at www.sunrisepublishing.com.

OTHER ELITE GUARDIANS NOVELS

Elite Guardians Collection

Driving Force

Impending Strike

Defending Honor

Elite Guardians Series

Always Watching

Without Warning

Moving Target

Chasing Secrets

AN ELITE GUARDIANS NOVEL

IMPENDING STRIKE

USA TODAY BESTSELLING AUTHOR

LYNETTE EASON

PRESENTS

SAMI A. ABRAMS

Turn the page for a sneak peek of the next Elite Guardians novel, *Impending Strike* …

SNEAK PEEK

IMPENDING STRIKE

THURSDAY, 11:00 P.M

Did the crazy girl want to get herself killed?

Elite Guardians Agency bodyguard Lizzie Tremaine parked her older model silver BMW out of eyeshot of the biker bar and hefted herself from the driver's seat. She'd bought the car for the safety ratings but had to admit the sleek design gave her a sense of luxury. Not exactly the type of vehicle that one drove around these parts of Columbia, South Carolina—but with no time to exchange it for a rental, she didn't have a choice.

Lizzie strode toward the entrance of Dirty Dogs, her boots crunching on the gravel. The song "Welcome to the Jungle" poured from the open door. She slowed her approach. *Jungle is right.* The bar was known for more than bikers looking for a good time. Rumor had it that girls disappeared from the establishment on a regular basis, but the cops had no evidence to close the place down.

The interior lights flowed from the building, glowing against the dark veil of night. The seedy bar on the outskirts of town was not one anyone in their right mind would pick for a nice evening out. Bridget Rutledge, the underage daughter of Lizzie's recent celebrity client, Bodie Rutledge, had chosen the place as a slap in her father's face.

The rumble of Harleys in the parking lot threw off the rhythm of Lizzie's heart. Or maybe it was Mr. Tall Dark and Scary bouncer guarding the door. She craned her neck and caught a glimpse of the missing sixteen-year-old.

Go in or wait? She'd called one of the other agency bodyguards, Charlie Lee, for backup, so help was on the way. And while Lizzie hated pulling him from his undercover assignment as a drug dealer, going into *that* bar without a male counterpart equaled foolishness. Just as she'd set herself up to wait on Charlie, a hard-eyed, tattooed man moved in on Bridget.

Fabulous. If someone pulled the girl out the back door...

Nope. Charlie or not, she had to get in there before the girl got herself killed—or worse.

Lizzie tugged at her too-short leather skirt and steeled her spine. She hated undercover assignments in places like this but refused to let Bodie down. The man was beside himself with worry for Bridget. With good reason. Lizzie stepped forward. The bouncer held up his hand, inches from her chest. Inked numbers adorned his fingers, and the three teardrop tattoos next to his right eye told her the man had seen the inside of a prison.

Shoulders back, Lizzie smiled. "I need to see my friend." She motioned inside.

"Don't think so." The man crossed his tree-trunk-sized arms over his chest. "Lady doesn't want to be bothered."

"Is that so?" Lizzie leaned in. "Listen, I really don't think you want cops showing up. I'm guessing someone in there isn't twenty-one." Lizzie raised her chin. She'd studied her opponent. He had weaknesses, but she'd rather not explore them.

A low growl rumbled in the bouncer's throat, and his glare zinged daggers at her. "Fine." He stepped aside.

She brushed past him and released a long breath. Once inside, she meandered her way across the postage stamp room. The smoky haze stung her eyes.

"Hey, baby."

Lizzie raised a brow at the man clad in black leather, who, by the looks of him, had joined the three hundred club years ago. "Not your type."

He belly laughed. "Maybe. Maybe not." He slid a rough knuckle down her cheek.

The mixed scent of body odor and beer curdled her stomach, but she refused to cringe at his touch.

Hurry up, Charlie.

She jerked her face away from the man. "Paws off."

"Feisty little thing, aren't you?" He reached for her again.

She didn't have time for this. Lizzie snatched his thumb and twisted it to the breaking point. He let out a howl. "You don't want to find out." A quick push and the man stumbled. Lizzie took advantage of the opportunity and found a stool at the bar with a perfect view of Bridget.

The Dirty Dogs bar, small compared to the local places in downtown Columbia, had four red plastic booths that lined the far wall and six four-topper tables in the center of the room. Easy enough to keep her target in sight.

The bartender slid a glass of amber-colored liquid in front of her then continued wiping the bar top with a white cloth.

She sniffed the drink. Whiskey. "Excuse me. I didn't order this."

He jutted his chin at the guy wearing a black doo-rag skull cap with red and yellow flames. Skull and rose tattoo sleeves covered both arms.

Great, another one. A single woman in a bar full of testosterone and attitude—there'd be more. And it was the entire reason she'd called Charlie. Where was he, anyway? She lifted the glass in a silent toast, then brought it to her lips and pretended to take a sip. Her gaze zeroed in on Bridget. The young girl sat between two men in a booth, flirting like her last meal depended on it. Lizzie had to get her out of here before one of the big dudes took Bridget up on her unspoken offer.

The thump of the bass increased, and the murky cloud of cigarette smoke around her thickened. A massive hand landed on Lizzie's shoulder. Her eyes trailed the meaty fingers and up the thick inked arm to a bearded face. The same doo-ragged man that had bought her a drink peered down at her.

He stepped into her line of sight of Bridget and leaned down, pressing his hand on the bar top, trapping her. His rancid breath brushed across her cheek. "Drinks aren't free around here."

Lizzie's patience waned. What was it with this type of nean-derthal? She had no doubt about her abilities to handle him, but getting physical might encourage him to bring his friends into the action. And as skilled as she was in self-defense, not even she dared to take on the whole pack. She gritted her teeth and focused on a spot on the far wall, forcing in three shallow breaths, pushing her anxiety aside.

"Then stop buying drinks." With a flick of her hand, she flipped her long hair over her shoulder. "Not interested."

The man rose to his full six-foot-plus height. "I think—"

"Hey, gorgeous." Lips pressed against her temple. "This guy a problem?"

Charlie. Her partner of three years had never looked so good, even in his scruffy undercover state with that wicked temporary dragon tattoo on his forearm.

"Hi, baby." Her sickening sweet drawl made her want to gag.

His hand wrapped around hers, Charlie tugged her behind him and widened his stance. "I think you better leave my woman alone."

His woman? Lizzie refrained from rolling her eyes.

After a long stare down, the man rejoined his friends.

She pivoted and gazed up at Charlie. *Play the part, Lizzie.* She let a coy smile curve her lips, and she ran her hands down his arms. "Thanks, Drago."

He pulled her in close and nuzzled her neck. "Why didn't you wait?"

"Bridget's playing a dangerous game. I couldn't leave her alone."

"Where is she?" He kissed her behind the ear.

A jolt of electricity zipped down her spine, muddling her train of thought. "At your four o'clock."

"Got her." Charlie slipped his hands to Lizzie's waist, pressed the Glock 43 she had tucked in the waistband of her leather skirt against her skin, and grinned. "Nice."

"I don't leave home without it." She winked.

"Uh oh, looks like Tiny and friend are planning to make their move." Charlie shifted and slid his hand into hers and squeezed.

Tiny scooted from the booth and hauled Bridget up next to him. His partner slipped from his seat and exited out the back door of the bar.

"Showtime." Lizzie sauntered toward Bridget. "Hey, girl! Haven't seen you in forever."

Wide eyes of the sixteen-year-old stared at her, lower lip quivering.

Tiny's beefy hand clutched Bridget's thin bicep.

Charlie's warm touch on the small of Lizzie's back centered her. His quick tap on her right side indicated she go for Bridget while he took care of the big man. Her focus tunneled in on the task at hand and even the loud music faded into the background.

Charlie brushed past her and bumped into Tiny.

"Watch it, boy." Tiny's deep timbre rose above the din.

"Boy?" Charlie's fists rested on his hips. "Don't think so, dude." Without warning, Charlie's hand chopped against the pressure point on the side of Tiny's neck, and his knee connected with the man's stomach. Tiny lost his hold on Bridget and staggered backward.

"Let's go!" Sending up a quick prayer for Charlie, Lizzie grabbed Bridget and pushed her out the backdoor. Lizzie blinked, forcing her eyes to adjust to the dark alley. She scanned the surroundings. Dumpsters to her left with cardboard boxes lining the brick exterior walls. The exit to her right. A dim streetlamp glowed at the end of the alleyway.

"Come on." She dragged the girl toward the parking lot.

Bridget's hand trembled in hers, but she stayed with Lizzie.

Tiny's partner stepped from the shadows. "And where do you think you're going?"

"Get in that alcove," she whispered to Bridget.

The girl rushed to the opening while Lizzie kept her eyes on the man in front of her. Charlie had better not have gotten himself killed.

The huge man rushed her. She stepped back and spun with a roundhouse kick to his face. His head snapped back. He staggered. Lizzie grabbed his shoulders and brought her knee up full force. With a howl, the guy dropped like a rock to the pavement.

Lizzie yanked her Glock from her holster and aimed it at him. She sucked in air, trying to catch her breath. "Don't move." She shifted, but never took her eyes off the man lying on the ground. "You okay, Bridget?"

"I-I think so."

The back entrance to the bar crashed open, and two figures fell out into the alley. Tiny and Charlie. Tiny took a swing, but Charlie dodged it. He grabbed the man's arm, wrenched it behind him, and shoved him against the dumpster. Charlie whipped out zip ties and secured his attacker to the metal handle.

He pivoted and took in the scene. "Y'all good? No problem taking him down, right?"

Brat. "Nah. Six-five and two hundred eighty pounds is a walk in the park. Come secure him so I can get Bridget out of here, will you?"

Before Lizzie got her Glock holstered and helped Bridget to her feet, Charlie had the guy flex-cuffed next to Tiny.

"Let's get your package in the car."

Sandwiched between her and Charlie, Bridget shuffled, head down. Lizzie held on to the girl's arm and led her toward the vehicle.

Lizzie opened the passenger door and all but shoved Bridget in. If the night's events didn't open the young lady's eyes, Lizzie didn't know what would. She shut the door and turned, coming nose to nose with Charlie. A little too close for her sanity after the canoodling in the bar. She had no business being attracted to any man, especially not Charlie.

Lizzie skirted around him and headed for the driver's side. "Thanks for the assist."

"No problem." He scratched his beard and grimaced.

"Ready to see the light of day again?" Lizzie grinned and lowered herself into the vehicle. She rolled down the driver's window then hit the locks.

"More than." Charlie rested his forearms on the top of the car and leaned in. "You take the princess back to her tower, and I'll take out the garbage."

"Deal. See you in the morning?" Each week, the agency had a team meeting, and Charlie had been hit and miss lately due to his undercover assignment.

"Unsure. Now, get out of here. Kiss Addy goodnight."

Her twelve-year-old daughter. Once again, Lizzie had left her mother to watch over Addy while Lizzie rescued someone else. Her pulse raced, and her breathing shallowed. She struggled to tamp down her reaction. No one could know about her condition. Not now. Not ever. She swallowed hard and peered up at Charlie. "As soon as I drop off Bridget. Stay safe."

His knuckles rapped on the roof. "Always." Charlie sauntered off into the shadows. He'd call Detective Quinn Holcombe to pick up the two jerks from the bar and head off to his undercover world of drug deals. And she'd drop Bridget into the hands of her worried father, then head home to Addy.

She glanced at her passenger and tightened her grip on the steering wheel, causing the laces to dig into her fingertips. "That could've ended badly."

Tears trailed down Bridget's cheeks. "I know." The mousy voice surprised Lizzie. She prayed the young lady had learned her lesson.

"Good."

Only one thought entered her mind as she drove through town in silence. What if it had been Addy in that bar, and Lizzie hadn't arrived in time?

Charlie hated living within the depths of depravity.

And yet, that's where he found himself once again. God had called him to a life of service and protection, so here he was. He just wished it didn't include undercover work.

Charlie slinked past the dingy apartment that Mayor Eliza Baker had arranged for him and sauntered down the sidewalk, aiming toward his next drug deal—one that might land him the big fish and stop the new flood of drugs into Columbia, South Carolina.

The fingers of moonlight touched the neighborhood, creating eerie shadows along the edges of the street. Poorly lit streetlamps gave no relief in illuminating the dark corners. Why must the big deals take place in the dead of night? The temperatures had dropped but the humidity hung on, causing sweat to bead on his upper lip.

Three warm blocks later, he slipped into the opening of a

dark alley. The stench of vomit and alcohol turned his stomach. One of the many effects of the drug-invaded world that he hated.

Two years ago, his sister Olivia Edwards Savage—one of the founders of the Elite Guardians Agency—had assigned him to guard Darrell Hewitt, the son of the biggest crime boss on the East Coast. Due to Charlie's contacts from that assignment, the mayor had begged him to use his former police training to go undercover and help shut down the newest influx of drugs coming through Columbia. She'd confided in EGA and two detectives, his friends Quinn and Steven, that she felt if they stopped the drug flow, the uptick in gang activity might slow. The mayor wanted the best for her city, but she worried about a leak in the office and had kept the operation under wraps.

He leaned against the building, folded his arms, and closed his eyes, relishing the cool brick on his back. A skitter at the back of the alley had him searching the darkness for the little four-legged critter that had captured his attention. Unsuccessful in his visual hunt, he turned away from the distraction.

He strained to peer around the corner and settled back in. Where was his contact?

Charlie ignored the nighttime noises and allowed his mind to wander to earlier that evening. He'd chanced sneaking out of the neighborhood and going to the bar. But Lizzie had called, so he'd gone. The image of the large man's hand on Lizzie popped into his mind. His teeth clenched. If that man had hurt her... He shook off the direction of his thoughts. She'd handled herself like a pro. Always did.

Petite, full of spunk and deadly skills described Lizzie perfectly. She never backed down from a challenge and loved to learn new things. Everything from archaeology to computers to the latest in self-defense techniques. Something that had captured his attention when she'd started working for EGA. But he'd never acted on his interest. As the only male on the team, he refused to put his coworkers, especially Olivia or Lizzie, in an uncomfortable position. Besides, getting his heart stomped on once in life was more than enough.

Friends. That's where Lizzie landed, and that's where she'd stay. He liked her way too much to ruin their friendship. But if he ever wanted to wade into the dating pool again, Lizzie would be the girl.

Shoes shuffled on the pavement. A grunt and thud echoed through the night air. Charlie jolted. He instinctively went for his weapon at the small of his back, but suppressed the reflex to yank it from the holster. He squinted into the darkness. A drunk had fallen and lay curled in the fetal position at the end of the passageway.

Get your head in the game, man. Now wasn't the time to lose focus. No more thinking about Lizzie. He settled back against the brick wall and waited for his new *friend.*

The sticky August humidity continued to hang in the air. Sweat trickled between Charlie's shoulder blades and his tattered black T-shirt stuck to his chest like a second skin.

Thirty miserable minutes later, Jimmy appeared from the shadows and made Charlie a drug deal offer that he gladly accepted. One that would clean up more filth from the streets.

"You got a deal, bro." Charlie gave the drug runner the required gang-type handshake. The glint of the streetlight illuminated the flaming skull and crossbones tattoo covering the man's forearm. Its glowing eye sockets gave Charlie the creeps. He retracted his hand and had a strong desire to shower away the slimy feeling from dealing with the lowlife.

Jimmy grinned, revealing several missing teeth. "Thanks for the business." With a nod, the man disappeared around the corner.

Charlie released the proverbial breath he'd held during the transaction. His shoulders sagged. With his forearm, he wiped the sweat from his brow. One more successful deal for a delivery made him that much closer to ending the undercover charade of drug dealer.

Each planned drug buy raked on Charlie's nerves. The lifestyle wore on him. After a year of setting up his presence in the drug scene and five weeks of full work undercover, he wondered how much more he had in him to continue.

He shoved his hands in his pockets and fiddled with his burner phone. His touchstone. His lifeline to the safe world. No names, only speed dial numbers of his Elite Guardians Agency teammates and Quinn. The women had insisted that he include their numbers. He'd resisted, not wanting to put the members of the agency in danger. But they'd reminded him that's what a team did. They had each other's backs. He was honored to be included among the top bodyguards in the nation, even if he was the only male. Not that he had a problem with that. He trusted them more than he trusted the police officers he'd served with on the Atlanta PD. And that said something.

Knowing that God was watching over him and that the team was a phone call away allowed him to maintain his calm demeanor and play the part of the cocky, confident dealer of his alter ego, Rod. He left the phone in his pocket and strolled down the sidewalk like he owned the neighborhood.

"I can do the hit." A gruff voice drifted on the night air.

Charlie froze and scanned the area, searching for the source of the words.

"Not so fast," a second man argued. "You can't mess this up. We have one shot at killing her, and if we miss, they'll close ranks."

The hair on the back of Charlie's neck rose. He ducked behind a row of trash cans next to an apartment building, grimacing at the strong garbage odor, a mixture between fish and rotten eggs. Forcing himself to focus, he strained to hear the conversation, but the men moved out of earshot.

Charlie slipped from his hiding spot and clung to the

shadows on the edge of the street, following his targets. His ratty shirt and stained jeans, not to mention his unkempt hair, gave him the ability to blend into the neighborhood, but a hinky feeling of being watched crept in and stayed.

He itched to call his sister and Quinn for backup, but he shoved the desire away. His imagination had kicked into high gear. That was all. With the Crips territory only a couple blocks away, it was probably some gangbangers planning their next attack.

A light breeze cut through the warmth, rustling the leaves on the trees that lined the street. Shouts and raised voices filled the night. A baby cried in the distance. Typical evening sounds for this part of town. Why didn't that fact comfort him?

Charlie made a left turn at the corner and glanced at the path he'd taken. He caught a glimpse of two figures slipping into the tree line.

Ah ha. Gotcha.

Charlie backtracked and edged closer. The voices rose. He held his breath and listened.

A twig snapped behind him.

Charlie spun.

Something connected with his midsection, and he dropped to the ground, gasping for air. Another hit caught him in the ribs. He cried out and threw up his arms to cover his head, then twisted as his attacker connected with a third blow to his temple.

Lightning arched through his skull with piercing brightness. Then the world dimmed.

Charlie's eyes fluttered, and he floated in and out of consciousness. He lay curled up on his side, blood pouring from a gash on his head. Eyes closed, he tugged his phone from his pocket. The movement sent pain shooting through his torso and he moaned. His brain and stomach swirled.

He laid the cell phone beside his face and struggled to get his fingers to cooperate. He made contact with the buttons and tapped a speed dial number.

"You've reached Lizzie. Please leave a message." The female voice swam in the distance.

"Help," he gasped through the agony. "Help me."

Charlie struggled to hold onto the present—but failed.

ACKNOWLEDGMENTS

As I understand it, the acknowledgment section is where the author has an opportunity to redeem herself for all the craziness she pushed onto those around her during the novel writing process. Allow me to humbly thank these amazing people...

First and foremost, I'd like to thank Susan May Warren and Lindsay Harrel for listening to God and starting a publishing company as amazing as Sunrise Publishing. Cyborg Susie (as I lovingly call her) is gifted by God with a unique ability to see stories and decode them like she's reading the falling code from the Matrix. Without her, this story would be missing key elements. Thank you for your kindness in teaching me, and for sharing your brilliance with the world.

For me, working with Lindsay was a dream come true. I told her I was a total fan girl after reading her novels long before I ever decided to pursue my own author career. She probably wouldn't have been my roommate at our brainstorming retreat if she knew how long I'd been following her on Instagram and praying I could talk with her in person. I'm insanely blessed to know Lindsay. Thank you for being a true blue friend who gives it to me straight and provides massive encouragement all along the way.

Without the talented and ever humble Lynette Eason, the Elite Guardians Collection would not exist. As a new author it's terrifying and mind-blowing to work with one of the greatest Christian suspense authors of all time. Seriously, you guys. Lynette continues to shock me with her devious plots and amazing story crafting abilities. No pressure, right? I am so very humbled that she allowed me to write a book in her series. Lynette, thank you for walking me through the writing process, teaching me with a kind and firm hand, and being the biggest encourager of all.

A special thanks to my fellow Elite Guardians Collection authors, Sami A. Abrams and Kelly Underwood. We're not only fellow writers on this journey, but we are also close friends. Thank you both for putting up with my neurotic overthinking and helping me untwist myself from the giant plot mess I created for myself. I've learned so much from both of you and it's my prayer that we'll be friends for years to come. KISS!

Thanking my husband and family should probably be at the top of my list since they put up with me daily. Thanks for putting up with the early mornings and late nights of writing, long phone calls, plotting meetings, endless book talk, me forcing you to listen while I work out the plot, and all the times you had to fend for yourselves (especially the week you had to survive while I went to the writing retreat). I apologize for anything I said while stressed over deadlines. You deserve an award for putting up with all of it. Any success I have is because of your prayers, love, support, encouragement, and help. Thank you, Jerry, for your wisdom, Mom for your encouragement, and my kids Logan, Gavin, John, Haley, and Bella for your story help along the way.

I have several friends that I want to thank, but first is Stephanie, who told me about Sunrise Publishing and encouraged me to audition. I mean, you could have told me earlier so I didn't have to pull it all together in two days...but I'll let that slide. To Christy, for all your wisdom, kindness, and most of all your friendship. To Charity, my BFF and biggest fan. Without you I wouldn't have a head this big. Thank you to the amazing talented author, Lisa Phillips. You came in late in the game, but you've already made me a better author, and without our competitive writing sprints this book might still be in progress.

Barbara Curtis deserves an extra special thanks for her meticulous work in editing this novel. Without you, my character's hair and eye color would have changed a few times and we may have left gaping plot holes. Your comments along the way were so uplifting that it gave me hope that I've written something at least one other person enjoyed.

I'm not sure there will ever be a Sunrise book without a special thanks for Rel Mollet, but I took it one step further and made her a character in this book. It was long after I wrote her character that she told me, "Nursing is not my strength!" Oh, the irony! Rel, I love our friendship, our ability to work closely together, read each other's minds, spot each other's errors, love each other's dogs, and so much more. Thank you for your tireless work and your contribution to me and to the entire publishing world.

Thank you to the all the readers, including the advanced readers and those who have and will leave book reviews. Without you as a reader, it seems kinda lame to write a novel. I appreciate your time and pray that these characters touch your heart in a positive way.

There are so many others I'd like to thank, but because Lindsay knows me, she said I had to keep it short and it's too late for that. If I didn't thank you here, please bring your paperback copy to me so I can hand write a personal thank you!

ABOUT THE AUTHORS

Lynette Eason is the best-selling, award-winning author of over 60 books including the Women of Justice series, the Deadly Reunions series, the Hidden Identity series, the Elite Guardians series, the Blue Justice series, and the currently releasing, Danger Never Sleeps series. She is the winner of three ACFW Carol Awards, the Selah Award, and the Inspirational Reader's Choice Award, among others. Her Elite Guardians series, featuring strong, successful female bodyguards, has captured readers' hearts and minds. Visit her at www.LynetteEason.com.

Kate Angelo is an author, minister, and public speaker from Southwest Missouri who works alongside her husband strengthening and encouraging marriages and families through their ministry. As the mother of five mostly grown children, she is fluent in both sarcasm and eye rolls—subjects she never intentionally taught while homeschooling. With her chihuahua taking up half of her desk space, she writes suspenseful stories of imperfect people who encounter hope and healing through Jesus. Kate is a tech enthusiast, coffee lover, productivity guru, accomplished knitter, avid boater, prayer warrior, and known klutz. Visit her at www.KateAngelo.com.

CPSIA information can be obtained
at www.ICGtesting.com
Printed in the USA
LVHW032120040422
715267LV00008B/1039